ROOTER

A NOVEL

TEIRAN SMITH

ROOTER

Copyright © 2015 Teiran Smith

This book is a work of fiction. Names, places, and incidents either are a product of the author's imagination or are used fictitiously. Any resemblance to actual persons, living or dead, events, or locales is entirely coincidental.

ISBN: 1517391083
ISBN-13: 978-1517391089

To Haley,
I hope you enjoy the story!

Leiren Smith

DEDICATION

Scott, thank you for always believing in me and telling me to never give up on my dream. I love you.

Mom, I love you. Not a day goes by that I don't think of you.

THE BEGINNING

I am not a fan of extreme heat, humidity, or sweat. And yet here I am on a record breaking hot Mid-May Michigan afternoon sunbathing in my backyard. Not because I want to, but because even though it's eighty nine degrees of miserable outside, it's one hundred and eleven degrees of hell inside my house.

The old house I share with my roommates, Miranda and Mike, isn't equipped with central air. And even if it was, we couldn't afford to run it. So I figure if I'm going to be sweating profusely, I might as well get a tan while I'm doing it.

The only respite I receive from the sweltering heat comes from the overgrown blades of grass that tickle and cool the soles of my feet.

Our lawn desperately needs to be mowed, but it's not my turn. I've mowed it two weeks in a row. I'm always picking up the slack of my roommates. If not for me we'd be living in squalor. I don't know if it's because they don't mind the filth or if they're just that lazy. But I refuse to mow this lawn one more time out of turn.

I hear my favorite sound and turn to watch Rooter pull up to his garage on his motorcycle.

I live for the sound of Rooter's Harley when he comes home. He's lived next to me for a little over a year and we've never met.

We've exchanged a few nods in passing, but nothing more. I can't muster the courage to introduce myself.

The fact that he's a one percenter might have something to do with that. He's a member of the Double H Motorcycle Club, formerly known as Halsey Hellions. Locals claim the Mayor and the Chief of Police are on their payroll; that the club owns this town.

I snooped around and found out Rooter is the club President's son. According to the patch on his vest he is the Sergeant at Arms. The SAA is third in the MC hierarchy, under the President and V.P. Word on the street is he's a "vicious motherfucker." There's a story he nearly beat a man to death with his bare hands.

When I look at Rooter, I see the tough exterior, but I also see something... gentle. It's been said that it's what a man does when he's alone that determines his true character. Rooter plays ball with his pit bull, Dopey, works out and runs on a regular basis, and has a carefree, childlike laughter. He smiles often; and in his smile I see innocence.

It's his smile that draws me to him.

I wonder what it would feel like to be the reason for his smile.

I yearn to be the reason for his smile.

Rooter opens his back door and lets Dopey out. The dog dashes to the giant red maple tree to pee and then lunges at him almost knocking him down. Rooter laughs, picks up the dog's ball and throws it. For the millionth time I wonder what his real name is.

"Goddamn it, Sophie!"

My reverie is broken by my undesirable roommate, Mike. He's so freaking annoying. I snap my head in his direction. "What?"

Mike is a for real dickhead. I've known him most of my life. Miranda has been my best friend since I was five and he's her older brother. Once upon a time he and I were good friends, but I can't stand him anymore.

I've asked Miranda repeatedly to kick him out, but she refuses. She claims he can't make it on his own; that he's unstable from the death of their parents, both of whom passed away last year. I don't buy it. I think now he's just an asshole; a shame because he used to be a nice guy.

"I was supposed to be at work a half hour ago!" Mike complains.

I roll my eyes. "Then it sounds like you're late."

"No shit!" He waves his hand at me. "You knew I had to work tonight!"

"What's your point?" I hold out my arms to inspect the color. I burn easily, but because I want to get a tan I didn't bother to apply sunblock.

"Did it occur to you to wake me up?"

He's right, I knew, and I could've woken him up, but his work schedule isn't my concern. Nothing about him concerns me. "Um, last time I checked, I'm not an alarm clock, or your mother."

Shit. I shouldn't have said that last part about his mother. That was cruel.

Mike's face turns a deep shade of red and the vein in his forehead protrudes. "Worthless, fucking cunt!"

He goes in and slams the door. He's hated me ever since I shot him down when he told me he had feelings for me. Almost a year has passed, and the time has done nothing to soften his attitude toward me.

I turn back in my chair to find Rooter glaring at our back door before turning his attention to me. I'm mortified and my heart pounds wildly. This is not the first impression I was hoping to make. Of all the ways I'd hoped to get his attention, this is not one of them. I raise my hand to wave because I don't know what else to do.

Rooter carries himself with confidence, head held high, and shoulders back as he strides toward our fence. "Everything okay?" He asks.

"Yeah, he's just a dick."

I figure now is a good time to introduce myself. I take a deep breath and get up from the lawn chair to meet him at the fence. The sweeping motion of Rooter's eyes as he looks me up and down reminds me I'm wearing my neon yellow string bikini. I try to appear confident though I'm not. It takes all my strength to keep steady on my feet.

"So I've gathered."

I extend my hand and hope he doesn't notice it's shaking. "I'm Sophie, sorry about that."

Up close, Rooter appears even more youthful than I'd thought. A complete contradiction to the serious expression he wears. His face is smooth and flawless, unlike most of his biker friends. His complexion is dark, not necessarily from a tan, indicating a possible Latino heritage and he has a chiseled, square jaw. He's taller than I realized, which compared to my considerable height is a good thing. I'd put him at six three, possibly taller. He's strikingly muscular, though not bulky and his dark brown hair is cropped close, though not quite buzzed. A trail of tribal tattoos cover his right arm; disappearing underneath the short sleeve of his black t-shirt.

"No worries," he says and takes my hand for a quick shake. His hand is rough and sturdy as it clasps mine. "I'm Rooter."

Damn. I was hoping for his real name.

I hear Mike's repugnant voice again. "Where the fuck are my black jeans?"

I turn to my back door to face the bane of my existence once more. When he sees I'm conversing with the badass one percenter who lives next to us, he turns pale white. He looks to Rooter, then back to me and softens his expression.

"Why would I know where your jeans are?" I ask with my hand on my hip.

"Because you did laundry after me and I had left them in the dryer."

I shift my weight from my left leg to my right and cross my arms. "Well, they weren't in the dryer when I used it."

"Then where are they?"

I huff, tired of this conversation. "I don't know, Mike. I don't keep track of your shit."

"Bitch," he mutters under his breath, goes back in and slams the door.

I turn back to Rooter. His jaw is clenched. It's sexy.

"Are you sure everything is okay?" He asks without taking his eyes from my back door.

I wave my hand casually. "He's just a blowhard."

Rooter turns his gaze to me. His right hand is balled into a tight fist. "Seems he could use a lesson in manners."

Rooter, a badass biker, teaching anyone manners seems ironic. I roll my eyes and nod in agreement.

"Look, Sophie," I like how it sounds when he says my name, "you don't know me, but if he ever gets out of hand," he motions to his house, "I'm right here, just let me know."

A smile crosses my lips. I didn't expect that. "Thanks, I appreciate it."

"I'm serious." He looks me square in the eyes. "I take that shit seriously." His phone rings which seems to irk him with the way he snatches it from his back pocket. When he looks at the screen his expression conveys it's an important phone call.

"It was nice meeting you, Rooter," I say and back away, excusing myself so he can answer the call.

"You, too, Sophie." He looks me up and down again. "Remember what I said." He smirks before answering the phone and walking away.

He smiled at me!
Oh my God.
He smiled at me!
I'll never be the same.

And I'm not. A few days have passed and I haven't run into Rooter once. I'm like an adrenaline junkie looking for her next fix;

constantly looking out the window for him or listening for the roar of his Harley. His schedule isn't at all conducive to mine. He works days and I have class every weekday except Wednesday and wait tables at the Grand four nights a week.

It's not until a few days later, on Saturday, that I see him again. I'm getting into my car, headed to work when he and one of his biker friends pull into his driveway. I've seen his friend before. He comes around a lot. According to his patch, his name is Bear. He's scary looking; hulk-ish, with a beard and he never smiles. Not even when he laughs.

Rooter waves. "Hey, Sophie."

I wave back. "Hey, Rooter."

No smile. Damn.

After a long, hard shift I pull into the driveway a little before one in the morning. Saturday's are always busy, but tonight was one for the books. The local DA rented the private room for a party with his hoity toity friends. Of course, I was assigned to it. I'm always assigned to the jerks. Randy, my boss, says it's because I'm pretty and it helps keep them in line.

I'm not that pretty. I'm too tall, with a lanky, athletic build. My hair is straight and so dark it's almost black. I have a baby face complete with dimples and blue eyes. I'm twenty one, but look fifteen. Not exactly a guy's dream come true.

The DA and his friends were complete chauvinistic jerks. They treated me like a lesser life form simply because of my sex and profession.

The highlight of the evening was when one of the men tripped me—I'm not convinced it wasn't on purpose—causing me to spill water on the DA, who ripped me a new one. I spent more than half my shift serving them and the bastards didn't even leave a tip. Water incident aside, I killed myself making sure everything was perfect. Their meals were cooked to order, and they never had to wait on a drink. The DA left a note telling me what a shitty waitress I am and that I need to work on my dismal personality.

Saturday's are when I make the majority of my money for the week. Saturdays pay my rent. This one is going to severely cripple my bank account.

Rooter's unexpected voice scares the shit out of me. I screech and nearly climb the tree when he says my name. I turn and find him sitting in his screened in porch. He's always there when I get home from work, but this is the first time he's ever acknowledged me upon arrival. He chuckles and apologizes for scaring me. With a laugh like that, I forgive him at once.

"Hey, Rooter." I wave.

Rooter points at my house. "Your friend, Mike, has been on-a-tear tonight."

"He's not my friend," I point out. I want it to be perfectly clear I'm not romantically linked to that jerk.

I peer at the house. Mike probably got drunk and took some Xanax. It's been his thing lately and every time he does it, he turns into a gigantic asshole.

"You might not want to go in there," Rooter warns.

I listen for a ruckus. There's nothing.

He continues. "They've been quiet for the past five minutes, but it's been like that all night. He screams, she screams back then it gets quiet again."

I rest my head on the roof of my car. I have nowhere to go at this hour. I'm drained and all I want is to pass out in my bed. I don't have the patience to deal with this shit.

No choice but to face it. Might as well get it over with. I stand tall and straighten my shoulders. "Thanks for the heads up."

"If you have any trouble, I'll be here."

"I appreciate it," I say and lumber toward the house.

When I open the front door the smell of marijuana and stale alcohol assault my nostrils. The only light in the living room comes from our twenty year old television. Mike is on the couch playing video games. Not surprising. It's all he does when he's not working. Hell, I'm surprised he manages to hold down a job. He's not the most motivated person in the world these days.

It's a shame. Back in high school, Mike was the most popular guy, and was voted most outgoing. He didn't know a stranger. He was the quarterback and captain of the football team, an avid runner, and very into fitness. Laughter followed him everywhere he went. With shaggy dark blonde hair, gentle dark blue eyes, and a bright smile, Mike was every girl's dream. Although I wasn't romantically interested in him, even I found him attractive. He's still attractive. He's not as active as he once was, but he still works out and lifts weights, which has bulked him up considerably. It's his ugly attitude and new found drug addiction I find repulsive.

"I've been waiting for you," he slurs, angrily.

"I'm tired, and really not in the mood." I roll my eyes and march past him toward the staircase.

"Bitch, I'm talking to you!"

"Sleep it off," I snipe and start up the stairs.

When I hear footsteps coming after me I run. I make it to my room just in time to slam the door shut and lock it. I push my desk chair under the door knob for added security.

"Move out," he screams and pounds on my door.

"Leave me alone!" I scream back.

This isn't the first time he has yelled at me to move out, but it's the first time he chased me down to confront me.

"Mike!" Miranda yells. "Go to bed, dammit!"

"I'm not putting up with her shit anymore. She has to move out."

"If anyone should leave it's you," she says. "So shut the hell up and go to bed!"

I hear a thump, followed by Miranda's cry. Mike's an asshole, for sure, but it's the first time he's ever laid a hand on one of us. I start to open the door but think twice about it. I can't help her if he beats the shit out of both of us.

"Miranda," I shout and lean on the door. "Are you okay?"

"Shut up, bitch," Mike growls. "You're next."

"I'm calling the police," I say and dig through my purse for my phone.

Both of them yell at me not to make the call.

Fear creeps up my spine as Mike kicks and punches my door. "Bitch, open this door or I'll bust it down."

I dial 911. He continues to scream obscenities and pound on my door while I tell the operator what is happening. The operator stays on the line with me until the police arrive. The moment they put Mike in cuffs he starts crying and says he's sorry.

I file a report and the police take Mike into custody for the night. At Miranda's urging, I don't press charges. Rooter watches from his front porch as Mike is taken away in the squad car.

Once the cops leave with Mike, Miranda and I sit on the sofa in the living room. I glance at the old fashioned wooden clock on the wall. It's two thirty. I rub my face, exasperated.

"This can't continue, Miranda."

Her shoulders are hunched and her elbows rest on her knees. "I know."

"I don't think you do," I counter. "He's been like this for almost a year. Now it's turned physical. I won't live like this."

"He's had issues ever since mom died. You know that."

I roll my eyes. Here come the usual excuses. "Maybe so, but it doesn't give him a license to attack us."

She cocks her head. Her eyes are sad and tired. "What do you want me to do? Put him out on the street?"

Brother or not I can't understand why she puts up with him. "Yes. That's what I want. He's a grown man who knows right from wrong. He needs to be held accountable for his actions."

"I can't throw him out with nowhere to go."

I take a deep breath and sit up straight. "It's either him or me."

Her eyes go wide, full of shock and fear. "You can't leave," she begs. "You're the only one I can count on. I can't afford this house on my own."

She says on her own because Mike rarely makes rent.

The house is her childhood home. Her mom left it to her when she died. Her parent's had taken out a second mortgage out on it before her dad passed. The small inheritance her mom left behind, after burial fees, wasn't enough to cover the entire loan. Miranda was left with a seven hundred dollar a month mortgage payment. She was a full-time college student who worked part-time when it happened. Now she works full-time and takes classes over the internet.

"It's him or me," I reiterate with crossed arms.

I'm putting on a good show, but I won't leave. I can't. I'm a full-time college student working part-time. I can't afford my own place. I have no parents and I've never met my only brother. All of my friends are in the same predicament as me. I have nowhere else to go.

"I think going to jail will scare him straight," she rationalizes.

For both our sakes, I hope she's right, though I seriously doubt it.

Later that morning I sit on the sofa and drum my fingers anxiously on the end table while watching a lame B movie when Miranda walks in with Mike.

He looks at me with a contrite expression as he stands before me. "I'm really sorry, Soph," he says.

I don't buy it. "The only thing you're sorry about is going to jail."

"That isn't true," he pleads. "I had way too much to drink, which I'm quitting by the way. No more alcohol or pills." He crosses his heart. "I promise. I really am sorry."

Bullshit. "For your sake, I hope you quit the drugs and drinking. You're ruining your life. But as for your apology, I don't believe a word of it."

I snatch my soda from the table and go to my room. Not five minutes later, the doorbell rings, followed by a loud commotion in the living room. I rush down the stairs, taking them two at a time.

Miranda stands in the far left corner screaming. Blood is smeared on Mike's cheek as Rooter pins him to the wooden floor.

FEELINGS & *ACCUSATIONS*

"You think you're a man?" Rooter growls and smashes Mike's face against the grain of the wood.

Mike whimpers in response. A pitiful sound. I'm almost embarrassed for him.

"Real men don't hit women!" Rooter roars and digs his knee into Mike's back between the shoulder blades. "If you ever so much as raise your voice to either of these girls, I'll hit you so fucking hard you'll dribble for the rest of your life!"

In one swift motion Rooter yanks Mike up to his feet keeping a hold of his hands. I stand in shocked silence. I've never seen or heard anything so menacing in my life. Or sexy. I shouldn't be turned on right now, but damn I am. Rooter and I lock eyes as Miranda continues to scream.

"Quiet," Rooter tells her, still looking at me. "Apologize to them," he snarls into Mike's ear.

"I'm sorry," Mike says, his voice trembling.

"Be specific," Rooter insists and squeezes Mike's wrists causing him to grimace.

Mike looks at Miranda. "I'm sorry I hit you." Then he turns to me. "And I'm sorry for being a dick to you all the time."

"Tell them it won't happen again," Rooter demands.

Humiliation swims in Mike's eyes. "I promise it won't happen again."

When Rooter lets go of his wrists, Mike dashes to Miranda's side.

Rooter looks at me. "You make sure to let me know if he pulls anymore shit on either of you."

I nod and watch as he turns and leaves without another word.

I am breathless and my mouth hangs open as I stare at the front door with disbelief. *Did that really just happen?*

Mike runs up the stairs and slams his bedroom door, jarring the entire house. I almost feel sorry for him. Almost.

Miranda looks at me, her eyes bulging from their sockets and asks, "What the hell was that?"

"I have no idea," I lie. Rooter told me he'd be there if I needed him, but I hadn't expected him to come along and handle the situation on his own.

Miranda darts up the stairs after Mike. I hear Rooter's motorcycle roar to life followed by him speeding away. After several minutes of pounding on Mike's door, begging him to open up and talk to her, Miranda gives up. A moment later she sits next to me on the sofa.

"He really is sorry, Soph. It's all he talked about on the way home."

Miranda is hands down, the most beautiful girl I've ever seen. She has an exotic appearance to her which most blonde's lack. Her face is heart shaped with flawless tan skin, a button nose and full, pouty lips. The exact opposite of me, she's short. Petite, yet curvaceous in all the right places. Men and women alike drool over her bust size. I call her a "mini Jessica Rabbit."

I gape at her and wonder how she can possibly believe him. Her warm brown eyes plead with me to forgive Mike. Most of the time, her puppy dog face wins me over, but not this time.

I'm sure Mike vomited apologies on their way here. And he probably promised to change and be better and to never, ever attack us again. It's what he always does. He'll act nice for a few days and then *bam*, dickhead Mike will be back just like that.

She constantly defends him and I can't understand why. I willfully gave him the benefit of the doubt when it first began. Both of his parents had just died unexpectedly, I'd rejected him when he admitted he was in love with me. But at twenty three he's a grown man who should know right from wrong and be willing to take responsibility for his actions and for his life.

My life hasn't been a cake walk by any means. In my opinion, his problems don't even compare to mine, yet I don't treat people like shit or attack them. What makes it worse is most of the time he appears to feel justified in his actions.

"I don't care." I don't say it to be mean or to piss her off, I'm just unwilling to lie.

Miranda pulls her eyebrows together in a frown. "That's a messed up thing to say."

"But it's honest. How many times are you going to allow him to lash out and get off with a simple apology?"

The afternoon sun leaks into the house illuminating dust on the old hardwood floors. I want to remind Miranda it's her turn to clean them, but now isn't the time.

She sits upright and crosses her arms. "As many times as I have to, he's my brother."

I shake my head in exasperation. "Have you taken a look in the mirror?" I ask. The right side of her mouth is swollen and bruised. "I won't allow him to do that to me and get away with it."

She waves her hands in the direction of Rooter's house. "Is that why that guy came here today? Did you send him here?"

My mouth falls open. How can my best friend of sixteen years think I'd do such a thing? She can't possibly know me at all if she thinks this of me. "Of course not!"

Mike comes rushing down the stairs. He stops in front of the sofa and points at me. He must've been eavesdropping. "Bullshit!" He hollers. "Admit it. You sent that goon here to scare me."

"No, I didn't!" I protest. "But from the look on your face when he was here, I'd say you were pretty fucking scared."

"If you didn't send him, why was he here?" Miranda asks calmly.

My head twists in her direction. As I open my mouth to respond Mike interrupts.

"Because she's fucking him!" He answers for me.

Miranda shoots me a questioning glance.

I stand and face Mike head on, infuriated by their accusations. "I am *not* fucking him." My voice escalates with each word. "I don't even know him."

"Lie," Mike growls and stares me down, his chest rising and falling with rapid breaths. "I caught you flirting with him the other day."

Miranda's eyes dart back and forth between the two of us.

"I wasn't flirting with him." I put my hands on my hips. "He wanted to make sure I was okay after you screamed at me."

"Why would he care if he doesn't know you?" He asks through gritted teeth.

I sigh, tired of this conversation. "I don't know, maybe it's because he's a decent person who doesn't like to see girls being bullied by guys."

Mike throws his head back and lets out a boisterous laugh. "He *is* a bully! He's Double H!"

He's a master at deflecting. It's just like him to take the fact I've just called him a bully and put it on someone else instead.

"That doesn't make him a bully," I counter.

"Right," he snorts. "You're obsessed with him so you choose to ignore all the stories about them."

"That's just it!" I yell and throw my hands in the air. "They're stories. Rumors. We don't know if they're true." I point at his face.

"You on the other hand, *are* a bully. You're mean to me and Miranda all the time. *That* is a fact!"

"Stop it!" Miranda wails. She puts her hands up in protest and steps in between us. "Enough! This isn't helping anything."

Mike points back at me. "I don't want her here if she's seeing that guy," he commands. "He's dangerous."

"I think you're dangerous," I counter.

"I said stop it!" Miranda screams at the top of her lungs. She turns to me, takes a deep breath, and speaks calmly. "Please let me talk with Mike alone. Will you wait in your room for me?"

Fine with me. I'm finished with this conversation. I stalk up the stairs to my room and slam the door behind me.

My adrenaline surges. It's impossible to sit still so I pace back and forth. How do I always end up in situations defending myself against things I have nothing to do with? I raise my shaking palms to my temples, fingers splayed.

The sound of Mike's voice as he hollers grates on my nerves. After everything he's put me through this year I've come to truly despise him.

Living here isn't working out. It hasn't been working out for a while. If Miranda wants to baby Mike and put up with his crap for the rest of her life that's her problem. I don't want it to be mine any longer.

I'd give anything to have enough money to stand on my own two feet. Maybe I can fit in another job. I wouldn't have any life, but if I could afford my own place, it might be worth it. Miranda will be able to find another roommate. She has tons of friends and acquaintances.

I come to a halt and shake my head. Who am I kidding? At my current rate of pay, I'd need to work sixty hours a week to afford my own place. If I worked sixty hours a week and attended college full-time, I wouldn't have any time to study. I'd be stressed all the time. I resume pacing and try to listen to what they're saying downstairs.

Fifteen minutes later there's a knock on my door. I know it's Miranda because I heard Mike peel away in his Camaro a moment ago.

"May I come in," she asks in a gentle voice.

I open the door and gesture for her to enter. She looks nervous as I close the door. She takes a seat on the bed and fiddles with her fingers. I recommence my pacing. God, I hate it when she acts timid.

"How can you believe I'd send someone here to attack Mike?" I beseech.

"I don't necessarily believe it," she explains, looking at her hands as she continues to fidget. "It was just a question."

"I didn't send him here," I snap.

"Are you seeing him?"

I gape at her. "No. I've talked to him once. The day Mike yelled at me outside, Rooter saw it and asked if I was okay. That's it."

"Okay." She looks up at me with pleading eyes. "I believe you."

I come to a screeching halt. "Okay?" I turn to her. "No. None of this is okay! It's not okay that I have to answer such questions. That I, yet again, am defending myself against something I didn't do!" And I don't stop there. "What would it matter if I was seeing him? It's nobody's goddamn business what I do."

She holds her hands up in surrender. "All right. You're right. I'm sorry."

I don't give a damn that she's sorry. She's always sorry. "I'm so done with this shit Miranda. I'm especially done with Mike."

"I get it. I really do," she speaks softly. "Will you give me a little time to figure out what to do?"

I throw my head back and groan. If I had a dollar for every time she's asked me that I could pay my rent for the next six months. "What is there to figure out? He and I can't live together any longer and out of the two of us, I am by far the better roommate."

"Yes, you are," she concedes and sits hunched over and grips the edge of the bed. "But he's my brother. My throwing him out would be another rejection. Another loss. Can't you understand at all why that is hard for me?"

"Of course I understand." I take a seat next to her. "But Miranda, it's not getting any better. Mike's not getting any better. Time won't change what needs to be done. You're only delaying the inevitable."

Miranda sobs into her palms. "I know."

I take her into my arms while she cries. I rub her back in an effort to soothe her the same way she did for me after my rape last year.

After a few minutes, she looks up at me with sad, puffy eyes and says, "I can't lose my brother too."

Miranda explains that while she and Mike were downstairs talking, he broke down at her feet and cried. He claimed last night was a wake-up call for him and said he'll meet with a therapist to discuss his anger issues. He begged her forgiveness and promised to never be violent with us again. She believes him, just as she always does. I'm a bit more skeptical. She thinks I'll change my mind if I talk to him. I doubt there's anything he can say to change how I feel, but she begged me to talk to him so I will.

After enough time has passed to calm my nerves I decide it's now or never. If I don't talk to Mike now, I won't bother to at all. I stand and head to his room. Once at his door, I take a deep breath before knocking. I hear his bed creak and then he opens the door a crack.

"Can we talk?" I ask. *Please say no.*

He opens the door wide enough for me to enter. Once inside his room, I stare apprehensively at the dark wood door as he closes it. He stands in front of me wearing a blank expression and doesn't say a word.

"I guess I'll start," I offer and wring my hands together, nervous. "I don't want to fight with you."

"Me either."

He's standing a few feet from me, and yet I feel as though he's right up against me. It has been eons since the last time I was in a closed room with him. This conversation has to happen, but this may not be the best place for it. What if he blows up on me? What will I do then? It's too late now. We're already here.

I swallow. "Then why do you start so many?"

He opens his mouth as if to speak and then shakes his head. "Sometimes, I can't control myself."

"Do you hate me that much?" I implore.

A pained expression crosses his face. He shakes his head in response.

"You have to stop treating me the way you do," I assert.

He takes a small step forward. "You don't treat me much better," he accuses.

My heart pumps hard within my chest. I take a step back. "I'm only reacting to the things you say and do."

"Not always. Some days, you walk in the door and cringe when you see me. You walk by me like you wish I wasn't here." The tone in his voice is accusatory, yet sad.

"I never did those things until you started being so mean," I justify.

"You broke my heart." He loses his cool and throws his hands in the air. "I didn't take it well, I admit it. But you knew for years how I felt about you." I start to say something, but he holds a finger up to stop me. His body shakes. "First, you let me kiss you, and then blew me off. Then, when I needed you most, I told you I loved you and you acted like I was inconveniencing you. It doesn't get much crueler than that. So before you start pointing fingers, you need to realize how you are partially to blame."

His words have knocked the wind out of me. He's never been this open or vulnerable with me. My knees shake and I need to sit. The only place to sit is on the bed which isn't preferable, but since it's my only option I take it.

It's all true. The day his father died, I went to see how he was doing. He broke down in front of me and afterwards, kissed me. And

I kissed him back. When he confessed his feelings for me, I wasn't prepared for it. I think my exact words were, "Please don't do this. I've been through enough already."

"The way I handled things with you was wrong," I admit while staring at the matted down gray carpet. "I let you kiss me because I wanted you to feel something other than the agony of your father's death. I'd just been raped by Adam. I wasn't prepared to deal with your feelings for me."

"Then why didn't you say that?" He asks. I hear him take a step. "Instead, you got up and walked away like I was nothing. And then the next time I saw you, you ignored me. You don't do that to someone you care about."

I peer up at him. "I wasn't ready to talk about the rape. I'm so sorry I hurt you. It wasn't my intention."

He sits next to me on the bed, hunched over with his head in his hands. "If I'd chosen a better time to tell you, would it have made a difference?" Mike looks at me with inquisitive eyes.

He's not asking if it would've changed my reaction. He's asking if I would've been open to the idea of being with him.

"It would've changed the way I handled the situation."

"How would you have handled it?" He puts me on the spot.

"I don't know, but Mike…" I can't say the words. I look away, uncomfortable.

"But you never felt the same," he finishes for me.

I shake my head.

"Why?" He puts me on the spot again.

I rub the tips of my fingers together. A nervous gesture. "I don't know."

"I devoted my entire life to you." He taps hard against his chest. "I've tried everything I can think of to be the guy you want, but it's never enough. Is it because I'm not bad enough for you? Because let's face it, I've tried that too."

"I don't see you that way."

"But you like that thug next door." The vein in his forehead throbs, and he clenches his fists.

I don't answer. This conversation is heading in a bad direction so I raise to leave. Mike races me to the door and barricades it with his body; his hands balled into fists as his thick arms hang at his sides.

THE WARNING

Mike's angry eyes bore into mine. "Did you send him here?"
My fear transforms to anger. "No."

He leans forward until our faces are no more than an inch apart.
There's a haunting gleam in his eyes. "Are you fucking him?"

And so we're back to this. I refuse to answer his question. "What
difference would it make?"

"Because if you could be with a piece of trash like that, you're not
the person I thought you were."

"Well, you're not the person I thought you were either." I jut out
my chin. "Because the Mike I grew up with wouldn't act this way and
he certainly wouldn't attack me or his sister."

Mike winces at my words and leans away.

"Please let me go, Mike."

He backs away from the door and lets me leave.

An hour later, I hear the rumble of Rooter's motorcycle and peek
out my bedroom window to watch him pull up to the side door of his
house. Once he's off the bike, he glances up to my window and our
eyes lock. My heart slams in my chest. Did he look up here because
he knew I'd be watching or because he knows it's my room? I can't

read his expression. After a moment, he motions for me to come outside.

As I make my way outside I check for any sign of Miranda or Mike. If they catch me going out to talk to Rooter they will be pissed. Not that it'd matter. Nothing they might say would stop me. But I don't want to put up with more of their attitudes or accusations. I breathe a sigh of relief when I don't run into either of them.

As I approach, Rooter stands next to his bike with his hands in his pockets. If I thought my heart was beating hard when he looked up at me through my window, I was mistaken. It's like a jackhammer in my chest as I stand before the object of my affection.

"I'm sorry if I scared you earlier," his voice is soft. "That wasn't my intention."

One wouldn't expect such softness from a "vicious" biker, and yet it seems natural coming from him.

"I wasn't scared."

His eyes go wide with amazement. They're such a dark brown, they're nearly black. I've never seen eyes so dark. They're captivating. "You weren't?"

"Surprised, maybe." I smile.

He smiles back and I melt. There has never been a more gorgeous smile than his. He doesn't just smile with his lips. His entire face lights up, like a child on Christmas morning.

"I bet," he admits and rubs the back of his head and rocks front to back on his heels and toes. "How's your friend... What's her name?"

"Miranda. Now, she was scared." I chuckle.

"I could tell," he says regretfully, his brow furrowed. "Look," he holds his hands up in front of his chest, palms facing me, "what happened yesterday, believe it or not, is completely out of character for me. I'm not some weird dude who busts into people's houses and attacks them. It's just... I have a problem with guys who hurt girls."

Swoon. I try to conceal my excitement of standing here talking with him. "That's an admirable quality."

He smiles and rocks back and forth again. "I wish I'd handled it differently. But when I saw him get out of the car… I lost it."

"Well, the good news is, I don't think he'll be attacking us anytime soon." I say it jokingly, but I mean it. Mike may act like a hard ass and be willing to attack a couple of girls, but I doubt he has balls enough to go up against a guy like Rooter. If he was to go after me or Miranda again he knows as well as I do Rooter will jerk his ass into a knot.

Rooter perks up to this, his eyes hopeful. "You kicking him out?"

I shake my head. "I just think he'll be too scared to try again. You scared the shit out of him."

His nostrils flare. "Why aren't you kicking him out?"

"He's Miranda's brother," I explain, "and she owns the house. I don't really have a say in the matter."

Rooter shakes his head and grits his teeth. "You should have one if you pay rent to live there."

I look to the ground. "It's complicated."

"No, it's not," he asserts. "He's an abusive ass. He needs to go."

"If anyone will leave, it would be me."

His eyes bore into mine. "Maybe you should consider that option."

"Easier said than done on my income," I explain. "And Miranda can't afford this house without me. Besides, I don't think it'll happen again." Not necessarily because Mike's remorseful, but because he's scared of what Rooter might do.

Rooter throws his head back and laughs sarcastically. "Are you kidding me? Of course it will."

"Mike is working through some issues." I say it more in my defense than Mike's.

"Sophie, do not make excuses for that asshat."

24

Rooter's hands clench into fists, but it doesn't scare me. Most girls would be intimidated by or even scared of him, but I'm not. I find it incredibly sweet he's willing to step up to my defense.

My mother was a drug addict who paid no attention to me whatsoever except when she was smacking me around and screaming. My dad bailed when I was a toddler. I haven't seen or heard from him since. I never met any aunts, uncles, or grandparents.

Once, while high, my mom admitted she never wanted children. The only reason she got pregnant with me was to keep my dad around which backfired because he never wanted kids either. When I turned sixteen I moved in with Miranda and her parent's. My mom got pissed, but only because her maid was gone.

The only boyfriend I've ever had took my virginity by raping me. Miranda has always been there for me, but when it comes to Mike we're at odds.

"I appreciate your concern, Rooter. Truly. But the situation is complicated."

His bitter expression tells me he wants to argue this point, but instead he says, "Well, just know, if I find out he hurts either of you again, I won't be as easy on him as I was before."

I don't doubt it. "Understood."

His phone rings and he looks as relieved as I feel. This conversation was a bit deeper than I'm comfortable with since I don't know him all that well. He snatches the phone out of his pocket, looks at the screen, then back to me.

"I need to take this."

I nod and turn to leave. He calls my name and I spin back around.

"If you ever need anything, I'm here."

"Thanks." I wave.

I watch as he answers his phone and strides to his door. Once he's inside I turn around and find Miranda standing in the doorway glaring at me with arms crossed and pursed lips.

"What was that about?" She whispers so Mike won't hear as I walk in the door.

"He wanted to make sure we were okay and apologize for scaring us."

"How very nice of him," she snorts. "Did he happen to apologize for attacking my brother?"

I stalk past her to the kitchen, but she follows on my heels. "Don't be like that, Miranda. He's genuinely concerned about our safety."

The kitchen looks exactly the same as it did when we were kids. Same pastel wall paper. Same old gray and white formica countertop. Same old reddish brown vinyl flooring. It has always been my favorite room in the house. It's where I spent the majority of my childhood.

Loraine, Miranda's mom, would bake cookies and cakes, while quizzing me and Miranda for upcoming tests. There's a scratch on the countertop from me cutting a head of lettuce without a cutting board when I was ten. Loraine had been so kind and patient with me about it. Every time I see this scratch, I want to cry.

"Did you tell him there's nothing to be concerned about?"

I turn and face her. Her arms are still crossed. "He's not an idiot. He hears what goes on over here."

"We argue. Who doesn't?" She protests.

I roll my eyes. "It goes way beyond that and you know it."

I grab a glass from the cupboard. Some of the glasses are from when we were kids. Loraine wasn't one to upgrade. She'd simply buy more when needed. I choose one of the oldest ones.

Miranda's defensive stance becomes even more rigid. "We have issues like everyone else. It's not anyone's business but our own."

I open the refrigerator, remove a two liter of soda, and fill my glass. "Well, Rooter hears those issues on nearly a daily basis, and he doesn't like it."

"I still don't understand why he'd even care."

I plunk the glass on the counter a little too hard and she flinches. "Don't start with your accusations, Miranda."

She uncrosses her arms and softens her expression. This is how it always goes with her. She comes on like a hard ass then the moment I reciprocate, she backs down at once. "I'm not accusing, just making a statement."

"Rooter doesn't like guys hitting women. He hears us over here fighting with Mike all the time. He heard what happened last night," I motion toward the bruise on her face, "and then he saw your face."

She picks up my glass and takes a drink. "So your big bad biker has a soft spot for abused women?"

"Apparently so." I tap the counter with my fingers. "He's not letting this go."

"It's none of his damn business!" She squeals like a petulant child.

"Quiet," I urge with wide eyes and glare at the ceiling. The last thing we need is for Mike to hear us.

Miranda points at Rooter's house and whispers harshly. "That guy needs to keep his nose out of our business. He's going to cause more trouble."

"Don't make Rooter out to be the bad guy here, Miranda. Mike caused all of this. And just so you know, I don't think he'll be going away anytime soon so Mike had better keep his anger in check."

I'm half asleep when I pull into the driveway after work. It's been a long, hard Monday. I had class from ten until three thirty then had to be at work by five. With all that's been going on, I'm lucky to be averaging four hours of sleep each night. To say I'm exhausted is putting it mildly. I am utterly dead on my feet.

As usual, Rooter sits in his regular spot on his front porch when I pull into the driveway. I climb out of the car and wave. He waves back, but says nothing. As tired as I am I'd like to chat with him. Not about anything in particular. I just like talking to him. But I don't know what to say. It's difficult for me to initiate a conversation with a person I don't know well. Asking about his day or commenting on the weather would be trite.

Since he doesn't speak, and I don't know what to say, I plod to my front door. As I unlock the door, I see movement to my left. I turn my head to see Rooter enter his house. All of a sudden, I get a crazy notion he may have been waiting for me to get home so he could make sure I got in safely. The thought gives me butterflies and a warm sensation fills my chest.

Our neighborhood is no longer the safe, family oriented place it once was. It has become overrun by criminals and prostitutes. A registered sex offender lives four houses down from ours. Last week there was a home invasion on the next street over.

I carry a thirty eight special everywhere I go. A birthday present, along with ammunition, from my mom on my sixteenth birthday. One could imagine my reaction. Saying I wasn't pleased is an understatement. Now, I'm glad to have it. Although I've never fired it, I have wielded it on a few occasions. Works like a charm.

To my surprise, the house is dark and quiet. Mike isn't in his typical spot on the couch playing video games. I creep up the stairs, listening for signs of life. Nothing. I take a deep breath, relieved. Tonight I will be able to sleep soundly, for at least a few hours, until I have to be up at seven to get ready for my nine o'clock class.

Thank God it's the last week before summer break. And to think I considered taking summer classes. Sure, graduating early would be nice, but I need a break. Plus I'll be able to put in more hours at the restaurant or even consider getting a second job and finally save a little money. As it stands, most of my money goes towards books and rent. There's hardly enough left over at the end of the month to splurge on something as simple as instant cappuccino.

I turn on the lights in my bedroom, drop my purse and keys to the floor and quickly strip down to my panties. I'm so tired I don't even bother to put on pajamas. I stretch my arms out wide and yawn. Just as I get ready to turn out the light, I see Rooter staring at me, bug eyed, from the window across from mine. We lock eyes for maybe three seconds. I'm frozen in place. He rushes and closes his blinds. I grab my comforter, wrap it around me and turn out my light.

How long had he been standing there? Had he watched me the entire time I undressed? He wouldn't do that. Would he?

My heart pounds within my chest and I giggle with my hand over my mouth. I can't believe that just happened. I've only been that exposed to one other guy. Adam. The night he raped me. Somehow, this exhibition doesn't bother me. Even if Rooter had been standing there purposely watching me undress, I don't care. In fact, I find it exciting. A fact that takes me wildly by surprise. Ever since Adam raped me, I've been rather timid around guys.

But as I stand giggling I find myself hoping Rooter liked what he saw. For the first time in my life, I genuinely want someone. I want Rooter, and I want him to want me.

The next day, after running an errand, I find Rooter straddling his bike as I pull into the driveway. Our eyes meet, the same as they had the night before, and my pulse quickens. I step out of my car and he climbs off his bike. He saunters over with a rueful expression.

"Hey." He puts his hands in his pockets and rocks back and forth, uneasy.

"Hey."

"I'm so sorry about last night. I'd just walked in my room and there you were." He waves his a hand up and down at me.

Yeah. There I was. In all my glory. I feel my face flush and have a burning desire to know what he thought when he saw me. "It was my fault. I should've closed my blinds. I was just so tired."

"I don't want you to think I'm a creepy, peeping Tom."

"I don't." It wouldn't bother me if he was. "Like I said, my fault."

"It's just that, in a year's time, we haven't spoken a word to each other. In the past few days, I've burst into your house, assaulted your roommate, and watched you undress."

Wait. "Watched?"

"In my defense, it was kind of hard to look away." He rubs the back of his neck looking sheepish.

"Did you like what you saw?" I ask, taking myself, and by the way his mouth hangs open, Rooter by surprise. Where the hell did that come from? I'm never that brash.

He shakes his head and all of my excitement and brazenness disappear in an instant.

"Sophie," he says and his phone rings. He retrieves it from his back pocket, checks the screen.

I'm relieved by the interruption. Now is a good time to make my escape. I look at my house and take a step back. Rooter holds up his index finger as if reading my mind and answers the phone.

"Yeah?" He answers curtly and listens. I hear a male voice on the other end of the line, but can't make out the words. "I'm on my way. Be there in fifteen." He hangs up and looks at me. "I have to go," he says and takes a step closer, looking intently in my eyes, "but to answer your question, yes, I liked what I saw. A lot. And that isn't a good thing for either one of us."

"Why?" I whisper, relieved by his admission. His nearness makes my stomach do back flips.

He looks me up and down with a glint in his eye. "Because you need me to stay away from you and that was nearly impossible to do *before* I saw you in your panties."

I blink and just about lose my footing. His intensity is overwhelming. "It was?"

"You have no idea." His voice is strained. "If you're smart, you'll stay away from me." With that, he turns and walks away. "Consider yourself warned."

He climbs on his bike and fires it up.

What the hell does that mean?

Before I can ask he tears out of his driveway.

ANOTHER RESCUE

After tidying up my room and putting away my laundry, I go to the bathroom to pee. As per usual, the toilet seat is up—there's no convincing Mike it should be down—and when I reach it, I gag immediately. Disgusting brown flecks cover not only the inside, but the seat as well.

Seriously? How the hell can you miss if you're sitting down?

My urge to pee has suddenly taken a backseat to my disgust and irritation. I march to Miranda's room.

The worst part about living with Miranda and Mike is the mess. I like a clean house. I don't understand what's so difficult about picking up your empty pop can and putting it in the garbage can. But the absolute worst part is the bathroom. Miranda has a habit of getting toothpaste all over the counter. I mean, the entire counter. Mike can't ever seem to hit the water when peeing. Basically, I never go into the bathroom unless I'm wearing shoes. But today it has hit an all-time high on the disgusting meter. Last week was Miranda's week to clean the bathroom. It never got done. Big surprise.

I am not happy.

Not one little bit.

"Miranda," I holler and open her door without knocking. She's sitting at her desk with her iPod on. I dart over and yank one of the ear buds out of her ear.

She jumps. "What?"

"Have you seen the bathroom?" I ask with my hands on my hips.

"I'm so sorry I didn't get to it over the weekend. I'm going to clean it."

"It needs to be cleaned right now." I demand and stomp my right foot.

"I'm painting my nails." She holds her hands up to show me her perfectly manicured pink fingernails. Not even her perky cuteness, with her hair bunched up on top of her head is enough to calm me.

"I don't care! There's shit all over the toilet!"

Her eyes go wide. "What?"

"Go see for yourself!" I wave toward the bathroom.

The moment she sees the mess she gags. "Mike!" She shouts.

"He's not here," I inform her.

"He's going to have to clean that. I'm not going near it." She goes back to her room and I follow.

She may have better manners than to crap on the toilet and leave it there, but her room is an absolute pigsty. Dirty clothes cover a third of the floor while her hamper remains empty. There are three empty glasses, one on her nightstand and two on the dresser. Almost all of her drawers are open with various items hanging out of them and her bed is unmade. I don't know how she lives like this. She takes such great pride in herself and in her appearance that she sometimes showers twice a day which includes clean clothes, fresh makeup, and newly done hair. How can she care so much about personal hygiene and so little about cleanliness in her room, or the rest of the house for that matter?

"The shower, sink and floor need cleaned as well," I remind her.

She points toward the bathroom. "I'm not going in there until he cleans that up. That's nasty."

"Who are you telling? Just when I'm sure it can't possibly get any worse, I'm proven wrong."

"Look at it this way," she goes back to painting her nails, "it's a good education for when you get married. All men are pigs. Chris was just as bad."

Chris is her boyfriend. They've been going out for a little over a year. I'm not a huge fan of his. He's hot, and he knows it and it shows. I'm not entirely sure what, other than his looks, Miranda sees in him. He treats her like crap until he wants sex, then it's all "Baby, I love you." Yuck.

Then it hits me. She said "was just as bad."

"Was?" I ask with an arched brow.

"I caught him with a stripper." She doesn't sound surprised. "And not a classy one from a gentleman's club. We're talking straight out of the gutter, not even hot, white trash."

"Ew!" I push back her comforter to make room to sit on the bed. "When did this happen?"

"Last weekend. He butt dialed me in the middle of the night. I heard Brian's voice in the background and assumed they were home," she gets up and joins me on the bed, "so I went there, and sure as hell, there they were, the three of them."

"The three of them?" I ask with wide eyes. Holy shit!

"Yep. The slut was on all fours getting fucked by my boyfriend while sucking Brian's tiny cock."

"What did you do?"

"I stood in the doorway for a minute while Brian screamed "Brandy, Brandy" over and over again. They didn't even notice me. So I said, "Care if I join?" You should've seen Chris' face."

"What did he do?"

"I never saw anyone move so fast in my life. He jumped off her and came after me, but I was out of there." She motions animatedly with her hands. "I ran as fast as I could to my car while he chased me butt naked with a flopping boner. All I could hear was "Please forgive me, baby, I love you." Yeah fucking right. Go love Brandy fuckwad."

The visual of Chris running after Miranda with a hard-on, coupled with her boisterous explanation make me want to laugh, but I stifle it. "I'm so sorry."

She shrugs. "I was tired of his crap anyway."

"Are you sure you're okay?" I ask even though she doesn't appear to be the least bit upset.

She nods. "It sucks and I'm pissed, but yeah I'm okay." She pauses and takes a deep breath. "The worst part of it was when he blamed it on me. He told me it was my fault for not giving him enough sex."

"What?" I ask, stunned. That's low, even for Chris.

"Apparently, five times that week wasn't enough."

"What an asshole." Who the hell cheats on Miranda? She's the hottest girl I've ever seen. And to cheat on her with a nasty stripper? You'd have to be a complete moron! Now I feel sorry for yelling at her about the bathroom. I wrap my arm around her shoulder. "Well, if you decide you're not okay, I'm here for you."

"Thanks," she says and wraps her arms around my waist.

"Can I ask, why you didn't tell me?"

She leans away and looks at me. "I don't know. I wanted to, but things haven't been that great between us lately. I didn't feel like I could come to you."

"Miranda," I say her name gently, "you're my best friend. You can always come to me."

She looks away, sad. "It's just that, I know you're upset with me for always defending Mike, even when he hurts you."

I turn her chin so she's facing me. "Mike aside, you are and always will be my best friend. You have always been there for me. You're all I have in this world, Miranda."

She gets a little misty eyed. "You know I love you, right?"

I take her back in my arms. "Yes, I know. And I love you, too."

We sit and hug for a moment and then I get an idea. "How about we order a pizza, pop in a chick flick, and veg out together tonight?"

She looks at me with her pretty, sad brown eyes and bounces up and down. "I'd love that."

"I'll order the pizza, while you pick out the movie."

For the next two hours Miranda and I lay on the couch, legs entwined, like we used to when we were little. Occasional giggles and Miranda's lip smacking, are the only sounds we make. For the first time in a while, I feel content.

And then Mike walks in the house.

"You need to clean the toilet before morning," Miranda tells him, before he can run up the stairs.

"It was your turn to clean it," he protests.

"Yes," she agrees, "but you're the one who crapped all over it."

"How do you know it was me?"

She sits up with a perturbed expression. "Seriously? Only three of us live here Mike, and it wasn't me or Soph."

He groans, irritated. "Fine, I'll clean it in the morning."

"It better be clean before six!" She snipes as he darts up the stairs.

"Whatever!" He yells back and slams his door.

"I'm not kidding!" She shouts.

I stand up and yawn. "I'm going to bed."

"Thanks for tonight." She smiles and turns off the television.

"It was fun. I've missed this."

"Me too."

I'm sitting at the dining room table, staring at Rooter's house, drinking a cup of coffee when Mike appears before me.

"The toilet's clean," he says and stands, staring at me, waiting for acknowledgment.

I'm not going to thank him for cleaning his mess. "All right."

He stalks out of the house and slams the door behind him.

I sigh. I'd love to go back to the way things were before Loraine and John died. Before Mike told me he loved me. Mike and I never really hung out just the two of us, but we had a good time when we were around each other. Sure, we got on each other's nerves from time to time, but that's how it is with family. He was like the brother I never had, which is how I viewed him.

When the three of us were in high school, we'd crawl through the attic window onto the roof and drink Red Bull in the middle of the night. He'd tell us jokes and make us laugh until tears streamed down our faces and our stomachs hurt. He was there when I first got my period and made fun of me when I got my first training bra. There's really very little Mike doesn't know about me, and I about him. Why can't we get back to that? Is it even possible?

On my way to my car I hear the rumble of a motorcycle. Assuming it's Rooter, I look to my right and watch him come down the street. I only have twenty minutes to get to work and it takes me fifteen to drive there. Yet I fully intend to find out what he meant by "Consider yourself warned."

Rooter pulls into the driveway and turns his head in my direction right as I trip on an exposed tree root and fall face first, twisting my ankle in the process.

"Ow!" I wail and grab my ankle.

"Shit, are you okay?" His voice is thick with concern as he rushes to my side.

I try to stand on my own, but can't. I hiss in pain.

"Let me see." He lifts my left pant leg to assess the damage. He removes my shoe, feels the bone, and rotates my foot a couple times. I moan in pain. "Already swelling. If it's not broken, it's a hell of a sprain. You need an x-ray."

Before I know what's happening, he puts his right arm under my knees and his left around my back and scoops me up. He carries me with little effort to the passenger side door of my car and sets me inside as gently as possible. With each tiny movement, it's like a knife is tearing through my ankle.

"I'll be right back." He disappears into his house. A minute later, he appears with a Ziploc bag of ice. "Keep this on your ankle," he orders and jogs to the driver's side and hops in.

I hand him my keys and watch in silent awe as he pulls out of my driveway. I put the bag of ice down to retrieve my phone from my purse.

"Keep that ice on your ankle," he orders.

"I need to call work and tell them I'm not coming," I explain while still digging through the mess in my purse trying to find my phone.

He takes the purse from my hands. "Keep the ice on your foot." The moment he looks inside the bag he sees the revolver. "She packs," he mutters to himself, seemingly impressed as he continues to rummage through my purse. "How do you find anything in this trash pit?" He asks with a chuckle.

I'd laugh in return, but I'm in too much pain. And I'm scared. He should be looking at the road, not in my purse.

Finally, he gives up and retrieves his phone from his back pocket and starts typing something. "What's your boss's name?"

He knows where I work? "Randy."

"I need to talk to Randy," he says into the phone and I continue to stare. "Hey, Randy, I'm calling for Sophie Holt."

He knows my last name, too?

"She's on her way to urgent care. Might've broken her ankle." He listens to whatever Randy is saying. "I'll have her call you when she's out." He hangs up.

I stare at him with a slack jaw.

"You have a nice boss," he says flippantly.

"You know where I work?"

"Mm-hmm," he admits cautiously.

"And my last name?"

He turns to me with an arched brow. "Does that scare you?"

"No. It just seems you know quite a bit about me," I say, wondering what else he might know.

Rooter's expression is intense, and he clenches his jaw. "You have no idea."

I gulp and stare, astounded.

"Does that scare you?"

My already racing heart speeds up. "No." Actually, it turns me on. A lot.

He looks away and makes a right at the stop sign. "Well, it should."

"Why?" I ask.

He chuckles eerily. "You have heard of my club?"

"I've heard the rumors."

"Rumors," he scoffs and shakes his head, "that's what you think they are?" He's trying to intimidate me, but it doesn't work.

"Life has taught me to only believe what I see firsthand."

We come to a railroad track and he slows way down in an obvious attempt not to jostle me too much. Rooter looks out of place behind the wheel of a car. Especially in my grandma-esque two thousand and four Toyota Camry. "Well, let me tell you, first hand, they're not all rumors." He shoots me a stern look, trying to convey a message.

"Is that what you meant when you said," I raise my left hand to make a quote, "consider yourself warned?"

He looks back to the road. "That's part of it."

"If you're so bad, why are you helping me?"

Another Argument

Rooter hesitates, lets out a deep breath and his shoulders sag. "I don't know."

"I have a hard time believing you do anything without a reason."

He shakes his head infinitesimally and raises an eyebrow. "You're perceptive, you know that?"

I lean in his direction, ignoring the searing pain it causes. "So what's your reason for helping me?"

He pulls over and turns to me with a conflicted expression. "Fuck it," he throws his right hand in the air, "here goes. I've been watching you since I moved in three years ago," he admits.

My eyes go wide and my breath catches. *Holy shit. He's been watching me for three years?*

"The first time I saw you," he continues, "was when you thrashed the girl across the street."

He's referring to Janelle. She rents the house across the street from us. There's no parking on her side of the street, so when she moved in she claimed the spot in front of our house. Miranda parked there one day and Janelle went off. A fight ensued and poor Miranda, unsurprisingly, was on the losing end, so I stepped in and ended it. A quick left hook and a knee to her nose was all it took.

"The second time I saw you, you came to help Mrs. Frank in the garden. You had the face of an angel."

I gape at him in total disbelief.

"I watched as you came and went, visiting the Frank's. You washed their cars and helped around the house. But the day you moved in I decided to learn more about you."

I can tell there's more he wants to say, but he stops there, allowing me to process the information.

"You watch me?"

"More than you watch me."

Shit! He knows. I stare at him, mouth agape. Without another word, Rooter puts the car in drive.

Rooter pulls into the Urgent Care parking lot, parks, and shuts off the engine. He turns to me with a mixture of sadness and worry etched into his face. "Sophie," his voice is so gentle, "I wasn't kidding when I said I know a lot about you." He turns in his seat to face me. "I know about your childhood. About your mom. About how you left home after she put a gun to your head." He pauses long enough that I think he's done, but then speaks again, softly. "I know about the rape."

Tears pool in my eyes and a lump forms in my throat. He knows about the worst moments of my life. My chest aches. How does he know all these things? More importantly, what else does he know? The pain in my ankle takes a backseat to the wave of emotion I'm experiencing. "You know a lot about me."

He nods. "You're like a walking contradiction. So strong, and yet so frail."

With those words, it seems he understands me better than anyone. I wipe a tear away with the back of my hand.

"Now are you scared?" He asks.

"No." I should be. A normal person would be.

Rooter shakes his head, gets out, walks to my door and helps me out as gently as possible. He lifts me into his arms and carries me to the Urgent Care entrance.

"How can I be afraid of you when all you do is help me?"

An X-ray confirms my ankle isn't broken, but severely sprained. The doctor wraps it, prescribes Vicodin for the pain and recommends RICE: rest, ice, compression, and elevation. I can't work for two weeks.

I hobble to the car on crutches with Rooter at my side. We haven't spoken since we walked into the Urgent Care facility. The silence is awkward as he pulls out of the parking lot. I start to say something, anything, when his phone rings.

"Yeah," he snaps into the phone. "I'm tied up right now. I can be there in an hour."

He hits a manhole which sends a shooting pain to my already throbbing ankle and I lean my head back and grimace. He turns to me and mouths he's sorry.

"I'll call when I'm on my way," he says to the caller and hangs up the phone.

"I never knew sprained ankles hurt this bad. Miranda had one once, and I thought she was such a wuss."

He laughs. "A wuss?"

We both laugh. I love the sound of his. It has a higher pitch than that of his speaking voice. The laughter is a pleasant departure from the awkward silence.

Rooter pulls into the pharmacy parking lot and turns to me. "Where's your script? I'll go in and get it."

"I'm not filling it."

He faces me, incredulous. "What? Why?"

"I'll just take ibuprofen."

"Ibuprofen won't touch that." He points at my foot.

I slouch and gaze into my hands. I know the ibuprofen won't work, but I don't have insurance and money is a finite resource for me.

"Give me the script." He snaps his fingers.

"I can't afford it," I mutter, feeling helpless.

"Sophie, you need the pills. Give me the script."

I shake my head. "I can't let you buy my medicine."

"Give. Me. The. Script."

I gape at him, on the verge of tears. "You barely know me," I say and then remember he actually does know me pretty well. "Well, I barely know you. You're not paying for my prescription."

He yanks my purse away and takes out the prescription.

"Rooter, no!"

I watch as he jogs into the pharmacy. I'd run after him if I could. All I can do is sit, stewing and biting my nails. I appreciate his willingness to help me, but I also value my independence, greatly. His taking pity on me over my lack of money is embarrassing.

Fifteen minutes later, he's back in the car and hands me the bag.

I must pay him back. "How much was it?"

"Don't worry about it." He starts the car and backs out of the space.

My jaw drops. "I want to pay you back."

"Sophie, I said don't worry about it." The stern tone of his voice tells me this conversation is over.

"Thank you." I hold up the bag. "Again."

He shrugs. "No problem."

I watch with veneration as Rooter drives, careful to avoid any bumps in the road. I've never seen him drive a car. He owns a truck, but rarely drives it. I doubt he's this cautious when he does. He holds the steering wheel with his left hand and rests his right hand on his leg. When he turns the radio on, it comes on blaring. Rooter jumps, almost hits his head on the roof, and swears before turning it down.

I cackle. I like my music loud and I'd forgotten to turn the radio down last time I drove. My CD of choice, a former boy bander turned solo act, is playing.

Rooter eyes me, unimpressed. "Seriously?"

"It's a good song," I protest.

He puts the radio on and turns it to the local hard rock station and bobs his head to the music. "Now this is good music."

"It is."

"You like this?" He gapes at me.

"I'm nondiscriminatory when it comes to music."

The right corner of his lip rises and he nods once as though he's taking in another new tidbit of who I am.

When the song finishes and the station goes to commercial, I turn down the volume. "This makes three times you've helped me."

Rooter shrugs, acting as though it's no big deal.

But it is. Especially since his confession. I get an idea. "Since you know so much about me, it's only fair you tell me a little about yourself."

A moment passes, and he glances at me, unsure. "You don't want to know me, Sophie. Take my word for it."

"Yes, I do."

Another moment passes.

"I'm waiting." I purse my lips.

"Give it up, Sophie," he groans.

"If you can find out things about me, I can do the same."

He laughs. "Go ahead. Maybe you'll learn something that'll convince you to stay away from me."

A wave of anger and exasperation come over me. "Obviously that's not what you want."

"It's what's best for you."

"But it's not what you want," I challenge.

He looks at me, deflated, and shakes his head and looks back at the road. The muscles in his forearm flex as he squeezes the steering wheel. "Fuck."

"I'll decide what's best for me. All I'm asking is to get to know you."

"Sophie, I'm a bad guy." He clenches his jaw.

"You keep saying that, but I beg to differ. You came to my defense after Mike tried to attack me. You took me to the doctor today and paid for my prescription. Bad guys don't do things like that."

We're a block from my house when he slams on the breaks and pulls over. The vein in his forehead protrudes and his face is red. His irritation is obvious and yet, I still see gentility.

"What is the matter with you?" He snaps and throws his hands up in frustration. "How are you not freaked the fuck out right now? I've basically admitted that I've been stalking you for three years. I'm a fucking one percenter, Sophie! Any other girl would run in the opposite direction, terrified."

He has a point. But it doesn't change the fact I'm not scared. Even I don't understand it. "I'm not afraid of you."

He leans his head against the headrest, rubs his denim covered thighs and exhales. A moment later he puts the car in drive and pulls away. Not another word is spoken as we make our way to my house.

Rooter takes my purse and the prescription bag before helping me out of the car, taking care not to jostle me too much. Once at my front door, he hands me my keys so I can unlock it. When the door is open I reach for my purse and pills, but he motions for me to go inside.

"What happened," Miranda says and jumps up when she sees me. Her eyes twitch to Rooter when she sees him come in behind me.

"It's a bad sprain," he informs her.

"Why didn't you call me?" She asks me and looks at Rooter again.

"It happened really fast," I explain and shuffle to the sofa. "Rooter was there when it happened."

"Where?" She asks.

"In the front yard on my way to work."

"She needs a glass of water to take her pills," Rooter tells her.

"Sure," she says, looking surprised, and walks to the kitchen.

Rooter takes my crutches and helps me onto the couch.

"Thank you," I say.

"You gonna be okay here?" He looks toward the kitchen where Miranda is.

"Yeah, Miranda will help me."

"What's your number?" He asks and pulls out his phone. I tell him and he programs it into the phone. "I'll text you with mine so you'll have it if you need anything."

"You don't want me to know you, but you're giving me your number so I can call you for help?" My phone pings from within my purse.

His lip twitches. "I'm aware of the irony, but I want to make sure you have the help you need."

"I'm sorry, where's the bad boy persona you keep warning me about?" I joke.

He rolls his eyes. "I gotta go," he says when Miranda appears before us.

I give him a rueful smile. "Thanks, again."

"See ya, Sophie." He turns and leaves without acknowledging Miranda.

Miranda hands me a glass of water with a questioning eye. "You two friends now?"

I open the pill bottle and dispense one into my hand. "I'm not sure."

"Not sure?"

I pop a Vicodin into my mouth and wash it down with water. "He thinks I'm better off not knowing him."

Miranda crosses her arms. "I think he's right."

I roll my eyes. "I'm getting really tired of people telling me what's best for me."

"He's in a biker gang that does bad shit, Soph. You *are* better off not knowing him."

"He's also a guy who has come to my rescue, three times now. And while you were in the kitchen getting my water, he gave me his number in case I need any more help. So you'll have to excuse me for disagreeing."

"I'd bet the only reason he's helping you is because he wants in your pants." She taps her foot the exact way Loraine used to do when she was unhappy about something.

"If that was true, he wouldn't tell me I'm better off not knowing him."

She shakes her head. "You're hopeless."

I slam the glass down splattering water all over the coffee table. I grab a dirty paper towel from the end table to wipe up the mess. "What does that mean?"

"That guy is bad news."

I feel my pulse in my forehead. "That guy has a name."

"What kind of name is Rooter, anyway?"

I throw my head back and sigh. "Leave it alone, Miranda. Please."

"Fine. Do what you want. But mark my words," she points toward Rooter's house, "that guy, Rooter, is trouble. If you get involved with him, it's going to lead to trouble."

Miranda stalks out of the room. She means well with her concern, but she needs to chill the hell out. She's my best friend. I like Rooter and I want to talk to her about him the way normal best friends would. I want to tell her how it felt in his arms when he carried me and describe to her the look in his eyes when he told me he knew about my past. I want her to share my excitement with me. It's not like she hasn't dated her fair share of bad guys. She's being a total hypocrite.

Later that night, while lying in bed, I see the light come on in Rooter's bedroom. I pick up my phone from my nightstand and contemplate texting him. I stare at the screen, ready to type, but can't think of what to say. I've already said thank you, so I simply write: *Good night, Rooter.* My index finger hovers over the send button for a few seconds before pressing it. I peek out my window to his, waiting to see if he'll reply. A few seconds later he does: *Good night, Sophie.* I stare at the screen and then clutch the phone to my chest.

This is just the beginning.

JEALOUSY?

The next morning while sitting at the dining room table, I get a text from Rooter.

Rooter: *I saw Miranda left. Will she be gone long?*

Me: *She went to work. She'll be home after 5:00.*

Rooter: *U gonna be okay while she's gone?*

Me: *I think so.*

Rooter: *Do u have everything u need?*

Me: *For now.*

Rooter: *If u need anything, text me.*

Me: *Okay. Thank you.*

That he thought about me and checked on me makes me giddy. His concern for me gives me butterflies and I smile.

I wait to see if he'll text back. After a couple minutes I assume the conversation is over, but continue to hold my phone, looking at the screen. My suspicion is confirmed when I hear his bike roar to life and he pulls out of his driveway. Another couple of minutes pass when my phone pings with another text. I know it's Rooter by the sound because I've set his ringtone to a revving motorcycle engine.

Wait... He just left his house. How can he be texting me?

Rooter: *Will u be alone with Mike all day?*

Me: *I'm not sure.*

Rooter: If u have any trouble with him text me. I can be there in fifteen minutes.

My heart skips a beat and a goofy smile spreads across my face.

Me: *And you call me a walking contradiction…*

The guy told me he's been stalking me for years and that he's a bad guy I'm better off not knowing. Yet, he goes out of his way to protect me and take care of me? He's giving me a severe case of whiplash.

A couple minutes pass and he doesn't text again. I regret my choice of text, worrying it might make him over-think things. Not wanting the conversation to end on that note, I text him again.

Me: *Thank you for everything, Rooter.*

The morning passes and I don't hear from Rooter again. Mike leaves around noon, and surprises me when he asks if I'll be okay alone. I say yes, although to be honest, I'm not sure. My ankle hurts like hell. The only movements I've made are to the couch and the bathroom.

Starving, I painfully hobble to the kitchen to figure out something for lunch. There isn't a morsel of food in the house. I lean against the counter and contemplate my options. I could order Chinese or pizza for delivery, but both would require a minimum purchase of twenty dollars. Since I won't be able to go back to work for at least a week, I can't afford it.

I consider texting Rooter to ask him to bring me lunch, but he already paid for my prescription, which I'm sure was expensive. Just thinking about it makes me cringe. He probably wouldn't let me pay for my lunch either.

Suddenly, it occurs to me that Ryan doesn't work today.

Ryan works with me at the Grand as a bartender. The first time I met him, I thought it was love at first sight. He's tall and lean and covered with random tattoos. He's British and when he speaks with that deep voice… But then I found out he's gay in the most mortifying way.

I'd had a tad too much to drink and confessed how hot I thought he was. He gave me a sincere smile and said, "Thank you, love, but I have a boyfriend." Sensing my humiliation he covered with, "But if I ever decide to bat for your team, you're the first girl I'm calling." We've been buds ever since.

We don't hang out as much as I'd like to. Mostly just at work. He spends the majority of his time with his boyfriend, Seth. That Mike is a serious homophobe doesn't help matters. The one and only time Ryan was here, Mike made his distaste perfectly clear. He even ordered Ryan not to look at him because he didn't want "a flaming fag having fantasies" about him.

Since Mike isn't home I text Ryan and ask if he'll bring me a bite. Thirty minutes after placing my order, he shows up with bags in hand. Even though I told him Mike is gone, he looks around for him the second he walks into the house.

"He isn't here," I assure him.

He smiles. "Good, because I have zero patience right now and I'd totally massacre that homophobic, woman hitting tosser."

I laugh hard and accidentally bump my foot on the coffee table. It hurts badly enough that tears form in the corners of my eyes. Ryan rushes over and drops the bags on the table.

"Shit, babe, you okay?"

I lean over, clutch my ankle. The pain has rendered me speechless so I nod. We sit in silence for a minute until I regain the ability to function. I glance at the clock and realize I missed my dose of Vicodin.

"Do me a favor?" I ask. "My Vicodin are in my purse." I motion to my bag on the dining room table.

While I swallow the pill, Ryan lays out the food on the coffee table. It's not what I ordered. I shoot him a questioning glare.

He shrugs. "I know you prefer the real chicken club."

"Yeah, but I can't afford it," I explain.

"That's why it's my treat." He flashes his megawatt smile.

Anyone who doesn't know Ryan would never guess he's gay. He's not the least bit effeminate. He has masculine style and mannerisms. Even the way he sits. He looks like a guys, guy. No pun intended.

"You didn't need to do that."

"I wanted to do it."

"Thank you. You're the best."

Ryan takes an obnoxiously large bite and chews with his mouth open because he knows I hate loud eaters. "Yeah, I know," he says after he swallows. "Randy said to take as much time as you need, but he knows your money is tight. He mentioned having you work in the office if you can't work on the floor straight away."

My eyes go wide. I know I don't have anything to worry about as far as my job is concerned. When I spoke with Randy, he told me not to worry. However, he didn't mention working in the office. I make a mental note to call him tomorrow.

"Really? That would be great, but it'll still be at least a week. I can barely get around the house."

I take my first bite of the chicken club and am at once thankful for my friend's generosity. I do prefer the real sandwich. I hate eating the cheap sandwich because I know it's processed and ground up chicken parts soaked in food coloring to make it appear appetizing.

"So I have news," he says and sticks out his bottom lip.

"Yeah?"

"Seth is moving out."

"What?" I ask, but I'm not shocked. "What happened?"

"*Mark* happened."

"Mark?"

"Yeah, some wanker he works with. They've been working closely and," he puts his fingers up in quotes, "they just couldn't deny their feelings any longer."

I can't hide my lack of surprise so I simply tell him I'm sorry rather than I told you so.

"Thanks." He gives me a sad smile.

"You don't sound very surprised."

With a mouth full, he shakes his head, indicating he isn't. "He's packing right now, so I was super thankful when you texted."

"It's a stupid question, but is there anything I can do?" I take a sip of my drink.

He shakes his head and dries one of his eyes with his middle finger. "So, anything new with your biker?"

"He texted this morning to make sure I'd be okay and told me to text him if I need anything."

Ryan scrunches his eyebrows together. "But yet, he thinks you should stay away from him."

"Exactly."

"Makes sense," he says sarcastically.

"Right?" I chuckle.

He motions to the food in front of us. "So, why didn't you have him bring you lunch?"

"I thought about it, but I don't want him helping me all the time."

"It may be the only way he'll come around."

That thought has crossed my mind. I don't expect Rooter to come knocking on my door asking to hang out although I desperately wish he would.

"I guess I'll have to be the one who does the coming around."

"And if he won't allow it?"

That, too, has crossed my mind. "Then I'll be persistent," I giggle.

After Ryan has cleaned up our mess, he and I sit on the couch watching salacious daytime television. Mike walks in, takes one look at Ryan and opens his mouth to say something. Likely something rude to my friend. He must think twice about it because he shuts his mouth and goes upstairs to his room without a word. Still rude, but much better than it could've been.

"I wish he would've said something," Ryan says. "Would've given me an excuse to punch something."

I rub his shoulder in an attempt to soothe him.

"Speaking of punching someone," he continues, "do you mind if I spend the rest of day here? If I go back to the house, I'm sure to beat the living hell out of that knob head. That or get completely pissed which could very well lead to me beating the bloody hell out of the both of them."

"Of course you can," I say with a sympathetic smile and pat him on the leg. But then Mike comes downstairs and saunters into the kitchen. "But maybe we should hang out in my room."

Ryan and I spend the rest of the day reading and watching movies in my room. We lay side by side on my bed until I fall asleep with my head rested against his shoulder. When I open my eyes, he too, is asleep. It's dark outside and the only light in the room comes from the television. I reach over and turn on my bedside lamp. Ryan is adorable in his sleep. I run my fingers through his silky hair.

"Wake up sleepy head."

He snuggles against me. "Would you mind if I stayed here tonight? I don't want to go home."

"Sure you can." I kiss his temple.

I take a pair of pajamas to the bathroom to change. On my way back to my room I run into Mike in the hall.

"Have you converted the fairy?"

Only one sentence from him and my blood is boiling. "Shut up."

"Hey, I'm all good with it. Anything's better than that dickwad next door."

"Perhaps I should tell that dickwad you called him a dickwad."

Mike turns gray. "Good night, Sophie."

I have to stop myself from slamming my door. I don't want to have to explain myself to Ryan. The last thing I need is a confrontation between those two. The television is off, but the bedside lamp is still on. Ryan lies on his stomach under the covers. He lifts the blankets for me to get in beside him. As I crawl into the bed, I see Rooter staring out his window before he closes the blinds. I can't make out his expression. Surprise? Jealousy? Relief?

"Shit." I whisper, although Rooter can't hear me.

"What?" Ryan asks.

"Rooter just saw us."

Ryan perks up a little. "Oh."

I grab my phone and start to text Rooter, but I don't know what to say. I want to explain this isn't what it looks like, but that's much too presumptuous. After debating for a few minutes I place the phone back on the table and lie next to Ryan. The bed is small and Ryan is huge, so we're forced to snuggle.

"Maybe this will make him jealous enough to make a move." Ryan suggests.

"I doubt it," I admit, but secretly hope he could be right.

"A guy doesn't stalk a girl for three years unless he's interested. Trust me, he's jealous. And look at me," he gestures the length of his body, "I'm like an Adonis."

We both burst out laughing. Once the laughter subsides neither of us speaks again. I lay and stare at the ceiling in silence. After a few minutes Ryan's breathing evens out, indicating he's asleep.

He has a point. Rooter wouldn't go to all that trouble to find things out about me if he wasn't interested. Surely seeing another guy in my bed has piqued his curiosity.

WHITE LIES

It's after two o'clock and Rooter hasn't texted to ask if I need anything. I try not to read too much into it. He already told me to let him know if I need anything and likely doesn't see a need to repeat himself. At least that's what I'm trying to tell myself.

I'm not convinced.

He saw me get into bed with another guy. Since he doesn't know Ryan's gay, he likely assumes I'm seeing him.

Damn it! I should've just texted Rooter and had him bring me lunch.

If it wasn't for the throbbing in my ankle, I'd be pacing the room.

On his way out this morning, Ryan gave me a pep talk. He said a little jealousy is a good thing. It could very well be the thing that changes Rooter's mind about being in my life. I just need to find a way to use the situation to my advantage.

I decide to text Rooter.

Me: *Hey. You busy?*

More time than I'm comfortable with passes. Six minutes seem like eons.

Rooter: *Yeah. What's up?*

Shit. I don't want to bother him if he's busy.

Me: *Nothing that can't wait. Call me when you're free?*

I purposely use the word call because I want to hear his voice.

I wait close to ten minutes for a response, but never get one. I may not know Rooter all that well, but I get the impression something is off. If yesterday was any indication, he would've checked in on me this morning and would've responded to my last text to confirm he'll call me back.

Four hours have passed and I still haven't heard from Rooter. It's about the time he gets home from work so I'm sitting on my porch so I can catch him. My pulse quickens when I hear the rumble of his motorcycle coming down the street.

When he pulls into his driveway I wave to get his attention. He nods once and rides his bike to the back of his house. So far, this plan isn't working out the way I'd expected. I'd thought he'd stop and at least say hi. Not wanting to miss the opportunity to talk to him, I pick up my crutches and hobble to the side of the yard as fast as I can. Rooter has let Dopey out to go to the bathroom. His back is to me.

"Hey," I call out.

He turns around and opens his mouth to speak when Dopey charges toward me at full speed.

"Shit," Rooter hollers and takes off after the dog. "Dopey, stop!"

But the dog doesn't listen. He bounds toward me as fast as his four legs will carry him and as he reaches me, he jumps and knocks me over. If it wasn't for the stabbing pain in my ankle, I'd laugh from being covered in drool by this adorable pit bull. Rooter yanks Dopey off me, scolds him, and orders him to sit.

"You all right?" His voice is cloaked with agitation.

I can't tell if he's irritated with me or the dog. Perhaps both?

"Yeah." I wince and sit up.

Rooter wraps his arms around me to help me stand and then hands me my crutches. "Sorry about that."

"It's okay."

He appears unsure, looks at my ankle.

"Really." I try to assure him.

"Sorry I didn't get back to you. It was a busy day."

I shrug, acting like it's no big deal. But it is a big deal. It's a *huge* deal. I've been tweaking all day from lack of a response by him. "No worries," I say, trying to hide my frustration.

Rooter smiles, but it doesn't reach his eyes. "So, what did you need earlier?"

I didn't really need anything, and I can't remember the lie I was going to tell him earlier. I could go with the truth and tell him I wanted to hear his voice, or I called to say hi, but I don't have the guts. We're not anywhere near that level in our new friendship. Hell, I'm not sure this even is a friendship. He has made it perfectly clear I should stay away from him. And the way his deep brown eyes bore into mine right now has rendered me completely incoherent. I decide to tell a version of the truth.

"I don't remember now."

"Oh, okay." He pauses, seemingly unsure of what to say or do next, as am I.

This is completely new territory for the both of us. I can't think up anything to say so I'm grateful when he speaks again.

"How's the ankle?"

"Hurts like hell," I admit. "I can't do much of anything for myself."

"Miranda helping you?" He asks.

"When she can, but she has her job and school. She hasn't had time to even get to the grocery." I get an idea. I think it resembles the lie I was going to tell him earlier. "Which reminds me why I texted you earlier."

"Yeah?" He sticks his hands in his pockets and rocks back and forth.

I love it when he does that. I try to hide my smile. "Would you mind running me to the grocery store?"

Rooter eyes Miranda's SUV in the driveway. "Miranda isn't able to go?"

I shake my head. A lie. Of course she can. In fact, she's planning on leaving in about an hour. However, this is the only thing I can come up with to talk with Rooter and hopefully finagle a way to spend time with him. "She's completing an exam online and midnight is the deadline." Where is this coming from? I despise lying, and yet I seem to be quite good at it.

Rooter's expression deepens as he contemplates my request. After a few seconds, which take much too long to pass, he lets out a deep breath and rubs the back of his neck. "I'm kind of busy, Sophie. Is there anyone else who can help you?"

I get that he's alluding to Ryan, but am not quite sure how to address it. "Not really, but if you aren't able to, I understand. No worries," I repeat. I never said that until I heard him say it.

He takes another breath and several seconds pass. "Okay," he says and my heart falls. "I'll take you."

Unable to contain my excitement I smile wide. "Thank you so much! You have no idea what this means to me."

He chuckles. "It's not that big of a deal. I'm just taking you to the grocery."

I try to cover. "There's literally *no* food in my house, so yes, this is a *very* big deal."

Concern and discernible irritation washes over his features. "No food? Are you serious?"

"Completely." I'm starving right now.

"Why didn't your," he pauses and clears his throat, "friend, take you shopping last night?" His jaw clenches and my stomach flips.

He's so damn sexy. I fantasize about running my fingers over and kissing the stubbly skin of his cheek. Again, I'm rendered incoherent and have a difficult time coming up with a plausible explanation. "He brought me dinner."

"Well, at least he did that much."

His disapproval makes me giddy inside, but I don't respond.

"Give me ten minutes and I'll come get you."

I wait at the front door like a teenage girl waiting for her date to arrive. True to his word, Rooter appears before me in exactly ten minutes. He escorts me to his truck and takes care when he lifts me into the cab. After tossing my crutches into the back he slides in next to me and asks which store we're going to.

"Aaronson's?" I answer with a question because I realize it's much farther away than any other store. The distance is precisely why I chose it. I want to extend my time with Rooter as much as possible. Only thing is, Aaronson's isn't cheap, which is probably why he's giving me a questioning look. "They have the best produce," I explain and he nods and starts the engine. At least it isn't a lie. Even if it costs three times as much, I do prefer their produce to anyone else's.

Inside the truck, I'm overwhelmed by Rooter's scent, a mixture of leather, aftershave, and peppermint. I inhale deeply and a warm, calm sensation falls over me.

"Why couldn't Mike go to the store?" Rooter asks. "He lives there, too."

"Mike, go to the store? No thanks." I chuckle. "Only if I wanted a cupboard full of junk food and canned soup."

Rooter chuckles at my response. "There's this thing called a shopping list."

I roll my eyes. "Not even that would work, and besides, I don't trust him with my debit card."

He shakes his head and grips the steering wheel. "I still don't understand why you both allow him to stay there."

"I don't allow it." I sigh and pick at my cuticles.

"You should have a say in who lives in the same house with you."

Yes, I should. "My name isn't on the deed."

"But you pay rent to live there." He presses his lips into a thin line.

"Miranda has faith he'll change and go back to the Mike of old."

Rooter's head snaps in my direction. "You mean he wasn't always a woman beating pussy?"

I laugh at his choice of words. "No. He used to be a nice guy."

"What changed?"

"His parents died and apparently, I broke his heart."

Rooter's posture stiffens, and he looks at me with a raised brow. I can tell he's replaying the chronology of the things he's learned about me. "Broke his heart? When were you two together?"

"Never! Oh, God, no," I quickly answer. "A while back, he told me he was in love with me and I didn't reciprocate."

Rooter visibly relaxes. His death grip on the steering wheel loosens. "Well, that explains a lot."

"Yeah."

"Doesn't make it right, though."

I shake my head in agreement. "No, it doesn't."

"Do you have the same faith as Miranda that he'll go back to being a decent guy?"

I shake my head. "I wish he would, but I lost hope for him a long time ago."

Now would be a good time to tell Rooter that Ryan is just my gay friend, but I'm not sure how to approach it. I don't want to appear presumptuous. Maybe he didn't think anything of it. And if he did, and he was jealous, I need to find a way to use it to my advantage. So for now I'll keep that tidbit to myself.

Once in the store Rooter grabs a cart and follows me as I fill it with items from my list. We're only a third of the way down the list when I grimace in pain and come to an abrupt halt. He rushes to my side wearing a worried expression.

"You okay?" He asks.

"I'm fine."

He cocks his head, not buying it. "I should've just taken the damn list and come for you."

"I'm okay," I insist, touched by his concern. "I prefer to do my own shopping. I'm picky about brands."

Rooter reaches into the cart and holds up store brand cereal and generic Hamburger Helper. "Really? Because everything in this cart is generic."

"Not everything." I blush and point to the Velveeta cheese and Stewarts Root Beer in the cart. The only reason they're in the cart is because Miranda wanted them and paid for them, but he doesn't know that.

"Pardon me," he chuckles. "Let's make sure to get brand name processed cheese."

We both laugh. A fellow shopper is annoyed that we're taking up the entire aisle. He tries to squeeze past us and bumps my ankle. I cry out in pain. Rooter grabs the guy by the shoulder and forces him to turn around and face him.

"What the fuck, man?" Rooter snipes. "You hit her."

"I—I'm sorry," the guy stammers. He's a big guy, and looks like he could hold his own, so the fear in his eyes as he gapes at Rooter takes me by surprise. "I didn't mean to hurt your girlfriend, I was just trying to get by."

"The words excuse me exist for a reason shithead." Rooter's grip on the guy's shoulder gets tighter causing him to wince.

"I'm sorry. Really," the guy says.

"You're sorry? Did you not see her crutches or didn't that matter to you when you rammed your cart into her?" Rooter's entire body trembles as he struggles to keep his anger in check.

While I appreciate Rooter's concern for me, I don't want him beating the hell out of this guy. We were taking up the entire aisle after all. It's not worth getting into a fight over and I'd hate to see what kind of shape he'd leave this guy in.

I reach out and put my hand on his shoulder. "I'm okay, Rooter."

"No, you're not!"

"I really am sorry," the guy says. Beads of sweat appear on his forehead.

"Why are you apologizing to me?" Rooter growls. "She's the one you rammed with your cart!"

The guy turns to face me. "I really am sorry, miss."

"It was our fault," I say. "We were taking up the aisle."

"Do not make excuses for him, Sophie!" Rooter orders. His face is a deep shade of red.

"I could've said excuse me," the guy admits.

"Yes, you could have," Rooter agrees with a menacing tone.

"It's done now," I say to Rooter. "Let him go."

"Watch where you're going from now on." Rooter lets go of the guy.

I watch the guy scurry out of the aisle, unable to believe that just happened. I find myself torn between feeling irritated and being turned on. Rooter didn't need to take it to that level, but damn, it was hot.

"You act like he took my leg off. It wasn't that big of a deal."

"It was to me."

"Why?"

"Because it was inconsiderate. He saw that you're on crutches. He could've said excuse me."

"Maybe he thought he could get by."

Rooter shakes his head and pinches the bridge of his nose. "He fucked up and deserved to be called out on it."

"The guy was scared to death. I'm surprised he didn't piss himself."

Rooter chuckles. "Now that would've been funny."

I have to turn around to hide my smile. I can't be mad at him. As I start to hobble away I'm stopped by his warm hand on my arm.

"I wasn't going to hurt him, Sophie." His expression is soft, but worried. "I was just trying to teach him a lesson."

"I'd say you succeeded."

"Are you mad at me?"

"No." I shake my head. "I appreciate you standing up for me, but you took it a little too far."

The ride back to my house is a quiet one, but the silence isn't awkward. Rooter pulls up in front of my house and helps me out of the truck.

"I'll walk you to the house and then bring the bags in."

Once inside we find Mike sitting on the sofa. His expression is a mixture of fear and displeasure. The way his eyes are scrunched together and his upper lip is raised in disgust makes me want to laugh.

"We gonna have a problem?" Rooter asks him.

"No." Mike says and softens his expression.

Rooter turns to me. "I'll be right back."

I shuffle to the coffee table and set my purse on it. Mike looks at me like he wants to say something, but isn't sure he should.

After a moment he asks, "Why is he here?"

"He took me grocery shopping."

"I thought Miranda was going to the store tonight because you aren't supposed to be walking."

I don't know what to say. I'm not about to tell him I lied to Rooter and convinced him to take me so I could spend time with him. But when I turn around, Rooter is standing only a few feet away from us. The look on his face conveys he overheard our conversation. He carries the bags into the kitchen and then heads out for more.

"Thanks for offering to help," Rooter snipes at Mike with his arms full of bags, on his last trip. "I assume you won't be eating any of this."

Once he's in the kitchen, Mike goes up to his room. I gimp into the kitchen after Rooter.

"So, you lied to get me to take you to the store?"

"Rooter, I'm sorry. I just..." I can't finish the sentence. Mortified, I look to the floor.

I hear him step closer, but don't have the courage to look up. "Why?" He asks.

I can feel the heat radiating off his body. My breath hitches. "Because it's the only thing I could come up with to get you to hang out with me."

He laughs loud. "What?"

Exasperated, I look up, which is a mistake because the amusement in his eyes only increases my humiliation. "You're dead set against me getting to know you, so it wasn't like I could call to chat or ask you to come over."

He sighs and pinches his eyebrows together. "Sophie, it's for your own good. Deep down, you know I'm right."

"No, I don't and you won't give me a chance to prove you wrong."

Rooter exhales sharply and rubs his forehead. The look in his eyes conveys that he's torn between his conviction and mine. "What you saw in the store tonight... That's who I am. Do you really want to be around that?"

"You were defending me."

"Why do you constantly make excuses for people?"

"I'm not making excuses. It's what I believe."

He exhales and takes a step back. "You know what I believe?" He asks but doesn't give me a chance to answer. "You need to forget about me. Forget about me and focus your attention on the guy who woke up in your bed this morning."

Miranda suddenly appears before us. Talk about bad timing.

"Can you put these away?" Rooter barks at her before I can state my defense.

Shit!

"Of course," she says, her eyes are wide, and she's frozen in place.

"Rooter, last night wasn't what it looked like," I try to explain but he's already walking away and I'm in no shape to run after him. "Rooter," I shout.

He throws a hand in the air. "It really doesn't matter," he yells and stomps out of the house.

"It does to me!" I say, but it's too late, he's already gone.

"What was that about?" Miranda asks.

"More of the," I make air quotes with my fingers, "I'm better off not knowing him shit."

She makes a face that reiterates she thinks he's right.

I hold my hand up to her. "Miranda, don't."

She puts her hands up in the air and steps away. "I didn't say anything."

"Your face said it all."

"Well, he seems pretty persistent about it. Maybe you should spare yourself the trouble and let it go."

"Maybe you should leave me alone and quit telling me what to do!"

"I'm not telling you what to do, dammit!" She kicks a bag and sends frozen pizzas flying across the kitchen. "Excuse me for caring about my best fucking friend!"

I desperately want to run after Rooter and explain Ryan is just a friend. A gay friend. I pick up my phone to text him, but my battery is dead and my charger is upstairs in my room. If it wasn't for my injury I'd run and get it so I could text him, but that isn't an option. And there's mint chocolate chip ice cream melting in one of these bags.

Fifteen minutes later, I've managed to put away the contents of two out of the nine bags of groceries when Miranda plods back into the kitchen.

"Here," she says with a gentle smile and takes the canned vegetables out of my hands. "I'll finish this. Go sit down."

"Thanks." I shuffle to the dining room table, relieved to be off my foot. Tears brim in my eyes, whether from the pain in my foot, or the argument with Rooter, I'm not sure.

"I'm sorry," she says, and comes over to me when she sees the tears in my eyes. "I don't want to fight with you."

"Me either."

"Can I ask you a question?"

"Sure," I answer, although I really wish she wouldn't because I have a sneaking suspicion I won't like it.

"Why does getting to know that guy matter so much to you?"

I roll my eyes. "Rooter," I correct her for what feels like the hundredth time.

She gives me a contrite smile. "Sorry, Rooter."

"I know it seems silly, crazy even. There's just something about him. He makes me feel things I've never felt."

"Like what?"

Where do I start? I exhale a long breath. "Safe."

INTRODUCING THE SLUT

Miranda's eyes bulge from their sockets and she takes a deep breath. I can tell she's trying to stay steady and calm so not to upset me. "Safe?"

"Yes," I respond defensively. "Safe."

She shakes her head. "I honestly don't get it."

How many times must we have the same conversation? I realize she doesn't understand my interest in Rooter. There's no way I can explain it to her, when I don't completely understand it myself. All I know is we don't get to choose to whom we are attracted. I didn't choose to be attracted to him. I just am.

"I know, Miranda." I won't bother to try explaining it. All I want to do is get a hold of Rooter, so I stand and grab my crutches. "I'm going to my room."

The look on her face tells me she wants to continue the conversation. Whether it's due to genuine interest or if she wants to try to rationalize the situation with me, I don't know. Though, I'm sure it's the latter.

She's always been that way. Whenever I date or like someone she doesn't care for, she tries to get me to see her point of view and change my mind. She has my best interest at heart, but it's annoying. While it's her prerogative not to agree with everything I say and do, she doesn't have the right to control me. I wish she'd just let me live my life my way.

Sure, I make mistakes, but so does she. It's a part of living and learning. Maybe this situation with Rooter is a mistake, but there's only one way to find out. As my best friend, it's her job to be there for me when I need her, not to tell me how to live my life.

Once in my room, my eyes go straight to Rooter's bedroom window. The light is off. I lean my crutches against the wall, sit at my desk and plug my phone into the charger. I'm super impatient and the forty seven seconds it takes for my phone to power on pisses me off.

"Hurry up!" I yell at the device.

As soon as I'm able to enter my passcode, I call Rooter. After three rings, it goes to his voice mail, indicating he rejected my call. "This is Rooter," the smooth sound of his voice gives me goosebumps, "leave a message." Forget that. I hang up and hit redial. It rings twice before going to voicemail.

"Seriously?" I gripe to myself and hit redial a second time. This time, it rings, and rings, and rings before going to voicemail yet again. "Rooter, please answer the phone. I need to talk to you."

I hang up and hold the phone in my hand, staring at the screen hoping he'll hear my plea and call me back. After five or six minutes, I figure he isn't going to call me back. Rather than calling again, since I know he won't answer, I send a text instead: *Please call me.*

I wait a couple of minutes and after no response, send another text: *Just so you know, that guy who woke up in my bed this morning is gay. Call me.* I pray that this will convince him to call or at least text me back. After another long four minutes, I conclude he isn't going to.

As I sit in my chair staring at Rooter's window, I get an idea. His blinds are open. At some point he'll go to bed. I'll get his attention then.

Four hours and thirty nine excruciating minutes have passed. My eyelids are getting heavy when I see the lights come on in Rooter's room. I jerk upright in my bed and stick my head out the window, flailing my arms like a mad woman.

"Rooter," I holler. "I need to talk to you!"

Our eyes lock as he walks toward his window. My pulse races. His expression is a mixture of amusement and irritation.

"Open the window!" I yell.

He continues to stare at me a moment and I move my arms in an upward motion, indicating I want him to open his window. Instead, he reaches for the string on the blinds and snaps them shut.

"Fine!" I slam my window down and turn around to find Miranda standing behind me.

"Everything okay?" She asks.

"What do you think?" I snipe.

She lets out a deep breath, closes my door and sits next to me on the bed. "Talk to me," she says gently.

I shake my head. "I can't."

"Yes, you can. I promise not to judge or tell you what I think."

I want to so bad. I need to someone to talk to and I want that someone to be her. I decide to give it a shot, but I'm not sure where to start.

First, I come clean about the depth of my infatuation with Rooter and when it began. Then I tell her about our conversation the day I sprained my ankle, of all the things Rooter found out about me, and how he paid for my prescription. Everything. Just as she promised, she listens until I finish without saying a word.

"And now, he won't talk to me. I don't know what to do," I whine.

A moment passes while Miranda processes the information. She looks me in the eyes and takes a deep breath. I prepare for the worst.

"He can't ignore you if you're standing right in front of him." She grabs me by the arm and tugs me from the bed.

"You want me to go over there right now?" I ask, ignoring the pain in my ankle from Miranda's jerking.

"No time like the present."

I glance at my alarm clock. "At present, it's almost two in the morning. I can't go over there."

"Then you'll go first thing in the morning," she says with a sympathetic smile and when she yawns I do the same.

"You should go back to bed. Thanks for listening," I say and reach out for a hug.

"I realize I haven't been very supportive when it comes to him, but if this is what you want, I'll support you."

"Thank you."

I set my alarm for seven, so I'm stunned when I'm woken by the sound of Rooter's Harley. I check the clock. It's only six thirty. He never leaves this early. I peek out the window and watch as he pulls out of his driveway.

So much for going to his house first thing this morning. I guess I'll have to wait until he gets home later. Since I have nowhere to be I roll over and drift back to sleep.

When I wake again it's after ten. I check to see if Rooter's bike is in his driveway even though I'm sure I would've heard him pull in. It isn't there, but there's a suped-up, red convertible Mustang I've never seen before.

Three hours later the car is still in the driveway. I'm in the dining room when Rooter's back door opens. Dopey runs out and a skanky blonde with a mammoth rack follows. I choke on my soda. *Who the hell is this chick?* I've never seen her around. In fact, I've never seen anyone at his house other than his biker friends and an older woman I can only assume is his mother. Does Rooter have a girlfriend or is this his way of making a point to me to back off?

Unconsciously, I pick my phone up and dial his number. It goes straight to voicemail which surprises me because I can't imagine he'd leave his phone off.

I spy on the girl through the dining room window. She doesn't appear to be familiar with the dog. She doesn't like it when he jumps up on her and gets grossed out by his drool covered ball when he brings it over for her to throw. I cackle at the face she makes when she wipes her hands on her leggings. I hope this means she isn't Rooter's girlfriend and that she's as unfamiliar with him as she is with the dog, though I seriously doubt it. Rooter doesn't strike me as the kind who would allow someone he doesn't know well into his home.

By nightfall, the blonde is still there and Rooter hasn't come home. I've called him four times today and each time it went straight to voicemail. I'm beginning to suspect he blocked my number.

I'm in bed trying, and failing miserably, at paying attention to the sitcom playing on my television. All I can think about—all I've been thinking about—is the girl at Rooter's house and why I can't get through to him.

The light comes on in his bedroom, but the closed blinds obstruct my view. *Why is that skank in his bedroom? She needs to get out of there now.* I keep my eyes on his window until the light goes out a few minutes later. I can only assume she's sleeping in his bed. *Bitch.*

Knowing the slutty blonde is sleeping in Rooter's bed keeps me up most of the night. I can't take my eyes off his window. This is the worst kind of torture.

At six I give up and get out of the bed, but not before flipping the bird at his house.

It's somewhat of a warm morning, so I take my coffee out to the back porch. Not an easy task in my condition. I stumble on my way out, and my cup shatters on the concrete.

"Fuck!" I holler and throw my crutch into the lawn.

The grass is overgrown, again. I'm not surprised. It's not like Miranda or Mike can possibly find the time in their busy schedules to help with shit around here.

"You okay?" A strange, female voice asks.

I turn to my left and find miss perky boobs staring at me. I hate that she looks perfect this early in the morning. Without a word I turn around and hobble into the house.

"Slut," I mutter and slam the door.

"Who?" Mike asks.

"No one." I try my best to shuffle to the coffeemaker without my crutches. When I grimace in pain Mike gently takes me by the elbow.

"Just sit. I'll make you a cup."

"Thanks." I peer up at him in surprise as he helps me to the dining room table.

Blondie is still outside when Mike hands me a new cup of coffee.

"That the slut?" He asks.

I nod and take a sip. Not near enough creamer, but I can't bring myself to ask him for more.

"She's hot." He ogles her through the window.

Yeah, she is. "You would think so."

His head snaps in my direction. "What does that mean?"

"Just that she would be your type."

"Because my type are sluts?" He scowls.

I shrug and take another sip of my coffee. The last girl he brought home didn't look much different from this chick. They met in a bar and spent a couple nights together. He got what he wanted and sent her on her way.

"And what does that say about you?" He asks.

I furrow my brow, confused. "Why would that say anything about me?"

"I seem to remember a time when I found you attractive. If I'm attracted to sluts, wouldn't that make you a slut?"

I roll my eyes. "Fuck off, Mike."

He leans down closer to me. "The only reason you're calling her a slut is because he fucked her instead of you."

I shove away from the table causing pain to shoot up my leg.

"Don't bother. I'll leave," he barks and stomps out of the room.

"What was that about?" Miranda asks with squinty eyes and her hair bunched up on her head.

I motion to the girl sitting on the stairs of Rooter's back porch.

She pulls her eyebrows together. "Why are you arguing over her?"

"Because I called her a slut and Mike said the only reason I called her that is because I'm jealous."

Miranda crosses her arms. "And he's right, isn't he?"

"Miranda, look at her!" I wave my hand in the trollop's direction. "She looks like a slut!"

She shifts her weight to one foot. "Perhaps, but you wouldn't even care if she wasn't at Rooter's house."

I sigh. I have no response because she's right.

Another day has passed. Rooter still isn't home, and the girl remains at his house. I assume she's staying there to take care of the dog which gives me hope there isn't anything going on between them. But it also piques my curiosity. Where did he go? Vacation? Has something happened? Is he okay?

I try calling and texting him a few more times, but each time it goes straight to voicemail. I've officially concluded that he blocked my number. One way or another, I'm rectifying that shit the moment he gets home.

Finally, fifty six hours and thirteen minutes later, I hear the rumble of Rooter's Harley. I watch and wait for the bimbo to leave so I can go over there and make him talk to me. But hours pass and she never leaves.

Rooter's bedroom light comes on and his blinds are open. I sit on my bed and watch as he walks to the window with the blonde right behind him. Our eyes meet and he closes the blinds.

Yep. She's definitely a slut.

Moving On

"I think you're doing the right thing," Miranda says, picking at the salad in front of her.

We're sitting in Skyles, the local sports bar. They have the best food in town even if it's a bit overpriced. It's not the most glamorous of places. It's dingy and dark with posters of sports players and scantily clad women on the walls. My kind of place.

I gander at the ginormous bacon cheeseburger in front of me. I always do this. Whenever I'm upset about something, I turn to food for comfort. I don't care what they say about emotional eating. I refuse to deny myself the happiness this greasy burger can give me.

The morning after Rooter took Blondie to bed, I decided to take his advice and forget about him. It's been four days and I haven't bothered trying to reach him, nor have I been inclined to. My urge to run to the window to watch as he comes and goes has greatly diminished.

Seeing him with her changed everything for me. I no longer view him the way I once did. No way could I ever be interested in a guy who'd have sex with a tramp like her. I get a cold chill merely thinking of it.

"I'm so over my infatuation with him."

"Good, because you can do way better than him."

"Yes, I can." I hope. I always seem to get mixed up with bad guys. But, there's always a first for everything.

"Speaking of doing better, you'll never guess who I ran into the other day." She claps her hands and bounces up and down.

"Who?" I feign interest. I'm not a fan of Miranda's matchmaking skills. The last guy she set me up with was a complete jackass. Besides, the only reason she's doing this is because she doesn't trust me to stay away from Rooter.

"Hayden Cross. I ran into him at the gas station. He asked about you right away."

We've known Hayden since grade school, but never ran in the same crowd. He was such a geek. He graduated high school a year early, promptly went to college and now works as an investment advisor at his father's wealth management company. I haven't seen him in forever, but last time I ran into him, he'd grown out of his awkward phase; put on a little muscle and his face had grown into his nose.

I raise a brow, skeptical. "Just because he asked about me doesn't mean he's interested, Miranda. We haven't seen each other in close to two years."

"Trust me, he's still interested. He was all like, "How is she? We should get together soon. Please be sure to tell her I said hi.""

"I faintly remember you telling me once that if I ever went out with him, you'd disown me." I chuckle and it feels good. I can't remember the last time I laughed.

"Well, that was before he grew up. I mean, you should see the guy. He's hot. And he comes from a great family."

I always hated that saying. As if coming from a well to do, educated family somehow makes you a good person. Puh-lease.

"He has a great career, and he just bought his own house. He's exactly the type of guy you should date."

She acts like she knows him so well when she hasn't seen him in as long as me. I resist the urge to roll my eyes and smile instead. She's only trying to help me.

"I don't know about going on a date, but we could all get together sometime soon." I'd like to catch up with him and say hi. The way he used to always follow me around was annoying, but he was always kind.

"Yay! I'll set it up." She claps her hands together like a three year old excited over a chocolate chip cookie. If she wasn't so cute, it would be obnoxious.

When we pull into our driveway a half hour later, I fight the urge to look at Rooter's house and win. I smile and do an internal happy dance over my small victory. I almost make it into the house when I hear the roar of several Harley's coming down the road. My head involuntarily turns and I watch Rooter, followed by three of his biker friends, pull into his driveway. If I'm not mistaken, I could swear Rooter's head turns in my direction, though infinitesimally. Not that I care. I don't want him to ever look at me again. Hopefully he'll take his own advice and forget about me the same as he wants me to forget about him.

Several hours later I'm in my room trying to sleep, but the noise from the party at Rooter's house is overwhelming. At least a half dozen more bikers and a few skin baring harlots have shown up there since we got home this afternoon.

Earlier, Miranda and I tried to watch a movie, but the howling and rock music was so loud we couldn't concentrate. She threatened to call the cops, but I begged her not to. Rooter would assume it was one of us. No one else would dare call in a complaint on him.

Unable to resist, I lift a blind to get a peek of what's going on. Rooter stands next to his fire pit. A smile dances on his face as one of the bimbos leans into him and says something. She's even skankier than the blonde from a few days ago. She's wearing a midriff baring tank top, booty shorts, clog high heels and her dark hair hangs down to the middle of her back. There's a tattoo of some sort on her right leg. It makes its way from her inner thigh right above her knee to the outside of her leg, disappearing under her skirt.

I shake my head in disgust. He has seriously nasty taste in women. Not wanting to see anymore, I huff and flop onto my mattress, but not before wondering if he'll take her to his bed later.

Two hours pass and his party is still going strong. I can't sleep. Can't watch television. Can't even read. So I lay on the bed, picking my cuticles, trying—and failing—not to think about Rooter. I lift a blind and look to his backyard. I wish I hadn't.

The slutty blonde from a few nights ago is back and sits on Rooter's lap. He's got one arm wrapped around her, his hand rests on her thigh. They must be in a relationship. I bet she wouldn't appreciate the fact that he was cozying up to the brunette earlier. I know I wouldn't. Yet another reminder that I indeed dodged a bullet.

Why do I even care? Why am I concerning myself with this shit? Rooter isn't a part of my life. He never really was. He can do whatever and whomever he chooses.

And so can I. I need to find something or rather someone better with whom to spend my time. I've heard people say the best way to get over someone is to find someone new. But why do I even need to get over him? We were never together! We were and are nothing to each other. God, I'm pathetic.

Miranda is right. I need to find someone to date. I spring from the bed and go to her room, entering without knocking.

"Miranda?"

"Yeah?" She sits up on her elbows.

"Find me a date."

I've gone back to work, and not a moment too soon. I'm just about broke. Randy has me working in the office, helping with employee schedules and vendor orders. If I had it my way, I'd continue working in the office instead of on the floor as a server. But my foot is much better, so it's only a matter of time before I'm back to taking orders and schlepping beverages.

Ryan pops his head into the office doorway. "Want to grab a movie tonight?"

"Sure," I say, even though I can't afford it. It's the best offer I've had in a long time so I refuse to turn it down.

"Great." He smiles sweetly. "My treat."

"No, I'll pay for myself."

"I invited you, so I'll pay."

I know what he's doing. He's aware of my financial woes. "Ryan, it's okay. Really."

"You're doing me the favor, Soph. I hate going to the movies alone, and I really want to catch the latest Seth Peterson flick. He's such a hot piece of ass."

One of the many things Ryan and I see eye to eye on is Seth Peterson's ass.

"Fine," I agree, knowing he won't back down, "but you have to let me buy the popcorn."

The movie is a Rom-Com and makes me feel even lonelier than I already am. Apparently, it does the same to Ryan.

"Stay with me tonight?" He asks as we walk to his car. "I still haven't gotten used to sleeping alone."

His invitation sounds lovely. I could use a little time away from my house. Away from Rooter's house. "Sure."

Though Ryan and I are just friends, lying next to him in his bed relieves my loneliness. The warmth of his body next to mine, though we aren't touching, is comforting. For a moment, I allow myself to pretend he's my boyfriend and snuggle a little closer.

I've never known real love. Never been held by a guy who loves me. I yearn for it. I ache for it. My insides feel hollow. When will I find the one who completes me?

When I wake, I don't recall falling asleep, and for the first time in weeks I didn't dream of Rooter. I smile, thankful for my dear friend, who's still asleep next to me.

Later that morning Ryan drives me home. Just before we reach my house we pass Rooter, on his morning run. We pull up in front of my house and he jogs by as I climb out of the car. We glance in each other's direction and our eyes meet, but only for a second. He doesn't say hi. He doesn't even nod the way he used to. He simply looks away and continues jogging to his house.

"Thanks for last night," Ryan says. "I needed that."

"Me, too." I smile. Ryan has quickly become one of my best friends. In fact, history excluded, he's giving Miranda a run for her money.

"See you later babe." He winks.

"See ya, babe," I say with a chuckle and close the door. Babe is our new mutual name for one another.

I turn around to find Rooter standing in his driveway stretching. He watches Ryan's car as he drives away. Without bothering to acknowledge him, I stride to my door.

"Hey, Sophie," he says nonchalantly as if we talk all the time.

His greeting takes me by surprise, but I don't let it show. "Hey," I state simply, open my door, and go inside.

The gall of him! How dare he say hi to me! Technically, he didn't say hi. He said hey, which is more than hi in my opinion. Hey is what you say to a friend. Hi is a kind greeting you say to anyone including a stranger. I'd prefer that he said hi. In fact, I'd prefer that he said nothing at all. He warned me I was better off not knowing him, and now I believe he was right. He needs to leave me alone.

Yet the mere sound of Rooter's voice saying my name is enough to make my entire system go haywire. My pulse races and a warm sensation washes over my entire body. My breathing has picked up and my knees are weak. I lean against the door and try to regain my composure.

As the hours tick by I try not to think about the sound of Rooter's voice as he said my name. Instead, I focus on tonight's double date with Hayden, Miranda and Ian. The closer it gets the more eager I become. I look forward to a fun night out, and after talking to Hayden on the phone for two hours yesterday, I'm excited about seeing him.

Miranda begs me to let her fix me up. My style is much more conservative than hers, so we have to compromise. After trying on at least half of the dresses in her closet, I settle on a little blue dress with an open back and bell sleeves. It's a little shorter than I prefer, but at my height, most dresses fit me this way. We pair it with silver high heeled sandals and crystal embellished dangle earrings. My hair is up with a few loose tendrils. Miranda applies my makeup, giving me a sultry appearance with smoky eyes and red lips.

After a final appraisal in the mirror, the doorbell rings. Miranda wasn't lying. The guy standing before me isn't the Hayden I remember. This guy is cool and confident. His outfit is sleek; a crisp, fitted, white collared shirt with the sleeves rolled up, a black tie, dark jeans, and trendy boots. He's definitely no longer awkward. His dark hair is perfectly shaggy. He has a very handsome face with just the right amount of stubble. I'm totally swooning.

"Sophie," Hayden says and flashes a confident smile. His voice a little higher in pitch than I prefer in a guy. "It's so good to see you."

"You, too," I answer honestly.

He pulls me in for a quick, yet warm embrace and then steps away and gives me a good once over. "You are breathtaking."

My face heats up. No one has ever said that to me before, but the way he says it is so sincere that it doesn't sound cheesy. "Thank you."

Hayden guides me by the elbow to the passenger door of his car—a shiny black BMW. I hear a noise, a choking sound, and glance at Rooter's driveway. He's straddling his bike, eyes on mine, mouth hanging wide open. I smirk at him and get in the car. Rooter fires up his bike and speeds away, full throttle.

THE ATTACK

The date hasn't gone well. Hayden may have grown out of his awkward, dorky phase, but he's turned into a real prick. He's elitist and conceited. So is his friend, Ian.

The drive home feels like it takes a decade. When we finally pull up to my house I hurry out of the car. Hayden does the same.

"I would've gotten that for you," he says, referring to the car door.

I spy Rooter sitting on his front porch. We make brief eye contact.

"Sorry," I flash a sweet smile, not for his sake, but for Rooter's. Hayden offers me his arm and I take it as we walk to my front door.

"I really enjoyed tonight." Hayden gazes at me with a smile.

"Me, too," I lie as compellingly as I can, but just saying the words makes me cringe.

"It was so nice to see you after all this time." He turns to face me and takes my hand.

"Yeah it was." I lie again.

"I'd love to take you out again, soon." He looks to Miranda and Ian who aren't saying anything to each other. "Just the two of us."

"That would be nice." And the lies keep on rolling. I smile to add to the effect.

"Next week?"

No way am I committing to anything with this jerk, but I want Rooter to think I like him. "I'll need to check my work schedule. Can I get back to you?"

"Please do."

He smiles and my stomach roils with the knowledge of what's coming next. He leans in slowly for a kiss. I debate what I should do. I don't want to kiss him. At all. But I want Rooter to see me kiss him. When he's about eighty percent in I try not to tense up as I lean in the rest of the way until our lips meet. There's nothing remarkable about the kiss and I'm thankful when he doesn't slip me the tongue.

"I've dreamt about doing that since sixth grade," he admits with an excited smile. It reminds me of the guy I used to know and not the asshat I just had dinner with.

"Thank you for tonight, Hayden. It was lovely."

Miranda unlocks the door while the guys go back to the car. Not able to resist, I turn in Rooter's direction to find him staring at me with a blank expression.

The moment we close the door, Miranda apologizes for the evening. "Worst date ever. This one's on me. I was entirely wrong about Hayden."

"It was pretty awful." I sit on the sofa and remove my heels.

Ryan made me promise to text him the second I get home to tell him how the date went. Not thirty seconds after I press send he responds: *Mind if I come over since it's early?*

It is early. It's only ten o'clock. I respond to his text with: *Abso-bloody-lutely.* He thinks it's hilarious whenever I say bloody or bollocks since I'm American.

"Ryan's coming over," I tell Miranda.

"Yay," she says gleefully and claps her hands.

Miranda fell in love with Ryan after he gave her one of his famous back massages. The man has magical hands. He once rubbed my back for an entire hour. I thought I was in heaven. Yet another reason I wish he was straight. I've yet to meet a guy willing to give one, let alone one good at it.

Ryan, Miranda, and I sit in her room discussing and laughing about what a disaster our date was.

"That's the absolute last time you set me up," I warn her. "You suck at picking guys for me."

"Tonight was a flop, I admit it, but it's not my fault. There aren't any good guys out there!"

"Hey," Ryan says hand over heart, feigning offense, "I'm a good guy."

"Yes, babe, you are." I mess his long hair. "You're the last good guy alive, and as luck would have it, you don't like girls."

"I love girls," he says. "I just don't want to shag them."

Miranda yawns. "It's been a long day for me. I'm going to call it a night."

"In other words, get the fuck out, right?" Ryan says with a laugh.

The British accent is by far my favorite. I love when Ryan says any word with a 'u'. He pronounces them with an ooh sound rather than an uh sound.

When Ryan and I enter my room I see Rooter's light is on and his blinds are open. I turn my light on and hurry to the window to close my blinds when Rooter comes into sight. He's shirtless, showing off all of his tattoos; the one on his arm continues onto his shoulder, down his side. I've never seen anything so magnificent. His sweatpants hang low on his hips revealing a perfect V on his abdomen. His eyes switch from me to Ryan and back again; his face giving nothing away. We both close our blinds at the same time.

"Bloody hell, that man is gorgeous!" Ryan says.

Sadness and emptiness sweep over me. "Yeah, tell me something I don't know."

I don't sleep well. I spend the night tossing and turning, dreaming of Rooter. We kiss, we hold hands, he tells me he loves me. And then I wake up and am smacked by the reality none of those things will ever happen.

An hour later I walk Ryan to his car. We hug and give each other a quick, friendly kiss.

"See you tomorrow, babe," he says and opens his car door.

"See ya, babe."

When Ryan pulls away I turn around to find Rooter standing in his driveway watching me. Without a word I start walking to my house.

"I really didn't take you as the revolving door type," he snipes.

I come to a screeching halt and spin to face him. "What did you say?"

"Fucking one guy, going out with another a couple days later, then calling the first guy over after being dropped off by the second. That's high traffic if you ask me."

"I didn't ask you, Rooter, so fuck off!"

He simply shrugs which pisses me off even more.

I charge toward him. "And who the hell are you to judge me? I've seen the skanks you run with."

He throws his head back and laughs, a booming sound. "Apparently, you aren't any better than them."

"I'm not a slut!"

"Your actions would prove otherwise." He purses his lips.

"You have no fucking idea what you're talking about!"

"No? You fuck," he makes air quotations, "*babe*, go out with another guy, kiss him, agree to another date then bring *babe* over to fuck again? Pardon me, but that is a perfect definition of a slut!"

Evidently, Rooter never got my text about Ryan being gay, and seeing me with both guys has given him the wrong impression. However, I'm too pissed to care about that right now. He just accused me of being a whore like the girls he hooks up with. I'm no slut! I've had sex with one guy in my life, once. And it was not of my own volition, so Rooter can go screw himself.

"For your information, not that it's any of your damn business, but," I make air quotations, "*babe*, the guy you think I'm fucking, is *gay* you asshole!"

His eyes go wide with shock and he takes a small step forward. "What?"

"That's right. *Babe* is one hundred percent take it up the ass *gay*! I'm not fucking anyone and I'm *not* a slut."

I turn to walk away, but am brought to a standstill by Rooter's firm grip on my arm. He spins me around and crashes his lips against mine.

I shove Rooter away and slap his face with all my might causing him to grimace and his body to tense. Both of us are panting.

"Don't touch me!" I roar.

"I'm sorry," he breathes with a pained expression. "I shouldn't have—" I don't allow him to finish.

"You're damn right you shouldn't have."

But then the memory of his lips on mine, however brief a time it was, comes to mind. They were so soft, and warm, and their sweet taste still lingers. My mind races. I'm pissed off and confused. I hate the way he's treated me and the things he accused me of. But I've wanted him for so long. Part of me still does. A really *big* part. But not this way. Not like this. I turn to walk away, and to my surprise, relief and dismay, he lets me go.

The moment I close the living room door, tears pour from my eyes. Not because I'm sad, but rather because I'm utterly overwhelmed.

"Oh my God." Miranda rushes to my side. "What the hell just happened?"

"Rooter accused me of being a slut and we got into a fight and then he kissed me and then I hit him." The words fly out in one rushed sentence.

Miranda takes me by the hand and leads me to the sofa. She sits next to me and rubs my arm in a comforting manner. I wipe my tears away with the back of my hand.

"Why would he accuse you of that?"

"He thought I've been sleeping with Ryan, and then he saw me with Hayden last night, and then saw Ryan leave just now."

"Then why did he kiss you?" She asks, confused.

"Because I told him Ryan is gay and that I'm not fucking anyone."

Her eyes go wide and a look of amusement forms on her face. "So, he was jealous."

I perk up. This hadn't occurred to me due to my state of upset. "You know, I think you're right."

Her eyes go wide. "Wow."

"Yeah, wow." My mind goes back to the kiss, my mind stuck on the idea that Rooter was jealous. There's no other explanation.

"How does that make you feel? That he might have been jealous?"

I take a deep breath, allowing myself a moment to think before answering. I feel a lot of things, and it's all difficult to sort through.

"Truthfully, I like it. But, after everything that's happened, I don't know…" I don't finish the sentence. There's no need because Miranda understands what I mean better than I do.

Shortly thereafter I hear Rooter's motorcycle as he speeds away.

I sit with Miranda in her room, reading gossip magazines and smutty romance novels about highlanders and damsels in distress while she studies for her upcoming exam. Though we don't talk much, her presence is enough to calm my nerves.

Around five thirty she takes a break from studying and we head to the kitchen to cook dinner; ramen noodles—the college girl special. Beef flavor for her, chicken for me. We sit at the dining room table and eat in silence. The great thing about Miranda is she knows when I need to be quiet; when I need to take time and sort my thoughts, but don't want to be alone while I do it.

I take the last bite of my noodles when Rooter's bike comes roaring into his driveway. After dismounting the motorcycle he stands, helmet in hand, staring at me as though he's debating coming over. Again, I'm both relieved and dismayed when he opens his back door and goes into his house.

"You want to talk to him," Miranda says. "I can see it in your eyes."

"Yeah," I admit, "but not yet. I'm not ready."

"Well, when you're ready, I have a feeling he'll be waiting." She gets up, takes our bowls to the kitchen and places them in the sink while I continue to stare at Rooter's house. "Want to watch a movie until we fall asleep?"

Mike walks into the living room and plops onto the couch and turns on ESPN. It's the only television with cable in the house. He pays for it so he can watch Sports Zone, so we can't very well tell him to go away. He may not be reliable on the rent every month, but he makes sure to pay the cable bill on time.

"We can watch a DVD in my room," I propose.

After changing into our pajamas and popping in a DVD we've watched a thousand times, we crawl onto my bed with a bag of microwave popcorn and two sodas. Twenty minutes into the movie, the light in Rooter's room comes on and grabs my attention.

He sits at the edge of his bed, arms on his knees, head in his hands. When he looks up his eyes meet mine. I watch as he pulls out his phone and types something. In an instant, my phone pings with his motorcycle ringtone. I pause the movie and grab my phone from the bedside table.

Rooter: *I promise to leave u alone, but I want to tell u I'm sorry. For everything.*

I stare at the screen, trying to process the myriad of thoughts coursing through my mind. I glance at him. He's looking at his phone, perhaps awaiting my response.

"Is it him?" Miranda asks and I nod. "What does it say?"

I hand her the phone. She reads the text then hands it back.

After a long minute and a half, I decide how to respond. I look to his window and he's still sitting on his bed, but this time, looking at me with a forlorn expression.

Me: *Thank you for your apology. I haven't decided whether or not I want you to leave me alone (and I will be the one to make that decision). I'll let you know when I do.*

I hit send and watch as he reads my text. A ghost of a smile crosses his lips. He shakes his head and types again.

"What did you text him?" Miranda asks and I hand her the phone. It pings again, and she gives it back.

Rooter: *That's fair.*

Assuming our conversation is over, I lay the phone next to me and we resume the movie. Although the movie is one of my favorites, I can't concentrate on it. All I can think about is the way Rooter's lips felt against mine, and the somber, sincere expression he wore when he was sitting on his bed texting me.

A half hour later, Rooter's bedroom light goes out. My window is open, allowing in the cool evening air. His bed faces his window so if he's in it he can see me. I wonder if he's watching me. My phone pings.

Rooter: *Good night Sophie.*

A warm feeling falls over me and I smile. I bet he's watching me.

Me: *Good night Rooter.*

I'm in a deep sleep when I'm abruptly torn from my bed. A deafening scream escapes my lips and a large hand covers my mouth to quiet me. I bite down on the skin until I taste blood. A man curses and I scream again.

"Let me go!" I thrash about, trying to pry myself from his grip, but it's useless. He's too strong.

I try to remember the instructions my self-defense teacher gave me, but I draw a blank. Not knowing what else to do, I continue screaming and writhing, terrified, trying desperately to get away.

"Shut up, or I'll kill you right now," the man snarls and hauls me from my room.

Miranda is screaming as I'm being dragged down the stairs. She and her captor are following behind. Once we're downstairs, the men toss us onto the living room floor. Mike is tied to a dining room chair across the room, his mouth covered in duct tape. He's crying.

"On your knees," Miranda's captor commands us.

I scramble to my knees and peer up at our assailants. The two of them are wearing all black with matching face masks.

"Your boy here owes us a lot of money," the man continues. "We've waited patiently for him to come up with it. We're done waiting."

My captor walks to where Mike is sitting. "We aren't leaving here until we collect in either cash or blood," he explains.

A chill creeps up my spine. This is the kind of story you hear about on the news and read in the paper. You never dream it will happen to you. My entire body trembles and my breaths are fast and shallow. I've never been so scared in my life. I don't know how much money Mike owes these thugs, but based on their actions, it must be a lot. Neither of us have any money. I presume there's only one way this standoff will end; with one or all of us dead. I glower at Mike, disgusted. How did he lose his way to this degree? I knew it was bad, but I didn't realize it was this serious.

"Mike says he knows where he can get the cash," the other man says.

"You girls are going to be—"

Before he can finish his sentence, Rooter comes around the corner, grabs him by the throat and puts a gun to his temple. Rooter's eyes flash to mine then to the guy standing above Miranda who reaches for his own gun.

"Move another inch and I'll put a bullet through this fuck's skull," Rooter threatens menacingly, eyes bulging, nostrils flaring.

DOUBLE H PROTECTION

"Sophie," Rooter says, never taking his eye off the perpetrator, "go get your gun."

Without hesitating, I sprint up the stairs taking them two at a time to my room to retrieve my thirty eight from my purse. I dash back downstairs and point the gun at the man across the room from Rooter. No one has moved a muscle.

"Keep it on him," Rooter tells me and then forces the man he's holding the gun on to the floor. "Tape his feet together," he tells Miranda.

She jumps up from her position on the floor and hurries to follow out Rooter's orders.

"If you even think about touching her, I'll blow your brains all over this floor," Rooter growls at the guy as she wraps the tape around his ankles. "Make it tight," he instructs.

When she's finished with his feet, Rooter tells her to tape his hands behind his back. Once finished, Rooter moves to the other guy and points his gun at him. "I've got him," he tells me. "Watch the other guy."

I back away and stalk to the thug on the floor and point my gun at him.

"Tape him up same as the other one," Rooter instructs Miranda, and she quickly complies.

Rooter places the men side by side on the living room floor. He kneels and shows them the tattoo on his inside of his forearm. Overlapping H's. Their eyes go wide with fear.

"That's right bitches, I'm double H. And that girl right there," Rooter points at me, his voice low and menacing, "the one you snatched out of bed in the middle night to do God knows what with; she's mine."

His words cause my heart to flutter even though I know he's only saying them as a scare tactic.

"You fuck with her," he continues, "you fuck with my club. I'm sure you've heard what happens to people who fuck with my club."

"I didn't know she was your girl, man," my captor squeals.

Rooter pushes the barrel of his gun to the guy's temple. "So what? You think it's okay to go around hurting innocent women?"

"We didn't hurt her, man," the guy shrieks.

"There's blood on her face!" Rooter shouts, furious, and I fear he'll pull the trigger.

"That's my blood. The bitch bit me!"

Rooter hits the asshole in the face with the butt of his gun. "Do *not* call her a bitch. Why are you here?"

"He owes Viper three large," Miranda's attacker says. "He sent us to collect."

Rooter saunters over to Mike and rips off the duct tape covering his mouth causing him to grimace. "This true?" He asks him.

Mike nods, too scared and ashamed to speak.

"You're fucking pathetic," Rooter spits. "I'll deal with you later."

"I should call the police," I say.

"No!" Rooter barks. "The police can't help you. Viper will just send someone else to finish his dirty work. I need to handle this."

My mouth hits the floor. "Do you know Viper?"

"Yes, and we need to finish this shit tonight."

How the hell does he know Viper? "What are you going to do?"

"I'm going to send Viper a message." He turns and glares at the perps on the floor. "That this house and its inhabitants are under Double H protection, and that the debt will be considered paid in full for the attack on you."

An instant later, the front door flies open and in walks Bear, followed by three other Double H members all of whom are rather large and scary looking. I've never felt safer in my life. The men take in the scene before them. First, Bear looks at Rooter, then to the two men on the floor, then to Mike, then to me, and lastly, Miranda. His eyes linger on her. She's wearing a revealing white satin pajama cami and panty set. He grabs the throw blanket from the back of the sofa and hands it to her so she can cover herself. The guy may never smile, but he's chivalrous. Who would've guessed it?

"Everyone okay?" Bear asks.

"We're good. Put these two in the van," Rooter instructs him, pointing at the goons. "Take them to the warehouse."

I watch as Bear and another club member hoist one of the men up and carry him out of the house.

"You okay?" Rooter asks and takes my gun from my hands and sets it next to his on the table.

I'm still shaking and can't answer his question. My breathing is erratic as the enormity of what just occurred hits me. He pulls me into his chest and wraps his arms around me. Before this moment, I hadn't noticed he is shirtless, wearing only a pair of dark gray sweats. I press myself against him in an attempt to lose myself in the comfort of being in his strong arms. The warmth of his skin against my face and the sound of his steady heartbeat is soothing. I try to mimic his even breaths. Just as I'm calming down, I'm startled by Miranda screaming.

"How could you do this to us?" She yells at Mike and slaps him in the face. "What the hell is the matter with you?"

"I'm so sorry," he cries.

"If it wasn't for Rooter, we could all be dead right now!"

Bear walks back into the room. "They're loaded," he says to Rooter, taking notice of the way he's holding me. "You staying?"

"Yeah. I'm not quite finished here," Rooter says signaling to Mike.

"All right," Bear looks at Miranda then back to Rooter. "Need anything else from me?"

"I've got this. Take care of them," Rooter says, referring to Viper's thugs. "I'll catch up with you when I'm done here."

"All right, man." Bear nods at me and Miranda before turning to leave.

"Okay, everyone have a seat," Rooter commands. "We're going to have a little family meeting." He motions for Miranda to take a seat on one end of the couch and leads me to sit on the other side. He pulls Mike over in his chair so he's facing us and then takes a seat in the middle of the couch and wraps his arm around my waist.

"Are you going to leave me tied up?" Mike asks.

"You will speak only when I've given you permission. Do you understand?" Rooter threatens, his tone ominous.

Mike doesn't answer, but it's clear he understands.

"You," Rooter points at Mike, "are moving out first thing in the morning. I don't care where you go or if you even *have* anywhere to go, but you are leaving."

Mike struggles not to argue, but remains quiet. Rooter turns to Miranda.

"Do you have a problem with this?"

Miranda cowers and glances down at her hands which are folded in her lap. "I agree that he needs to go, but..."

"No but's. I won't allow him to be here if Sophie's here. Do you want Sophie to leave instead?"

My head snaps in Rooter's direction. *He won't allow him here with me?* I glance down at his arm hugging my waist. Possessive. Protective. And sexy as hell. I like it. A lot.

"No."

"Then he's gone. First thing." He looks back at Mike. "If I need to, I'll personally see to it. I don't want you coming anywhere near this house or Sophie without my prior knowledge."

"That's a little extreme," Miranda complains.

"Extreme?" Rooter shouts. "He almost got you both killed tonight or have you already forgotten?"

Miranda shrinks back. "No, but he's my brother. This is my house. I'll decide whether he can come here."

I turn to Miranda, incredulous. "How long are you going to accept the shit he puts you through? The shit he puts both of us through?"

"You're acting like I should write him off. I can't do that," she cries. "He's the only family I have left."

"Fine." Rooter pulls me closer to him. "Sophie will move out first thing in the morning."

"What?" Miranda and I say in unison.

Rooter turns to me. "I won't have you here if he's here."

I'd venture a guess that tonight puts me and Rooter back in the friend zone, but he's acting like more than just my friend. He's being possessive in a boyfriend-y kind of way. I like it.

"Rooter, it's not that simple," I argue. Where does he expect me to go?

"It is that simple, Sophie." He looks at Miranda. "So who's it going to be? Your loving, reliable best friend or your precious brother who almost got you both killed?"

Miranda sniffles and wipes her face. She looks from me to Mike. Honestly, I'm hurt and offended that this decision is difficult for her to make.

"You have to go, Mike." Her voice is barely louder than a whisper.

"But," Mike starts and Rooter shoots forward in his seat promptly shutting him up.

"You heard her," Rooter says. "You're out. And I better not hear of any retaliation against these girls over it."

A few minutes later Rooter removes his restraints and Mike rushes upstairs without a word.

"You're doing the right thing," Rooter reassures Miranda.

She nods but her expression is sad and unsure.

"Thank you for helping us tonight," I say to Rooter. "I thought we were dead."

"Thank God your window was open or I might not have heard your screams." He tucks a lock of hair behind my ear and gazes at me with warm eyes.

"I'm going to talk to my brother." Miranda gets up and goes upstairs.

My eyes follow her. I'm peeved. The least she could do is thank Rooter for swooping in and saving her life.

"I've never been so scared in my life," I admit with a shudder and Rooter pulls me into his chest and rubs my back. "I can't believe what just happened."

"It's okay now. Those guys won't come near you again."

I look up at him. "How can you be so sure?"

"Viper won't mess with the club. He knows better."

I arch a brow. "Care to elaborate?"

He shakes his head. "Trust me. After telling those guys you're mine, I wouldn't be surprised if you receive a handwritten apology from Viper himself."

The clock on the wall says it's after four in the morning. I'm wired right now, but I'm supposed to be at work at ten. After being off work so long, I can't call off. I need the money and I really don't want to do that to Randy after how understanding and generous he's been. Today will be a very long day. I sigh. "Shit."

"What?"

"I have to be at work in less than six hours."

"You should try to sleep."

I rub my eye with my middle and index finger. "I doubt I'll be able to, but I should try. I'm working a double."

"I need to go deal with… things." He clenches his jaw.

I'm still shaken up so the last thing I want is for Rooter to leave. "Will you stay… a little while until I calm down?"

Rooter's face softens, and he smiles. "Sure, but I thought you were going to try to sleep?"

I flush, embarrassed. "It's just that I'm completely on edge and won't be able to sleep until I calm down. Your being here… makes me feel safe." I've never felt so exposed and vulnerable in my life.

"Okay. I'll stay." He stands and holds out his hand.

Rooter leads me, hand in hand, to my room. He pulls the sheet back for me and I crawl into the bed facing the wall. He gets in and curls himself around me from behind.

"Is this okay?"

"Yeah." The memory of being dragged from my bed less than an hour ago comes to mind and I cry.

He clutches me tight against him. "It's okay, Sophie. I'm here."

"I thought I was going to die." I shudder from heavy sobs.

"I'll never let anyone hurt you."

"My life is so fucked up," I say between sniffles. "This is the kind of shit that always happens to me. No matter how hard I try to get away from it, it finds me."

"It'll never find you again. I won't let it." His voice is resolute.

Rooter holds me tight while I cry myself to sleep. The last thing I remember is him kissing the back of my head and telling me everything will be okay.

We jerk upright in the bed when awoken by the sound of my alarm.

"Shit," Rooter says groggily. "What time is it?" He rolls over and shuts off the alarm. It's only seven o'clock.

The air coming in from the window is cool and gives me a shiver. I lay back down and pull the blankets over me. "Let's go back to sleep."

"I should go deal with things at the warehouse."

Rooter looks at me, smooths my hair away from my face. The rock hard muscles in his abdomen contract as he shifts into a sitting position sending tingles from my head to my toes. I could lay here and stare at him all day.

"You sure about working today?" He asks.

"I have to."

"I'll send one of the guys to escort you there. What time are you off?"

"You don't need to do that." I start to sit up, but he stops me.

"It would give me peace of mind."

My pulse quickens. "I thought you said nothing else would happen."

"It won't once I get word to Viper. Right now he's probably wondering where his guys are."

I rub my face. "This is so messed up."

"Yeah," he agrees. "I'll come get you from work. Are you getting off at your normal time?"

"Yes."

"Damn, that's a long day." He sighs and rubs the back of his neck.

I shrug. "Got to pay rent somehow."

Rooter gazes at me for a long time with a serious, thoughtful expression. "You're very strong, Sophie."

I laugh, sarcastic. "Yeah, right."

"You are," he asserts and lies on his side to face me. "You've been through so much. And you were great last night. So calm, collected. Did everything I told you to."

"I was freaking the fuck out."

"It didn't show. You know, that's one thing I've noticed about you. You have a great poker face. You never give anything away."

"From years of practice."

Growing up, I was always sad, scared, or angry. Though I refused to pretend to be happy to appease my doped up mother, I also couldn't let my true feelings show. I feared she'd beat me or lock me in my closet for being ungrateful for the wonderful life she had given me.

Tears well in my eyes and I look away. I hate being emotional. When people are around I despise it even more.

Rooter places his finger underneath my chin and gently turns my face to his. His eyes are sad. Sad for me. And I hate that. I don't want his pity. "You don't have to hide from me, Sophie." His voice is so tender.

I shake my head. "Sometimes, I wish I could hide from myself."

He pulls me close, kisses the side of my head, and inhales deeply. "I didn't mean to make you sad."

I hug him tighter to me. No one else's embrace has ever comforted me more or made me feel safer than Rooter's. I wish I could stay in his arms endlessly.

He pulls away so he can face me, but keeps his arms around me. His eyes exude warmth and sincerity. He leans in slow. Right before his lips touch mine, he stops. "Is this okay?" He whispers.

"Yes."

When Rooter's lips meet mine they're soft and warm like I remembered, only this time, he's gentle rather than forceful. He gives me a sweet, serene, closed mouth kiss, but it lingers. This simple kiss holds more meaning and power than any passionate kiss I've ever shared with anyone else. When he pulls away and looks in my eyes, it seems as though he feels the same.

SOMETHING SWEET, SOMETHING SOUR

Darren, a member of Double H, shows up at nine thirty to follow me to work. He's the type of guy who when you see him you cross to the other side of the street; older, perhaps late thirties, with dark hair turning gray around the edges, and he's huge. Not fat huge. His tattooed skin covers loads of ridiculous muscle. He watches from his motorcycle as I walk to the back door of the restaurant and waves before he leaves.

This morning, Rooter instructed me not to say anything to anyone about last night. He said it's better it stays between those of us involved. He delivered the same speech to Miranda though with a little more urgency to drive home the point. This kind of story would spread across this town like a flu epidemic if not controlled at the source. Rooter insists the last thing we or his club needs is for the police to come barging through the door.

I make it through the first half of my shift on pure adrenaline alone. By the ninth hour, I sway as I walk and yawn uncontrollably while taking my customer's orders. Randy comes over to me while I'm loading a tray with drinks at the bar.

"I'll take this." He looks at me with concern. "You go lay your head on my desk."

"Are you sure?"

"You're due for a break anyhow."

"But we're busting at the seams." I point at the crowded dining room.

"That's why I need you to rest, so you can get back out here and hustle." He spins me in the direction of the office. "I'll come get you in thirty minutes."

The moment my head hits the desk, I'm dead to the world. No sooner than I'm asleep, I'm awoken by a kiss on the cheek.

"Time to wake up sleeping beauty," Ryan says sweetly and I lift my head. "Wow, you look bad. Are you okay?"

I shake my head. "Bad night."

"Drinking?"

I shake my head again. "Mike and his bullshit."

He crosses his arms. "What did he do now?"

"To make a long story short, he fucked up. Bad." I adjust my ponytail. "Got involved with the wrong people. Miranda kicked him out."

Ryan throws his hands in the air. "Yes!"

"Well, it wasn't exactly her choice."

"You finally stood up to her?"

I shake my head. "I would have this time, but no. Rooter told her he had to go."

He furrows his brow. "Wait, I thought you weren't talking to him anymore."

I grin. "Last night sort of changed that."

"What aren't you telling me?" He asks perceptively, with a grin.

"We kissed. Again." Ryan already knew about my argument with Rooter after he left my house.

"No shit! With your consent this time?"

"Oh, yeah." I smile, giddy.

"You feeling better?" Randy interrupts us, poking his head around the door.

"I think so," I lie. I actually feel worse. Napping does that to me.

"Then let's get to it." He claps, prompting Ryan and I to follow him.

The rest of the night passes in a haze. By the time my shift comes to an end my feet and back ache, and my eyelids feel like they have weights on them. On our way out of the restaurant, Ryan and I find Rooter straddling his bike. I've never seen anything sexier than Rooter on his bike waiting for me. Unable to conceal my happiness to see him, an enormous smile spreads across my face. To my delight, he smiles at me the same way.

"Hi," I say, breathless as I reach his bike with Ryan at my side.

"Hi." He dismounts his bike and extends his hand to Ryan. "I'm Rooter."

I'm relieved he saved me from a possible awkward introduction. What would I have said? Ryan, this is Rooter, my neighbor? My friend? When we each know we're more than both, even though we haven't labeled exactly what this is yet.

Ryan accepts his invitation to shake hands. "Ryan."

"Nice to meet you, Ryan."

"Same here." Ryan turns to me. "See you tomorrow night."

"See ya."

"What happened to *babe*?" Rooter teases when Ryan walks away.

"Well, I didn't want you to get worked up again."

He chuckles and rubs the back of his neck, embarrassed. "Now that I know he's gay, I'm sure that won't be a problem." We both laugh. "Ready to go home?"

"Yeah." I look at his bike and wonder what it would be like to go for a ride. I've never been on a motorcycle.

"Want to ride with me?" He asks, reading my mind.

"What about my car?"

"I'll bring you to pick it up in the morning." He grabs his helmet off his handle bars and sits it on my head and fastens it. After getting on the bike, he instructs me to do the same. "Put your arms around me like this." He guides my hands around his waist. "Hold on tight."

"Okay." I'm a bundle of excited nerves.

The bike roars to life. "If you get scared, let me know."

"I will."

"You ready?"

"Yeah."

So many times, I've fantasized about what it would be like to ride on the back of Rooter's motorcycle, never believing it would actually happen. It's unlike anything I could've ever imagined. Although we can't be going faster than thirty five miles per hour, it gives me an exhilarating rush. My fantasies didn't do the real deal any justice whatsoever. There's nothing like this in the entire world. The only thing I like better is the feeling of Rooter's lips on mine.

We pull into Rooter's garage, and he kills the engine. I climb off wishing the ride had been a little longer regardless of how tired I am.

"What did you think?" He asks, hopeful.

"It was amazing!" The air in Michigan turns considerably cool during the night, and I'm cold from the ride, but it was totally worth it.

He smiles wide and unstraps the helmet and removes it from my head. "I love riding. I can barely tolerate being in a car anymore."

"I can see why." I brush my fingertips across the smooth metal of the gas tank. "Maybe I'll get one of my own."

"Whoa, whoa," he chuckles, "slow down. One step at a time."

I smirk. "It's not like I can afford one anyway."

We walk side by side down the length of this driveway. "How'd you do today?" He asks, all trace of amusement gone.

"I was fine until the halfway point, but I persevered."

The corner of his mouth turns up. "I'm not surprised."

"Gotta do what you gotta do." I shrug.

"One day, life will be easier."

"I've been telling myself that for years."

"It will, I promise you."

He takes me by the hand, interlacing his fingers with mine. This is the first time we've ever held hands. I wonder if he realizes this.

"Thank you. For everything."

"No, Sophie, it's I who should thank you."

"For what?" I furrow my brow, surprised.

"For giving me a chance when I didn't deserve one. I've been awful to you."

"What?" I come to a halt. "You've done so much for me. I don't even want to think about where I'd be right now if not for you."

"I don't want to think about it either. But I've done some pretty nasty things too."

"You've also done some pretty great things. You saved my life." God, I want him to kiss me so bad I can hardly stand it.

He's quiet a moment, clearly processing his thoughts. "I thought you were better off without my influence, but now I believe you might actually be better off with me around."

"I've always believed that."

He scratches his head while rocking back and forth on his toes and heels, nervous and perhaps a little bashful. A total contradiction to his usual intense, confident demeanor.

"I'm done trying to stay away from you, Sophie. When I told those guys you were mine, I meant it."

My breath catches. I want to be his. I've wanted to be his for so long.

His confidence returns and his eyes convey a powerful determination. "I intend to make you mine."

"I think you'll find that won't be very difficult."

He smiles and leans toward me slowly until our lips meet in another soft, sweet kiss. I pull him closer to deepen the kiss, but he gently resists and pulls away, resting his forehead on mine. I whine in protest.

"I want to do this right," he breathes. "This will probably sound juvenile, but… will you go on a date with me?"

I smile wide and have to stop myself from jumping up and down. "I'd love to go on a date with you, Rooter."

His shoulders relax and he breathes what sounds like a sigh of relief. Had he been worried I'd say no?

"When's your next day off?"

"Wednesday."

He beams, excited. "Then Wednesday it is."

"So, how did today go for you?" I ask as we walk, hand in hand, the rest of the way to my door.

"It was fine," is all he says, but he can tell I want more. "I've taken care of everything. Don't worry."

Truth be told I'm not worried. I have every confidence in Rooter's ability to handle the situation and to protect me. "I was just curious."

"It's done now." He kisses the top of my hand. "You rest. We'll talk tomorrow."

When I enter the house, it's dark and quiet. I turn on the stairway light to go to my room. When I get to the top of the stairs, I hear Miranda crying in her room. I'm exhausted, desperate for sleep, but I can't ignore my best friend in a time of need.

"Miranda?" I tap on her door.

"Come in," she croaks.

She's sitting on her bed, propped up against the headboard. Her face is a red, puffy mess. I don't dare ask her what's wrong because I already know.

"Want to talk about it?"

"I lost my brother today. I put him out on the street."

"You aren't blaming yourself are you?" I take a seat at the foot of her bed.

"I blame all of us, Sophie."

"What do you mean *all* of us?"

"Me, you, Rooter, Mike. All of us."

This is just like her. "That's bullshit! Mike did this to himself. To us! We could've been killed because of him."

"He has nowhere to go!"

I try my best to stay calm in order to talk sense into her. "I'm sure that isn't true. He has friends."

She rolls her eyes. "Yeah, druggie friends."

"Again, his choice." I wave my hand at an invisible Mike. "Not ours."

"Yeah and I made my choice to turn my back on my brother," she smacks a pillow, knocking it off the bed. "Who knows what will happen to him now."

"Whatever happens to him will be his own doing, Miranda. Not yours and not mine."

"He'll never get the help he needs out there." She waves toward the window.

I take a deep breath. "It wouldn't matter whether he's here or out there. He won't get the help he needs until he realizes that he needs help."

"You don't understand," she groans and waves me away.

This infuriates me. My mother was a drug addict. No matter how much I begged her, she refused to get help. It was her choice to make. She made it. And as a result, I turned my back on her and left home. She killed herself a little more than a year later. If anyone understands what Miranda is going through, it's me.

"Have you forgotten who you're talking to?"

She groans. "Can you not make this about you?"

I laugh, sarcastically. "You're the one making this out to be about me. You're mad and you blame me for the fact Mike is gone."

"It's partially your fault. You broke his heart at the worst possible time in his life, then you let your new psycho boyfriend make me throw him out."

I rise from the bed and glower at her. "Wait a minute, are you saying I should've gone out with Mike out of pity? Or are you actually mad at me for not having those kinds of feelings for him?"

"You should've handled it differently."

I lean into Miranda's face, pointing my index finger at her causing her to recoil. "I'm not to blame for Mike's bullshit," my voice is low and foreboding. "He's grown. He knows the difference between right and wrong. He's responsible for his actions. And as for my new *psycho boyfriend*," I motion toward Rooter's house, "he's the only reason you and I are alive right now. He saved us both from your fucked up brother's stupid ass decisions!"

"Maybe he wouldn't be making such stupid ass decisions if he had a little more support from the people he loves."

I back away and throw my hands in the air, exasperated. "I can't believe you're blaming me for his problems."

"Well, you certainly didn't help them."

"You're unbelievable." I clutch the sides of my head. "You know what? I should've been the one to go."

She crosses her arms and juts out her chin. "I think you're right."

"Fine. I'll leave first thing in the morning. I'll be expecting a refund for the rest of the month's rent." I stomp out of her room and slam the door behind me.

"Fine!" Miranda screams.

FIRST DATE

I'm in a deep sleep when I'm awoken by the sound of my door opening. Visions of the night before give me a start and I jerk upright. It's only Miranda, but it doesn't make me feel any better.

"Sorry I scared you," she whispers and enters my room cautiously. Her eyes are still puffy from crying last night.

"What do you want?" I rest on my elbows.

"I'm on my way to work, but I wanted to apologize for last night. I didn't mean any of it."

I shake my head, incensed. "Sure you did. You're just afraid of losing a reliable rent paying roommate."

She cries. "That's not true, Soph. I really am sorry."

"Miranda, I'm exhausted." I fall back onto my mattress.

"I know, but you work tonight so this is my only chance to talk to you. Please don't leave. Not until we talk. If you still want to move out after that, I won't try to stop you."

"Fine," I grumble, but only because I'm truly not sure where I'd even go. I think Ryan would take me on as a roommate, but if not I don't know where else I'd go.

"Do you mean that or are you saying it to get me to leave?"

I glare at her. "Only one way to find out."

"Please, Soph. Promise me you won't leave," she frets.

"I said I would stay."

She stands at the edge of my bed looking at me, reluctant to leave.

"Are you going to stand there and stare at me all day?" I snipe.

"Sorry. I'll see you tonight?"

"Yeah."

"Okay." She walks to my door and turns to look at me once more. "I really am *very* sorry about last night."

What am I supposed to say? Thank you? It's okay? I'm not thankful for her apology and it's not okay. So rather than respond I simply nod. Once she closes my door behind her I pull my blankets over my head hoping to go back to sleep, but my phone rings. The ringtone tells me it's Rooter. I roll over and pick it up from my nightstand.

"Hello?"

"I'm surprised you're up so early."

I don't think I'll ever become immune to the sound of his voice. I glance out my window and see him standing at his. "Stalking me?" I jest with a smile.

"Always," he chuckles. "I saw you talking to Miranda."

"Yeah, she and I got into it last night. She begged me not to move out."

"You're moving out?" His voice is thick with concern.

I drag my fingers through my hair and when they get stuck in a tangle it occurs to me I probably look like hell. "I doubt it."

"You doubt it?"

I check my appearance in the mirror and it confirms my suspicion. My hair is matted to the right side of my head and my eyes are ringed with dark circles. I must've slept hard. "It was a stupid fight. We'll get over it. We always do."

"Let me guess, it had to do with kicking Mike out."

"You guessed it."

"And she blames you and me."

"You guessed it again." Having this conversation on the phone while looking at each other through our bedroom windows is somewhat strange, but I like it. I like seeing his face as he talks; the shape of his lips when he forms his words and the way his body moves when he shifts on his feet. "You ready to take me to my car?"

"That's why I called. I need to run an errand. Shouldn't take longer than a few hours."

"That's cool. I could use a few more hours of sleep. Maybe you can take me to work later. I don't go in until four."

"That'll work." He flashes me a smile.

After an extremely busy night the last thing I want to do is have a talk with Miranda at a quarter to one in the morning. I pull into the driveway and when I open my door, Rooter walks toward me.

"Hi," I smile, happy to see him.

"Hi." He kisses me on the cheek. He takes me by the hand and walks me to my door. "How was work?"

"Kicked my ass." After a couple steps I muster the courage to ask him a burning question. "Can I ask you something?"

"Of course."

"All this time, you sitting on your porch when I get home from work, have you been doing it to make sure I get in safe?"

He rubs his neck. "Yes, I have."

I knew it! "You truly are amazing."

"This is a bad neighborhood. I don't want anything to happen to you."

"My own personal bodyguard." Swoon.

"I guess I am."

We stand and stare at one another in front of my door. I'm dying for him to kiss me.

"You going to unlock your door or do you want to hang out here all night?" He snickers.

"I'm waiting for my good night kiss."

Rooter leans in and gives me a peck on the cheek.

"That's all I get?" I pout.

He leans in again and presses his lips to mine, quick and soft, but it's enough to make my heart race.

"I want a real kiss," I whine like a petulant child.

He smirks and shakes his head. "I'm not kissing you until after our date."

"Why?"

He squeezes my hand. "Because I want to do this right."

The tone of his voice conveys how important this is to him, so I let it go. "Okay." I unlock the door. "Thank you for walking me to my door."

"My pleasure. Good night, Sophie."

"Good night, Rooter."

Miranda is sitting on the couch, waiting for my arrival. Her expression is pensive. The television is on, but muted. She must've heard me pull up.

"Hey," she squeaks.

"Hey." I'm still on a high from seeing Rooter. I hope this conversation won't ruin it.

"How was work?" She rubs her hands on the top of her legs.

"Busy. I'm tired."

"I'll try to be quick."

I plod over and sit in the Lazy Boy next to the sofa.

"I was wrong to blame you for Mike's issues."

"Yes, you were." I press my lips together in a tight line.

"Mike and I got into it over kicking him out. He said a lot of really awful things and I was upset. I took it out on you."

No shit. "I get that, but, he had to go. You agree with that, don't you?"

Her eyes tear over. "Yeah. I do. I just hate that it's come to this. He hates me."

"He hates everyone, Miranda." I take a deep breath. "There's something I need you to tell me."

"What?" She wipes her eyes with the sleeve of her shirt.

"Are you mad at me for how I handled it when he told me he was in love with me?"

"No." She shakes her head emphatically. "I'm not. It was shit timing. He chose the worst possible time to come out with that."

"I never wanted to hurt him."

"I know that, Sophie. And you're right. Mike is an adult. He's responsible for his actions. He needs to be held accountable for the things he's done to us."

"Yes, he does."

"It's so hard for me," her soft cries turn into sobs. "He's the only family I have left. Losing him is killing me."

I sit next to her and cradle her in my arms. "I know."

"I love him so much."

"He loves you too, sweetie. But he's really messed up right now. We have to hope he gets the help he needs."

She scooches closer while she cries. I rub her back and tell her everything will be okay even though I'm not one hundred percent sure it will be.

When date night rolls around, I'm not the least bit nervous. I'm anxious to get this show on the road. I've been waiting for this moment ever since I first laid eyes on Rooter.

Miranda wants me to wear one of her sexy dresses, but I assume wherever Rooter and I go, we'll be going on his motorcycle and wearing a dress wouldn't bode well. I settle on a pair of ripped skinny jeans, a black blouse with sequins, and a pair of black flat boots. I pair it with bangle bracelets and black stud earrings. My hair is down in loose waves and Miranda applies my makeup giving me smoky eyes the way I like.

The doorbell rings at exactly five thirty. I shoot up from my seat on the couch, jacket in hand. It's way too warm outside right now for a leather jacket, but it'll be much cooler by this evening.

"He's here," I squeal just loud enough for her to hear.

"Have fun." She kisses me on the cheek.

When I open the door, I'm blown away. Rooter is in a pair of crisp dark wash jeans and a muscle hugging light gray, long sleeve V-neck shirt with the sleeves pushed up his forearms. I'm taken aback by seeing him sans his leather MC cut. He's beyond perfect. And he's eyeing me questioningly.

"I wasn't going to make you ride the bike tonight."

I peer down at my clothing and frown. "Is this not appropriate? I can change," I offer, suddenly wishing I'd taken Miranda's advice and worn a dress.

"You look amazing, but I don't want you to think you always have to dress for the bike."

I breathe a small sigh of relief. "Rooter, you hate being in cars. Of course I dressed to be on the bike."

"This is our first date. I'd be happy to take my truck."

"I like riding with you on your bike."

He smiles wide and when he kisses my temple it sends shivers down my spine. "You are too good to be true."

Rooter and I walk hand in hand to his garage to get his motorcycle. I can't stop staring at him, even when he notices.

"No cut?" I ask.

"Not tonight."

"It wouldn't bother me."

"That's not why I chose not to wear it. Sophie, there's more to who I am than the club." Rooter's smoldering expression is hot enough to make me melt. "Tonight I just want to be a guy on a date with his girl."

Swoon. "As long as you aren't doing it for me. I don't have that kind of expectation."

He smiles and sets his helmet on my head. "We need to get you a helmet of your own."

This one statement makes me happier than I can possibly explain. It means he's looking ahead, and he sees me in his future.

"So, where are you taking me?"

Rooter shakes his head and gives me a mischievous grin. "Have to wait and see."

I climb onto the back of the bike and wrap my arms around his waist the way he instructed me to the last time. The scent of his cologne is a mixture of oak and fruit. Before I'm aware of what I'm doing, I lean in to his neck and inhale deeply. He pats my calf affectionately before firing up the engine.

We pull up to a beautiful lakefront cottage. What is this place? A friend's house? He's bringing me to a friend's on our first date? I didn't have any set expectations, but I thought we'd be alone. Rooter helps me off the bike and removes the helmet. I rake my fingers through my hair hoping it still looks nice.

"It's perfect," Rooter assures me and takes me by the hand.

He opens the front door of the cottage without knocking and motions for me to go in ahead of him. The place is stunning. The walls are white, the ceiling is vaulted with dark wooden beams, and the floor is a dark, wide plank hardwood. The furniture is white, and the décor is in light blues and neutral tones. Sunlight shines in through the abundance of windows. Beautiful.

"Wow," I gasp.

Rooter flashes me his signature panty wetting grin and takes me by the hand. "Come."

He guides me through the house to a set of french doors leading to the backyard. The doors open to reveal a beautiful beach side dinner complete with candles and soft music. An elegant table setting awaits us beneath a pergola draped in white curtains and red rose vines.

"Rooter, this is…" I try to think of a word to describe the beauty before me. "There are no words for what this is."

He kisses my hand. "I'm glad you like it."

"I more than like it. I've never…" I get choked up.

No one has ever done anything even remotely this romantic for me. No one has ever done *anything* romantic for me. Period. I was beginning to think this sort of thing only happens in the movies. Rooter pulls me close.

"I want to give you the things you deserve, Sophie." He tilts my chin up to look at him. "This is what you deserve."

"Rooter, please kiss me."

He leans in so close I can feel the heat radiating from his skin. "I'm going to kiss you Sophie."

My stomach is floating in my chest, warmth cascades over me and my pulse races.

He continues. "I'm going to kiss you like you've never been kissed in your life. Like you'll never be kissed by anyone else ever again."

Yes. That's what I want. I've waited my entire life for a kiss like that. I knew Rooter was the one to give it to me the moment I first laid eyes on him. My lips part in anticipation.

He backs away with a smug grin. "But not until the end of our date."

"That's cruel," I pant.

"Anticipation makes it better." He winks.

My God that was hot. My stomach does a back flip. "I've been anticipating it for a year, a few more hours can't possibly make a difference." My face lights on fire. I hadn't meant to make that admission.

"Have you now?" He taunts.

"I—I…" Am at a loss for words. Embarrassed, I look away.

Rooter chuckles again. "I've been anticipating it for three." He turns my face to his. "Stalker, remember?"

He knows exactly what to say to calm my nerves. "I remember."

Rooter clasps my hand and leads me to the candlelit table, pulls out a chair for me to sit. Once in his seat, he waves his arm toward the house which takes me by surprise. I hadn't seen anyone when we were inside. Moments later, a pretty brunette who appears to be in her mid-fifties comes out and walks toward us.

"What will you be drinking tonight?" She asks.

I glance at Rooter. This is someone's house. I don't know what they have.

"I'll have a Corona," he says to the woman. "You like whiskey and beer, right?" He asks me.

"Yes." It shouldn't surprise me that he knows this. He knows a lot about me.

"I had them stock Jack Daniels for tonight. Have you tried Corona?"

I nod and look at the brunette. "I'll have Jack on the rocks and an ice water, please."

"Sure thing," she says before walking away.

"You really are something else."

"What?" He feigns ignorance.

A few minutes later, the lady reappears with our drinks. "Would you like to order now or do you need a few minutes?"

It's at this moment I spy a small menu before me on the table. On it are three options: Filet mignon, Chicken Florentine, and Lasagna. All three of which are my favorite meals.

"Give us a few minutes," Rooter instructs with a smile.

"Wave when you're ready," she replies and goes back to the house.

"Just how close of attention have you been paying?" I accuse playfully.

He shrugs as if it's no big deal.

I take a sip of my Jack and savor the flavor. It's my favorite alcoholic beverage, though on my income I rarely get to enjoy it. This is a real treat. "Thank you, Rooter. This is perfect."

"I aim to please." He winks and it just about kills me.

"Mission accomplished." I wink back and hope I don't look like an idiot.

It's a gorgeous, sunny evening. I gaze out at the breathtaking view of the lake. Waves crash onto the beach and the sun sparkles like gemstones on the water. There are a few boats floating in the distance. A gentle wind blows through my hair. I lean my head back and inhale the fresh lakeside air. A few minutes pass in a comfortable silence as we both take in the scenery.

But my mind isn't settled. Something has been bothering me ever since Rooter asked me out. I figure now is as good a time as any to clear the air. I'd rather get the answer now than spend the entire night wondering.

"Can I ask you a question?" I take a large swill of the chilled liquor.

"Of course." He sits up straight.

"What about the blonde? Are you two still together?"

Rooter shakes his head vehemently. "We were never together, Sophie. That should've *never* happened." The last part he seems to say more to himself than to me.

I don't know whether this makes me feel better or worse. "She stayed at your house while you were gone and then with you. I've never seen any other girl at your house before, so I must assume you've known her a while."

"I've known Candace a while, but we were *never* in a relationship. It was just…" He halts, appearing uncomfortable.

"Sex," I finish for him.

He squeezes his eyes shut and his expression conveys he really doesn't want to be having this conversation. After a few seconds opens his eyes. "Yeah, but it's done, Sophie. You have nothing to worry about."

Except for the fact that you had sexual relations with a whore. I still don't feel very good about being with a guy who had sex with someone like her. Though there probably aren't many guys who wouldn't have sex with her. Hell, there probably aren't very many who *haven't* had sex with girls like her.

"Sophie," he takes my hand, "I'm not the kind of guy you need to worry about. I'd never hurt you."

I open my mouth to speak but stop. I can't say it. I don't even know why I started. I shake my head. "Never mind."

He scoots close. "No. Say it. I need to know what you're thinking."

I open my mouth then close it again and take a large sip of my whiskey. "I can't."

"Well, you have to because I won't let this go until you say it."

"I don't want to ruin this." I wave around at the beautiful setting.

"You won't ruin it," he insists. "Sophie, I want you to always be honest with me. Tell me what you're thinking."

I stare into his eyes seeking confirmation that I can indeed say anything to him and that he'll understand. "She and I are nothing alike. If that's the sort of thing you go for, how can you possibly be attracted to me?"

"Sophie that's *not* the sort of thing I go for. She was just… available."

The word "available" causes me to flinch. Again, I'm not sure if his honesty makes me feel better or worse. This conversation quickly reminds me that Rooter is indeed human and not the perfect being I've often dreamed him up to be. "I don't know how I feel about that."

"Sophie, you must believe me." The look in his eyes is earnest. "I have never wanted *anyone* the way I want you. Tonight is a case in point. I have never dated. *Ever.* You make me want things I've never wanted."

This revelation rocks me to the core. He must be in his mid-twenties and he's never dated? How is that even possible? "Never dated? How old are you?"

"Twenty five, and no, not even in high school."

"How do you go twenty five years without dating?" I ask skeptically.

"I was never interested in relationships," he answers frankly.

"Oh." He was only interested in sex. I take another swig and drain the glass.

"Like I said, you make me want things I've never wanted. I want to date you." He shakes his head. "No. I want to make you mine."

My pulse quickens. "Why me?"

"Because you are unlike anyone I have ever met. You're everything I never knew I always wanted. And I knew it the moment I first laid eyes on you."

LAST FIRST KISS

I gasp, unable to breathe. Did he really say that or has the whiskey already gone to my head causing me to hallucinate? In all the times I've fantasized about being with Rooter, not once in my wildest dreams did he ever say anything as amazing as those words. I think I just fell in love.

"I feel the same way," I admit, breathless.

Rooter leans in and gazes into my eyes so deep I'm sure he can see my soul. Part of me wants to shrink away and hide while the other wants for him to never look away. The moment he opens his mouth to speak my stomach growls wildly, and we burst into hysterics.

"Hungry?"

"Starved."

"Let's order."

I glance at the menu in front of me and I'm reminded how much he knows about me. This is my chance to learn some things about him. I waver between ordering and asking the question I've been longing to get the answer to. When my stomach growls again, I nod and Rooter waves at woman in the house.

After ordering—lasagna for me, steak for him—I ask the burning question. "It occurs to me I'm on a date with a guy whose name I don't know."

"You know my name." He pulls his eyebrows together.

"Your real name."

"You know my real name."

My brow furrows. "You were born with that name?"

He chuckles. "What? You don't like it?"

"Of course I do. I just… assumed it was a road name."

"You're right. It isn't my birth name. But it is my real name." Rooter must sense my confusion because he continues before I can ask him to clarify. "Birth names are chosen for us before we figure out who we are. Our road names are chosen when we become men. After we learn who we are."

"So, your road name is based on who you really are?" This confuses me more. What the hell could "Rooter" stand for? It's not even a word in the English dictionary.

He laughs. "My road name was chosen for me by Bear, my best friend. You've met him."

"Does it have a meaning?"

He pauses, hesitant. "It does."

"Which is?"

He wags his index finger at me. "Privileged information which you must earn."

"Seriously?"

"Dead serious."

His tone infers he's not going to budge on the topic which only serves to make me even more curious. I go back to the original question. "Then at least tell me your birth name."

"Jace Alexander Russo."

Sexy. I smile. "I like it. You look like a Jace."

Rooter shifts in his seat. He looks concerned. "You like Jace better than Rooter?"

"No." It isn't a lie. I bite my bottom lip and smile. "I think both suit you well."

"Good, because no one calls me Jace."

"Not even your parents?"

Rooter shakes his head. "It took a while for my mom to accept the change, but I've gone by Rooter for years now."

I'd love to change my name. Sophia is such an old lady name. When I was younger, the kids at school used to tease me. In middle school, I tried to get my friends to call me by my middle name, Noelle, but they didn't take to it.

By the time we've finished our meal, I've learned that Thirty Seconds To Mars is Rooter's favorite band, and he prefers rock or rap music, though he likes some top forty stuff. His favorite color is gray, his mother's name is Camilla, his parents are still happily married, and he has two uncles, both of whom are members of the club, and one aunt named Pam; the woman waiting on us tonight. In fact, this house belongs to her. Rooter spends a lot of his free time here at the beach to "get away from all the noise."

Rooter stands from the table and extends his hand. "Take a walk with me?"

"I'd love to." I smile.

We walk down a set of white wooden stairs to the beach. The wind has picked up and the air off of the lake is cool. I'll be glad I have the jacket for the ride home.

Rooter looks at my hand in his. "You have the softest hands."

I blush and shake my head. He has to be lying. They're rather manly if you ask me; big with long fingers. I've always been self-conscious about them.

"You don't take compliments very well."

He's right. My mother used to always say I was too masculine. She wanted a ballerina and a pianist. I was neither, and she made her displeasure very well known.

"Where'd you go just then?" Rooter asks.

We've stopped walking though I'm not sure when that happened. "Nowhere I want to be."

We stroll again. "I'm a fantastic listener. You can talk to me about the things you think about. Your memories."

"I don't want to talk about them," I admit. "I don't want to think about them, although I do."

"I respect that. I'm just throwing it out there so you know you can if you ever want to."

"Thanks." I peer at him with a diminutive smile. "So, tell me more about yourself. When did you join the club?"

His face glistens from the sunlight. He wears a soft, thoughtful expression. "My pop started the club with his best friend, Wrench, when they were nineteen, so it's been a part of my life forever. I started working for them at eighteen and became an official member when I turned twenty one."

"Growing up, did you always want to be a member?"

"Off and on. There were times when I thought it was more trouble than it was worth, but those guys are my family, so I suppose it was inevitable."

"Was there anything else you wanted to do?" I stop walking and pick up a neat, multicolored rock with my free hand and put it in my pocket. A memento of our first date. We move again.

"Not really. I always wanted to run the shop with my pop." Rooter's family owns a custom bike shop in Halsey. They're fairly well known. They draw bikers from states as far away as Colorado. "Everything I know I learned from him and Wrench."

"Can I ask you a question?"

Rooter stops walking and looks me in the eye. "Sophie, you don't have to ask if you can ask me things," he murmurs. "Just ask. I'll tell you anything I can."

"Your shop is successful. Makes a lot of money. Why get involved in other... bad things?"

"It's not exactly what it seems. All we've really done is fight to keep drug dealers and prostitution out of Halsey. That was the reason for the club's inception. To do what the cops can't do. What they don't have the balls to do. But they can't possibly have the locals knowing we're doing their job better than they are, so they have the media spin it a different way to make their tiny little dicks look bigger."

"But you even said you do bad things. It was why you wanted me to stay away from you."

"Sophie, to keep this town safe, we get involved in very risky shit with extremely dangerous people on a regular basis. Anyone who is involved with us is a target. Being with me means wearing a bulls-eye. That's why I was reluctant to get involved with you."

"But you changed your mind."

"I still think this is dangerous, but I can't not be with you."

My breath catches in my throat. "I can't not be with you either."

He shakes his head. "I don't get your interest in me at all. Explain it to me."

I don't have a clue how to explain it to him, so I use his words. "You make me feel something I've never felt."

"What's that?"

"Safe."

He shakes his head and laughs.

"What's funny?"

"I just told you that being with me could be potentially dangerous to your health and you feel *safe*?"

"Rooter, I've always felt safe around you."

He rests his forehead against mine. "I will always do everything in my power to make sure no one ever hurts you."

"I believe you," I whisper.

Rooter places his hands gently on the sides of my face and spreads his legs to lower his stance. "You can always believe in me Sophie," he declares. "You've been through so much. You've been hurt and mistreated so badly by those who were supposed to love you. I promise you I'll never hurt you."

"I hope not," I murmur without meaning to.

Rooter's face is mere inches away from mine. His tender hands radiate warmth. I search his eyes and they convey a silent vow. This man will never hurt me. I've believed it all along. He is my protector. The one I've been waiting my entire life for. Overwhelmed by such powerful emotions, a tear escapes my right eye. He catches it with his thumb.

"You are safe with me."

He leans in so slowly that every molecule of my being begins to ache. My pulse races, my breathing has stopped, and I'm frozen. He's well aware of what he's doing to me. It's as if he takes pleasure in torturing me this way.

He shifts his head a bit to the right and just as his lips are about to touch mine and put an end to my agony, he speaks. "Open your eyes."

I obey and find him staring intently at me with smoldering brown eyes.

"Once I kiss you, you're mine, Sophie. Do you want to be mine?"

"I've never wanted anything more."

Rooter finally closes the tiny gap between us and places his lips on mine. They're warm and soft, precisely as I remembered, only this time they move against mine with purpose and intensity. He kisses my top lip and then my bottom, running his tongue along it, coaxing me to open for him.

All of a sudden I'm nervous. He's surely kissed a lot of girls. He intends to be my best—and I'm sure he will be—but what if I don't live up to his expectations? I haven't kissed very many guys. When he gently nips my lower lip, I part my lips and silently pray he won't be disappointed in me.

The instant our tongues meet, he moans. It's the sexiest sound I've ever heard. Rooter's in total control of the kiss. He kisses me expertly and passionately, doing just what he said he'd do; kisses me like no other ever has or likely ever will. I let out a desperate moan of my own. His tongue is smooth as it explores my mouth. Our kiss vacillates between fervent and tender, but his lips never part from mine. My knees become weak and I wrap my arms around his waist for stability. The kiss becomes slower and softer before he gradually pulls away. For the first time in my life, I know what it's like to be thoroughly kissed by a man.

His hands stay on my face as we stare into each other's eyes. "Oh my," is all I can say.

"Even better than I imagined." He smiles and strokes my cheeks with his thumbs.

"Best first kiss ever."

"Your last first kiss." His voice is cloaked with determination.

I pull my phone out of my back pocket, turn on the camera and hand it to Rooter. "I want to record this moment."

Rooter holds the phone out and takes two pictures; one of us smiling and another of us kissing. After he's done, he texts them to his phone.

"Good first date?" He asks as we sit in the sand staring out at the sparkling water, my back against his chest.

"My last first date."

He chuckles and kisses the side of my head. "Good answer."

The Tease

I'm still on a high from last night's date with Rooter. Ryan and I are both on break sharing a plate of sirloin tips and rice topped with an oriental sesame vinaigrette. I've just finished telling him all about the date. "It was perfect, Ry."

"Damn, for someone who's never dated, he sure does it well."

"Right?" I chuckle and take a bite of the steak, savoring the flavor. If it wasn't for Randy feeding me gourmet meals for free on work nights, I'd probably be on a ramen noodle diet.

"Sounds like he knows quite a bit more about you than you thought."

"Yeah. Part of me would be glad if he already knows all my shit, but the other part—not knowing exactly what he knows—is somewhat embarrassed by it."

Ryan is hogging the rice like he always does so I scrape some to my side of the plate.

"You have nothing to be ashamed of, babe." He squeezes the top of my knee. "A lot of really fucked up stuff happened to you and none of it was your fault."

"I don't want him to think I'm damaged or broken because of it."

Nearly everyone who knows my story—and few do—thinks of me that way. Including Miranda and her parents when they were alive. It's part of the reason she treats me the way she does. Miranda wants to control what I do and who I do it with so no one can hurt me again. She thinks being mentally and physically abused by my mom—the only family I've ever known—has left me emotionally inept. She thinks I tend to let the wrong people in push the right people out; that I'm not a good judge of character. Perhaps she's right, but I'll never admit it.

"I doubt he thinks of you that way."

"It worries me because I want him to see *me* when he looks at me, not my past."

"That might be tough, Soph. Our pasts are a part of who we are, good and bad."

That's what I know and I don't like it.

"Take me for instance," he continues. "My father stopped talking to me for three years after I came out. It's why I have a hard time living out in the open as a gay man."

"Wow, I didn't know that."

The sadness in Ryan eyes is overwhelming and my heart breaks for him. My issues with my mother and a lack of a father help me to understand what that derision must have felt like for him.

"It's why Seth did what he did," he continues. "I wasn't comfortable living life together out in the open. He couldn't take it anymore."

It's my turn to comfort him. I lean my head against his shoulder and hold his hand. "I'm so sorry, babe."

He shrugs and wipes a stray tear from his cheek with his sleeve. "Nothing I can do to change it now. It's a lesson learned. That's all we can do. Learn and grow through the pain."

I believe in soulmates. I always have. But I believe there are many kinds of them; not just romantic. Ryan is one of mine. He and I are kindred spirits. We understand and have empathy for each other's pain. In the short time I've come to know Ryan, he's become a positive, solid force in my life. When I'm down, he raises me up.

When I'm happy, he shares in my joy. I'm eternally grateful he has come into my life.

"I love you," I admit for the first time, knowing he'll understand my meaning.

"I love you, too, babe."

When I pull up, Rooter is standing in my driveway. My stomach does a little flip at the sight of him. He opens my door and helps me out of the car.

"Hi," he murmurs and kisses me. His lips are light as a feather against mine giving me goosebumps.

"Hi." I beam at him.

"How was work?" His thumb massages the top of my hand in gentle strokes.

"Good. Made a ton in tips." Hand in hand, we walk to my front door, my eyes on him the entire way. "Want to come in?" I ask once we reach my door.

"Wish I could. I have to be at the shop by six. We're running behind on a build."

I feel guilty. It's almost one in the morning. He should be sleeping. "You didn't need to wait up on me."

"I'll always wait up on you, Sophie. Your safety is more important than sleep."

Swoon. I place my hand on his cheek and he leans into it. His stubbly cheek is warm against my palm. "But you'll be so tired tomorrow."

"No worries. I napped earlier."

Likely because he knew he'd be up late to make sure I got in safe. He really is too good to be true.

"Thank you for walking me to my door."

"Maybe we can grab lunch together tomorrow. I'll call you around noon."

"Okay."

He leans in slow for a kiss and my entire body goes haywire. My pulse speeds up, my breathing becomes uneven, and my stomach does somersaults. At first the kiss is soft and sweet, but then he takes my bottom lip between his teeth and licks it, erupting a fire inside of me. I moan a little too loudly. His smirk tells me he's aware of the effect he's having on me.

Rooter does something to me I can't explain. It's as though his entire being is a magnet that draws me to him. I can't wait another second. I need to taste him now. I wrap my hands around the back of his head and pull him into me. He kisses me, but barely. He teases me with the tip of his tongue causing me to whimper. I need more. But he pulls away and removes my arms from his neck. There's a gleam in his eyes.

"Don't tease me," I pant.

"But it's so much fun."

"Not for me."

"No?" He leans in, the side of his face grazes mine. His breath is hot against my ear. His heat, his scent, is intoxicating. "I think you like it," he taunts in a low voice. "Look at how you're responding."

My chest heaves and my breath is ragged. He laughs, mockingly. He has me right where he wants me.

"I hear payback is a bitch," I threaten.

He pulls back and looks at me, amused. "Is that right?"

"Yeah." Two can play this game.

He cocks his head to the right. "And exactly how do you plan on paying me back?"

"Maybe next time, I won't *let* you kiss me."

"Oh Sophie," he takes a lock of my hair and twirls it between his fingers, "we both know better than that."

"Guess we'll have to wait and see." I hate that I'm still panting.

"Good night, Sophie." He winks and I nearly collapse.

"Good night."

I watch him through the front door window as he walks away, finding it hard to comprehend how such an indecently hot human being exists. And finding it even harder to fathom that he's mine.

"Holy fuck," Miranda says and I jump two feet in the air.

"I didn't know you were there." I hold both hands to my chest.

She doesn't notice she almost gave me a coronary. "I may not be completely sold on that guy, but he sure knows what the hell he's doing."

"Torturing me is what he's doing."

"I'd like someone to torture me like that." We both laugh.

Rooter calls me at noon exactly to tell me he's on his way to get me. He pulls in front of my house less than fifteen minutes later. I dart out of the house and upon seeing the look of amusement on his face regret my eagerness at once.

"Happy to see me?" He smiles wide making the skin around his eyes wrinkle.

I shrug. "Just hungry."

"Is that right?"

"Yep."

"Well, I'm *very* happy to see you." He leans in to kiss me and I take a step back. "Playing it like that, huh?"

"Just giving you a taste of your own medicine. How is it?"

"Pretty damn good from what I can remember." He winks.

My heart skips a beat. "Well, that memory is going to have to hold you over a while."

"We'll see."

"Yeah, we will."

Rooter secures his helmet to my head and I climb on to the back of his bike. He kisses the palm of my hand giving it a featherlike lick that sets my skin ablaze before wrapping my arms around him. He's playing dirty.

We pull into Skyles' parking lot and hop off the motorcycle. Rooter takes me by the hand and leads me into the bar. Joe Skyles, the owner, is working the bar. I've gotten to know Joe pretty well over the years. He used to ask me out all the time, but he's way too old for me. I'd put him at thirty, at least, though he's a very attractive thirty. When he sees me walking hand in hand with Rooter, he looks surprised.

"Hey, Joe," I say as we take a seat at a high topper near the bar.

"Hey, Soph." He sets two menus before us and looks from me to Rooter and back to me again.

"Joe, this is Rooter." I wave between the two men. "Rooter, this is Joe."

"Nice to meet you, man," Rooter says and extends his hand.

"I've seen you in here before. Nice to meet you." Joe's voice is flat as he shakes Rooter's hand. "What can I get you to drink?"

"I'll have my usual." I smile.

Rooter looks at me with an expression I can't decipher. "I'll have a coke."

Joe goes back to the bar and Rooter chuckles under his breath.

"What's funny?"

"Joe doesn't seem very pleased to see you with me," he whispers.

"He's probably just surprised. I usually come here with Miranda."

"Yeah right. That poor man is heartbroken." Rooter is simply delighted with himself.

Joe arrives with our drinks. "One sweet tea and one coke. Ready to order or do you need a minute?"

"Give us a minute," I say.

Joe stands and stares at me a little longer than he should before returning to the bar.

"And I thought you came here for the food," Rooter jests.

"I do!"

"Yeah, that and the exceptional service."

I shake my head and smirk. "Jealous?"

Rooter shakes his head, his expression now serious. "Not at all. I simply find it interesting."

"Find what interesting?"

He takes my hand and brushes his thumb across my knuckles. "The fact that you can have any guy you want and you chose me."

"You should remember that next time you think about teasing me."

He leans in close. "That a threat?"

I lean in to close the gap. Our faces can't be more than an inch apart. "Try me and find out."

"Sophie, if you want me to kiss you, I will. Right here. Right now."

My stomach flips and my body tingles. God, I want him to kiss me. Badly. But I need to teach him a lesson so rather than give in to my desire, I sit back in my seat and cross my arms. "You just want to mark your territory."

He sits back and shakes his head. "You and I both know I don't need to."

"What does that mean?"

"Simply that I know how much you want me."

"You're so full of yourself!" But he's right. I've never wanted anything as much as I want to be with him.

He cocks his head with a leer. "Just telling it like it is."

I scowl and shake my head in mock disgust.

He leans in again, his expression profoundly resolute. "I want you just as much, Sophie. And mark my word, before this day is over I will kiss you."

Getting Comfortable

"Do you have a little time or do you need to get back?"
Rooter asks after paying for our meal.

"I have time." And if I didn't, I'd make the time.

"Want to ride out to the Westlake Boardwalk?"

The Westlake Boardwalk is hands down one of the most beautiful lakeside destinations in all of Western Michigan, though somewhat overpopulated by tourists. Tourists from all over the US vacation there each year. Most people call ahead for reservations two and even three years in advance to secure their lodging; especially the campers. It's also popular with photographers both local and from afar. But even the overcrowding can't take away from its magic.

The boardwalk expands two miles with the lighthouse pier on the far northern end. It's one of my favorite places on earth, not that I've seen much of the earth. I've never stepped a foot outside of Michigan.

"I'd love to go. I haven't been there since last fall."

Rooter nods. I can't be sure if it means he knows when I was there last or if it's in agreement that we'll go.

The ride takes close to an hour because Rooter takes the scenic lakeshore route to get there. Whenever I drive up to the boardwalk, I take this route, but it's a wholly different experience on the back of

Rooter's Harley. Riding on the back of his bike, I feel as if I'm a part of the scenery, even though it's passing by at speeds upward of sixty miles per hour. It's a little cooler along the lakeshore than inland, but the pure exhilaration I get from the ride is worth the shivers and goosebumps.

"Were you warm enough?" Rooter rubs my arms, his concern evident. "I wasn't thinking about how much cooler it is along the lakeshore when I took that route."

"It was p-perfect," my teeth chatter. "So beautiful."

"We'll take the main roads home."

He laces his fingers with mine as we walk through the parking lot. We've only been dating a few days and yet I feel completely at ease; as though we've been together for years. The main entrance to the boardwalk is to the right of the parking lot, but he guides me to the left.

"I thought we were going to the boardwalk." I point toward the entrance.

"Going in the back way," he says as though I should know this.

"There's a back way?"

He looks at me with amazement, the corners of his eyes crinkle when he smiles.

The walk to the back entrance is long, maybe a half mile, but I don't mind. Walking alongside Rooter is a fascinating experience. People's expressions are priceless. They look from him to me and back to him again, trying to understand why we're together. Rooter is wearing his club cut with a pair of ripped black jeans and a snug white t-shirt that showcases his tattoos. I'm in a pair of white skinny jeans, a coral colored floral blouse and a pair of Toms. Our arms are wrapped around each other's waists signifying we are indeed a couple. We make quite an interesting looking pair, but the looks Rooter is getting bothers me. Women glare at him as though he's a rapist or murderer. Men eyeball him like a dirty thug who has no right to be near me.

Who the hell do they think they are? They aren't any better than he or I. Do they assume they look better in their capris and loafers? Do they believe their yuppie style makes them better people? Well, I hate to break it to them, but by the looks of them I'd say half of the women here suffer from a severe lack of self-respect and self-esteem, with the way their boobs are on display for everyone to ogle. And the husband's? Please... Most of them are ignoring their breast baring wives and panting over girls half their age. I haven't seen Rooter check out any other women, or their boobs since we got here. He's twice the man any of these judgmental schmucks are.

Rooter comes to an abrupt halt causing me to lurch forward. Luckily he keeps a hold of my hand or my face would be plastered on the sand covered concrete.

"Do you want me to take you home?" He asks, out of the blue, looking straight ahead instead of at me.

I furrow my brow. "Why would I want that?"

"Please, Sophie. I can see how uncomfortable you are."

"What? No." I panic. What did I do to make him think that?

"Yes you are," he insists and jerks his hand away from mine. "Everyone's staring and judging you for being with me and it bothers you." He backs away from me, offended.

"No. Rooter," I grab a hold of his hand and hold it tight, "I don't care what anyone thinks about me being with you. I don't like the way they're looking at you."

"What?" His shoulders relax and he unclenches his jaw.

"These judgmental assholes are looking at you like they're better than you and it's pissing me off!" Each word escalates in volume until I'm hollering. One of the judgmental housewives gives me a dirty look provoking me to glower at her as she walks by.

Rooter cackles. His earlier irritation is long gone. "Whoa, killer. Back down." He comes close and takes hold of both my arms as though I might pounce on someone at any second. "It doesn't matter what they think."

"But they're wrong!"

"Again. Doesn't matter." He rubs my arms in a soothing fashion to calm me. "Don't let it bother you. I don't."

This takes me by surprise. Rooter doesn't strike me as the type to allow people to look down on him. "Never?"

He shakes his head emphatically. "I don't care what strangers think of me."

"It doesn't piss you off even a little that they're looking down on you when they don't even know you?"

"They're strangers, Sophie. I'll never see any of them again, so why should it bother me?"

"Yeah, but it still pisses me off."

Rooter smiles and leans his forehead against mine. "I like protective Sophie."

His gaze holds a depth I've not yet seen. His face is at once serious and thoughtful, with the right corner of his mouth turned up diminutively. For a moment, I fully expect him to lean in for a kiss. Instead, he pulls his forehead from mine and brings my hand to his lips and places a gentle kiss on the top without ever taking his eyes off of mine.

My heart rate speeds up and I can barely breathe. Forget my earlier declaration that I won't let him kiss me. I want him to. No. I need him to. Right here. Right now. In front of all these jackasses giving him dirty looks.

Rooter gives me a wink and gets up from the bench. Dirty devil. He knew I wanted him to kiss me.

We come to a small opening between two towering sand dunes. The opening is narrow, so I follow Rooter until we come to a small clearing of beach. Roughly a hundred yards to our right is the boardwalk and public beach. I've seen people on this side, but never knew how they got over here. There's a gate blocking access from the public beach side which is always manned by a guard so that no one can enter that side without paying the entry fee. There's a few people here on the beach with us; a woman under a multicolored beach umbrella reading a novel, a few couples, and one family with a toddler, a boy not older than four.

"This is a private beach."

"No one ever says anything," he says dismissively.

"You come here often?" I never once pictured Rooter kicking back on the beach. I always envisioned him hanging out in his shop or in bars with his biker buddies.

"Mostly in the winter."

"The winter?" I definitely wasn't expecting that. The sole idea of it causes me to shudder. Lake Michigan winters are brutal to say the least. I've seen pictures of the ice banks on the lake. That's good enough for me. I have zero interest in experiencing them firsthand. I don't even want to witness my yard in the winter. I'm talking subzero temperatures and three feet of snow on the ground from the end of December throughout most of March. One of these days, I'm moving south where it never snows.

"Yeah. When the lake's iced over, the sunset here is phenomenal. Have you ever seen it?"

I shake my head. "Not much of a cold weather person."

He chuckles. "Well, I'm bringing you here this winter. You must see it."

Although I like him talking about us in the future tense, there's no way I'm coming here in the freezing cold to watch a sunset. I don't care how amazing it is. I've seen a lot of sunsets I can't imagine one pretty enough to make me brave getting frostbite. "Take a picture."

"No pictures. You have to see it in person to really capture the beauty of it."

I giggle at my hot, badass biker talking about capturing the beauty of a sunset. He never ceases to surprise me.

"What?" He asks.

"You and phenomenally beautiful sunsets seem like a bit of an oxymoron."

"What? I'm not phenomenally beautiful?" He feigns offense.

Although he isn't truly offended by my words, I am. The more I get to know about him, the more attractive he becomes. And I thought he was a God before I met him. "Actually, you are."

Rooter cups my face with his large, callused hand and looks into my eyes. "I think you're phenomenally beautiful."

My breath hitches. *Kiss me, please.* Just when I think he might, something hits me in the head.

"Sorry," the little boy says, embarrassed and runs off with his beach ball.

Rooter and I laugh. I gaze up at him, hoping for a kiss, but apparently the moment has passed.

I remove my Toms and Rooter follows close behind as I mosey to the edge of the water. The sand on this side is pristine. No bottle caps or toy cars pressing into my feet. No towels and chairs to maneuver around. No dogs or kids running into me full speed ahead. No one yelling at me for accidentally kicking sand onto them as I walk by. Only soft, white sand and the sound of the waves rolling onto the beach. The sun sparkles like diamonds on the water. I close my eyes and inhale as a gentle wind blows through my hair.

"I could spend all day here." I open my eyes and look to my right to find Rooter gazing at me with a smile.

"I'm game."

He takes a seat at the edge of the water and I do the same. I lift my face to the sky to absorb the warmth of the sun.

"I wish I could, but I have this thing called a job and unfortunately I need said job to pay another thing called rent."

Rooter grins and laces his fingers with mine. "I'll bring you back when we can spend an entire day together." His grin turns mischievous. "Preferably with you in that yellow bikini."

My mind goes back to the day we met and I flush. I lean into Rooter for a kiss, but my phone rings and interrupts the moment. *Dammit.*

"I thought you weren't kissing me," Rooter jokes.

"I changed my mind." My phone is still ringing with Miranda's ringtone.

"Is that right?"

We're still leaning into each other. All I'd have to do is inch forward and my lips will be on his.

"Yeah," I breathe.

"Well, so have I." He pulls away.

"What?" I stare at him, bewildered. Finally my damn phone shuts up.

"I'm going to make you work for it."

"Work for it?"

"Yeah. You're going to have to earn it."

How am I supposed to *earn* a kiss? I'm not exactly the most experienced person in this thing called dating and I'm pretty sure I suck at flirting. Trying not to overthink it, I cross my arms and say the first thing that comes to mind. "I won't go out with you again until you kiss me."

He leans in close. So close I know he's going to give me what I want. "Sophie, be realistic. You know you can't stay away from me."

Denied, yet again. I lean back and prop myself up on my elbows. "You so need to get over yourself."

Rooter leans down further, hovering over top of me. "Actually, I think it's *you* who can't get over me."

My heart palpitates and I can barely breathe. His face is inches from mine. I hate this game, but I love it. I lean forward to close the gap between us. "Kiss me," I plead.

And then my phone rings again. He pulls away and sits upright with a smirk on his face.

This is the second time Miranda has called. Since she knows I'm out with Rooter it must be important, otherwise she'd just send a text. "Hello?"

"I need you to come home." Her voice quivers with panic.

"What happened?"

Rooter's head jerks in my direction.

"Mike just called. He's wasted, and he's pissed. Says we're going to pay for kicking him out."

"I'm on my way." I end the call and turn to Rooter. "I need to get home."

"What is it?"

"Mike just called Miranda and threatened her."

When I open the front door, Miranda is sitting on the couch trembling as she cries. She stares at her phone on the table before her.

"Has he called back?" I ask and sit next to her.

"What did he say?" Rooter asks, taking the chair next to the couch. He hunches over and rests his arms on his knees.

"He said this is his house as much as it is mine and I had no right kicking him out. And said I was wrong to choose Sophie over him and he's going to make both of us pay for it."

"He can't be stupid enough to try something," I say to Rooter. "You warned him to stay away."

"He was seriously pissed off," Miranda counters. "And you know how he gets when he's high."

"If he's doped out, there's no way of knowing what he might do," Rooter agrees and sits upright, rubbing his chin. "He probably won't come here, but he could show up somewhere else. I wouldn't put anything past him."

"He's never sounded like this," Miranda whimpers. "He was serious."

Rooter picks up Miranda's phone and hands it to her. "Unlock it."

She hesitates and stares at the screen. "What are you going to do?"

"I'm going to call him." He snaps his fingers, impatient.

"That'll only piss him off more, especially if you call from my phone. He'll think I had you call him."

"That's the point," Rooter explains, still holding his hand out for the phone. "If he thinks you called me for help it might scare him enough to drop it."

Miranda unlocks the phone and hands it to Rooter, her reluctance showing by how slowly she hands it to him.

Rooter finds Mike's number and calls it and I hear screaming blaring through the speaker. "Stop talking and listen fucker," he growls into the phone.

PERSONAL SPACE

Miranda's face is pale and turning a strange shade of green which only happens when she gets upset enough to throw up. I consider backing away but then she grabs a hold of my hand and squeezes it tightly.

"Did I or did I not say no retaliation against these girls?" Rooter doesn't allow Mike to answer. "If you want to keep your limbs, you will *never* threaten these girls again. Do you understand?"

Silence.

"Tell me you understand!" Rooter bellows, startling Miranda. "Good. Now promise me you will stay away from them... Good boy." Rooter hangs up the phone and places it on the table. It amazes me how he switches from pissed to utterly calm in an instant. "I think he got the point, but to be sure, either me or one of my guys will keep watch over you both for a while."

"Thank you," Miranda says and cries again. "I never believed he'd actually hurt me, but now I'm sure he will."

"I won't let that happen," Rooter assures her.

"It'll be okay," I tell her.

Miranda leans into me and her body shakes as she cries. "No, it won't. I've lost my entire family."

Her words break my heart. I know what it's like not to have any family. I don't want this for her. As much as I hate seeing her hurt like this, I'm glad she finally sees Mike for what he's become and is taking his threats serious. There was a time when I thought his threats were empty, but not anymore. Not since the night he hit Miranda. The Mike I grew up with is gone. Maybe not forever, but certainly for now.

"I know it feels like the end of the world to you, but it will be okay," I assure her. When she doesn't respond, I continue. "Your parents may be gone, and Mike is messed up, but you're not alone. You will never be alone, Miranda."

"What would I do without you?" She sniffles and balls my blouse into her fists.

"You'll never have to worry about that." I watch Rooter go into the kitchen.

"Promise me you'll never leave me, Sophie."

"I promise."

Rooter is talking on his phone, but I can't make out what he's saying. Miranda wipes her eyes as he walks back into the living room.

"Bear will be here in a while." He turns to Miranda. "He'll stay with you while I take Sophie to work."

"Is he the scary one with the beard?" Miranda asks me and Rooter laughs.

"That's the one," I say.

"Good. He'd scare the shit out of Mike."

"He scares most people." Rooter chuckles.

According to the clock, I'm due to be at the Grand in less than an hour. "Speaking of work, I need to get ready."

"I'll wait here," Rooter says.

I had expected he'd go home, but if he's going to stay, I'd rather he was with me. "You can come with."

Rooter looks around my room as though he's never been in here. He reads the quote stenciled in black paint on the wall behind my headboard: *I crave a love so deep the ocean would be jealous.* I turn to my dresser to retrieve my work pants so he doesn't see me blush. When I turn around he's sitting on my bed sifting through the romance novel I've been reading. Of course it's a smutty bad boy meets good girl story. He grins at me with a questioning brow.

"Have a thing for bad boys?"

"I thought that was obvious." I try to sound nonchalant, but my insides are churning.

I'd never given much thought to how much a person's bedroom says about them until this moment. This room is filled with personal mementos and tidbits like this book, revealing who I am. There are pictures of me and friends, old and new, all over the room. Perhaps most revealing is the collection of postcards pinned to the wall of the places I dream of going to such as Bali, Paris, and the Grand Canyon. Rooter gets up and walks to the postcard covered wall.

"What are these?" He points at a postcard of Cabo San Lucas, Mexico.

"Places I hope to visit one day."

"There's a lot of them here."

"I dream big." I sigh.

"That's a good thing."

I flick one of the postcards. Who am I kidding? I'll be lucky to make it to the Rock and Roll Hall of Fame in Cleveland. "Yeah. Good for setting myself up for big failure."

"Don't say that." Rooter turns to face me. "You can do anything you want with your life. You're strong enough to make your dreams come true."

"Yeah, well, strong or not we don't always get what we want in this life." My track record proves it.

"You're right, we don't," he agrees. "But the fact you have these on the wall proves you haven't given up hope."

"Sometimes, I feel like hope is all I have." I regret the words as soon as they slip out.

"You have so much more, Sophie," he strokes my cheek with his thumb, "but hope is one of the most important things to have. My Nona always said that without it, we have nothing."

"She sounds like a wise woman." If only I had someone like her. I walk away from the wall to put space between myself and my unreasonable dreams.

"She was." He pauses and surveys me with a thoughtful expression. "You remind me of her."

"I do?" I look at Rooter through my dresser mirror as I grab a fresh pair of panties, hoping he won't see and quickly wad them up into the pants.

He comes up behind me so close I can feel his heat. "Your demeanor is the same. Incredibly sweet and strong."

"I'm not that sweet," I counter and fiddle with the things in my hand.

"Yes, you are." He leans in to my neck and inhales deeply. My body goes haywire when he snakes his arm around my waist places an open mouth kiss just below my jawline. "And you taste even sweeter."

Right now the only dream I have is of Rooter's lips on mine. I drop my things to the floor, spin around and attack his lips with mine. He doesn't hesitate to kiss me back and relief cascades over me at finally being this close to him. Evidently, I'd been yearning for this kiss even more than I realized. I throw my arms around his shoulders and pull his body against mine, deepening the kiss. Rooter's mouth is heavenly. He tastes delicious. His hands creep low on my back. He's barely touching my butt and yet it's enough to set my body on fire.

Everything he does is perfect, yet it's not nearly enough. I crave this guy in a way I hadn't even realized was possible. My hands move down the front of his chest beneath his cut, over his pecs to his taut abdomen. I can feel every line and curve of his muscles through his thin shirt. Rooter's hand slides even lower and cups my ass firmly. His other hand reaches up and grabs a fistful of my hair and tugs just hard enough to convey his desire. *Oh my.* A wild groan escapes my lips prompting him to kiss me deeper, harder.

I reach under his shirt to touch his skin with my fingertips. The moment our skin meets Rooter throws his head back and moans, deep and raspy. My fingers trace the lines of his six pack. When his eyes land back on mine they convey a carnal hunger that sends tingles straight to my core. No man has ever looked at me in such a way. My legs quiver.

Rooter leads us to my bed and lays us on the mattress. His mouth moves from my lips to my neck and I arch my back to give him better access. His tongue teases my skin with soft, languid movements. I fantasize about his mouth, his tongue on my entire body. His lips leave a trail of wet kisses as he makes his way upward. When he nips my earlobe it sends sparks throughout my body. He breathes, warm and ragged against my flesh. The temperature in my room spikes to a hundred degrees.

The hand that was in my hair travels down my side. Rooter raises my legs up to his hips and wraps them around his waist. He glides his hands along the outside of my thighs, gripping tightly once they make it back to my hips. The timber of his tone is desperate when he moans my name right before grinding his hardness into me.

Images of Adam hovering over me flood my mind. Panicked, I gasp and jerk away from Rooter. Sensing my distress, he jumps off of me with a curse.

"I'm so, so sorry, Sophie." Fear and remorse are thick in his eyes. "Are you okay?"

What the hell is wrong with me? Embarrassment quickly replaces my panic and I fold my arms over my chest. Unable to speak, I nod in response.

"Talk to me," he coaxes gently. "I need to know you're okay."

"I'm fine," I squeak and cover my face to hide my shame. "I'm sorry."

"Hey," he tugs my arm away and looks into my eyes. "You have nothing to be sorry for. I let it go too far."

Too far? We barely did anything. "I don't know why I reacted that way."

"Because you're not ready for this, that's why." He pushes away from the bed and stalks to the far end of the room facing away from me. "I can't believe I did that," he fumes.

"It was my fault. I started it." Exactly like me to take a perfect moment and crap all over it.

He spins around. "Don't make excuses for me Sophie. You should be able to kiss me without worrying about me jumping you. I just..." He rubs the back of his head. "I'm not used to... having to control myself. That's not an excuse. There is no excuse." He rushes over to me and drops to his knees, his arms lay at his sides. "You know I wouldn't have... let it go any farther, don't you?"

"Of course I do." So why did I freak out? And why the hell would I think of Adam in that moment? Rooter is nothing like him. And unlike Adam, I actually want to be with Rooter. I've only been fantasizing about it for a year. I finally get my chance and I wig out.

"Sophie, I'd never do anything you aren't ready for. Shit." He jumps up and away from me. "What am I saying? I just *did* something you weren't ready for. I promise, it won't happen again. I never want you to be afraid of me."

"I could never be afraid of you," I assert.

"But you were, just then," he motions toward the bed, "when you jerked away. I scared you."

"No. I wasn't afraid of you. I was..." I can't find the right words. Yes, I panicked, but not because I was afraid of him. "It was a stupid memory."

The way he screws his eyes shut tells me my words make him feel worse not better.

I stand before him and take his hand into mine. "Listen to me, I'm fine with what happened."

He opens his eyes and scans my face for proof that my words are true.

"I am," I insist. "Actually, I really liked it and I feel stupid for freaking out." Embarrassment creeps over me again.

"Of course you freaked out, babe." He reaches up and grazes my cheek with the back of his hand. "That was way too much, way too soon."

"I didn't exactly do anything to stop you." *Wait. Did he call me babe?*

"I know," he sighs and drops his hand. "But for the first time in my life, I want to be with someone. In a relationship. But I want to do it right and I'm already screwing it up."

"You haven't screwed anything up."

"I told myself I'd take things slow with you. One step at a time. But when you kiss me, it's like I can't think straight. All I can think about is how good it feels."

His emphasis of "good" sends my insides into somersaults. I'll never get over this guy, a living deity, actually wanting me. *Me.* "I feel the same way."

He smiles, but it doesn't meet his eyes. "You're trying to make me feel better."

"Yes, but I mean it."

Rooter pulls me close and kisses the top of my head when there's a knock on my door.

"Bear is here," Miranda calls through the door.

"You should get ready for work." Rooter says and turns to the door. "I'll go downstairs."

"Hey." I tug his hand. "We okay?"

"Of course, babe." He winks before leaving the room.

Babe? He seriously just called me babe. Twice. And then he winked. Holy hell. That. Was. HOT. I go to my bed and plummet face first, silently screaming into the mattress. Why the hell did I have to go and freak out and ruin everything? I'm such a spaz. Like a toddler throwing a tantrum, I kick the bed.

"Um?" Rooter's chuckle sends a jolt through my body and I cease all movement. "I left my phone."

Forget embarrassment. That has nothing on the utter mortification I'm experiencing at this precise moment. I lay completely still as Rooter reaches down next to me to retrieve his phone.

"You might want to hurry," he suggests, his voice filled with humor. "We need to leave in fifteen minutes."

"Mm-hmm," I mumble into the mattress and wave him away. He chuckles again on his way out.

Scary Beary

Miranda is sitting in the recliner, her knees pulled to her chest, staring at Bear like a petrified rabbit waiting to be pounced by a cheetah.

"I don't know if this is a good idea," I whisper to Rooter.

"What?" He whispers back.

"Miranda is scared to death."

His lip turns up at the corner. "Bear won't hurt her."

"I know, but look at her." I wave in her direction.

Rooter snickers. "She might as well get to know him. He's my best friend, and he's going to be around. Besides, I talked to him and told him to be a little less—"

"Scary?" I cut him off.

"I think I used the word intense."

"I mean, does the guy ever smile or is he pissed off all the time?"

Rooter snorts. "He's not pissed, Sophie. He's just a very serious individual."

That's an understatement. "I'd say."

Rooter takes me by the hand. "He's a good guy, trust me."

"I do trust you." I believe him because I can't imagine the person Rooter chose as his best friend would be anything less than a great person.

"Good." He checks his watch. "We really need to get going."

While I believe Rooter, I still need a little peace of mind. "I'll be right back." I say and tread toward Bear who's scrolling on the screen of his smart phone. The closer I get to him, the harder my heart pounds. "Can we talk?"

I lead him to the far end of the dining room. "Don't take this the wrong way. I'm so thankful for you coming and keeping watch over Miranda, but—" I'm losing my nerve. Man this guy is freaking huge. I'm a tall girl and he makes me feel like a dwarf. I clear my throat and straighten my posture. "Miranda is in a delicate state of mind and you're kind of…"

He cracks the teeniest hint of a smile. "Intimidating?" He finishes for me.

"Yeah."

Bear has a nice smile. Maybe if he shaved his beard, he'd look a little less daunting. Then again, maybe not.

"I know. I'm working on it. She'll be okay, I promise." He gives me an awkward, closed mouth grin. I find it to be quite endearing.

When Rooter and I enter the living room after my shift at the Grand we find Miranda sitting next to Bear on the sofa, doubled over in laughter. Bear is wearing an amused yet perturbed expression. I spy several bottles of craft beer on the coffee table.

"Oh my God, Sophie, you have to see this!" Miranda slurs and sloppily motions for me to come over to her. "I found out why he never smiles."

"I think it's time for me to go," Bear says, clearly embarrassed and tries to stand up, but Miranda lurches forward and clutches his arm. I expect him to become irritated with her, but he smirks instead.

"Show her," Miranda whines at him. "It's so cute."

Cute? Since when does Miranda think Bear is cute? Rooter laughs behind me.

"See?" Rooter's voice is barely louder than a whisper. "I told you she'd be okay with him."

"Show her," Miranda demands with her hands on her hips. Bear shoots her a stern look, and she changes tactics and bats her pretty, long eyelashes at him and flashes a smile. "Please?"

"Okay," he relents and shakes his head. In only ten hours, Miranda has wrapped this big bad biker around her pinky finger. There really is no man on the planet immune to her charm. "But you have to make the face," he tells her.

Miranda makes her funny face where she squishes her cheeks together, crosses one eye and sticks out her tongue. Bear's mouth spreads into a huge, genuine smile with the straightest, brightest white teeth I've ever seen.

Damn! The guy could be in a dental commercial with those puppies. He must whiten them every day. I burst out laughing, Rooter joins me.

"I care about dental hygiene, okay?" Bear grumps which makes the three of us laugh harder.

"Is that seriously why you never smile?" I ask him.

"Yes," Rooter answers for him and cackles. "The guys all call him Pearl."

Bear flips him the bird. "I think it's time to go."

Miranda is still clinging to his arm, and her smile turns to a frown. "Stay a little while longer," she begs.

"Can't," he says. "I have to be at the shop early."

"Boo." She sticks out her bottom lip. "You're no fun."

"How did this happen?" I whisper to Rooter.

He shrugs and whispers back, "I have no idea."

"I'll come back after work tomorrow," Bear promises Miranda.

"But who will protect me tonight?"

"Rooter is right next door." He points at the wall toward Rooter's house.

"Actually, I'll be staying here tonight," Rooter says and I gape at him in surprise. "I'm not leaving you alone until I'm sure this thing with Mike has blown over."

Before he leaves, Bear helps me get a drunken Miranda upstairs to her room where she once again asks him to stay. Miranda is a lot of things, but easy isn't one of them. But when she gets drunk, she loses her inhibitions. Luckily, Bear is chivalrous enough to turn down her advances and tells her he'll see her tomorrow.

Once Bear is gone, Rooter runs to his house to get Dopey and change into something to sleep in giving me a chance to catch up with Miranda. Rooter already brought me up to speed on the issue with Mike. Thankfully, he hasn't attempted to call Miranda again. Now I want to find out about her day with Bear.

"So, I take it you made a new friend," I say.

"I think I'm in love."

I laugh and fall back onto her bed.

She rolls over and looks at me with a wide smile. "He's not scary Beary anymore."

"Scary Beary?" I hoot and turn to face her.

"He's not scary at all," she slurs. "He's hot."

"So what did you two do today?"

"I made dinner for us and Beary helped me wash the dishes. His real name is Max. Maxim. He's s-so funny Soph. And he took me for a ride on his motor," she hiccups, "cycle to get ice cream. We watched a movie and drank beers. It was the best date ever."

"Date?" I raise an eyebrow.

She grins. "Yep."

"Does he know it was a date?"

"He will soon enough," she giggles.

"I have no doubt."

Miranda always gets what she wants and if she still wants Bear after she's sobered up, he's in serious trouble.

Rooter appears at the top of the stairs in loose, gray sweatpants and a white t-shirt with Dopey at his side.

"Hey Rooter," Miranda calls out, drunkenly emphasizing the ooh sound. "Thank you for int-introducing me to my future husband."

"No problem," he laughs and takes Dopey into my room.

"Future husband?" Rooter asks after I've closed my bedroom door. He's sitting on the edge of the bed. Dopey is curled up at his feet.

"I think Maxim has created a monster." Upon hearing my voice the dog jumps up and trots over to me. "Hey, boy," I say and scratch his ear.

"He told her his name?" He asks, shocked.

"Yeah."

"He doesn't tell anyone his name."

Dopey follows me to my dresser as I get a pair of pajamas. I really need to keep up on my laundry. The only clean ones I have left are a tank top and boy short ensemble with a Wonder Woman symbol on the top and stars on the bottoms. A birthday gift from Miranda last year. We both loved Wonder Woman as little girls. It's either this or wear something dirty from the hamper which is only a slightly worse option.

"Maybe he likes her, too."

"Evidently."

"I didn't see that coming," I admit.

"Me neither." He shakes his head and grins.

"I'll be right back," I say and go to the bathroom to change into the most embarrassing pair of pajamas anyone could possibly own.

I stand in front of my door, stiff as a board with my hands balled up at my sides, for several long minutes trying to muster the courage to open it and go inside. I can only imagine Rooter's amusement when he sees me in this ridiculous get up.

Exactly as I suspect, he howls in laughter when he sees me dressed as Wonder Woman. My face goes up in flames.

"They were a gift."

"Indeed, they are." His body shakes from his boisterous laughter.

"Shut up." I smack his arm and nudge him so he'll make room for me on the bed.

"You're too cute. Where's my phone?" He reaches past me to get it from the nightstand.

"No pictures!" I swipe his phone before he can get to it and tuck it underneath me.

"That isn't going to stop me," he taunts and reaches under me to get it. We roughhouse and when I fight back, he tickles me.

"Agh!" I squeal. "I give up." He tickles my side again anyways. "I said I give up!" I arch my back letting him retrieve the device.

A cool wind blows through the window giving me goosebumps. I hear a deep intake of breath and catch Rooter staring at my chest where my chill is evident.

"You cold?" He asks through a strangled voice and backs away.

"A little." I pull the blankets up around me.

"I'll close the window." He reaches over and starts to pull it shut.

"No." I tug on his arm. "I like it cool at night."

"You won't be too cold?"

"No." I grin. "I like to cuddle in the blankets."

An eager smile spreads across Rooter's face and he gets under the covers with me. "Me, too."

He rolls onto his back and pulls me against his chest. My head lays above his heart and I can hear its thrum, strong and a little fast.

Rooter leans down, presses his face against my head and inhales. "You smell so good."

There's no possible way that can be true after being in the kitchen at the Grand all night. "Yeah, like garlic and onion."

He inhales again. "Sweet, like flowers."

"I like this," I admit, drawing circles on his chest with my index finger. I think I feel him shudder but it's so slight I can't be sure.

"Me, too."

"It kind of makes me glad Mike called."

"Look at me." His tone is serious, making me think I have upset him, but when I look up, his expression is soft. "You never need an excuse to be with me, Sophie. Want me to stay here, ask. Want to stay with me, tell me. Okay?"

Giddy, I smile and my voice shakes when I speak. "Okay."

"It's late." He kisses my forehead. "Let's get some sleep."

When I wake up, I'm in fetal position with Rooter's body enveloping mine. His quiet snores are the only sound in the room. Dopey sits on his hind legs staring at us, patiently waiting to be let out. According to the clock, it's almost nine.

"Rooter." I reach back and tap his thigh to wake him up. He grumbles a response and starts snoring again.

I roll out of bed as gently as I can so I don't disturb him. I can take the dog out on my own. When I hear Rooter move I turn around to see if I woke him. He has rolled over onto his stomach, but he's still asleep, clutching the pillow. Sun pours in through the window illuminating his muscular back and strong shoulders. The man is simply mouthwatering. *When did he take off his shirt?* I stand a moment, daydreaming about caressing the gorgeous lines of his muscles with my fingertips and am broken from my musing by Dopey pawing at my side.

When I bring Dopey back inside Rooter is standing at the kitchen sink with a glass of water in his hand. He's still shirtless and his sweatpants are hanging dangerously low on his hips. Fantasies of running my tongue along his perfectly formed V stream through my mind.

"My eyes are up here." Rooter points at his eyes with his index and middle fingers.

My face catches on fire and I turn away.

"Good morning, babe." He walks over and pulls me in for a hug.

The skin on his chest is warm against my face. "Good morning," I squeak.

"Sleep well?"

"Amazing," I admit.

"Me, too." He kisses the top of my head. "You're an excellent spooner."

"I am?" I've never done it.

"The best."

Visions of him spooning with other women come to mind, and it irritates me. I'm sure he's had a lot of sex with a lot of women, but I don't want him comparing me to them. Ever. I might be a great spooner, but being an almost virgin I'm sure I'll suck at everything else in comparison.

"Coffee," I grumble and pull away. "Must have coffee. Should I make enough for you?" I ask and measure out the grounds.

He shakes his head. "What are your plans for today?"

I look down at my heavily worn black yoga pants that I dug out of the hamper before letting Dopey out. "Don't have any plans, but I seriously need to do laundry."

"That's cool." He finishes his glass of water. "We can hang here for a while. I need to run by the shop later. The three of us can grab lunch."

"Rooter, you don't need to babysit me."

"I'm not." He wraps his arms around my waist and grins. "I'm just hanging out with my girlfriend on her day off."

The way he says "girlfriend" is so casual and natural sounding it nearly makes me forget the conversation we're having. I tilt my head to one side. "You're babysitting me."

"I'm spending time with you and in the process making sure you're safe. That's what any good boyfriend would do."

And now the word "boyfriend" has my insides stirring. Rooter— Jace Alexander Russo—is my boyfriend. It still doesn't seem real. I don't think it ever will. "Well then, you can help with the laundry." I smirk.

"I'd love to fold your delicates." He smirks back.

"I bet."

First Fight

"You two are sickeningly cute." Miranda stumbles into the kitchen. "Is there coffee?"

"Almost." I pull away from Rooter to grab two mugs from the cupboard.

Miranda fishes through another cabinet for aspirin.

"We're out. I have ibuprofen in my purse," I offer.

"Is it upstairs?" She leans her head against the cabinet door.

"Yep."

"I can't make it all the way back up there," she whines as the coffeemaker chimes that it's finished.

"I'll get it," Rooter offers and runs upstairs.

"So," I start once he's gone. "You have a thing for scary Beary now, eh?" I pour us both a cup of the coffee and add hazelnut creamer.

"He's so fucking hot, Sophie," she says making me chuckle. Never in a million years would I expect to hear that from her. "Do you think he likes me?"

"We both do." I'll never get used to referring to me and Rooter as we.

"Really?" She asks, her eyes turn bright, exuding excitement.

Rooter pads into the kitchen and hands me my purse. I fish out the bottle of ibuprofen and hand it to Miranda.

"Later," I mouth to her when he's not paying attention.

Rooter wasn't kidding when he said he'd fold my delicates. He almost looks excited when I dump them on to my bed. Another tickle war ensues when I try to shoo him away from them. Of course, I lose. I don't know whether to be glad or embarrassed that I only wear nice underwear. Collecting cute bra and panty sets is kind of my thing. It has nothing to do with sex or guys. I simply have an issue with wearing ugly or mismatch bras and panties. Miranda thinks I'm nuts. Maybe I am.

"Do you really need this many bras?" Rooter laughs. There must be fifteen of all different colors and materials laying in a pile before us.

"Yes, I do. They all go with their own matching panties," I explain.

Rooter's face changes from amused to desirous and it gives me tingles.

He clears his throat. "This is something I didn't know about you."

He picks up a bra and mimics the way I'm folding the one in my hand. When he's done he pulls a purple, lacey thong from the pile.

"Do you actually fold these?" His voice is low, sultry.

I think this is turning him on. I like it.

"Yes," I take it from his hand and demonstrate how I fold them. "Like this."

"Seriously?" He asks. "There isn't enough material to bother with."

"I prefer things to be neat and in order. Makes it easier to find when I'm trying to pair things together."

Rooter grabs another thong and folds it the way I showed him, followed by a few more pairs. When he comes across a red see through lace bra with black satin laces on the cups he stops and holds it up to me. A gasp escapes his lips followed by a curse. "You actually wear this just to wear it?" He's staring at me slack jawed.

"Yeah," I mumble, bashful.

"Go put it on," he growls.

Now it's my turn to go slack jawed. "What?"

"Knowing you have it on will be hot as hell." He winks.

For grins, I do as told and go into the bathroom to change. When I return, we—or rather I—continue folding and putting the rest of the laundry away while Rooter stares at me.

After a putting a third load of laundry into the dryer, Rooter suggests the three of us grab lunch before heading to his shop. We can't all fit in his truck so we take my car. He insists on driving and when he starts the ignition, my favorite former boy bander blares through the speakers. He jumps and shouts a curse before turning off the radio. Miranda and I laugh.

"Do you ever listen to anything else?" He asks.

I shrug. "Occasionally." I turn the radio back on, but at a quieter volume.

"I seriously need to educate you on what real music is."

"Oh, really?"

"Nirvana," he holds his right hand up to count as he backs out of my driveway, "Radiohead, Soundgarden, Alice in Chains. Four of the greatest rock bands of the nineties."

"Nirvana? No, thank you."

"What? They are *legendary*."

"They're greasy and grungy, and that guy, Kirk whatever, couldn't even sing. All he did was scream."

Rooter stares me down with a dead serious expression that makes my heart skip three beats. "Do. Not. Ever. And I mean ever, hate on *Kurt* Cobain. The man was and always will be a legend."

"Pay attention to the road." I turn his face back to the windshield.

"Where do you girls want to eat?" He asks.

"Let's go see Joe at Skyles," Miranda suggests.

"You in love with him, too?" Rooter asks, amused.

"He is hot in an old guy sort of way," she responds and I laugh. She leans up to my seat. "Poor Joe will be heartbroken when he sees you have a boyfriend."

"He already knows," Rooter tells her and winks at me.

Did someone turn on the heat in here?

After lunch, Rooter drives us to his shop to check on the bike he's working on with Bear. I'm eager to see where he works and what he does, and he appears equally excited to show me.

Miranda totally geeks out over the opportunity to see Bear. She spends the entire ride from Skyles touching up makeup and making sure her hair is perfect. I haven't seen her this excited about a guy since she first hooked up with Chris.

"This bike will be sick as shit when we're done with it," he brags as we pull into the lot. His smile turns to a frown. "Fuck."

I turn my head in the direction Rooter's staring and see Blondie's red Mustang parked in a visitor parking space in front of the main entrance. He parks my car by the employee entrance across the lot.

"What is she doing here?" I ask.

"Probably checking on her bike." Rooter opens the car door and steps out.

Great. Not only is she hot, she rides a motorcycle.

He waits impatiently as Miranda crawls out of the backseat and then hurries us into the building. When we step inside he scans the immediate area, nervous. *What is he worried about? He said they're done. Was he lying?*

Rooter leads us into a dark room at the end of the hall and turns on the light. It's a well decorated conference room with expensive, modern furnishings. The entire front wall is covered in glass and I can see the parking lot through a window across the hall.

"Wait in here," he tells us.

"Where are you going?" I ask, already knowing the answer.

"I'm only going to see what she wants." He speaks slow and cautious.

"Why can't I go with you?" I cross my arms and shift my weight to my right leg.

"It's just business, Sophie."

"Then why are you hiding me in here?"

"I'm not hiding you."

"That's what it looks like to me," Miranda smarts off and Rooter shoots her a warning glare. "Sorry."

"Look," he turns back to me, "I told you that was done and I meant it."

"And yet, you're stowing me away in a conference room." I wave my arms at our surroundings.

He exhales and combs a hand through his short, dark hair. "You don't want to come with me, trust me."

"Why not?" I cock my head to the side.

"Sophie, it was just weeks ago that she and I…"

"Were fucking?" I finish for him.

He flinches. "Yes. And I don't think she'd appreciate seeing us together."

"Too bad."

"Sophie, please," he whines, impatient. "Trust me."

I shake my head, exasperated. I do trust him. At least I thought I did until now. I look in his eyes trying to determine if he's telling me the truth. Honestly, I can't tell.

"I'll be five minutes. I promise."

"Fine. Go."

"You're pissed."

How very observant of him. "Yeah," I huff.

He shakes his head. "I'm sorry." He leans in to kiss my cheek and I have to fight the urge to pull away. "I'll be right back."

"Do you think he's telling the truth?" Miranda asks as soon as he pulls the door closed.

"I have no idea." With gritted teeth, I stare at the skank's car through the window.

I pace the length of the vast room over and over for ten agonizing minutes. I'm getting dangerously close to going to find them. Or leaving. How fucking rude to leave me here while he goes to "talk" to his ex-trollop. Visions of Candace traipsing around in a slutty little outfit, leaning on and putting her hands on Rooter flow through my mind. I grip the back of a chair so hard that I snap off the end of a fingernail.

"Dammit!" I holler. "He's got another two minutes and I'm the fuck out of here."

"Look." Miranda points to the window, her mouth hanging open.

Rooter is following a scantily clad Candace to her car. They're both wearing shit-eating grins which piss me off even more. And then that bitch leans in, grabs Rooter's crotch and kisses him. He jumps in surprise, but doesn't push her away like I'd expect.

"What the hell?" We both gasp in unison.

The bitch lets go of Rooter's junk, but leans in and says something to him that makes him smile before she gets in the car. I swear he even blushed! What the actual fuck? Rooter closes her car door, looks to this end of the building and walks back to the door he just came out of.

"Fuck this! I'm out of here." I snatch my purse and dart out of the room.

Miranda follows me as I run down the hall to the door we came in through. "Hurry and get in the car," I holler. And then I realize Rooter has my keys. "Shit!"

"Here." Miranda tosses me her key ring. After we got locked out of her car at the movie theatre in the pouring rain a year ago, we started carrying each other's spares.

As soon as we jump into the car I start it and throw it into reverse as fast as I can. I tear out of the parking space and hear Rooter scream my name. I watch him run after us through the rearview mirror as I speed out of the parking lot.

"He fucking lied!" I scream at the top of my lungs and punch the steering wheel sending a blinding pain up the entire length of my arm.

"What an ass. Watch that—" But she can't finish before the car jerks violently to the left as I hit the curb with the passenger side tires.

"He told me they were done!"

"What are you going to do?"

When I see Miranda gripping the dashboard for dear life I slow down. He's not worth risking my best friend's life. "I'm done with his ass. I should've known better!"

"No, I meant, he's just going to follow us to the house."

I hadn't thought about that. "You're right." I make a hard right and head in the opposite direction of our house.

"Where are we going?"

"Ryan's."

My knuckles sting as I furiously rap them against Ryan's front door until he opens it.

"What the—" Ryan barks until he sees my face. "Sophie, what's wrong?" He pulls me into his living room.

"He lied to me." In my purse, my phone rings incessantly. It must be the hundredth time he's called since I left the shop. I jerk the damn thing from my bag and scream into the receiver. "Stop calling me!" Knowing he won't stop I turn the phone off after hanging up on him.

"What did he lie about?" Ryan leads me to his sectional and sits beside me.

I rehash the entire scene for Ryan in one long run on sentence. "I am so done with him."

"I can't believe he did that," Ryan says, astonished.

"He did," Miranda confirms.

"I can't go back to the house," I tell him. "Is it okay if I stay here for the night?"

"Of course, babe." Ryan rubs my arm to comfort me. "Stay as long as you need."

"Thank you." I fling my arms in the air and nearly hit Ryan in the face. "God, I'm such an idiot!"

"He's the idiot," Ryan asserts and holds my hands in his.

"I believed everything he said. All that shit about how he never wanted to be with anyone until me. How I made him feel something he never felt before." I jump up and pace the room. "All bullshit!"

"He even had me convinced," Miranda admits.

"You warned me, though. I should've stayed away from him. Now what the fuck am I going to do?" I gesture wildly in the air. "He lives right next door!"

"Don't worry about that right now," Ryan says. "We'll figure something out."

"Yeah," Miranda agrees. "You need to put some space between you and him."

"I want to punch him in the face." I draw back my fist and look around for something, anything to punch, but give up after I find nothing. "I want to kick him so hard in the balls he'll never be able to fuck her or any other bitch ever again!"

"I know that feeling," Miranda says.

"Me, too girl," Ryan concurs.

"I hate men!" I bellow and fall back onto the sectional.

"Hey," Ryan feigns offense trying to lighten the mood.

"All men but you," I correct with a forced smile.

"I hate to do this to you," he says, "but I need to leave for work."

"You really don't mind me staying here?"

"Absolutely not. Make yourself at home. There's plenty of food and drink. Booze if you prefer. If you get tired, sleep in my bed," he offers with a warm smile. "But save room for me."

I laugh, but barely. "Thank you so much."

"Do you want me to stay awhile?" Miranda asks after Ryan leaves.

She can't stay with me. She has virtual class tonight. Virtual class is where she has to sign in and attend class online with the professor and other students. It'll count against her if she misses. I don't want her to get dinged on account of me and my boy problems.

"No. Go do your class thing."

"I feel terrible leaving you here alone."

"It's okay," I assure her with a smile. "It might do me some good to have time alone to think." I don't really believe this. In fact, I'm pretty sure being alone will be utterly miserable and could result in some sort of poor decision making.

"What should I say to him?" Miranda asks, standing in front of the door.

"Whatever you want, but do *not* tell him where I am."

"I won't," she assures me.

"I'm serious, Miranda. You have to promise not to tell him."

"I promise." She starts out the door, but stops and turns around. "Call me if you need anything, okay?"

When I wake I turn on my phone, curious as to how many messages and texts Rooter has left for me. My stomach is upset. I'm nervous about what he might say, but I'm more nervous about how I'll respond to it. I can't bring myself to check my messages. I need more time to calm down.

Finally, at ten thirteen I give in. The first message was left right after I peeled away from the shop.

"Listen to them with me?" I ask Ryan who is sitting across from me at his dining room table.

"Sure," he says and scoots into the chair next to me.

I take a deep breath and count to ten in an attempt to control the roiling of my stomach. After several long moments, I push play.

THE EXPLANATION

"Sophie," Rooter huffs, out of breath, "baby I'm sorry. Just let me explain. Call me or come back to the shop, please."

In the second message, he gets a little more desperate.

"Babe, I know you think you know what you saw, but it's not what you think. You need to call me back. Now."

By the third message, he's all but given up.

"Sophie, since you turned your phone off, this is gonna be my last message. I understand what you think you saw. If it was me I'd probably be pissed, too. But I wouldn't run away from you." There's a pause. "You can't hide from me forever so when you get this message, call me."

The next voicemail is from Miranda. "Sophie, I talked to Rooter. It was all a huge misunderstanding. I think you should call him when you get this message."

"Wow, he must've seriously done a number on her," I snort.

There's one more voicemail and I almost don't want to listen to it.

"I'm lying in your bed," my heartbeat quickens, "and I hate that you're not here. I hate that you're out there somewhere so mad at me that you won't talk to me. Sophie, I swear to God I'd *never* do anything to hurt you. I care so much about you. Knowing that you're sad because of me is killing me baby. Please come home and talk to me."

It takes everything I have not to get choked up. He sounds so sincere. But isn't that what cheaters and liars do? Play on others weaknesses and emotions? My mother did it to me until the day she died. She'd lie and do horrible things to me and then tell me how sorry she was. That she didn't mean to do it or that, as in this case, I misunderstood something. I can't go through that again. I won't go through it again.

"What should I do?" I ask Ryan.

"You live next door to the guy. You'll have to face him at some point."

I fiddle with the phone. "Do you think it might've been a misunderstanding?"

"If he convinced Miranda of all people, it might have been. There's only one way to find out."

"Okay." I take a deep breath. "Take me home."

On the way to my house, I absentmindedly gnaw on my lip while trying to mentally prepare myself for what's coming.

"You won't have any lip left if you keep that up," Ryan quips, trying to lighten the mood.

"I'm not sure I'm ready for this."

The buildings are passing by too fast. I need this drive to last a little longer. Will Rooter and I argue? Will he be able to convince me of his innocence or is this the end? Do I even want to hear what he has to say? Words are so feeble. They can be meaningless. A person can say anything. Actions prove our intent, our loyalty, and our trustworthiness. Yesterday, he let the girl he swore he was done with put her hand and her mouth on him. He even smiled for Christ's sake.

"It's like a Band-Aid. Just get it over with and rip it off."

I didn't get much sleep last night. Every time I nodded off, I dreamt of her touching him. Kissing him. Of him enjoying it. The way he seemed to enjoy it yesterday. The way he seemed to enjoy her touching him a few weeks ago. I'm not sure this is something I can forgive, regardless of how he tries to explain or justify it. But I'm also not sure I can walk away from him. We're barely even an "us" and already we're at the brink of ruin.

We're three blocks from my house. I exhale sharply and pull down the visor to check my appearance in the mirror. Of course I look like shit. My eyes are puffy, skin is blotchy. My hair is piled on top of my head in a messy bun. This is not the way I want to look when arguing with my boyfriend over being fondled by chick who's twice as good looking as I am on my best day.

"You're beautiful," Ryan declares.

I flip the visor up and lean my head against the headrest as we pull onto my street. Rooter is nowhere to be seen when we pull up in front of my house. His bike isn't in the driveway which gives me hope he might be gone.

"Thanks for everything, Ry."

"Call me if you need anything," he says as I climb out of the car.

I hurry to the hide-a-key rock that's buried in our mulch bed to retrieve the key to the front door. If I can get inside without Rooter seeing me maybe I can delay the inevitable a little longer. I open the door, close my eyes and take a deep breath as I step into the house.

"Sophie," Rooter's worried voice gives me a jolt. Dopey comes bounding to my side.

"What are you doing in here?" I snap and throw my purse to the floor. This is *my* house. *My* sanctuary. He has no right to be in here without my permission and he most certainly doesn't have it.

"I've been waiting for you to come home." He rises from the couch and rubs the back of his neck.

"Couldn't you have waited at your own house?" I clutch the back of the chair, angry.

Rooter ambles toward me, slow and cautious. "I was afraid you'd avoid me."

He's right. I would have. The dog paws at me but I'm too irritated to give him any attention.

"Sophie, I'm so sorry."

If I went by his tone and remorseful expression, I'd believe him. But I'm going by what I saw.

"You're only sorry you got caught." I squeeze the fabric tighter and deliver a warning glare not to come any closer.

"That's not true."

"You just stood there and let her…" I mimic the way her hands groped him because I can't say the words.

"Listen to me, I know how it looked and I'm sorry but—"

"Stop saying you're sorry," I scream and slam my fists on top of the back of the chair.

Rooter's eyes go wide, and he instinctively takes a step back.

"And don't you dare say it wasn't what it looked like!" I point my finger at him. "You fucked up."

Rooter takes a careful half step forward. "But, it wasn't what it looked like, babe."

His use of the word "babe" makes my stomach turn. I wonder how many times he called Candace "babe." I bet he called her that every time they fucked. The mere thought of it makes me want to vomit. "Don't call me that! I'm not your babe."

"Yes, you are." He reaches for me with worry etched into his features. "And I'm yours."

"No." I jerk away. "If you were mine, you wouldn't have let her touch you that way."

He clasps his hands over his head. "I should've handled it differently, it's just that…"

"No justs, no buts. It should've never happened. How'd you like it if you saw some guy do that to me?"

His jaw clenches and there's a spark in his eyes. "Honestly, I'd probably massacre the guy."

"Exactly, but now I'm supposed to say, oh, don't worry, it's okay."

"No, you're not," he sighs, impatient. "That's why I'm trying to explain it to you."

"Please, by all means," I wave my hand in the air, "let's hear why you let your ex-slut kiss you and grab your dick."

Surprised by my choice of words, he raises both eyebrows before answering. "What she did is something she's always done—"

I cut him off midsentence. "So since she's always done it she might as well keep doing it? Is that what you're saying?"

"No. Sophie," he rubs his face, "will you please let me speak without interrupting?"

"Fine. Go ahead."

I walk around to the front of the chair and sit cross legged with perfect posture as though I'm at a job interview. Rooter takes a seat on the couch to my right.

"I've known Candace all my life," he begins. "We grew up together. Her dad was one of the original club members. When he died a few years back, she ran off with a guy from school. About a year ago, she moved back here after he nearly beat her to death. We started hooking up a few months back.

Rooter stops as though to gauge my response. When he seems to be convinced I won't fly off the handle he continues, "We made a deal. It was just sex. No strings attached. If either of us met someone new or if one developed feelings and the other didn't feel the same, we'd stop. So, after the night of your break in, I ended it with her. She put two and two together and figured I'd met someone. She flipped out.

He closes his eyes and takes a deep breath. "She admitted she was in love with me. Begged me to give her a chance. She threatened to kill herself. Said I'm all she has. The club is her only family. I knew that if she saw me with you, she'd lose her shit. She's not stable. She could've hurt you or herself. I was taking the path of least resistance."

"And part of that path is continuing to let her kiss and touch you inappropriately?"

"No. I told her it had to stop."

"Then why were you both smiling?"

"What?" He furrows his brow seemingly confused.

"After she grabbed you, she said something to you that had you blushing."

He bows his head and looks to the floor. "I don't remember."

"Bullshit," I snarl and lean in close. "Do *not* lie to me or you can leave right now."

He looks up at me earnestly. "She said to call when I realize how much I miss her."

I shake my head. "That wouldn't have made you blush. Tell me what she said."

He rubs the back of his neck. "You don't want to hear it."

I smack the arm of the chair. "Yes, I do!"

He speaks through gritted teeth. "She said to call her when I realize how much I miss pounding her tight pussy."

We both stare at one another for a long moment. He's gauging my reaction and I'm trying to calm down.

I squeeze my eyes shut. "Do you miss it?" I ask pointblank.

"No," he asserts as though I should already know this.

"Of course you do! Who are you trying to fool? Me or yourself?"

He's certainly not fooling me. Rooter is the kind of guy who gets around. The kind of guy who is used to lots of sex with lots of women. And after my little freak out the other day, he's got to be thinking he made a mistake with me.

"You want honesty? I'll give it to you. If sex was all I was after I'd probably be with her right now." His words cut me to the bone and I flinch. "But that's not what I'm after, Sophie. I want something real." He gets on his knees before me. When he places his hands on my legs I lean back. "I never thought I'd be saying this, but I want to be with someone I can fall in love with. That's you. I want to give you my heart and I hope you'll give me yours."

Forgiveness

I draw in a sharp breath and blink repeatedly while Rooter stares at me with hopeful eyes. I can feel my heart reaching for him from within my chest. Did I hear that right? He wants to fall in love with me?

I want him to fall in love with me and I thought I'd fall in love with him. But Candace is a huge complication. A complication I'm not sure I can accept. I can accept that he has a past. However, I can't accept that past being a part of his present especially if it will be flaunted right in front of my face.

Worse yet is the idea of what goes on—and what will continue to go on—between them when I'm not around. I don't want to deal with a slutty ex-whatever constantly throwing herself at my boyfriend. But if I continue this with him that's what I'll be signing up for. But then I see his gorgeous face anxiously staring at me, begging for a chance. Even though I believe what he said, I'm not sure what to do.

I fall back in the chair and rub my face. Rooter's hands grip my legs conveying his panic.

"Please don't let one mistake ruin everything."

"That's just it!" I exhale sharply. "This probably isn't even the first time something like this has happened and I seriously doubt it will be the last."

"I'll handle her."

"Like you did yesterday?" I push his hands off my legs. His touch is too much. I can't think clearly when his hands are on me.

"Sophie, please." He sits back on his haunches.

"Your situation with her is a lot more involved than you led me to believe," I sigh. "You've known her your entire life which means she'll always be around."

He leans forward again, but I hold my arms out to keep him at bay. "You have absolutely nothing to worry about, I promise."

"I believed that until yesterday."

He shifts forward again and takes hold of my hands so I can't stop him from getting close. "I won't let that happen again. Sophie, please give me a chance."

I must say something, but that something can't be yes or no because I'm far too inclined to say yes. It scares the hell out of me. "I need time to think."

Without hesitation Rooter shakes his head. "No."

"No?"

"That's right. No." He leans in temptingly close. "You want to pull back and be distant and pissed off, go ahead. But I'm not going anywhere. I'm going to stay right here and prove to you that this is where I want to be."

Utterly fucking astounded, all I can do is blink and stare him in the face which isn't even two inches from mine. If he kissed me right now I wouldn't stop him. I wouldn't be able to. His close proximity is jarring my senses and ability to think.

"So you go ahead and do what you need to do," he continues, "and when you're done being pissed at me, let me know."

There's nothing I can say to that so all I do is stare at him, mouth agape.

It's a slow night at the Grand so it gives me and Ryan time to chat while I help him clean behind the bar. I've just told him about my conversation with Rooter and what he said at the end.

"Nice one, Rooter!"

I immediately stop hanging wine glasses and suck in a breath. "What? Nice one?"

"Not to excuse what happened, but the man is owning up to his shit and is willing to take whatever heat you dish out. Good for him."

"I hadn't looked at it that way," I admit and go back to hanging the glasses while Ryan organizes one of the beer coolers.

"I'm not happy about what happened, Soph, but I think Rooter's a good guy with good intentions." He comes over, lays a hand on my shoulder and looks at me with caring green eyes. "I mean, he's never had a girlfriend. He's bound to cock up every now and again."

Ryan and I exit the restaurant to find Rooter sitting on his bike next to my car. I won't admit it to him—I have a hard enough time admitting it to myself—but I'm happy to see him. His being here to make sure I get home safe proves he does indeed care for me.

"Go a little easy on him," Ryan whispers before heading to his car.

"How was work?" Rooter asks and dismounts the Harley as I approach him. He's wearing a long sleeve, fitted black shirt that clings to his muscular physique. When he reaches up to rub the back of his neck it lifts just enough to reveal a hint of his midsection.

God why does he have to be so perfect? It'd be a hell of a lot easier to be pissy if he wasn't so ridiculously hot. "Slow and very boring."

"Want to ride home with me?" He puts his hands in his pockets and he rocks back and forth on his heels.

One moment I want to reach over and pull him in for a kiss and in the very next moment, I see Candace's mouth on him and I want to slap him. I shake my head. "I have my car."

"I can bring you back to get it tomorrow."

I open my car door. "I have a doctor's appointment in the morning."

Rooter lifts an eyebrow. "Everything okay?"

"Just an annual. But it's an early appointment so I'll need my car."

"Okay, I'll follow you home." Rooter leans in for a kiss and I turn my face and give him my cheek. I can't have his lips on mine when all I can think about is those same lips kissing another woman.

The drive home takes forever. I'm so tired that I have to blast music and bite my tongue to stay awake. Ryan's words keep playing in my mind reminding me I need to take it easy on Rooter. It would be different had Rooter been the aggressor in the kiss, but he wasn't. And I need to keep in mind I'm his first girlfriend. He's not used to having to think of another person's feelings when women hit on him.

But it's thoughts like this that make it worse. He probably has tons of women throwing themselves at him. Women willing to do anything and everything for just one night with him. He says he wants to have a relationship with me and we've only made out once. And then I remember how he said he likes that I'm different; that I make him want things he's never wanted. He said it himself, he isn't after sex. He's after something real. So should I suck it up and give him a pardon or do I take a few days to digest everything?

I'm so wrapped up in my thoughts I almost drive past my house. At the last possible second, I slam on the brakes and make a hard right into my driveway nearly smashing into the trash can.

"Forget where you live?" Rooter jokes, but his voice is thick with concern.

"Wasn't paying attention."

We walk in an awkward silence to my door. Walking side by side without holding hands or touching in some way feels... wrong. *Does he sense it too?* I blow out a heavy breath as I unlock my door.

"I'll be right back," he says when I step into the house.

I whip around to face him. "Rooter, you don't need to stay tonight. Mike won't come around here."

"Sophie, you don't know that."

"Yes, I do. And so do you." I look at my feet. "The only reason you want to stay here is because of what happened."

"Fine, you're right." He lifts my chin so I'm facing him. "I told you I wasn't going to give you space."

He's making this so hard for me. My stomach is in knots. I want him to come in with me and hold me through the night. But every time I look at him, I see *her*. Her bouncy blonde waves, her perfect body, her red lips pressed against his.

"No, you said you wouldn't give me time to think. You didn't say anything about space."

"Well, I'm definitely not giving you space."

He's got to be kidding me. I'm elated and frustrated at the same time. But who is he to decide that he's spending the night? "Well, you can't stay in my house without my permission."

He lifts his chin in consternation. "I won't let you push me away."

"I'm not pushing you away," I half lie with a huff. "I'm tired. I want to go to my room and go to sleep."

"Fine, then let's go to your room and sleep. We don't have to talk and I won't lay a finger on you."

Why lay your fingers on me when you can lay them on Cand-ass? God, these thoughts need to stop. "Rooter," I lay my head against the door jamb, "just go home. Please."

"That's what you really want?" He challenges.

No. I don't know. "That's what I want."

Rooter reaches out and cups my face with his palm. "There's really very little I wouldn't do for you," he says with a sad smile before walking away.

What the hell does that mean?

The first thing I do when I get to my room is close the blinds. Seeing Rooter in his room would be far too tempting. I know I'd text him and tell him to come back. No matter how much I want him here, no matter how much I want to put this whole thing behind us and move on, if I give in this soon, he won't take me seriously. I need to put my foot down now. He needs to know how much it hurt me to see him with Candace and he needs to know I won't tolerate that kind of behavior.

Five minutes later, I'm lying in bed staring at the ceiling wishing Rooter was here with me. I don't want to talk and touching would be a really bad idea since it clouds my judgment, but I want him here. I want to be near him. Close enough to feel his warmth and smell his scent without any words or contact. I peek out of my blinds and Rooter's window is dark. *Is he in his bed? Is he doing the same thing I'm doing right now?*

I grip my sheets tight and exhale in frustration when I hear the wood floor creak outside my door. Miranda must be up. Maybe talking to her would help. As I sit up my door opens and Dopey trots over and pokes my arm with his wet nose. Rooter's silhouette stands before me in the dark. Happiness, relief, and astonishment cascade over me.

"What the—" Rooter's fingers gently brush my lips to hush me. His touch relaxes and excites me all at once.

"Remember me saying there's very little I wouldn't do for you?"

I nod and inhale deeply allowing his scent to envelop me.

"Well, I refuse to give you time or space."

"So you break into my house?" I ask, trying to sound annoyed when he removes his fingers from my lips. I can't let him know how happy I am he's here.

He chuckles. "I didn't break in. I used the hide-a-key."

"I honestly don't know what to say."

"Don't say anything. Let's go to sleep." Rooter kisses my forehead and crawls past me into the bed against the wall. I remain upright staring at him in disbelief. He pulls me into a spooning position and drapes a protective arm over me. "Good night, Sophie."

"Good night, Rooter," I say, hoping he can't hear the relief in my voice.

Somehow, in the night, I must've turned around. When I'm woken by the sound of my alarm, I'm tucked face first into Rooter's bare chest with our legs intertwined. His head rests on the pillow above mine. I suck in a deep breath and inhale his masculine scent. It feels so good to be in his arms. Actually, it feels better than good. It feels *right*. Rooter reaches out and shuts the alarm off. When I try to roll over I'm stopped by two strong arms pulling me tight against him.

"Stay here a little longer," he murmurs and I happily obey. He reaches down and massages my back and I can't stifle my moan. "I like waking up like this," he admits.

Me, too.

"I need to get up," I say after a few minutes.

I tear myself from the bed and rummage through my closet for something to wear while Rooter leans back against my headboard and watches me. I force myself not to stare at his perfectly sculpted chest. I bet he wouldn't stop me if I touched him. I bet he wouldn't stop me from straddling him and licking his neck, and collar bone, and earlobe, and…

The sound of his raspy morning voice snaps me back to reality, but I don't know what he said. "What?"

"What time is your appointment?" He asks.

"Nine thirty."

Rooter snickers as I pair a bra and panty set together to match my outfit and I flash back to him helping me fold them.

"Want to grab lunch afterward?" He asks and swings his legs over the side of the bed.

"What part of I'm mad at you do you not understand?"

"I understand it perfectly, babe." He reaches for me and pulls me to stand between his legs. "What part of I'm not giving you time or space do you not understand?"

"You're not going to be one of those possessive, clingy boyfriends are you?"

"So you're saying you're still my girl?" He smirks. His callused hands feel incredible as they travel up and down the backs of my legs.

"Do I have a choice?"

"No." He chuckles as if he's joking, but he's being completely serious.

His touch is driving me crazy. I try desperately to keep my breathing steady, but my heart is racing. "I'm meeting Ryan after my appointment."

His hands stop moving and his expression changes from amused to worried. "For real? Or are you blowing me off?"

"I really am meeting him," I assure him with a smile while fighting the urge to reach out and touch his face. Rooter in the morning is a magnificent sight with his sleepy eyes and morning stubble. "We're going shopping for Miranda's birthday."

"Oh, okay." Relief rings evident in his voice. He pulls me to him and rests his face against my left boob in a completely innocent act. The way he wraps his arms around me and exhales is so sweet. It's as if he misses me even though I'm right here in his arms. I can't fight the urge to run my fingers through his hair. He hums in delight at my touch. "Please don't stay mad at me long, babe."

I can hear the aching vulnerability in his voice and it nearly tears me to shreds. It's at this moment I know I'll never be able to deny him anything. If he wants me, he can have me. "Look at me," I say

186

and he doesn't hesitate to do as told. "Seeing you with her like that hurt me."

His hand grips me tightly. "I can't begin to tell you how fucking sorry I am."

"I need for you to set her straight on what is and is not acceptable behavior."

"I promise, I will."

I tug at his hair, holding his head firm in my hands. "I also need you to promise you won't let her or any other girl kiss or touch you."

"I promise."

"Do you also promise to be loyal to me?"

"Always, babe."

I pull his hair just hard enough to make him wince. "And do you agree that I reserve the right to castrate you if you break any of those promises?"

"Happily. I'll even provide the knife." He peers up at me with an eager smile.

"Okay." I give in. "I forgive you."

Rooter roars and pulls me onto the bed with him. He snuggles against me, wraps his legs around me, and plants a sweet kiss on my collarbone. "Thank you."

DOUBT

Doubt is an extremely powerful emotion. I once vowed to never be in a relationship unless I have one hundred percent trust in the guy. I have a lot of trust in Rooter, but I also have doubts. Serious ones.

I know he cares for me. He's proven it on several occasions. I trust he truly wants a relationship with me and that he intends to be faithful. But I'm not positive he's capable of it. He has no track record to prove that he is. If anything, his track record proves he isn't capable of being in an exclusive, monogamous relationship. That scares the shit out of me.

I don't believe that we as a human race are monogamous by nature. However, we are—or at least I am—extremely possessive of our partners. I refuse to share and I don't think Rooter would either. So, even though we may be or become attracted to another person, our possessive instincts command us to be faithful so we don't lose that which we possess.

Two days have passed since I made up with Rooter over the Candace incident. That's what I'm calling it now. The incident.

Ryan and I are sitting at the break table. I was hungry when I ordered my food, but suddenly have no appetite. I've pushed more chicken around my plate than I've eaten.

"The bitch calls constantly," I complain. "What part of he has a girlfriend does she not understand? I mean, does she have any self-respect? It's pathetic."

Ryan gives me a sympathetic look. "They have history and she probably feels like she had him first so she's trying to reclaim what was hers."

"But he wasn't hers," I huff and push more chicken around my plate. Ryan grabs my hand to stop me.

"In her mind he was and still is. She's trying to run you off because you're new and therefore irrelevant. That's the way those bitches work."

"Yeah, well I'm not going anywhere and if she doesn't stop this shit I'm going to pay her a visit."

Ryan sits back in his seat and shakes his head. "I'm not sure that's such a good idea. Take the high road. Be the better person. She'll give up eventually."

"I'm not so sure."

In an attempt to be open and honest, Rooter has allowed me to read her texts. Her last text was a picture of her in bed wearing pink lingerie with the caption "Remember this?" When he opened it, he choked and turned bright red. I flipped out and demanded that he either change his number or block her. We argued over why he couldn't do either. He said he couldn't change his number for business reasons and blocking her wouldn't stop her. She'd just find other ways to make her point and it would probably make matters worse. Again, Candace wins and I'm stuck dealing with her crap.

That was the last conversation we had before I came to work. He's been texting me cute little messages all day telling me he's thinking of me and hopes I'm having a good night. I'm still pissed.

"It's only been two days. Give it a couple of weeks. She'll go away on her own."

"I don't know if I have another two weeks of this in me. I seriously want to choke the skank."

Ryan laughs and pulls me into an embrace. "I know, babe."

Girls like Candace don't give up and go away easily. Sure, she might go and pole vault off of some random loser to make herself feel better—because let's face it, that's what sluts do—but she's made up her mind that Rooter is the one she wants. She's known him and wanted him for way too long to walk away without a fight. And if she's truly in love with him, it'll get a lot worse before it gets better.

"Why must relationships be so complicated?" I whine.

"That's what makes them so much fun!" He squeals, sarcastic. The way his kind, green eyes sparkle when he laughs brings a smile to my face.

"What would I do without you?"

"I wouldn't want to know."

As per usual, Rooter is sitting on my steps with Dopey at his feet when I pull into the driveway. I'm at once happy and annoyed to see him. The dog comes loping over the moment I'm out of the car.

"Hey, boy," I say and pat his head.

Rooter gives me a small, unsure smile upon my approach. I can tell he's on edge, uncertain of how I'll react to him since I never responded to any of his texts tonight.

"How was your night?" He asks as I unlock my door.

"Fine." I pause and peer up at him before opening the door. "I don't think you should stay here tonight," he opens his mouth to protest so I continue before he can, "and not just because I'm mad."

He crosses his arms. "Why then?"

"Because, we don't live together and it's not a good idea to get into the habit of spending every night together."

Rooter grabs my hips and pulls me against him. "I think we should definitely get into that habit."

"I'm serious," I insist and push away.

"So am I." He tugs at me again.

"You're not staying here tonight. Mike hasn't been an issue, so there's no need."

He lets go and takes a small step back with a crestfallen expression. "This is because you're mad."

I wish he wouldn't look at me that way. It makes it nearly impossible to stand by my conviction. "Yeah, I'm mad, but I don't think we should spend every night together."

"Too much, too soon?" He tilts his head to the side. His expression changes from worried to hopeful.

"Yeah," I whisper. *I never thought I'd say that.*

"Okay, I understand." He wraps his arms around my waist. "Just so long as you aren't pushing me away because of Candace."

"Thank you for understanding," I say, even though Candace is the biggest reason I'm sending him home.

I've been thinking about all the nights we've spent together. At first, it was about making sure Miranda and I were safe in case Mike tried anything. But, he never did and at this point it seems Rooter is staying with me more because he wants to than for our protection. We've only just started dating. It's too soon. And on nights like tonight, when I'm tired and pissy, it's better for both of us if he gives me space.

"Are we still spending the day together tomorrow?" His gentle dark eyes are disarming.

"Yeah," I agree even though I have my reservations.

As much as I love spending time with Rooter, I'd like a little time to myself to digest everything. Maybe spend the day with Ryan or go to a movie with Miranda. Everything with Rooter has happened so fast. We've seen each other every single day—and nearly every night—since we started seeing each other. I realize this is what I wanted, and I still want it, but it would be nice to have a minute to take it all in. And honestly, hearing his damn phone go off every few minutes is becoming a little more than I can stand.

Rooter waits until I'm inside and have locked the door before he leaves. Although I'm irritated with him, I still watch him walk to his house. Even in loose sweatpants, the guy has an irresistible ass. Maybe I should've let him stay.

I get out of bed way earlier than I normally do after a work night so Miranda jumps in surprise when I enter the kitchen.

"What are you doing up?"

"Couldn't sleep." I rub my eyes and yawn.

It was strange being in my bed alone. I was cold and lonely and kept looking at Rooter's window all night long. Even though it's way too early to be spending every night together, I hated being without him last night. I like the way it feels to lay in his warm, strong arms. The way our bodies come together perfectly when we spoon. I especially like it when he mumbles in his sleep and when he kisses the back of my head when he thinks I'm asleep. It's like we were made to sleep together.

"I didn't make enough coffee for you since you're not usually up this early."

"I'll make some," I say and slowly pad to the coffeemaker.

"So, Rooter didn't stay last night?"

I shake my head and rinse the carafe.

"Everything okay?"

"Yeah. There's no need for him to stay here. Mike never did anything and I doubt he will."

"So, I have news." She bounces with a silly smile.

It's entirely too early for this level of excitement.

"Yeah?" I hit the side of the coffeemaker with a measuring spoon full of coffee grounds and spill them all over the counter and floor. *Shit.*

"I had dinner with Bear last night."

I can't see Miranda's face as I wipe up my mess, but I can hear her smile. "Oh?"

"He went to Rooter's first. He saw me on the porch and we got to talking. He ordered a pizza and stayed until eleven thirty."

"Was Rooter with you guys?" I try to sound casual.

"No." She shakes her head. "He left before the pizza came. Oh my God, Sophie," she squeals much too loud. "I swear I'm going to fall in love with this guy. When he's around, I can't think straight. I can barely breathe."

"I know that feeling," I chuckle. *How can anyone possibly be this perky this early in the morning?*

Miranda clutches my arms. "I know I gave you a hard time about Rooter being a biker, but I must tell you, I'm so sorry. I was completely wrong. And if it wasn't for you, I wouldn't have met Bear. So thank you."

"You're welcome."

"I have so much to tell you," she grabs her purse from the counter and slings it over her shoulder, "but I'm seriously going to be late for work. Will you be home later?"

"I don't think so. Rooter wants to do something since it's my day off."

"I swear I never see you anymore." She sticks out her bottom lip.

"I know." I mimic her pout. I love her, but this is way too much conversation before my first cup of coffee.

"You're still coming to the Red Door for my birthday party aren't you?"

"Of course."

"And you invited Ryan?"

"He'll be there."

"I'm considering inviting Bear. Do you think it's too soon?" She's speed talking in typical excited Miranda fashion. "I mean, we've never actually gone on a date."

"Ask him as a friend," I suggest and lean against the counter. "Tell him all your friends will be there and that he's welcome to come if he wants. Be nonchalant about it."

"That's perfect!" She bounces again. "That's exactly what I'll say." She scurries to the pantry, grabs a breakfast bar and flings it into her purse. "I've got to go! Maybe I'll see you tonight!" She says as she rushes out of the house.

"I'm switching her to decaf," I mutter to myself and close my eyes.

At noon on the button, Rooter calls to tell me he's on his way. Although I thought I wanted time to think and do my own thing today I find myself excitedly anticipating his arrival.

"How'd you sleep?" Rooter asks and kisses me softly when he strides into the room.

"Good," I lie snidely. "You?"

"Terrible," he groans and wraps his arms around my waist. "I missed you."

"Yeah?"

"Did you miss me?" He leans in like he's going to kiss me, but I know the game he's playing.

I shrug. "Maybe."

"Maybe?" His eyes go wide and a mischievous grin plays on his lips. Next thing I know I'm on the floor screaming and thrashing about while Rooter tortures me by tickling my sides. "Still a maybe?"

"Yes," I holler, writhing on the floor. "I missed you!"

"How much?" He continues to tickle me for his own amusement.

"A lot!"

"Be specific."

If I don't say something good here, he might never stop this torment. "I missed you so much I barely slept at all." *Dammit. I really didn't want to admit that.*

He stops tickling me and stares intensely into my eyes. "Really?"

"Yes," I huff, out of breath.

"Does that mean I get to sleep with you tonight?"

I look at him, afraid to give him my answer. I really hate being tickled.

"Hmm?" He presses with a wicked glint in his eye.

"Rooter—" But he doesn't let me finish and begins his tickle attack again.

"All you have to do is say the words I want to hear and I'll stop," he taunts.

"Okay, okay!"

He stops tickling me. "Yeah?"

"On one condition."

His head tilts to the side. "Which is?"

"That we sleep in your bed." We're always at my house. I've never once stepped a foot into his. I wonder if there's a reason he's never invited me over.

"Okay." He agrees easily with a shrug and helps me off the floor. When his phone rings he seems hesitant to answer it, but does so anyway. "Hey," he answers and turns away. "Yeah, I'll be there in thirty minutes."

I watch him curiously while he finishes his conversation.

"I know we said we would do something today," he begins and scratches his head, "but something came up with the club and I can't get out of it."

"That's okay. Miranda asked earlier if we could do something when she got off work." It's not entirely a lie. I'm sure she'll want to hang out when she gets home.

"I'm really sorry, Soph." He bows his head as though he's committed a terrible offense.

"Hey, it's okay," I take a step forward and take his hand into mine and smile. "I understand. I just can't believe you drove all the way here from the shop to tell me. You could've just called."

He smiles, but it doesn't reach his eyes. Something feels off. "I wanted to see you before I left. You were so mad at me yesterday."

"Yeah, yesterday wasn't the greatest." I look to the floor. Rooter tilts my chin up to face him.

"You believe me when I say you don't have to worry about Candace, don't you?"

"Of course I do. I just wish she'd go away."

"You understand why I can't write her off?"

I turn away and cross my arms. "Yeah, I guess."

"You guess?"

I sigh and look back to him. "I realize you've known her forever and there's history there, but put yourself in my shoes. What if a guy I'd known forever who was in love with me was calling me and throwing himself at me constantly? Would you be able to sit back and be patient until he decided to stop?"

"Probably not." He pinches the bridge of his nose.

"I'm willing to give it a couple weeks and see what happens, but if she hasn't let up by then you'll need to do something about her."

Rooter holds a hand to his chest. "I know I'm asking a lot of you, but she's hurting right now Sophie and it's all my fault. I should've never…"

"Had sex with her," I finish for him.

In one aspect, his sympathizing with her pisses me off. But it also shows me how much of a caring, compassionate person he is. I like that he's considerate of other's feelings. But in this case, it means I have some chick calling my boyfriend all hours of the day and night, sending him slutty pictures and texts. In one of her texts she even said she misses the taste of his cum. That is not and never will be okay with me. I worry that sitting back and being patient is setting a bad example of what I will accept in our relationship.

"Let's just see what happens," he says. "I promise we'll figure it out."

IT'S OVER

Rooter insisted on giving me money so Miranda and I could go do something fun while he's gone on club business. She and I decide to go to the trampoline park for a little fun and invite Jess and Abby along to make it a foursome.

"How's it going with your biker?" Abby asks as we enter the park.

Abby is a sweet girl, but she lives for gossip. Unless I want my business strewn all over town, I need to make sure to offer as little information as possible. She doesn't do it with any malicious intent. She simply can't help herself. Abby grew up in a strict Catholic household and was never allowed to do anything. Ever. As a result, she spent her entire high school career living vicariously through everyone else. A habit she's not been able to shed.

"It's going okay," I offer.

"Miranda says you're practically living together."

I glower at Miranda. "That's not true," I snap. "We've only spent a few nights together. He lives next door."

She holds her hands up and steps away. "I didn't mean to piss you off."

I force myself to speak gently. "I just… Want to keep my private life, private. You understand, right?"

"How about a little dodgeball," Jess suggests, bringing an end to our conversation.

When Jess and Abby go to the bathroom, I grab Miranda by her shirt sleeve and yank her toward me causing her to spill some of her soda on the floor. "Why the hell would you tell Abby that Rooter lives with us?"

"It was only a joke, Soph." She lifts my hand away from her shirt. "She asked about you and him. I only meant to imply that you two are always together."

"Well, in the future, would you please not offer information about my relationship?"

"Sophie, I'm sorry, I didn't think it was that big of a deal."

I pinch the bridge of my nose and inhale deeply. "Abby is the town's loud speaker. I don't need everyone knowing my business."

"Honestly, what's the big deal?" Her tone is inquisitive. "So what if people know you and Rooter are together?"

"It's not that."

"Then what is it?"

I exhale sharply and look at my feet. "I don't want her finding out about Candace. The last thing I need right now are a bunch of people telling me I'm an idiot for trusting him, especially if they turn out to be right."

Miranda touches my arm and when I look up her eyes are filled with concern. "Do you think they might be right?"

"I can see it now. Little, innocent Sophie got involved with a big bad biker who's screwing a slutty, stripper on the side. Actually, that isn't right." I point toward my chest. "I'd be the side bitch."

Miranda raises her eyebrows and leans forward. "Do you really think that?"

"I don't want to, but I can't help it. He hasn't done anything to stop her from calling and texting." I grind my right fist into the palm of my left hand. "I swear if I see one more nasty picture on his phone, I'll give that bitch the worst beat down of her life!"

A young girl, not older than eight strolls by and when she sees my angry stance, a frightened expression forms on her face and she hurries away. I quickly drop my hands and try to calm down.

"If you have doubts about him, it might not be a bad idea to talk to her and get her side of the story."

"Like she'd tell the truth." I roll my eyes and take a swig of my water.

"That's why you take his story and combine it with hers. The truth usually falls somewhere in the middle. Trust me. I've been there."

It is a good idea. There's only one problem. "Rooter will be pissed if I go to her."

"That's his problem for not doing what he needs to do to get rid of her."

After spending two hours playing dodgeball, volley ball and doing backflips into the foam pit, Jess recommends we cap the evening off with a drink.

"I have seriously had too much to drink," Miranda says an hour and a half after arriving at Skyles. "Why do I always do this on weeknights?" She giggles and sways on her barstool.

"Saying you're drunk means you're not yet drunk," Jess says and swallows a shot.

"If I'm not drunk yet, I will be in seven minutes." Miranda says.

"Seven minutes?" Abby laughs and we all join in. "That was random."

"If you're drunk in seven minutes then I'll be drunk in three," I toss back a shot of Jack.

"Trust me," Joe says from across the bar, "you girls are all drunk."

I turn to Joe who looks back at me with the bluest of blue eyes. I can't tell if it's concern or lust I see in them. My gaze moves to his lips. They're nice. I bet he's a good kisser.

"Why don't you have a girlfriend, Joe?" I ask.

"The curse of the good guy." He wipes up drops of spilled liquor before me.

"You are a good guy," I agree and lean forward on the bar, resting on my elbows. "But you're a hot good guy. Women go crazy for that shit."

He flushes. "Oh yeah?"

"Ssssure," I slur.

"I think women would rather go out with guys like your boyfriend than a workaholic like me."

"That's not true." *Is it?*

"You wouldn't go out with me," he reminds me.

Miranda, Jess, and Abby stare at us in complete silence, but I try to ignore them. "Only because you're too old for me."

Joe stops cleaning and looks deep into my eyes. "I'm not too old for you."

"You're like, thirty."

"Twenty nine," he corrects me with a gorgeous, radiant smile. "And you're a grown woman, Sophie."

"Maybe I should've gone out with you."

"You still can." He winks. It's hot, but not as hot as when Rooter does it.

This is my cue for some serious flirting, but with Jess and Abby around I need to be careful. "I have a boyfriend." *I miss Rooter.*

"I'll tell you what," he leans in close, "when you've had enough of him, I'll be here waiting for my chance."

"Really?"

"Sophie, you're the perfect girl. Beautiful, smart, kind. I'd be the luckiest guy on earth if you'd go out with me."

"Hot and sweet." I poke his cheek. *Shit, I shouldn't have said that.*

"Are you flirting with me?"

"No. I have a boyfriend."

"Speaking of, where is he tonight?"

"I don't know." I haven't heard from him in hours. The last time we texted, he said he should be done around ten and that he'd call me. It's going on eleven. I pick up my phone and check to see if I've missed his call. I haven't.

"If you were my girl," Joe says, "you wouldn't have to sit around, checking your phone, waiting for me to call."

"Damn," Jess whispers into my ear. "If you don't want him, I'll take him."

Another twenty minutes pass and I still haven't heard from Rooter. I debate between calling and texting and calling wins because I want to hear his voice.

"I'll be right back," I say to the girls and take my phone outside where it's quiet.

Rooter picks up on the third ring. "Hey, hold on a minute." His voice is much too cool and there's music and loud people in the background. A few moments later he's back. "Hey, babe. What's up?" His voice is barely more than a whisper.

"Where are you?"

"Are you drunk?" He sounds surprised.

"A little. When are you coming home? I missssss you." That last shot is hitting me hard.

He chuckles, and it makes my pulse race. "I'll be there in a half hour."

"I'm not at home and we're all drunk."

He sighs. "Where are you? I'll come get you."

"I'm at," And then I hear that skank's voice.

"Rooter, what," she says and then the phone goes quiet.

What the fuck? Did he hang up on me? I check the screen of my phone and see we're still connected. "Rooter," I scream into the phone. My blood boils.

Nothing.

"Rooter!" I hear shuffling and then he's back again.

"Sophie—" He starts, but I cut him off.

"Are you with that bitch?" I seethe.

"Babe, listen—" I cut him off again.

"Fuck you!" I hold the phone to my mouth and scream at the top of my lungs. "I'm not listening to shit. You're with her! You lied to me. It's over. It's fucking over!" I throw my phone as hard as I can into the parking lot, tear the door open and march back into the bar.

The moment Miranda sees the expression on my face she rushes over and grabs my hands. "What happened, Soph?"

"He fucking lied!"

The other patrons in the bar turn their attention to me and Jess and Abby dart over to us. Joe is right behind them.

"Let's take this into my office," he says and guides us toward the back of the bar.

Joe's office isn't what I'd expect. It's large, and bright, and well furnished. He leads me to a couch to the right of his desk. The girls sit with me. My body is wracked by tremors. I'm too angry to cry. All I want to do is punch something. I ball my hands into fists on my lap. It's amazing how sobering your boyfriend cheating on you can be.

"He's with her. Right now! I called, and he acted all weird and then I heard her voice in the background."

"Who?" Abby asks.

"Candace! The skank ass bitch he's been fucking." And then it dawns on me and I turn to Miranda. "Apparently, he's been fucking her this entire time!"

"Tell me everything," Miranda says.

"I went outside to call him because he was supposed to have called me by ten, but he didn't. He didn't sound right when he answered and there was music and voices in the background.

At this point I'm speed talking and gesturing with my hands like a crazy person. "He put me on hold. He asked if I was drunk and said he'd come get us. Then I heard that slut say his name! And then he must have covered the phone because I thought he hung up on me. When he came back, I asked him if he was with her and he had the nerve to say "Babe, listen" as if he thought he could explain his way out of the shit!"

"What a jerk," Jess mutters.

"Holy shit!" Abby shrieks.

Miranda drapes her arm around my shoulder. "That's it! That bitch is getting an ass kicking."

"I'm the one who should get the ass kicking! I'm the," I make air quotations, "other woman. All this time I thought she was going after my man when it was the other way around!"

"You didn't know that," Miranda says.

"Well, now I do and I'm done. I never want to see his ass again."

"But he lives next door," Abby reminds me and I cringe.

"He better stay the hell away from me."

Refusing to allow us to drive drunk, Joe offers to drive each of us home. The absolute last place I want to be is at my house where Rooter will surely be waiting for me with his bullshit lies. Lies. It was all a lie. Why did he do that to me?

Ryan is still at work and won't be home for another hour or two, so I can't go there. Both Jess and Abby live with their parent's and in my current condition, neither of those places are an option.

"You're more than welcome to come to my house," Joe offers. "No funny business, I promise." He smiles.

I don't hesitate to take him up on his offer. "That would be great, Joe."

"I'll take you to my place first so you don't risk running into him."

I sit on Joe's couch, massacring my nails for a half hour wondering what the hell Rooter will do when Joe and Miranda pull up and he sees I'm not there. Maybe he won't think anything of it. Maybe he'll assume I'm with Ryan and leave it at that.

He's probably blowing up my phone, but I never went back for it after I hurled it across the parking lot. I was too upset to remember it. It's probably smashed into oblivion anyways.

When the phone rings I jump a mile high. Joe's voice comes through on the answering machine after the fourth ring. "Sophie, pick up!"

I hurry to the phone as fast as my wobbly legs will carry me. "Joe, what's wrong?"

"He's following me."

I hold my palm to my forehead, fingers splayed. "What?"

"Miranda passed out in the car, so I had to help her into the house. When he saw you weren't in the car, he lost it."

"Shit!" I pace the room and drag my fingers through my hair. "I should've known he'd do this."

"What do you want me to do? Should I call the cops and send them to the house before I get there?"

Fuck, fuck, fuck! "I don't know what to do," my voice quivers and I stomp my foot. I'm not prepared to deal with Rooter, but I don't want to call the cops on him.

"What do you think he'll do when we get there?"

He may be a cheating asshole, but I'm still confident he wouldn't hurt me. Joe on the other hand, may not be as safe. "Let him follow you. I'll deal with him when he gets here."

"All right, but get ready, I'm only three blocks away," he warns, and the phone goes dead.

The sound that used to bring me so much joy now sends waves of panic through my system when I hear Rooter pull up.

"Sophie," Rooter shouts and the door opens.

He pushes past Joe into the house. My heart pounds and adrenaline surges through me. I slap him with all my strength the moment he stands before me. He grimaces and rubs his jaw.

"What are you doing here?" I bark.

"What are *you* doing here?" He shouts, looks at Joe then back at me.

"Trying to stay the hell away from you!"

He throws his head back and laughs as though I've just told the funniest joke he's ever heard. "That's never going to happen. Let's go." He grabs my hand and tugs me toward the door. "Now."

I yank my hand away and take several steps backward. "I'm not going anywhere with you! Go back to your skank."

Rooter takes a deep breath and closes the distance between us. "Do you really want to do this here?"

"I don't want to do it at all." I point at the still open door where Joe is standing, watching us in disbelief. "I want you to leave!"

"I'm not leaving without you." His voice is ominous.

"Well, I'm not leaving!"

"Yes, you are."

If I didn't know Rooter the way I do, I'd be overcome with fear. As he stands before me, every muscle in his body is tense. His breathing is erratic, and he's staring at me with wild eyes. But I'm not afraid so I stand my ground and cross my arms in defiance.

"No, I'm not!"

He gives me an evil, eerie smile. "I'll carry you out of here if I have to."

"Touch me and Joe will call the cops."

Rooter glares at Joe, who is standing by his open front door, and bellows. "Fuck the cops. Call them. We'll be gone before they get here."

"Just go, please." My emotions switch from anger to blatantly overwhelmed and tears pour from my eyes.

Rooter reaches out for me but I step back when his hand makes contact with my arm. He no longer looks angry, but rather sad. His muscles relax a tiny bit and he sweeps a hand through his dark hair. When he speaks, his voice is pleading. "Sophie, it's not what you think."

I grab the back of my head with both bands and squeeze. "I'm so fucking sick and tired of you saying that! How dumb do you think I am?"

"I know what it seems like, damn it! But it really isn't what you think!"

I cross my arms again and grip my biceps much too tightly. The pain is a welcome distraction. "I don't care what it is, Rooter. I want this to be over."

"Well, that isn't happening."

Why won't he leave me alone? I wipe my tears with the back of my hand. "Why are you doing this? Is this some sick joke to you?"

"Baby, no. God no!" Rooter looks like I've struck him with a dagger and reaches out and touches my face.

"Stay away from me!" I smack his hand away and take yet another step backward. I'm running out of room. A few more steps and I'll be pinned to the wall. "Just go!"

Rooter makes a steeple with this fingers covering his nose and his mouth. "Sophia," he sighs and drops his hands, "you have two choices here. You can hear me out the easy way or you can hear me out the hard way."

ANOTHER EXPLANATION

The hard way? I don't even want to know what that means. "Rooter, don't you understand that I'm tired of hearing you out when it comes to her?"

"Yes, I do. But I'm telling you, what happened tonight was completely innocent."

"Innocent or not, you lied to me. You said you had club business, and you were with her!"

There's nothing he can say to change that fact. He told me one thing and did another. And he did it with the very person we've been arguing over for the past few days.

I glance at Joe and think back to the words he said earlier. Maybe I'd be better off with a guy like him. He's kind, funny, good looking, owns his own business, and lives in a nice house. He seems to live a nice, normal life and probably has zero drama. I bet I wouldn't need to worry about psycho ex-sluts if I was with him. He did say he'd wait for me. At this rate, he might get his chance sooner than later.

As though he's reading my mind, Rooter turns my face to his and orders Joe to give us a moment alone. Joe looks at me for approval and I nod prompting him to leave the room. This is humiliating. I can't believe this is happening at Joe's house of all places. I should've gone home. I cross my arms and glare at Rooter waiting for him to give me his lame ass excuse.

"Sophie, I didn't lie. I was with the club. I was at our annual summer party." Rooter looks down and rubs the back of his neck. His typical nervous gesture. "My mom throws it every year. I knew Candace would be there, so I tried to get out of it. But it's something my family does for the members and with my rank in the club I had a responsibility to be there."

Okay, so it's not a completely lame ass excuse, but I'm not appeased. It doesn't explain everything. "Why didn't you tell me the truth?"

Rooter looks at me, pensive. "I wanted to, but with everything that's gone down the past couple days with her, and you being pissed off at me..." He rubs his face with both hands. "I wanted to take you, but we both know what would've happened if I did. If I would've told you the truth about what was going on, it would've hurt you. I was protecting you."

I understand what he's saying and while his reasoning is better than I expected, it doesn't make me feel much better. Because of Candace and her bullshit antics, I was the one lied to and left out. "So again, she wins."

"What are you talking about?" He furrows his brow, confused. "Wins what?"

"No matter what, she'll always be around because of her history with the club. She gets to be there and I don't. I won't be in a relationship with you like that."

Rooter's eyes go wide with panic. He reaches out and clutches my arms. "Sophie, this shit with her ends tonight. I'm putting a stop to it. I'll tell her no more phone calls or texts. It's done."

I laugh, but instead of joyful, it's sinister. "Like that'll matter. She's not going anywhere."

"She'll always have ties to the club, yes, but not with me."

"Yes, she will." I pull away and shuffle to the large picture window. It's pitch black outside so I can't see anything. I close my eyes and bow my head. "She always will."

"Sophie, I'm asking you to trust me." Rooter comes up behind me and stands so close I can feel the heat that radiates from his body. His close proximity confuses me. It's both upsetting and comforting. Part of me wants to wrap my arms around him and never let go while the other part wishes he'd leave and never return. "Trust me that *nothing* is going on between her and me. Yes, I run into her from time to time and I probably always will, but it doesn't mean anything. She's just somebody I know."

But she's more than somebody he knows. She's somebody he's kissed and touched and had sex with. She knows him in ways I don't.

"How can I trust you when you lie to me?"

"I didn't lie."

Infuriated, I spin around and jab my index finger into his chest. "You lied by omission!"

He takes a half step back in surprise. "Can't you understand why I felt uncomfortable telling you?"

Yes. But it doesn't make me any less angry. "It's too much, Rooter. I can't deal with this." I try to step around him but he holds me firmly in place.

Rooter loses hold of his cool, controlled demeanor. His body tenses and he glares at me through narrowed eyes. "Well, you'll have to deal with it because I'm not going anywhere."

I ball my hands into fists and scream. "Fuck!"

"Babe," he says the word gently, but his disposition remains fierce, "there's nothing Candace can say or do to change the way I feel about you. You're the one I want. The *only* one."

I believe everything he has said. Especially the part that he isn't going anywhere. I measure my options, but the only one I have—the only one he's giving me—is to get over this right now and leave with him. But I'm not ready to get over it. *Dammit!* I am so pissed. But it doesn't matter. I've lost this argument. I close my eyes and bite my bottom lip. His hands are still on my arms holding me in place. I inhale slowly.

"If I leave with you, I want you to take me home and leave me alone for the night."

"There's no "if." You *are* leaving with me."

My eyes fly open. Who the hell does he think he is? He doesn't own me. Maybe I should stay to teach him a lesson. "You don't control me. I'll do what I want, Rooter. If I want to stay here, I will."

He tosses his head back and laughs. "I don't think so."

I try to jerk away but he grips me tighter, holding me against my will. Anger bursts inside me and it takes every ounce of my self-control not to knee him in the crotch. "You can't stop me."

Wildness flares in his eyes. "From staying the night with another man? Yes, the hell I can."

I roll my eyes. "I wouldn't be staying *with* him, Rooter."

"You won't be staying here at all." He lets go of my arms and strides to the kitchen counter, grabs my purse and points at the door with it. "Let's go."

Exasperated, I shake my head, which I shouldn't do because it feels like a bomb went off inside it. Damn Jack Daniels. "Let me go tell Joe I'm leaving."

I start toward the hallway, but Rooter cuts me off. His jaw is clenched.

"I'll tell him." He hands me my purse. "Wait here."

An excruciating throbbing in my head wakes me. The light streaming in through my window is much too bright. According to my alarm clock, it's just after nine in the morning. I spent most of the night tossing and turning, haunted by visions of Rooter's wild eyes, vacillating between anger and worry.

Rooter did exactly what I asked him to and took me home. After making sure I got in safe, he left me alone for the rest of the night. Though before leaving he said we need to talk after we've both had time to calm down. I don't know what the hell he needs to calm down about. I wasn't the one who lied to him and spent the day with my ex-boyfriend after telling him I was going to work.

As angry as I was, it comforts me that he refused to leave me alone and let me stay at Joe's. Remembering the way he threw his head back and laughed and told me he'd never let me stay away from him makes my skin tingle in a good way.

Rooter is a man who doesn't shy away from confrontation. He stands up for what he believes and fights for what he wants. If he wants me the way he says he does, he'll need to sort out this issue with Candace. I will not continue to be lied to. I won't tolerate him hanging around her behind my back, regardless of the reason. Just because I gave him a pass last night doesn't mean he can allow it to happen again.

When I sit up, my headache is joined by a loud whooshing sound and I become dizzy. I clutch the sides of my head and take slow deep breaths. Once the dizziness subsides, I roll out of bed and grab the bottle of ibuprofen from my purse. As I make my way down the stairs, I see Miranda sitting on the couch watching television. When she hears me her head snaps in my direction. She looks as hungover as I feel.

"When did you get home?" She croaks.

"Late." I hold up my bottle and head toward the kitchen. "I need coffee."

She follows me into the kitchen. "How did you get home?"

"How do you think?" I ask and fill a glass with water to take my pills.

"Rooter?"

"Yup." I pop the pills into my mouth.

Her mouth falls open and she leans against the counter. "How?"

"He followed Joe home and made me come back with him," I explain while filling the coffee carafe with water. "Should I make enough for you?"

She shakes her head. "I vaguely remember him freaking out when he saw you weren't with me. Did you fight?"

"Oh yeah."

"What did he say about Candace?"

Even though I'm hungover and my head is banging, I go ahead and tell Miranda the whole story. When I'm done, she leans back and stares, mouth agape.

"It's kind of hot that he refused to go away," she says.

"Yeah, well, it didn't seem hot at the time." I curl my legs under me on the couch and take a sip of my coffee. There's not enough creamer in it, but I don't feel well enough to get up and add more.

"But it does now, doesn't it?" She grins earnestly.

"Yeah, it kind of does." I smile back but it quickly fades. "But what I don't get is what he meant when he said he needed to calm down. I didn't do anything."

I smacked him and tried to get him to leave, but in the end I gave in and left with him. He has no reason to be mad.

"Yeah, that doesn't make any sense," she agrees. "I'm guessing you'll find out soon enough. When do you think you'll see him?"

I shrug and look at the clock. It's five minutes till ten. "Dunno. Hopefully not until I feel better."

Finally, at ten thirty I get in the shower. The hot water is soothing as it cascades over me. Miranda and I have a rule to make our showers as short as possible to save on the water bill, but today I take my time. After over thirty minutes, I shut the water off and wrap a towel around me. My headache is gone and I'm somewhat back to normal. After brushing my teeth, I amble into my room to get dressed. The unexpected sight of Rooter pacing the floor with a scowl on his face gives me a jolt.

"Is there a reason you're ignoring me?" He barks and comes to a sudden stop directly in front of me.

"Ignoring you?"

"I've been calling and texting all morning." His angry glare makes me feel small.

"Shit." I face palm. "I don't have my phone. I threw it across the parking lot after talking to you last night."

"Oh." His expression changes from furious to contrite. If it hadn't been for the whole Candace disaster I'd have my phone and I would've received his calls and texts. "I'm sorry."

I glimpse my towel covered body. "Can you give me a minute to get dressed?"

Rooter eyes me up and down, taking in my appearance with a ghost of a smile. When his eyes meet mine, they're kind and warm. "I'll wait in the hall."

I quickly throw on a tattered black concert t-shirt and a pair of shorts and open the door. Rooter leans on the wall across from my door, arms crossed with one foot resting against the wall behind him. I can't help but to marvel at him. His broad shoulders, muscular arms, and tan skin are displayed perfectly in a tight, charcoal colored t-shirt. Gone is any trace of anger or frustration for which I am thankful.

"Come in," I say and take a seat on my bed.

"How are you this morning?" The mattress concaves as he sits next to me.

"Tired and hungover."

"You still mad?"

I sigh and rake my fingers through my wet hair. "Yes and no." He furrows his brow in confusion prompting me to continue. "I understand why you felt you couldn't tell me the truth. But I need for this issue with Candace to go away."

"I get that," he rubs his hands along the top of his thighs, "and I told you last night it will."

"Okay, but how? How will you make it go away?"

"I'm going to talk to her." I raise a brow in question and he continues. "Today. I'll tell her the phone calls and texts must stop."

"And if they don't?" I grip the edge of the bed.

He pauses a moment to think and rubs the back of his neck. "I don't know. But I promise I'll figure something out."

"Fair enough." I turn my body to face him. "And do you promise not to withhold things from me in the future? Even if you think it'll hurt me or I'll respond badly to it?"

"Yes, I promise. But you need to understand that Candace is someone I'll always know. I can't make her disappear."

"Rooter, I need to know I can trust you." He rolls his eyes as though he can't believe I said that. "You sympathizing with her and allowing her to come between us makes it hard for me. Especially when you withhold information from me."

He breathes in and out slowly. "I get it, Sophie. It won't happen again."

I fall back onto the bed and groan. "I hate that I'm turning into one of those crazy jealous girlfriends."

Rooter chuckles and leans over me bracing his weight on his elbow. His face is mere inches from mine. "You have nothing to be jealous about. I'm yours."

Those words, "I'm yours," make my stomach do back flips. I gaze into his eyes and can see he means it. I reach up and stroke his cheek. My chest rises and falls with rapid breaths as he stares at me with a fierce, passionate expression.

These past couple days have been brutal. I've felt so disconnected from him. As I stare into his dark eyes and feel the heat of his body, I crave what is mine. I need to be as close to him as I can be. I need to feel his arms around me and taste his kiss. As I lean in, he pulls away and pins me down by my wrists.

"Are you mine?" He growls.

GETTING DISTRACTED

Rooter hovers over me, glowering at me intensely through narrowed eyes, his lips pressed into a tight line.

"Yes," I answer, breathless.

"Say the words," he demands in a rough tone.

"I'm yours."

He leans in close as though he's going to give in and kiss me, but then he stops and pulls away yet again. "I saw the way you looked at him last night. Do you want him?"

Now I know what he meant when he said he needed to cool down. Had I looked at Joe in anyway? In the heat of the moment I contemplated things last night that under normal circumstances, I never would. Yes, Joe is nice, and attractive and all the things I thought last night, but I could never feel about him the way I feel about Rooter. My desire for Rooter is undeniable and all-consuming. It's animalistic. It's why I get so crazy over Candace and why I'm scared out of my mind he'll break my heart. I've never wanted anyone this way. I never will. He is it for me. I feel it in my bones.

I answer him honestly. "No."

"Don't lie to me, Sophie." He speaks through gritted teeth.

"I'm not lying—" He cuts me off right as I'm about to admit to him the ways in which I want him.

"Were you going to let him kiss you? Were you going to sleep in his bed?" His body trembles and a glint of rage flickers in his eyes.

"No!" *How could he even think that?* Before I can ask, Rooter's grip on my wrists tightens, but not enough to hurt me.

"Just the thought of his hands or his mouth touching you makes me crazy."

"He didn't touch me."

"And he never will. No one will ever touch you, but me."

Two can play this game. If he doesn't want other men touching me he shouldn't allow other women, namely Candace, to touch him. I lift my chin and return his bold stare. "Then no one had better be touching you, either."

"You're the only one I want to touch me," he murmurs.

I'm undone by his words. Unable to take this any longer, I beg for what I want. "Kiss me, please."

Rooter's lips crash against mine and we both moan the instant our tongues meet. My body falls slack as he devours me, still pinning my wrists to the mattress above my head.

"You taste so fucking good." His voice is raspy and full of desire. He leaves a trail of soft kisses from the corner of my mouth to my jaw, just below my ear. When he gently nips my earlobe, I moan and arch my back.

I place a wet kiss on his neck close to his collar bone and a fierce groan escapes his lips so I do it again. His skin tastes delectable. I've never before been this brazen with anyone. The guy has always had to make the first move, even when it came to kissing. But I want Rooter in a way I've never wanted anyone. He makes me feel wanton and sexy and unafraid. "Do you like that?" I whisper in his ear.

"Hell yes," he groans.

I wiggle my hands that are still in his firm grasp. "I want to touch you."

Rooter lets go of my wrists and rests his elbows on either side of me. I place my hands on his biceps and move them to his wide shoulders, to his chest. His chest is rising and falling as fast as mine. The hunger I see in his eyes reflects my own.

"Take this off," I tug at the hem of his shirt. He doesn't hesitate to pull it over his head. The sunlight shining through the window illuminates his taut chest and abdomen. Becoming bolder by the second, I tell Rooter to roll over. Once he does, I run my fingers over his chest and begin to lower myself against him. Right before our bodies meet, he shoots me a warning look and grabs my hips to stop me, obviously concerned about what happened the last time we were in a similar position.

"It's okay," I assure him and take his hands into mine lacing our fingers together as I slowly lower myself against him.

This time I'm ready when I feel him hard against me. When I rock back and forth he bites his lower lip and arches his back off the bed. I lean forward and flick his neck with my tongue and he grinds harder between my legs.

"Fuck, that feels good," he mutters, giving me more confidence.

I slide my hands from his shoulders, over his chest to his waist. My mouth travels lower, planting small kisses until I reach his nipple. I've always wondered if guys like to have their nipples sucked. I take Rooter's into my mouth and feel it stiffen as I stroke it with my tongue. The dark skin surrounding the hard tip is soft and smooth. Rooter's fingers dig into my hips. With the way he hisses and moans with pleasure, licking his nipples could become my new favorite pastime.

Using my left hand, I trace the outline of his lips. He opens his mouth and sucks my finger. It's warm and wet and completely erotic. A deep ache builds between my legs. I want to feel his mouth on me. I raise up and peel off my top. His eyes go wide as he stares at my bare chest.

"My turn," I whisper with a naughty smile.

"Christ, Sophie." His voice is strangled and his chest heaves. "Are you sure?"

"Yes." I glide up and down his bulge.

Before I know it, Rooter flips us over so I'm the one on my back. He hovers over me, still between my legs, resting on his elbows. "You're so beautiful."

He nibbles my neck and grazes my skin with his warm tongue. I shudder as be blows on my wet skin. His lips trace my collar bone while his hand glides down my left side and reaches behind to squeeze my ass. Rooter groans as he rocks his hips against me again and again making my desire peak higher and higher. He pulls back and gazes hungrily at my naked chest again. Very slowly he takes my breast into his hand, brushing my nipple so delicately that I barely feel it. But God do I feel it.

"I've fantasized about touching you," he breathes and leans down. "About feeling you against my tongue."

"Me, too," I whisper.

His lips are so very close and his breath is hot against my breast. My desire churns deep within until I think I might combust from anticipation. And when he looks up at me with dark, hooded eyes my heart skips a beat.

"You're sure?" He asks again before going any farther.

"Yes," I pant.

Without breaking eye contact, he opens his mouth and swipes my nipple with his tongue causing me to arch off the bed. *Hot damn, nothing has ever felt so good.* He's still staring at me. Testing me.

"Again," I whimper and he circles my nipple slowly with the tip of his tongue before taking it into his mouth and sucking gently. The sensation of his warm, wet mouth against my delicate flesh is exquisite. He closes his eyes and moans as he continues to suckle.

"So soft." He pulls back and blows on my wet skin making me shiver. My eyes roll back into my head. "You like that?"

"Mm-hmm." I grip his shoulders.

"Should I kiss the other one?"

"Yes, please."

"Open your eyes, babe," he commands in a deep, lustful voice. "I want to watch you watching me."

I open my eyes and his expression is desirous as he flicks the other nipple and blows on it sending shivers from my head to my toes.

"I've laid in bed so many nights," his voice is rough and deep, intensifying the ache in my core, "looking at your window, fantasizing about what it would be like to touch and taste you."

God, I love the way he talks to me. "Me, too."

"Yeah? And is it as good as you imagined?" He flicks my nipple again.

My core tightens with need. "So much better."

"I agree." He moves to my other breast and slowly swipes his tongue across it.

"Rooter," I moan. Needing more, I pull his face against me.

His hands travel down my waist and reach beneath me, kneading my ass as he grinds his cock against my most sensitive spot. "Do you like feeling me against you?"

"Yes," I pant.

I wrap my legs around him and drag my nails over his back up to his shoulders and he moans into my ear. He nips and sucks on my earlobe as he rotates his hips against mine and grinds his hardness between my legs, up and down and back and forth over and over again until a heavenly pressure mounts in my center. My legs begin to shake and I pant and call his name again and again until I'm desperate for release.

"Oh, God yes!" I cry out loudly, not caring that Miranda can probably hear me all the way downstairs.

Rooter leans back to look at me, his brown eyes blazing. "Yeah?"

"Yeah," I moan and bite my lower lip. I'm so. Very. Close. I close my eyes waiting for my delicious release. When he comes to a sudden halt my eyes fly open.

"Keep your eyes open," he commands, staring at me with dark, lust filled eyes before he moves his hips again.

I watch the taut muscles in his abdomen constrict with every rotation and thrust of his hips. It doesn't take long for him to bring me back to the brink. I grasp his biceps tightly as I teeter on the edge, ready to go off.

"Let go, baby," he murmurs huskily. "I want to watch you come for me."

And that's all it takes to send me flying over the edge, shattering into a million pieces. Our eyes are locked as I writhe beneath him, crying out his name. Seconds later, Rooter collapses onto me with fast, shallow breaths of his own.

Completely spent and utterly sated, I lay still for several long moments allowing myself to catch my breath. It doesn't take long for the realization that I just had an orgasm while Rooter watched to hit me. *Holy shit.*

"I second that." Rooter rolls over onto his back. "That was hot as hell."

Had I spoken aloud? I clasp one hand over my face and cover my exposed chest with the other.

"Are you embarrassed?" His voice is laced with amusement.

Too self-conscious to speak, I simply nod my head.

Rooter pries my hand away from my face and looks at me with kind, warm eyes. "Why?"

My face is on fire. "Because I just... You know. While you watched."

"So did I." He gives me a reassuring smile.

"You did?" I look at his crotch and see a wet spot forming on his jeans. My face heats up again. "Oh."

"It's so cute how quickly you switch from bold to bashful." He chuckles.

"I'm glad I amuse you."

"Now what am I supposed to do about this?" He points at his groin.

"You do live next door." I point to his window.

"Miranda is downstairs."

"Forgot about that." I giggle.

"Shit. All right." He crawls over me to get out of the bed. "I'll be right back."

The moment Rooter leaves, I hear loud footsteps racing up the stairs followed by a furious knock on my door.

"Hold on," I say and throw my top on. "Come in."

"Oh my God, did you just…"

"Not exactly. But go back downstairs." I wave her away. "He's coming right back."

"I want to know everything," she says with a wink and goes back downstairs.

While Rooter is gone, I replay our make-out session in my mind and it occurs to me we did more than make-out. We dry humped. I've never dry humped. I've heard Miranda talk about it, but never quite understood what the big deal was. The words "dry humping" seemed painful to be honest. It seemed better to masturbate, or be fingered, or have actual sex. Now I know what the big deal is, and like Rooter said, it was "hot as hell." I want to do it again as soon as possible.

I sit on my bed with my legs pulled up to my chest when Rooter walks back in the room. He looks different now. Manlier. Sexier. More familiar. More mine. I'm definitely more his. We may not have had sex, but that was the closest I've ever come to it, of my own volition. I'd barely been to third base before today. I've given myself to Rooter in a way I've never done with anyone else. I may not be a virgin, but I've already decided that when the time comes, he will be the first and hopefully only one I give myself to.

Rooter sits sideways on the bed facing me, his eyes full of intensity. "That was amazing, babe."

"Yes." My face flushes again and I rest my head on my knees.

He reaches out and strokes my cheek. "But we need to finish the conversation we were having before I got distracted."

MEETING THE SLUT

I blink. Did I hear that right? "We weren't finished?"

Rooter shakes his head and his eyes drill into mine. When he speaks, his voice is cool and controlled. "I need you to tell me why you went home with Joe Skyles."

This is the last thing I want to talk about. Especially after what just took place. Doesn't he know he's supposed to be cuddling with me and whispering sweet nothings in my ear? We're not supposed to be rehashing our fight. The dour look he's wearing tells me I'm not getting out of this conversation. I sigh and hang my head.

"Because I was mad at you and didn't want to come here."

"That's the only reason?" He asks calmly, but I perceive doubt in his voice.

Offended by his insinuation, my head jerks upright to face him. "Of course. Why would you even ask me that?"

"Out of all your friends, you had nowhere else to go? No one else to call?" The gentility of his voice doesn't match his stern expression.

Does he truly not believe in me? Does he think so little of me that he believes I'd hook up with some other guy like that? How can he expect me to trust him if he doesn't trust me? "You don't trust me."

"Sophie, you told me it was over, refused to talk to me," he raises his voice. "Next thing I know, you're at another guy's house."

I roll my eyes and huff. "It was late, Rooter. He offered me a place to stay. That's all it was."

"I believe you. But, Sophie, I won't tolerate you going home with other guys." I start to interject, but he covers my mouth to stop me. "I don't care how mad you get at me. You don't go home with other men. Ever." His voice is eerily level and calm though his demeanor is anything but.

"I said it wasn't like that," I complain.

"I get that and I don't care," he narrows his eyes and pinches the bridge of his nose. "You don't go home with other men."

I throw my hands in the air. "I thought you cheated on me!"

Rooter takes a deep breath and speaks with a little more passion. "Because you wouldn't hear me out. Which is another thing we need to work on." He drags a hand through his hair. "This is all new to me, Sophie, and I'm trying, but you can't run off and refuse to talk to me every time I piss you off."

I straighten my legs and lean forward. "It's not just because I was pissed it was because of the *reason* I was pissed."

He closes his eyes and exhales. "I'm going to tell you one more time, and I seriously hope it will be the last," he opens his eyes and looks at me with a meaningful expression, "I'm completely loyal and faithful to you. I will never cheat on you. If you ever doubt me or have questions, talk to me. Don't assume, because I promise you'll be wrong every time.

He scoots closer and cups my face. "There's no way I'd ever risk hurting you or losing you. If you knew how damn much and for how long I've wanted you, there's no way you'd ever think I would."

I gulp. My pulse races. Rooter stares into my eyes, waiting for my response. "I'm sorry." I lean into him. "I promise, I won't ever go home with anyone again."

"Do you also promise that you'll hear me out next time you get pissed?"

This isn't really a promise I can make. But I'll try. "I promise."

Rooter leans his forehead against mine, and gazes dreamily into my eyes. "I'm crazy about you."

"Me, too," I whisper.

His phone rings and ruins our moment. I had him set Candace's number to a distinct ringtone so I'd know if it was her calling. It's her. Evidently, she can't go a single day without talking to him.

"Should I answer it?" He asks without leaning away.

"You did say you'd talk to her."

He pulls away and answers the phone. "Yeah?"

Our eyes are locked while he listens to whatever she's saying. He lays his hand on my thigh and delicately rubs small circles with his fingertips giving me goosebumps. The slightest touch from him and I turn to mush. Is he trying to distract me from the fact that he's talking to her?

"I'll send a tow truck and meet you at Molly's Auto. All right."

"What was that about?" I ask when he hangs up the phone.

"Her car broke down." He stops stroking my thigh but keeps his hand in place.

I raise a brow. "So she called you?"

He shrugs, sheepish. When he speaks he sounds like a five year old explaining to his mom why he stole a cookie from the cookie jar. "I'm sort of the one she's always called when she needs help."

Of course he is. I roll my eyes. "You're going to tell her that has to stop, too, aren't you?"

"Yes, babe." He sighs and rubs the back of his neck.

"Are you going there now?"

"Want to come with me?"

"Really?" I ask, wide eyed. "Are you sure?"

"I'm done letting Candace come between us. I'm going to show you, once and for all, that you can trust me."

This is what I have been waiting to hear. I look at the clock next to the bed. It's a little after noon. I definitely want to go, but I have to be at work by three. "Can you have me back by two?"

"Yeah."

The expression on Candace's face when we pull up is absolutely priceless. As per usual, she's dressed in a barely there outfit. She might as well just wear a thong and pasties since her clothes don't cover much else. She glares at our intertwined hands as we make our way to where she stands.

"I thought you were taking me to Nicole's." She addresses Rooter rudely with her hands on her hips. He can't very well take her if I'm with him. There isn't room enough for the three of us on his Harley.

"Bear's coming," he answers, flippant. "This is Sophie. Sophie, this is Candace." He squeezes my hand reassuringly.

After appraising me from head to toe, she turns her attention to Rooter. "You can't be serious, Rooter."

Fury boils inside me. It takes every ounce of strength I have not to break her perfect button nose.

"Candace, be nice." He speaks too calmly making his order perfectly clear.

"Be nice? Seriously?" She waves her hand at me. "You bring the bitch you dumped me for and expect me to be nice?"

Oh no she didn't. I lunge at her but Rooter grabs me by my arms and stops me. "You better watch who you're calling a bitch, skank."

"You better watch who you're calling a skank!" Candace steps up and Rooter turns me away from her.

"Let go of me!" I holler and thrash about trying to get free. She may have me in the looks department, but in a fight she wouldn't stand a chance.

"Stop it, now!" Rooter barks at the both of us. A couple of mechanics are standing in one of the garage bays observing us with smiles on their faces.

"Why would you bring her here?" Candace whines. "Are you trying to hurt me even more?"

"Bitch please—" I start, but Rooter cuts me off.

"Sophie, stop it," he growls through gritted teeth and keeps me pinned against him. He turns his attention back to Candace. "No, I don't want to hurt you. You're the one who called me for help. We were together when you called."

"You better stop calling!" I threaten, glaring in her direction.

"Sophie," Rooter snaps.

Candace gives an evil laugh complete with a taunting smile. "I'll call him anytime I want."

"Rooter, tell her," I demand.

He takes a deep breath. "Candace, you can't keep calling and texting me pictures."

"Come on, baby." She has the perfect seductive voice, deep and husky, and it pisses me off. How dare she call my man "baby." I start to say something, but Rooter covers my mouth. "We both know exactly how this is going to go. The moment the novelty wears off, you'll get bored with her and call me like you always do."

Like he always does?

"It's not like that with Sophie. I'm with her."

She chortles. "Yeah, this month."

"Candace, if we're going to stay on good terms you need to respect my relationship."

I roll my eyes. This chick doesn't respect herself. Does he really think she'll respect us? But I'm glad he's doing what he said he'd do and is telling her to cut the crap.

"Oh, you mean the way you respected me?" She asks. "One day I'm sucking your dick, the next I'm out with the trash?"

Her words make me cringe. Not because I feel bad for her, but because visions of her giving Rooter a blow job creep into my mind reminding me yet again of all the ways she knows him that I don't. My body shakes with anger. "You *are* trash!" I spit.

Candace lunges at me again and Rooter stands between us with his back to her and his arms holding me against his chest.

"Sophie, damn it!"

One of the mechanics jogs to us. "You need some help man?" He asks Rooter and looks at Candace.

"Put your hands on me and you'll be eating your balls for dinner." Candace glares at the guy.

The mechanic ignores her and laughs. "Got a pair of feisty ones on your hands."

Rooter nods in agreement. "Sophie," he murmurs against my ear, "will you please go inside and let me finish talking to her?"

"Are you kidding me?"

"We're not going to get anywhere like this." He kisses the side of my head. "Please? Five minutes."

He allows me to turn and face him, but he keeps his arms around me. "The last time you asked for five minutes it ended with her tongue in your mouth and her hand on your dick."

The knowledge that her hand has been in places mine hasn't only serves to piss me off more. I glare at her, but he turns me to face him.

"I promise that won't happen."

I stand and stare into his eyes for a long moment. If I refuse to go inside, he won't make me. But I agree that this conversation won't go anywhere if the three of us are together. "Fine," I give in.

"Thank you," he says and lets me go, but with a cautionary look not to try anything. "Take her to the office, man?" He asks the mechanic.

I watch them talk from the window in the office. I can't hear anything, but from the way Candace pouts, yells, stomps her feet, and points at me she's not happy with what he's saying. Bear pulls in and Rooter motions toward me.

Bear greets me in his typical fashion without a smile. "How goes it?"

"It could be better," I admit.

He nods. "Rooter seriously owes me for pawning that shit off on me."

I peer up at him and chuckle glibly. "You aren't fond of Barbie?"

Bear crosses his arms and stares out the window at them. Rooter rakes his hands through is hair which tells me he's losing his patience.

"Let's put it this way, she was barely tolerable before you came into the picture. Now she's fucking psycho."

I raise a brow. "Psycho?"

He chuckles. "That one is definitely short a few nuts and bolts."

"Should I be worried?"

He shakes his head and grins. "Nah. She's harmless."

"Yeah, well I'm not," I ball my hands into fists at my sides, "and if she doesn't cut her shit out things will get ugly."

Bear eyes me appreciatively. "If you ask me, that might be what it'll take."

"Yeah?" Through the window, I see Candace stomp her foot twice and pout about something.

"She's been obsessed with Rooter forever." He uncrosses his arms and rubs his forehead. "I told him not to go there."

"I wish he would've listened."

A moment passes in silence and then Bear turns to me. "Sophie, I realize I don't know you very well, but I've known Rooter my entire life." He pauses. "I probably shouldn't say this, but I think you should know."

Oh no. He's going to tell me to stay away from Rooter. That I won't win against Candace. That I'm one hundred percent completely out of my league here and I should walk away now before I really get hurt. "Know what?"

"The guy is certifiably crazy about you. I've never seen him like this. Believe me when I say," he points out the window, "that girl out there poses no threat to you whatsoever. No one does."

I stare at Bear in awe. Of all the times Rooter has said the very same thing, it never had the effect on me that Bear's words have on me at this moment. All the pent up anger and jealousy that has been living inside me the past few days washes completely away. I breathe a sigh of relief. "Thanks, Bear. I needed to hear that."

"I know." He turns back to the window and I do the same. We watch as Candace stomps away from Rooter into the garage bay where her car is. "But if you tell him I said it, I'll kill you." His tone is serious, but he gives me his silly, bright white smile.

THE SEDUCTION

Me, Miranda, Rooter, and Bear are meeting several of our friends—including Ryan—at the Red Door for Miranda's birthday party tonight. I sent Rooter home an hour ago so I could get ready. Usually, I'm not one to get dressed up, but tonight I want to look hot.

I made Miranda take yesterday off so she could go shopping with me. We found the perfect little red dress. A sheath halter with a plunging neckline that goes almost to my belly button. It's so short it barely covers my butt and has a dangerously low cut back. For a finishing touch, Miranda lets me borrow a gold body chain, and a pair of strappy gold heels. I want to wear my hair up, but she insists I wear it in long loose waves. As per usual, she applies my makeup complete with smoky eyes and red lipstick to match my dress. After putting on some double sided tape to make sure I don't suffer an embarrassing wardrobe malfunction, I'm all set.

When I look in the mirror, I don't recognize the girl in front of me. She doesn't look like a girl at all. The reflection staring back at me is all woman. A hot blooded, sexy woman. Before today, I never would've had the guts to wear something this revealing. But something in me has changed since my make-out session with

Rooter. I feel sensual and sexual for the first time in my life and I want to celebrate it. And I want Rooter to celebrate it with me.

But something has changed in him too since that day.

"He hasn't touched me, in that way, since the day in my room," I whine to Miranda. I watch as she sprays her swept up messy ponytail with at least a pound of maximum hold hairspray.

"That's weird." She repositions a few strands of hair and sprays again and I nearly choke. "Have you asked him about it?"

Miranda looks amazing in her white party dress. It has one strap with crystal beading mesh along the sides. I'd give anything to have her curves or at least her boobs. Though, I've been told on several occasions I have the perfect legs and ass. I turn and inspect my backside in the mirror. I don't really know. I guess it's decent.

"No. I don't know how. I mean, it's kind of embarrassing to talk about." I twist a lock of hair between my index and middle finger. "He said he thought what we did was hot, but now when we kiss, he stops before it can go any farther."

Last night, after work, he kissed me like he always does with full on passion. When I suggested he stay the night, I was dejected when he turned me down by saying he had to be at the shop by six. So then I said, "I promise to make it worth your while" and he kissed me on my forehead and still said he couldn't.

"Trust me, when he sees you tonight, he won't be able to stop himself. He's going to flip his shit."

"You think?" I pinch at the sides of my dress, unsure.

She turns and faces me with a serious expression and grabs me by the arms. "I know. Sophie, the man eye fucks you constantly. And that's when you're wearing capris and loose tops."

"He does?" She's probably misconstruing his typical intense demeanor for something else.

"Yeah," she says like I should already know this and laughs. "How do you not notice it?"

I shrug and look at myself in the mirror again for a boost of confidence. I hope Rooter likes what he sees. I want to make him want me so much that he can't keep his hands off of me. I've been going through withdrawals the past couple days, craving his touch. Yearning for the feeling of his wet mouth on my bare skin.

"Girl, listen, you may not even make it out of the house tonight once he sees you."

"I hope you're right."

"Trust me. I'm right."

I text Rooter to let him and Bear know we're ready. The limo is waiting. I stand in the living room fidgeting with the hem of my dress. Maybe it's too short. What if my tape gives away and a boob pops out while I'm dancing? What if Rooter thinks I look ridiculous? My heart pounds in my chest. I shouldn't have bought this dress. Who am I kidding? I can't pull this off. This isn't me. I'm not sexy. I'm cute, athletic Sophie who ran track in high school.

All the girls who ran track in high school constantly complained about their boobs hurting when they ran, but not me. My boobs weren't big enough to cause me pain. If there actually was an itty bitty titty committee, I could be the president. I take after my mom in that department.

"You look amazing, Sophie." Miranda squeezes my hand reassuringly.

I bite my lip. "I think this dress was a mistake."

"That dress is definitely not a mistake. You wait and see."

And then there's a knock on the door. Too late to change now. I begin to hyperventilate so I take a deep breath and hold my head high in an attempt to appear confident when Miranda opens the door. Rooter steps through the threshold and the moment his eyes land on me they bug out of his head and his jaw goes slack.

"Goddamn," he says and walks to me. His eyes trail from mine down the length of my body and back up.

"What do you think?" I ask, trying to masquerade my fear.

"It's so unlike you." He blinks and looks me up and down again. "You're hot as hell, babe."

"Really?" I ask and sigh in relief.

He licks his lips. "Oh yeah."

He's definitely eye fucking me.

"See, I told you he'd like it," Miranda chirps and ushers us out of the house.

In the car on the way to the club, Rooter can't take his wild eyes off me. His eyes vacillate between the body chain and my legs. He wraps one arm around my shoulders while gently stroking the top of my thigh with his free hand. He sucks in a breath and chews on his bottom lip.

"You look… Fucking edible," he whispers into my ear.

His words boost my confidence. "I might hold you to that," I whisper back and nip on his earlobe.

His jaw drops and longing swims in his dark eyes. I revel in what I'm doing to him.

"Keep doing that," his voice is deep and thick with desire, "and we won't make it out of this car."

"That would be okay with me." I take his earlobe into my mouth and suck.

"Christ, Sophie." The hand that's on my thigh travels upward and slides under the hem of my dress to cup my bare ass.

Miranda clears her throat reminding us we're not alone. Rooter removes his hand from inside my dress and tries to straighten up in the seat. His chest rises and falls with fast, shallow breaths. Miranda was right. This dress was definitely not a mistake. I have Rooter wrapped around my little finger, right where I want him. I'm going to have a lot of fun with him tonight.

The music is pumping as we enter the Red Door. Rooter places his hand at the small of my back and it's like fire on my bare skin. Miranda advises the door man we've reserved the VIP section tonight. We must make quite an entrance because all eyes are on us as we make our way to the back of the club where our seats are located. All of our friends are already there. Ryan hurries over and excitedly pulls me into an embrace.

"Babe!" He squeals.

"Babe!" I squeal back.

He grabs my upper arms and looks me up and down. "Holy fuck! You put every bitch in here to shame."

"Yes, she does," Rooter agrees. My head whips in his direction and he smirks at me. Desire still looms heavy in his eyes.

After greeting all of mine and Miranda's friends, Rooter and I sit on one of the red leather loveseats. His left arm is draped across my shoulder holding me close. I inhale his intoxicating scent and it sends pangs of yearning straight to my core.

"Do you want a drink?" He asks and I nod.

"Jack on ice."

He winks and waves for the VIP waiter to come over. "Two double Jacks. One on ice, the other neat. And whatever those two want." He points at Bear and Miranda. "I'll start a tab for the four of us."

We sit on the sofa talking with Ryan and my other friends. Jess and Abby are here tonight. They stare at Rooter like he's a God and hang on his every word. He is at ease and confident. Everyone seems to love him as much as I do. I take the last sip of my second glass of Jack and begin to feel the effect of the alcohol. Rooter's hand is on my thigh, stroking it lightly from the hem of my dress to my knee and back making me shiver. The way his eyes drill into mine and the curl of his lips conveys he knows what he's doing to me.

"Let's go say hi to Mario," Miranda suggests and points at the DJ booth with one hand and reaches for me with the other.

Mario is the DJ. We've known him for years. Miranda used to think she was in love with him, but he always had a thing for me. If it hadn't been for her affection for him, I might've gone out with him.

I glance to the DJ booth and see him waving at us. Rooter and Bear are engrossed in conversation so I decide not to interrupt them and stand to follow Miranda. Rooter tugs gently on my hand.

"Where are you going?"

"Miranda and I are going to say hi to a friend."

He nods and I follow Miranda to the DJ booth. When Mario's eyes go to me, he has the same reaction as Rooter did when he first saw me.

"Damn, girl! Looking good." He pulls me in for a hug and squeezes my ass.

I quickly pull away. "Watch it, pal," I say jokingly, but I mean it. I turn to see if Rooter saw anything, but he's not in his seat. I look around trying to find him when he suddenly appears before me. He wraps an arm around my waist and gives me a panty wetting grin. Mario's eyes go wide the moment he sees him.

"Mario, this is my boyfriend, Rooter. Rooter, this is Mario."

Rooter juts his chin out as his only means of greeting. He definitely saw Mario grab my ass.

"Nice meeting you, man." Mario extends his hand. The same hand he grabbed my ass with.

Rooter glares at his hand a moment before shaking it. "Want to dance?" He asks me.

I gawk up at him with surprise. "You dance?"

He holds his hand to his chest feigning offense. "I've been known to on occasion."

"Well then let's do it." I smile and lead him to the dance floor.

The dance floor is crowded to the point that it's more like a mosh pit than an area for dancing. But once people see Rooter they move away and create space for us. Mario spins a mix of the latest pop and dance hits. Rooter's hands go straight for my hips and we move in sync to the beat. Damn. The man has rhythm. I can barely keep up with him. His smug expression says, "I told you so."

The song changes to one with a slower tempo and Rooter pulls me flush against his body. His hands move from my hips to my ass and he squeezes. He leans in and speaks into my ear. "You have a fantastic ass."

My face heats up. "I'm glad you think so."

"Every man in here thinks so."

I shake my head at his grandiose exaggeration, but he continues.

"Every guy in this place wants to be me right now." He smiles, and it's not at all egotistical. He means it.

"You're the only one I want," I murmur into his ear. I think I hear him groan, but the music is so loud I can't be sure.

Rooter spins me around to face away from him and pulls me against him, my back to his front and rocks his hips to the music, grinding against my backside. One hand is on my hip while the other touches the center of my chest where the body chain rests. I let him lead me as I move my body in time with his. He leans down and grazes my shoulder with a trail of wet kisses up to my ear. Suddenly, all else falls away, and it's as though we're the only two people in the club.

His breath is hot against my ear. "I have never seen anything as beautiful as you."

I feel my face flush. We continue to dance in this manner for two more songs. The combination of the booze and this dress have me feeling brazen and sexy. Rooter is still behind me and I do my signature bend and flip which garners several hoots and hollers from other dancers on the floor. I strut slowly around him, grazing his ass as I make my way around to the other side where I grind against him, take it low and bring it back up. Our bodies move perfectly together.

Several dancers, mostly men have stopped moving and are now watching us. Rooter pulls me against his chest and swipes his tongue against my neck. He leads me as he sways his hips expertly. His eyes are focused on my chest where the body chain lies.

"You like?" I ask.

"One day," he reaches out and traces the chain, "I want to see you in just this, a thong, and these heels."

I lean in to his ear and try my hand at speaking seductively. "I'd be happy to show you tonight."

Rooter chokes and his eyes go wide. "You're killing me, babe," he groans.

Before I can tell him how serious I am, we're interrupted by Miranda and Bear joining us on the dance floor. Bear can't move like Rooter, but Miranda dances well enough to make them both look good.

Rooter takes me back to the VIP area and orders us another round of drinks. I sit on his lap on the loveseat and sip on my drink. His eyes never wander from me, even when he's speaking to someone else. He's a starved man and I'm his prey. A bead of sweat rolls down the side of his neck and I can't fight the temptation to lean down and taste it.

"You taste so good," I croon into his ear.

"You two need to get a room," Ryan teases.

"Yes, we do," Rooter agrees with a lust filled voice and plays with the chain on my chest.

I'm in heaven when I hear Rooter's deep, raspy voice call me "babe." His hands run through my hair, pushing it away from my face. I open my eyes and am blinded by streaming bright light.

"Hmm?" I ask and squint my eyes. "Where are we?" I don't recognize the setting. And then I notice the sensation of hot skin against hot skin. I'm draped across the top of Rooter with one leg between his.

"Sorry. I need to let the dog out."

"The dog?" I blink and look around. Dopey is at the side of the bed. When I see the headboard, I finally make out my whereabouts. We're in Rooter's bedroom.

"I'll be right back." He kisses the top of my head and gently scoots out from under me. When he stands, I'm shocked by the sight of his bare ass and I gasp. He turns around and gives me a devilish grin before pulling on his jeans.

What the...

Once he's gone, I lift the sheet and find myself in nothing but my thong. I squeeze my eyes shut, trying to remember what the hell happened last night. The last thing I recall is making out on the sofa at the Red Door.

MEETING THE FAMILY

While Rooter is letting Dopey out, I struggle to remember the events of last night. We both woke up naked so the only thing I can surmise is that we had sex. But I don't feel sore like I did when... I shake my head. I do *not* want to think about that. Ever.

Maybe Rooter was gentle? I'm sure he would've been. God, why can't I remember? We may have had sex for the first time and I don't remember a thing about it. I pull down the sheets to check for any visual cues that would indicate whether we did. Upon inspection I find a small love bite on my right boob, but nothing else.

I recall the sight of his gloriously sculpted ass and feel my face flush. Something must've happened. Why else would he have slept in the nude? We've shared a bed several times and each time he'd worn shorts or sweatpants.

Had I touched his naked body last night? I bet I did. And I can't remember! Argh! I could've done any number of things to him, and vice versa. I could've had the best night of my life and I can't recall a second of it. Frustrated, I kick the bed in a tantrum.

When I hear Rooter coming up the stairs I pull the sheets back over me. He ambles to the bed with Dopey at his side. His jeans hang deliciously low on his hips. Just above the waistline on the right where his V is, there's a purple love bite of his own. I lick my lips absentmindedly. Yeah, I had a good night.

"How do you feel?" He asks and slides into the bed next to me.

"Not bad at all." I furrow my brow. My lack of memory indicates that I had *a lot* to drink. "How is that possible?"

His lips curl up into a smile and he grazes my cheek with the outside of his hand. "I fed you a cheeseburger, two ibuprofen, and made you drink two glasses of water before we came up to bed."

That would explain it. Why do I never think to do that after a night of drinking? Probably because I don't drink very often. "Thank you."

"So you don't remember last night, do you?" His voice is laced with humor. He takes my hand into his and strokes my palm with his fingertips.

"Not all of it," I admit shamefully.

"What's the last thing you remember?"

"I remember showing you my double sided tape at the bar."

He shakes his head and laughs riotously. "Would you like me to fill you in?"

"I think you better."

Rooter shifts upward a bit and props a second pillow underneath his head. "First, you should know, we did not have sex."

"We didn't?" I perk up with relief.

"Of course not."

I eye him questioningly? What does he mean by that?

"Babe, our first time making love won't be when you're trashed."

He said "making love." Swoon. "Okay, so why don't you fill me in on what did happen?"

He rolls on his side to face me. "Do you want a play-by-play from the bar, or just the good stuff?" He chuckles and his eyes light up.

"The good stuff."

"All right then. After we got home and ate, you told me you had something you wanted to show me and dragged me in here," he points to the end of the bed, "where you proceeded to strip."

He smiles at the memory. I close my eyes and try to remember, but can't. Stripping doesn't sound like me. God, I hope I didn't make a fool out of myself.

"And this is where it gets interesting," he continues, "because of the tape. Apparently, it hurts when you try to remove it," he smirks, "which of course I was more than happy to help you with."

"Of course you were." I smile and bite my lip.

"So after getting you out of the dress and carefully removing the tape," he reaches over and picks up the body chain from his nightstand and dangles it in front of me, "I got my wish."

My entire body goes up in flames. I hope he liked what he saw. Nervous, I pick at a cuticle and swallow. "Okay, go on."

He reaches into his jeans and adjusts himself. My eyes follow his hands and I see his growing bulge. "Babe, Let me just say, hottest lap dance ever."

I clasp my hands over my face. No. I. Didn't. I had to have been blasted out of my mind to do such a thing. My stomach does a series of somersaults. Maybe I don't want to hear this after all.

Rooter chuckles and lifts my hands from my face. He pulls down the sheet to reveal my breasts and points at my love bite. "That's when you told me to put my mouth on you. A request I couldn't possibly refuse." He leans down and softly kisses the mark sending sparks throughout my entire body.

"Let's not get distracted," I say and turn his head to face me.

"I thought a reenactment might help you to remember." He winks, sending spasms to my core and props himself back up on the pillows.

As fun as a reenactment sounds, I really want to know what the hell went on last night. "Just tell me. You can show me later."

He rubs his hands together. "This is when it gets really good." He circles my love bite with the tip of his index finger. I'm almost afraid to find out what's next. "You told me you wanted to touch, kiss, lick, and suck every inch of my body and ordered me to get naked." All the humor is gone from his voice and has been replaced by deep intensity.

Although I can't believe what I'm hearing, it matches my fantasies perfectly so it must be true. I've always said alcohol makes us honest. While we might later regret our words or actions, everything we say and do when we're drunk reflects our true thoughts and desires.

"I stripped down to my boxer briefs, and that's when this happened," he points at the purple spot on his waist. We're finally getting to the good stuff.

"Go on," I urge, impatient.

He brushes a lock of hair away from my face and gazes at me affectionately. My heart palpitates, eager to know what happened next.

"I told you I thought we should stop. Save the rest for later. You said you were tired of waiting." He points at the swelling in his jeans. "You grabbed a hold of my dick and said you hated that other women have touched me and you haven't. You all but ripped my boxers off," he chuckles. "Do you want to know what happened after that?" He ever so slightly grazes my arm with the back of his hand.

I turn away and nod, unable to face him. Surely I'm about to learn something super embarrassing.

"Nothing."

I gasp and look back at him. "What?"

"It was so cute." He kisses the palm of my hand. "You were staring at my cock with eyes wide as saucers and then you passed out cold."

"Oh my God," I groan and roll over and bury my head in my pillow.

"Babe, it's a good thing you passed out because I honestly don't know how I would've stopped if you'd touched me."

"I'm *never* drinking again," I groan into the pillow.

"Hey," he rubs my shoulder, "look at me."

I turn my head to face him, but stay on my stomach. His lips are curled up into a reassuring smile. He delicately skims the small of my back with his callused hand.

"Don't be embarrassed."

"I'm not embarrassed. I'm mortified," I admit.

"Sophie, you have *nothing* to be embarrassed about. Last night was one of the best nights of my life."

I start to argue the point, but the intense expression he's wearing conveys that he means what he's saying. And truthfully, I just want to drop the subject altogether. "I need coffee."

He smiles, gets up from the bed and holds his hand out for me. I don't know why after everything that happened last night, but I suddenly become shy. He smiles knowingly and walks to his chest of drawers and retrieves a t-shirt and a pair of his sweat pants and lays them on the bed next to me.

"I'll put a pot on."

After pulling on the baggy clothes, I go across the hall to the bathroom. I'm a complete mess. My hair is ratted, my makeup is smudged and there are streaks of black mascara all over my face. I'd brush my hair, but can't find a brush or comb with which to do it. So I drag my fingers through it to smooth is out as best I can.

I wash my face and without thinking, use Rooter's toothbrush to brush my teeth. I've never used anyone's toothbrush. I always thought it was disgusting when couples did that. Being with Rooter is changing me in a lot of ways.

Rooter's house is immaculate. The décor is masculine, but there aren't any lame posters of motorcycles of half dressed women on the walls like I once imagined there would be. He has typical, but nice, bachelor-esque furniture; black leather sectional, huge flat screen television.

He sits at his dining room table drinking a cup of orange juice. A coffee mug sits in front of the coffeemaker for me, along with milk and sugar.

"I don't have creamer," he says and points to the milk and sugar. "Will that be okay?"

"It's perfect," I smile and pour the coffee into the mug. "Thank you."

His kitchen and dining room have obviously been renovated. The cabinets and granite counter tops weren't in style when this house was built. He has brand new, top of the line stainless steel appliances including a gas stove with a surface for grilling.

"I was thinking about making breakfast. Would you like some?"

"That would be great."

Rooter strolls into the kitchen and kisses the side of my head on his way to the refrigerator.

"I used your toothbrush," I admit with a shy smile. "I hope that's okay."

He shrugs like it's no big deal. "Sure."

I watch him in awe as he moves around the kitchen shirtless. This man truly is an Adonis. No. He's so much better. He's a God, a demon, and an angel in one.

"Can I help with anything?" I ask.

"No. Enjoy your coffee," he smiles and turns a burner on to fry some bacon.

Dopey comes over and lays at my feet at the dining room table. I sink back into my chair and take a sip of the coffee. The first sip is always the best. The warmth of the liquid is soothing. I'd close my eyes, but I can't take my eyes off of Rooter. His muscles constrict with every movement he makes. I feel a strong urge to go to him and trace his tattoos with my fingertips. And then I see the purple mark above the waistline of his jeans. *My mouth was on his skin. Right there. I'd like to put it there again.*

Rooter chuckles. "Penny for your thoughts?"

My face goes up in flames and I look down at my coffee mug.

A few minutes later, he comes into the dining room with two plates and places one in front of me before taking a seat across from me. I take a bite of the bacon and close my eyes, savoring the flavor. I rarely ever get to have bacon. It's a luxury I can't afford.

"This is *so* good," I mutter. "Thank you."

The corners of his eyes crinkle when he smiles. "You're welcome."

As I take another bite, I hear a motorcycle fire up. My head snaps toward my driveway.

"Bear stayed with Miranda?" I gasp and turn to Rooter in shock.

"Yep." He takes a bite of his fried egg.

My mouth hangs open. That's not like her *at all.*

Rooter chuckles. "Apparently we ruthless bikers have rubbed off on both of you."

"Apparently." She and I are going to have a very interesting talk when I get home.

"My parents are having a cookout this afternoon," he says casually. "Mom texted and asked me to come."

I don't know why he feels he needs to run it by me. Unless it's because Candace will be there. Reading my expression he speaks before I can even ask the question.

"Candace won't be there."

I sigh with relief. "Good."

"I'd like for you to come with me."

My eyes go wide. "To meet your parents?"

He shrugs and takes another bite. "Yeah, why not?"

"Okay." We eat in silence as thoughts about meeting his parents bombard my mind. I hadn't thought I'd meet them so soon. "Should I get dressed up?"

He shakes his head. "It's just a backyard cookout, hamburgers, hot dogs. We'll ride over on the bike."

Great, I'll meet his parents with helmet head. And then I remember, they're bikers too. Dressing up would be to them the equivalent of helmet head to most others.

"What time?" I ask and push some egg around my plate.

"We need to leave in an hour."

We pull up to his parent's house right on time. The quaint log house sits back off the road on a wooded lot. A huge pond wraps around three quarters of it. The garage is open with a screen door leading to the backyard where I hear classic rock playing in the background. Rooter takes my hand and leads me through the garage to the backyard.

A beautiful, exotic looking woman with long dark hair is watering the flowers in a nearby garden. The same woman I've seen at his house in the past. A girl who looks a lot like her is laying on a chaise lounge in her bikini. Rooter leads me to the woman whom I assume is his mother. Her eyes light up when she sees the two of us. She meets us halfway and wraps her arms around Rooter.

"Hey sweetie," she says with a thick Puerto Rican accent and squeezes him. When she pulls away to face me, her smile is genuine. "You must be the reason he's missed the last few Sunday dinners."

I look sideways at Rooter. *Sunday dinners?*

"I'm Sophie," I hold my hand out to her, but instead she pulls me in for a hug. And not a typical, quick, nice to meet you hug. She wraps her arms around me and squeezes me the same way she did Rooter. "I'm so happy to meet you." She pulls away. "I'm Camilla, but call me mama."

The girl who was in the chaise lounge sprints toward us with a shocked expression. "Rooter, what do we have here?" She asks with a mischievous grin.

"This is Sophie—" Rooter starts, but she cuts him off before he can finish the introduction.

"I'm Isabel, but everyone calls me Isa."

Camilla and Isabel seem a little over excited about meeting me. I can only guess it's because they didn't know about me.

"It's nice to meet you, Isa." I extend my hand.

"We don't shake hands in this family," she says and pulls me in for a quick hug and then hugs her brother. I think I hear her whisper to him, "Good choice," but I can't be sure.

Rooter leads me to the deck next to the pond and we sit side by side on a wicker couch. Isa takes a seat on the other side of him.

"I'll go get Papa," Camilla says and disappears into the house.

Rooter smiles at me and squeezes my leg.

"Did you wear a bathing suit?" Isa asks me and I shake my head. "You can borrow one of mine when you're ready to get in," she says casually and points at the manmade beach leading to the pond on the other side of the deck.

A few minutes later, Camilla comes out of the house followed by a tall man with grayish-blonde hair. I recognize Rooter's father from pictures I've seen in the paper and on the news. He looks at Rooter, then to me, and back at Rooter again and gives him what appears to be a nod of approval.

Upon his approach, Rooter stands to greet him so I follow suit.

"Pop, this is Sophie." He smiles proudly.

"Hey, pretty lady," his father says to me with a smile, "I'm Mick, but everyone here calls me Papa." He opens his arms for a hug. When he hugs me, it's in the same manner as Camilla.

"It's nice to meet you." I look at him with a smile. His eyes are blue, but they're kind like Rooter's.

The great thing about Rooter's family is they don't bombard me with a thousand questions to get to know me. Instead, we sit on the deck and make small talk. Camilla talks about her passion for gardening, which is evident as I take in their expansive lawn. Rooter and Mick talk about an old Harley they're rebuilding together. Isa, talks about school and the boy she just broke up with and Mick chimes in calling him a "little weasel." Rooter tells me if the boy hadn't been underage, he would've relocated his fifth appendage.

The only question asked is by Camilla

"So, how did you two meet?" She looks back and forth between me and Rooter.

"Sophie lives next door," Rooter explains.

"Lucky you," Mick says to Rooter and winks.

Rooter chuckles and nods in agreement.

"We're very happy to meet you, Sophie," Camilla says and touches the top of my hand.

A couple hours pass and I become more and more comfortable with everyone. They all listen intently as I tell them a little about myself. I've been corrected a few times when addressing his parents by their first names rather than mama or papa.

After getting to know everyone, we decide to take a dip in the pond before lighting up the grill. Isa leads me to her bedroom to get a swimming suit. The moment she closes the door she turns to me and says, "There's something you need to know."

Sunday Dinner

I hope this is the part where Isa tells me Rooter has never brought a girl home. But the intense expression she's wearing tells me it's likely something much more important.

"What is it?" I ask.

Isa leads me by the arms over to her bed and has me sit next to her. "Something tells me you don't quite understand the significance of my brother bringing you here today."

Maybe I was right after all and I am the first girl he's brought home. "To meet all of you, I guess."

She laughs and shakes her head. "Honey, if that's all he was doing, he could've done it on a Tuesday."

"I'm not following you." I furrow my brow. "Is there something special about today?" Maybe it's someone's birthday, or an anniversary.

When she speaks, she uses her hands to emphasize her words. "Sunday dinners at the Russo house are more sacred than Catholic mass at the Vatican. They're for family only. No friends, no acquaintances. Just family."

Now I get it. "Oh. I shouldn't be here."

She shakes her head again. "Honey, you're not getting it. He didn't bring you here to *meet* the family. His bringing you here today signifies that he's bringing you *into* the family."

I gasp and choke on the air. Isa pats my back. "What?"

"Looks like I have a new sister." She smiles and hops to her feet. "Thought you might like to know."

I sit slack-jawed trying to process what she just said. "Wait Isa, are you saying he's going to propose?"

She laughs again. "Well, I don't know about that, but if he's asking us to welcome you into the family he might as well."

"Oh my God." I lay my head in my hands. Is she serious? We haven't even been together a month! I inhale a deep breath and count to ten.

Isa tosses me a red bikini and pair of shorts. "We'll be downstairs... sis." She smirks and leaves me alone in the bedroom.

I take a few minutes to collect my thoughts before changing into the bikini. The top is a little big since I'm not blessed with Isa's Puerto Rican curves, so I tie it as tight as I can to make it work. When I make it back outside, Rooter and Mick are sitting side by side on the deck, engrossed in what appears to be a serious conversation. I can hear what they're saying from the doorway so I pause to listen.

"Of course, son," Mick says and shoulder bumps Rooter. "She seems great and sure is pretty."

"Yes, she is."

"But I gotta say, I thought I'd never see this day come."

"Me either, pop." Rooter pats Mick on the back. "There's just something about her."

"Hey, Sophie!" Isa hollers and waves at me from the pond.

I wave back and step out onto the deck. Rooter and his dad turn around to see me.

"If I was twenty years younger and single, you'd have some serious competition, boy." Mick bumps Rooter in the shoulder and laughs raucously.

Rooter holds his hand out for me. "This one's all mine." He smiles and pulls me onto his lap.

After dinner, I help Camilla and Isa clean up while the boys go out on the deck to talk. I wash the dishes, Isa dries, and Camilla puts away leftovers. The sliding doors are closed so I can't hear what they're saying, but Rooter keeps looking through them, smiling at me.

"Isa told me she explained to you the importance of today," Camilla says.

I'm glad she brought it up. I wasn't sure whether or not Isa was exaggerating. "She did."

"I can't tell you how happy I am that my boy brought you here today."

"Me, too." Isa chimes in. "I was seriously getting worried he'd try to bring Candace into the family."

Camilla swats Isa on the shoulder and shoots her a look.

"What?" Isa returns the look to her mother. "If she doesn't already know about Candace, she will soon enough."

"I know all about her," I grumble and then remember Rooter telling me how she's considered family to the club.

"If you have any trouble with her, you let me know," Camilla says. "You're family now and she knows better than to mess with family."

Camilla's statement moves me beyond words. She has known Candace her entire life while she's only known me a handful of hours and yet she's willing to defend me against her.

"Thank you, Camilla."

She swats me on the shoulder. "It's mama!"

"Sorry," I blush and just about drop the soapy plate in my hand. "Thank you, mama."

When we pull into Rooter's driveway I spy Bear's Harley in mine. Things are definitely moving fast with him and Miranda.

"My family loves you," Rooter says chin up, chest out after we dismount his bike. He's beaming with pride.

"I think they're pretty great, too." I smile up at him. "I'm glad you took me."

He scratches his head and rocks back and forth on his feet suddenly appearing nervous. "Isa told me she spoke with you."

"You mean in regards to the significance of taking me to the Russo Sunday family dinner?"

He stands with his hands in his pockets. "Yeah."

"I would've rather you told me."

He kicks at a beer bottle cap on the floor. "I was afraid you would think it's too soon and refuse to go."

"Everything about us is happening really fast," I admit, "but, it has been a year in the making. So…" my voice trails off.

Rooter closes the distance between us and leans his forehead on mine. "I want to give you all the things you don't have. You have a family now, Sophie."

His words nearly bring tears to my eyes. "I don't know what to say."

Rooter places his hands on both sides of my face and brings his lips to mine slowly for a tender, closed mouth kiss. I rest my hands on his sides and he places delicate kisses on my cheeks, nose, and eyelids. His breathing has picked up and when his lips find mine again, he skims my bottom lip with his tongue asking for entrance. He continues to hold my face in his hands and kisses me so. Very. Gently. His tongue caresses mine slowly, softly. It's as though we're making love with our mouths. I moan and fall flush against his body.

He takes me by the hand and leads me into his house. I'm left in a daze from his kiss and can't take my eyes off of him. But Dopey comes loping toward us and jumps up on him, taking his attention away from me.

"I'll be right back," he gives me an apologetic smile and takes the dog outside.

I stand in place, unable to move, until they return. Rooter takes my hand once again and leads me to his room. He turns on his bedside lamp and stands before me for a long moment, staring longingly into my eyes. He pulls his shirt over his head then tugs at mine. I raise my arms up and allow him to pull it over my head. My stomach does back flips.

This is happening. Rooter's going to make love to me.

There was a time, right after the rape when I thought I'd never want to be touched by any man, ever again. But in this moment, I'm absolutely sure I want Rooter. And even though we haven't been together very long, I don't want to wait. I crave the touch of his hands and the kiss of his mouth. I want to know what it feels like to be made love to. By him. I want to be his in every single way.

Rooter unclasps his belt slowly and winks, teasing me. God, if he only knew what that does to me. I lick my lips and back away so I can better see him. Never taking his eyes from mine, he unzips his jeans and lets them fall to the floor. My eyes go straight to his boxer briefs and I suck in a breath when I see his hardness straining against the black fabric.

He closes the distance between us, reaches around me with one hand and deftly unclasps my bra. I let it fall to the floor and he cups my left breast.

"So beautiful." His jaw is set and lust blazes in his eyes.

His gaze falls to my bare chest and he flicks my nipple with his thumb. He brings his free hand to my other breast and does the same with it. I throw my head back and moan with pleasure as he caresses me with his hot hands.

"I love looking at you and touching you."

He lowers his hands and unzips my jeans. He takes his time as he pulls them past my hips. I grasp his shoulders as I step out of them. His hands glide along the outside of my thighs as he stands back up to face me.

"I want you so much." He strokes my face softly. "Are you ready?"

I nod.

"I need to hear the words, baby."

"I'm ready," I murmur.

Rooter pulls the comforter back and lays me on the mattress. He hovers over me, propped up on his elbows. His hardness is pressed against my center and he leans down and places a wet kiss on my neck, just below my ear and blows on my skin making me shiver.

I place my hands at the small of his back and arch my spine until my nipples graze his chest. He grinds into me before leaning down and gliding his tongue along the edge of my nipple.

"That feels so good," I murmur and brush my fingers through his short hair.

"Yeah, baby," he says huskily, "talk to me."

He flicks the tip of my nipple with his tongue over and over again, sending shockwaves of desire straight to my core. He moves to my other breast and repeats the act.

"You're perfect," he groans and continues to work me with his mouth.

He makes his way down my body leaving a trail of wet kisses to my belly button. He looks up at me through hooded eyes and dips his tongue in. His eyes stay on mine as he licks me from one hip bone to the other. I bite my lip and whimper.

Rooter maintains eye contact with me as he slides his fingers into my panties. He's testing me, making sure I'm okay with this. Once he appears confident I'm ready, he slides his fingers lower. The instant he comes into contact with my clit, I throw my head back and moan. It feels so good. This is the touch I've been craving for so long.

His finger circles my clit slowly and I can't contain the pleasure I feel. "God, yes," I murmur. "Keep doing that."

He circles me a few more times and then moves his hand lower still, sliding his fingers up and down my wetness. He draws in a breath. "You're so wet, babe. I want to taste you."

I close my eyes in delicious anticipation of what's coming next. Yes. I want him to taste me. I want to know what it feels like to have his mouth on me. There.

He pulls his hand out of my panties and with the way he says the word "babe" I know something is wrong. I look down and he's holding up his hand for me to see. His fingers are covered in blood.

I clasp my hands over my face, mortified. *Oh God no! This cannot be happening.* I want to run away, but I'm frozen in place.

Rooter crawls up to my side. "Hey," he whispers and pries my hands away from my face. I keep my eyes screwed shut. "It's okay."

Unsure what to do, I cry. I don't have anything here to take care of myself with. Rooter picks me up and carries me into his bathroom. He puts me down and washes his hands.

"Tell me what you need. I'll go to your house and get it."

I look to the floor, squeeze my legs together, and clear my throat. "Tampons, clean underwear—the cotton kind—and something to sleep in. It's all in my dresser."

Rooter tilts my chin up and kisses me on the lips. "I'll be right back," he says and disappears from the bathroom.

While he's gone, I hop in the shower to wash away the evidence of what just happened. I'm not sure how long I stay in the shower, but when I step out, everything I need is sitting on the counter and the bathroom door is closed. I take my time getting ready. The idea of facing Rooter after what happened is nearly unbearable. He has to be completely disgusted. I would be. I am. How did I let this happen? I always keep track of my period. Now, when I have a reason to keep track of it, I don't.

I'm startled by a knock on the door. "Babe?" He speaks softly. "Everything okay?"

"No." I answer honestly, sitting on the lid of the toilet with my head in my hands.

"Are you dressed?" He asks.

"Yeah."

He opens the door, walks in and crouches before me. "Hey, don't be embarrassed."

I can't make eye contact with him. "I'm sorry, I didn't know."

"You have nothing to apologize for. It's a fact of life, babe. Not that big of a deal." He stands up and holds his hand out for me.

I peer up at him for a moment. He doesn't appear grossed out at all. How is that possible? I take his hand and follow him to the bed. He climbs in first and then holds his arms open for me to scoot in against him.

"Are you comfortable?" He asks and wraps his arms around me from behind. "Do you need anything? Tylenol, ibuprofen?"

"I'm okay," my voice shakes.

"Close your eyes and sleep," he murmurs and kisses the back of my head.

BAD NEWS

My eyes open at ten minutes to seven in the morning. I'm lying on my stomach and Rooter's arm is draped across my back. His light snores bring a smile to my lips. Dopey stares at me with his head on the side of the bed and wags his tail. He needs to go out. I reach out and pet his head. Rooter's arm pulls me snug against him.

"Go back to sleep, babe," he mumbles. "I'm not going in until later."

"Dopey wants out."

Rooter groans with displeasure. "Of course he does."

"I can take him," I offer.

Rooter kisses the back of my head. "I got it," he says and gets up. "Go back to sleep."

My cramps remind me of last night's events. Not that I'd forgotten. While I'm not quite as mortified as I was, I'm still a little embarrassed. I can't believe Rooter acted like it was no big deal.

Through the window, I hear Rooter and Bear's voices from the driveway, but can't make out what they're saying. After a couple minutes Bear fires up his Harley and rides away. Shortly thereafter, Rooter appears in the bedroom doorway, stretches his arms over his head and yawns.

"There's a problem at the shop." He walks to his chest of drawers and removes a pair of boxers and a dark gray t-shirt. "I'm going to grab a quick shower and head over there. You can stay here and sleep."

I sit up and throw my legs over the side of the bed. "I'll go on home. I have a lot to do today before work anyway."

"Okay." He walks over and leans down to kiss my forehead. "I'll see you when you get home from work."

I look at his face trying to decipher whether he's thinking about last night. Is he really okay with it, or was he as grossed out as I was? As I still am? Honestly, I hope he forgets about it altogether. However, the fact I know I'll never be able to forget it means he probably won't be able to either.

"And stop freaking out about last night," he says as though he's reading my mind.

I look up and smile at him sheepishly.

When I enter the house, I hear the water running in the bathroom upstairs. Eager to find out how Miranda's two nights with Bear went, I sprint up the stairs and knock on the bathroom door before letting myself in.

"Hey," I say and sit on the toilet lid.

"How was dinner with the rents?" Rents is our word for parents.

"It was good." I smile giddily and clasp my hands together. "How was your second night with Bear?"

She pokes her head out again and mouths, "Oh. My. God." She rolls her eyes back in her head emphasizing how good it was.

I laugh. "That good, huh?"

She shuts the water off and yanks the towel from the curtain rod. "We haven't even had actual sex and I've had more orgasms these past two days than I had the entire time I was with Chris."

"Two nights together and no sex?" Miranda isn't one to give it up easily, but being she spent two nights with the guy, I assumed it'd happened.

"Just about everything but," she giggles and opens the shower curtain. "I wasn't aware women could actually come from cunnilingus."

My eyes go wide. It's just like her to use that word rather than saying oral sex. "I wouldn't know."

"Two nights and still nothing?" She asks and drags her brush through her wet hair.

I proceed to tell her everything that's happened over the course of the last two days. When I'm finished, she's left standing with her mouth hanging open.

"That sucks, but periods aren't a big deal to some guys. It never stopped Chris."

"What?" I ask, disgusted. "You had sex on your period?"

She shrugs and goes back to fixing her hair. "Yeah."

I blanch. "That's gross!"

"It's only a little blood."

I shake my head. "No, thank you."

Miranda laughs and runs the flat iron over her already straight hair. I've never understood why she does this. It looks exactly the same after she irons it as it did before.

"So tell me more about you and scary Beary."

"He's so freaking amazing, Soph," she says and grips the closet doorway to stay upright while she slides on a pair of black heels. "We talk for hours. He's such a good listener, and so funny. And he's unbelievably sweet."

"He seems like a good guy," I admit.

"You have no idea." She pulls me into an embrace. "And I have you to thank for meeting him."

It's pouring rain when Ryan and I leave the Grand later that night. I make it halfway to my car when I come to an abrupt halt and gasp. I blink to make sure what I'm seeing is real.

"What the hell?" I say and sprint to my driver's side door. All four of my tires are slashed and the words whore, slut, bitch, and cunt have been carved into the door. I call Rooter immediately.

"Babe?" He answers on the first ring.

"My tires have been slashed." I stand in the rain utterly drenched, staring at my vandalized car. My entire body shakes from shock and anger.

"I'm on my way," he says. "Can Ryan wait with you until I get there?"

"Yeah."

Candace is the first person who comes to mind. If it had only been the tires I might've thought it was Mike, but the only person with the motive to key those specific words on my car is her. Ryan grabs me by my shoulders and leads me to his car. He opens the passenger door and helps me inside.

After what seems like eons, Rooter's truck pulls into the parking lot. He parks on the driver's side of my car and gets out to inspect the damage. I jump out of Ryan's car and dart over to him.

"That bitch did this," I say to him.

"Who, Candace?" He asks, staring at the curse words on the side of my car.

"Yeah." I stand with my hands on my hips.

He shakes his head.

"Why are you shaking your head?" I wave my hand at the words on my door. "This is her!"

"Get in the truck," he orders, irritated.

What's up his ass? "I should say goodbye to Ryan."

Rooter waves at Ryan from where we're standing and pulls me toward his truck. He opens the passenger door and helps me up.

"This was Mike," he says when he gets in and backs the truck out of the parking space.

I shake my head. "I don't think so. It was that bitch. I know it."

Rooter exhales sharply and pulls out of the parking lot. "Candace doesn't know where you work."

I give him my best are you serious face. "She could've followed me."

"Sophie, I realize you hate her," his voice escalates with each word, "but I'm telling you she did not do this."

"Why are you always defending her?" I shout.

"I do not always defend her!" He yells back. "But right now I am because I *know* she didn't do it."

The way he says the word "know" catches my attention. I jerk my entire body in his direction. "How do you know?"

He clenches his jaw and squeezes the steering wheel with a death grip. "Sophie, Mike did this. Plain and simple."

"Tell me how you know!" I demand.

His nostrils flare and he punches the steering wheel. He makes a hard right into a fast food restaurant parking lot and slams his foot on the brake bringing us to an abrupt stop. Because I'm not wearing a seatbelt my shoulder slams into the dash. It hurts like hell, but I'm not injured.

"What the hell?" I ask, rubbing my shoulder.

Rooter turns and looks at me like he's going to say something, but changes his mind. He takes my hand into his and grips it tightly. In his eyes is a level of intensity I've never seen. Not when he attacked Mike for hitting Miranda, and not even when those thugs broke into my house. I can literally feel the anger rolling off of him. Something is wrong. Something other than my slashed tires.

"Rooter, what's going on?"

He looks away from me to the windshield, still gripping my hand. When he speaks, he sounds defeated. "This entire day has been completely fucked up. I might as well make it a little bit worse."

His words trigger fear within me. Whatever he's about to say isn't good.

"What is it?"

He makes a steeple with this fingers covering his nose and takes a deep breath. "The reason I know Candace isn't the one who vandalized your car is because I was with her."

I take a deep breath and close my eyes, trying desperately to keep my emotions under control. I trust Rooter. If he was with her, he must've had a good reason. "Why were you with her?" I ask and open my eyes.

He turns to me with the saddest eyes I've ever seen. He reaches out, strokes my cheek and swallows. "She texted me earlier this evening. Said we needed to talk. I told her to forget it. That I wasn't playing any more games with her."

He turns back to the windshield, leans his head against the headrest and closes his eyes. I almost tell him to stop; that I don't want him to tell me what happened. I can sense that whatever he's getting ready to say will crush me. Crush us.

"She texted me a picture," he shakes his head and exhales, "of a positive pregnancy test."

My mouth drops to the floor. All the oxygen has been sucked out of my lungs and I begin to hyperventilate. I shake my head furiously. *This is not happening.*

"I went over there to call her out on more bullshit," he continues, "so she took another test. It was positive."

"You're sure it's yours?"

"I can't be sure without a DNA test," he rubs the back of his neck, "but there was one time… the condom broke."

I gasp. I want to punch something. Anything. So I lunge at Rooter and wail on his face and his chest. "How can you be so goddamn stupid?"

Rooter grabs a hold of my hands and pushes me back against the passenger door. He glares at me with wild eyes. "You're right. I am stupid. Sophie, I'm so sorry."

I'm tired of hearing him say he's sorry. "Take me home," I snarl and push him away.

The truck has barely come to a stop and I throw the door open and jump out into Rooter's driveway. He runs after me and catches up to me before I make it to my door.

"Sophie, please talk to me."

"I can't. Not right now." I need to get away from him so I can think. "Like you said, this day has been completely fucked up and all I want to do right now is sleep. Alone."

"I know you're mad—" I cut him off.

"Mad?" I scream and spin around to face him. "What I am goes way beyond mad, Rooter! There is no word in any language that can describe what I'm feeling right now!"

"I'm not comfortable leaving you alone knowing it was Mike who slashed your tires."

I stomp up the front porch stairs. "Well, you sure as hell aren't staying here tonight."

Rooter hurries past me and barricades the door. "I'll sleep on the couch. Who knows what that whacked out fuck is liable to try next."

"Then send Bear over, because you're not stepping one foot into this house."

Rooter appears to consider my words. "Promise me you'll talk to me tomorrow and I'll leave."

I roll my eyes and grip my keys so tightly it hurts. When I speak, it's through gritted teeth. "We'll talk when I'm ready and not before then."

"Tell me we'll talk tomorrow or I'm not leaving." He crosses his arms in defiance, but the panicked expression he's wearing tells me he's anything but confident right now.

I'm getting dangerously close to kneeing him square in the balls. "If you don't leave, I may never speak to you again."

"Tell me you'll talk to me tomorrow," he demands.

I ball my hands into fists and shout. "Fine! Just leave!"

"Say you promise we'll talk tomorrow."

I purse my lips and close my eyes. "I promise to talk to you tomorrow."

Rooter steps away from the door and waits while I unlock it. When I step over the threshold, he reaches out and takes my hand. "Good night, Sophie."

The moment I close the door behind me, every emotion I'm feeling hits me all at once and I sob. I run as fast as I can into Miranda's room and throw myself onto her bed.

"Sophie," she says, startled, and turns on her lamp. "What happened?"

"Can-dace is preg-nant," I choke through my sobs.

Complications & Arguments

I cry myself to sleep that night. When I dream, it's of him; him and me, and him and Candace, and him and his baby. Him. Him. Him.

When I wake up, he's sitting on the floor with his back against the door. I jolt upright.

"What are you doing here?"

"I had to see you."

"Maybe I don't want to see you." I feel bad the instant I say it. His being here is actually kind of comforting, but it also irritates me. I need time to process everything. It's just like him not to give me space.

Rooter gets up from the floor and crouches before me. It comes to my attention he's in the same clothes from last night. Then again, so am I. I was simply too exhausted to bother with changing.

"How long have you been here?" I ask and wipe the sleep from my eyes.

"I came in about three thirty."

I check the clock. "You've been here for six hours?"

Now that I take a good look at him, it's evident he hasn't slept. The skin beneath his eyes is dark and puffy. He looks haggard. Even haggard, he looks perfect. But this is exactly the kind of thought I can't afford right now. I shake my head to try to clear my mind. It doesn't matter how attracted I am to him. It doesn't matter how I feel about him. We have a huge, possibly insurmountable problem.

When he speaks, it as though he can read my mind. "I realize this situation isn't ideal. It's not what you wanted. But we can get through it."

"I'm not sure we can."

He lists forward, panicked, and takes my face into his hands. "Don't say that."

I pull away and scoot to the headboard. "You're having a kid. With Candace. How can you expect me to get past that?"

Rooter reaches out for me but I glare at him warning him not to touch me. He clasps his hands behind his head. "I realize I'm asking a lot of you, babe, but please…" He appears desperate. "I need you. I can't do this on my own."

He needs me? To do what exactly? Hold his hand? Tell him everything will be okay? Help him raise his kid? I'm not sure I can do those things. I don't want to do those things.

When I got into this relationship, I didn't sign up for a slutty, pregnant ex-whatever and I sure as hell didn't sign up for a kid. I'm twenty one freaking years old. I still have another year of college. I want to make a life for myself. I'd hoped Rooter would be a part of my future. But in that future, I don't see Candace and their kid.

"You're not on your own. You have *Candace*." I remark, snidely.

He shakes his head vehemently. His shoulders are tense and the vein in his forehead protrudes. "She's the last fucking thing I want or need."

You should have thought about that before you put your dick in her. That's what I want to say, but don't. "Well, that's too bad because you're stuck with her for the rest of your life."

"Fuck!" He punches my mattress. "What have I done?"

His distress makes me want to reach out for him and comfort him. But I, too, am distraught. I can't tell him everything will be okay or that we'll work this out because I don't know that it will be okay or if we will work it out. Yes, one way or the other, it will all work out, but not necessarily in the way he or I would hope. I'm very well versed in the harsh realities of life. In my experience, I'd say he'll go on, become a father, and in a year's time—give or take—our relationship will be a distant memory. I'll be a distant memory.

But on the flip side, as angry as I am about the situation, my feelings for him haven't changed. And that's what makes this so damn hard.

"I need time to figure out if this is something I can do." I push myself off of the mattress and go to my dresser. The reflection in the mirror can't possibly be mine. The girl before me looks as though she's aged ten years overnight. Her eyes are swollen and face is splotchy. "You're not just asking me to deal with Candace now. You're asking me to deal with you having a kid."

Through the mirror, I see the muscles in his face tighten. "It doesn't have to change us."

"But it does change us." I spin around to face him. "It changes you." *Can he really not see that?*

Rooter explodes off of the bed and saunters to me, his face is red. "So that's it? You're done?"

"I—I didn't say that."

"It sure as hell sounds like it."

"I…" I look to the floor unable to face him. "I just need some time."

"If this was happening to you," he tilts my chin up to face him, "I wouldn't bolt. I'd stick by you."

I furrow my brow and hold my hand to my chest. "Are you seriously trying to make me feel guilty?"

"I'm just telling it like it is. I thought you were stronger than this."

"Don't you understand?" Tears threaten to spill down my face. "I'm tired of being strong. I'm tired of being let down and left out."

Rooter's eyes bore into mine. "Sophie, I didn't do this to you. I did this before you. For what it's worth, I am sorry." He turns his back to me and drags a hand through his hair. "I'm not letting you down or leaving you out of anything. But if you walk away that's exactly what you'll be doing to me."

Without looking back, he opens my bedroom door and leaves me alone in my room. A few seconds later the front door slams shut.

Ten minutes later I'm still in my room reeling from our conversation when he texts me.

Rooter: *I had ur car towed to Molly's Auto for repairs. I can take u to work later, or u can drive my truck. Let me know.*

This is why I'm so crazy about him. Even though we're fighting, even though we may never get past this, he's still taking care of me. I text him back.

Me: *Thank you for helping me. I'm not going to work today.*

I literally just decided not to go to work when I read his text. I can't go. I'm completely spent mentally and emotionally. Randy is better off without me today. Tuesdays are a light day anyway so it shouldn't be a big deal. After pressing send, I call Randy to inform him I won't be coming in. While I'm talking to Randy, Rooter texts me again. After I hang up, I read the text.

Rooter: *I'll be here all day if u need anything or need to go anywhere. Or if u want to talk.*

Rooter is sitting in his house, not thirty yards away, and we're texting. Texting! I stare at my phone and debate whether I should call or text. I decide to text.

Me: *I don't want to fight. Please don't be mad at me.*

Four seconds after pressing send my phone rings. It's him.

"Hey," I answer on the third ring.

"I'm not mad at you, babe," his voice is soft and kind. "I'm just mad in general. Mad at myself. And I'm scared. I'm scared of losing you. Of having a kid I didn't plan for with a girl I don't want to have it with."

The vulnerability in his voice tugs at my heart. I can hear his fear. He really needs me. I know what it's like to be let down by those I've needed when I needed them most. I can't do that to him. Like he said, he didn't do this to me. It's simply an unfortunate circumstance; even if it was brought on by poor decision making on his behalf. We all make mistakes. He doesn't deserve to be persecuted for his. What would it say about me if I was to tuck tail and run? The least I can do is try.

"I can't promise you anything, Rooter, but I'm willing to take things day by day."

"That's all I'm asking." His voice is barely more than a whisper. We're both quiet for a moment before he speaks again. "Is it all right if I come over?"

It's strange to hear him ask to come to my house. "Yeah."

"Good, because I'm in your living room," he chuckles, but it's not an entirely happy sound.

Now that's just like him. How did I not hear him come in? "I'll be right down."

I examine my appearance in the mirror again though I don't know why. I look exactly the same as I did last time I checked. Like hell.

When I reach the top of the stairs, Rooter is standing at the bottom with his hands in his pockets. When he sees me, his lips curl into the slightest of a smile. I return the gesture.

I stop and stand on the last step making us almost the same height. He takes one hand from his pocket and hooks a finger through my belt loop to pull me against him. He nuzzles his face into the crook of my neck and inhales. I drape my arms around his neck and breathe a sigh of relief at his nearness, swathed in a quiet calm. We stand in complete silence and hold one another for several minutes. Eventually he reaches for my hand and leads me to the sofa.

"I hate to bring this up, but we still have the issue of your car to deal with."

I pull my eyebrows together, confused. "You said it was at Molly's."

He strokes the top of my hand with his thumb. His voice is quiet and soothing. "I'm talking about Mike. He needs to be dealt with."

I roll my eyes and sigh. Fucking Mike. Since it wasn't Candace, I must assume it was him. "What do you think we should do?"

He shakes his head. "*We* aren't going to do anything. *I* will handle it."

There's a picture of Mike—the old Mike from high school—on the wall. He's wearing his football Jersey, throwing a football during practice. Next to his picture is a photo of him and Miranda posing together the night of her Senior Prom. She didn't have a date, so he escorted her. Those were much happier times for the both of them.

"Rooter, he's Miranda's brother. I need to know what you plan on doing."

"He may be Miranda's brother, but you're my girl and by fucking with you, he fucked with me. He's going to pay for it."

Hearing him speak so possessively makes my heart flutter. I am his. Completely. And we both know it. It's either going to work for me or against me.

"Pay how?" I ask, not sure I want to hear the answer.

His jaw is set and there's an evil glint in his eyes. "I'm going to show him what happens when he messes with me."

"Rooter, I realize you're used to handling these situations a certain way," I reach out and take his hand, "but we have to be careful here. You need to keep Miranda in mind."

"Why? He wasn't keeping her in mind when he did this."

"Because she's my best friend. Mike is the only family she has left." I point at the pictures on the wall. "It would kill her if something happened to him."

"It's not like I'm going to kill him," Rooter sighs. "I'm just going to… Temporarily limit the use of his hands."

"Rooter—" I start but he puts his index finger against my lips and cuts me off.

"If we ignore this, the next thing he does will be much worse. I'm not willing to take that risk."

"Can't you just talk to him or something?"

Rooter shakes his head. "I've tried that. The only way I'll get through to him is by paying him a visit."

"We don't know where he is."

"That's why I need his cell phone number."

If Mike is the culprit, and he probably is, I want him to pay for what he's done. But I'm not sure if exacting the kind of revenge Rooter is known for is worth the pain it would cause Miranda. "If Miranda finds out I had anything to do with Mike getting hurt, including giving you his phone number, she'll hate me forever."

"You don't have to give it to me. Where's your phone?"

I wave toward the stairs. "It's in my purse in my room."

Rooter gets up and sprints up the stairs. Thirty seconds later he appears before me with a scowl and a clenched jaw. His eyes are narrowed at the screen of my phone. He looks at me with a glint of anger in his eyes then looks back at the phone. His hands are shaking. He chucks the phone at me angrily, though not so hard as to hurt me, and hits me square in the chest.

"What the fuck is that?" He growls.

I look at the screen. There's a text from Hayden: *Hey beautiful. I'm thinking about you.*

The first thought that comes to my mind is that Rooter knows my passcode. How the hell did he get it? I've never given it to him. But I don't dare ask while he's in his current state of mind. That's a conversation for another time. Besides, I don't have anything to hide.

I shrug in response to his question because I honestly don't know why Hayden is texting me after all this time. And I don't care. Frankly, it's the last thing I'm worried about. I—we—have much bigger issues to deal with right now.

Rooter points at the phone in my hand, his nostrils flare. "Put an end to that, or I will and neither one of you will like the way I do it."

I toss the phone on the coffee table and exhale harshly. "Rooter, it's not a big deal. We went out once. It was nothing. He knows I have a boyfriend."

My words do nothing to appease him. He's just as agitated, perhaps more so. "Then remind him and make sure he doesn't contact you again."

I tilt my head to the side, not sure whether to be irritated or amused by his behavior. "Wait, so you're telling me you're pissed about a text from a guy I went on one date with and yet I'll always have to deal with Candace?"

Rooter snatches my phone from the table and enters my passcode. He scrolls through and for an instant I think he's going to call Hayden himself.

"What are you doing?" I ask, but he ignores me. Very well. If he wants to make a fool out of himself with Hayden that's just fine with me.

Rooter retrieves his phone from his back pocket and dials. "Rat, I need you to run a trace for me." He rattles off Mike's number.

Once he hangs up with Rat, he tosses my phone at me. I catch it and set it back on the table.

"You gonna call that guy or what?" He grumbles.

"Right now?" I ask.

He eyes me questioningly. "Is there a reason you don't want to?"

"I think we have bigger issues than some guy sending me a random text."

"Call him, now," he growls, "or I will."

I fling my head back and laugh. I can't help myself. Rooter jealous over Hayden is priceless.

"You think this is funny?" He seethes through gritted teeth.

"You being jealous?" I snort. "I think it's hilarious."

Rooter's face turns a deep shade of red. He's severely pissed, and it makes me laugh harder. "Stop laughing, Sophie," he barks.

Anyone else would quake in their shoes at the sight of him in this moment. He looks as though he might attack at any second, but I know better. He'd never hurt me. My phone, on the other hand, may not be as safe with the way he's staring it down.

"I can't! It's just so ridiculous." I clutch my stomach in hysterics.

"Ridiculous?" He raises an eyebrow. "I'll show you ridiculous." He picks the phone up from the table and urges me to take it.

"You already have."

"Call. Him. Now," he fumes.

"He's nobody, Rooter. He doesn't warrant a phone call."

"Fine, I'll do it myself." He punches something into the screen. "Hayden?" He snarls into the phone then pauses while Hayden speaks. "This is the guy who will shred your dick with a fork if you ever text or call Sophie Holt again… Good," he says and hangs up the phone.

I'm not laughing anymore. "That was so unnecessary." I yank my phone away. "And how do you know my passcode anyway?"

Rooter shrugs and sits casually on the sofa. How can he be so calm when only seconds ago he was a raging lunatic? "I've seen you enter it a thousand times."

"And you remembered it?"

He shrugs again. "Is it a problem?"

"Of course not," I cross my arms and tilt my head. "*I* have nothing to hide."

"Are you insinuating that I do?"

"Suspicious minds are often the result of a guilty conscience, and with your slutty, pregnant exes and all…" I trail off.

Rooter pulls his phone out of his back pocket and tosses it my way. "Code is zero-nine-two-six."

My eyes go wide. Not because he told me his code, but because my birthday is September twenty-sixth. Maybe it's coincidence. I hand his phone back to him. "I don't need your code."

He leans forward and slips it back into his pocket. "It's one, not plural. And she isn't my *ex*."

I roll my eyes and cross my arms. "Yeah, it's hard for her to be an ex when she's still around."

Rooter groans and rakes his fingers through his hair. "I thought you said you don't want to fight."

I sigh and fall back against the sofa. "I don't. You started it."

Rooter scoots closer, his thigh brushing the side of mine, and takes my hand into his. "I'm sorry. I lost my shit when I saw that text."

"Do you really think I'd cheat on you?"

He hesitates for a moment before answering. "No babe, I don't." He rests his head on my shoulder. "I'm just crazy right now."

That makes two of us. I drape a leg over his and squeeze his hand. We need a break so we can get back to being us. Actually, we need a break to figure out who the hell we are as an us. We've done nothing but endure turmoil since day one of our relationship. But I have a feeling we won't be getting a break anytime soon. With that knowledge, I close my eyes and take a deep breath, trying to relax and take in this quiet moment after the storm. And then his phone rings.

It's Candace.

FRIENDS & ENEMIES

If I was a smoker, I'd be chain smoking right now. Instead, I sit on the couch drumming my fingers on the arm rest. My palms are slick from sweat and my eyes dart back and forth between the door and the antique clock on the wall.

Please let this go better than I expect.

It turns out Mike isn't as dumb as one might believe. He no longer has the same phone number, and no longer has his job. Whether he quit or was fired remains to be seen. The sudden changes has Rooter on edge. He thinks Mike is up to something and wants to make it as hard to be found as possible.

To track him down, Rooter has asked me for a list of Mike's friends and possible addresses. I've prepared the list, but before I hand it over I need to tell Miranda what's happening. She should be home from work any minute.

I'm not asking for it to go well. There's no way it will. Just let it be better than her tearing into me and throwing me out on the street. And please let her be in a good mood when she gets home. If she's had a bad day at work, I'm screwed. Rooter offered to be here when I tell her, but that'd probably make things worse.

Miranda opens the front door right on time. I know I had hoped for her to be in a good mood, but seeing the enormous smile on her face makes me feel guilty because I'm getting ready to erase it.

The extreme heat isn't helping. It's an unusually hot day. It's nearly ninety degrees outside. A rarity for our area anytime of the spring or summer. And if it happens it's typically not until mid to late August. It's only June. A bead of sweat rolls down the side of my face and I wipe it away with the back of my hand.

The instant she sees me her face falls. "Oh no. What happened now?" She sets her purse on the table before sitting next to me. "Is it Candace again?"

I shake my head. "Mike," I croak.

She leans forward with bowed shoulders. "What did he do?"

"It's about my car. Rooter assumes it was he who did it."

She shakes her head with a sad expression. "He's probably right."

I look away from her. "He's looking for him."

"I figured as much," she responds casually. I glance up at her. She rubs her forehead with her thumb and index finger. "Do you know what he's going to do?"

I sit forward and wring my hands together. Rooter's admission that it would likely involve Mike's hands give me visions of him smashing his fingers with a hammer. "Not exactly, but I'm sure it won't be pretty."

"I love my brother." She places her hand on my leg. "But if it was him, and I'm sure it was, he deserves to pay for what he's done."

Wow. She's taking this a lot better than I thought she would. I sigh in relief. "I don't want this coming between us."

"It won't, Soph. It's his own fault. He's just so damn stupid!"

I pick at a piece of lint on my shirt. "Rooter has asked me for a list of all of his friends and possible addresses."

"You have to do what you have to do and I accept that, but I won't participate. I hope you understand."

She thinks I'm asking her to give me the information. I shake my head. "I didn't expect you to. I'm just letting you know what's going on and what my level of involvement is."

"I appreciate it, Soph." She rests her elbows on her legs and rubs her face. "Can you do me one favor?"

I have an idea what she's getting ready to ask. "Yeah?"

"Can you please ask Rooter to go easy on him?"

"I already have," I assure her, but don't bother to tell her it isn't likely.

"Thanks," she says and pats my leg and stands. "And in other, much more exciting news, Bear is on his way to pick me up."

"Yeah?"

"We're going to Skyles for dinner."

I'm envious of Miranda. It's too soon to be sure, but so far it would seem Bear doesn't have any pregnant skanks chasing after him day and night. Miranda gets to go on dates with him without being interrupted by texts and phone calls. She doesn't have to try to figure out where she'll fit in once his newborn child is born. She certainly doesn't have to put up with coming second to another woman.

Rooter and I got into another tiff after Candace texted him yesterday. Of course she said it was an emergency, and he rushed over to her place. There was no emergency. When she texted she claimed she felt cramps, but the moment he got there they passed. I don't buy any of it. Rooter on the other hand isn't sure. I asked him if he was going to run to her every time she faked a crisis. He said as long as she's pregnant he's obligated to be there when she says she needs him. At this rate, he'll be there every day. And I'll be sitting around, waiting in the wings.

It's Friday night and Ryan and I are in his living room having an after work drink. It's been a hell of a night. Ryan's house is the perfect place for a little rest and relaxation. The lights are dim and soft music plays in the background. Rooter wasn't thrilled when I told him I was staying the night here because he knows the reason why; I need a break from him, and us, and all of our issues.

Rooter is on edge about Mike. I'm on edge because of Candace and Mike. Between Rooter looking for Mike, running to Candace every time she calls, and our conflicting schedules, we haven't spent any quality time together. The only time we're really together is when we're sleeping.

He hasn't tried anything since the night of Miranda's birthday party. We barely even kiss. He can probably sense I'm not into it right now. Perhaps he's not into it either. There's too much going on. And it's difficult for me to feel romantic or sexy with him when he's been hanging out with Candace all afternoon. He's literally seen her every single day since he found out she's pregnant.

I sit cross legged on Ryan's gray sectional, he's turned toward me with one leg tucked under him. "She calls every day," I drone and take a swig of Jack. "Multiple times, whining about being sick."

"How far along is she?"

"A little over a month."

"She could have morning sickness by now."

The only sickness she has is mental. I take another sip of the whiskey. "Yeah, but she claims she has morning, noon, and night sickness. And that's not even the worst of it!" I slap the couch. "The lying cow claims she's having cravings already. Cravings don't start until the second month."

The way she calls freaking out over every little thing got me thinking. I figured a little research would help Rooter decipher a true emergency from her using her condition to get his attention. I must've spent four hours online reading everything I could about what to expect during pregnancy.

Ryan raises an eyebrow and takes a sip of his bourbon. "How do you know?"

"I looked into it." Ryan nods without asking for details and I continue. "I tried telling Rooter, so he'd stop running over there every damn time she calls, but he says as long as she's pregnant he has to go."

Ryan tilts his head to the side. "He's not entirely wrong, but it's not like she's bedridden."

I throw my hands in the air. "Exactly my point!" I pour another shot into my glass. "Wednesday night, we were curled up in his bed, halfway through a movie we'd rented on cable when she called begging him to take her some fried chicken."

Ryan's eyes go wide. "No fucking way!"

"Way!"

"And he did it?"

"Of course! Baby momma calls and he goes running."

Ryan sets his glass down and turns to face me directly. "He can't do that to you. She isn't bloody helpless."

"Oh, but it gets better." I scoot closer. "He asked if I wanted to stay or go. Of course I went. I stayed in the car and when she opened the door, the trollop was in red lingerie with her robe hanging wide open!"

Ryan's jaw drops. "That bitch didn't call him over for chicken."

"Hell no she didn't!" I toss back the rest of my drink and slam the empty glass on the coffee table. "Rooter told her I was in the car waiting and she grabbed the sack of food and slammed the door in his face."

Ryan shakes his head in disgust. "She probably throws herself at him every time he goes over there."

"I know she does and it makes me sick." I press my lips together in a thin line.

Ryan shifts forward and looks me in the eyes intently. "He has to draw a line. He can't allow her to dictate every second of his life. At this rate, you'll never have a relationship. Not a real one anyway."

He's right. I take a deep breath and sigh.

He cups my chin. "Put your foot down, babe. Demand that he makes uninterrupted time for you."

That would be nice, but it isn't completely possible. "Club rules state he can't turn his phone off."

"Fine, then he needs to not answer her calls when he's with you."

Like that'll happen. My shoulders bow as I sit hunched over and pick at a cuticle until it bleeds. I had nice nails before this whole Candace debacle. "It would be nice to have just one day to ourselves."

Ryan takes my hand into his. When I look up I see his caring, beautiful green eyes. "Babe, if he can't make time for you the relationship will never last. Tell him that. It might make him think twice."

"I don't want to put more pressure on him." I turn away. There's a very real chance I'll lose him as it is. If I add to his list of demands and stress, I definitely will.

"Hey," Ryan forces me to look at him, "he did this. Maybe not purposely, but he did it just the same. If he wants to be with you, he needs to do right by you."

An hour later, I'm lying in the bed next to Ryan who's already snoring when a light appears in the room. I turn to my left and see my phone is illuminated. I reach over and pick it up to see a text from Rooter.

Rooter: Can't sleep without u next to me.

My heart flutters. It's three in the morning and he's thinking of me. He may not be able to make time for me, but at least he thinks of me. I stare at the screen and ponder texting him back. Maybe I should let him sweat it out for the night.

Yeah. That's exactly what I should do.

I pull into my driveway at eleven thirty in the morning to find one of Rooter's club members straddling his bike. I've seen the guy before, but never met him. He's older, maybe mid-forties. By the time I open my car door, he's standing before me.

"I'm Sparrow," he says and extends his hand to help me out of the car. He has kind blue eyes, but his skin is like leather. "Rooter sent me to wait on you."

I take his hand and step out of the car. "Is everything okay?"

He nods. "Said he couldn't reach you. He found the guy who messed up your car."

My breath catches. Rooter has Mike. I yank my phone from my purse. Sure enough it's dead. "Where is he?"

Sparrow shakes his head. His shoulder length salt and pepper hair swings back and forth. "Can't say. But he told me to tell you to call him the second you get here."

Without a word, I dart for my front door to get my phone charger from my room. I swiftly unlock the front door, fling it open and sprint up the stairs as fast as my legs will carry me.

"You gonna call him?" Sparrow hollers up the stairway.

"Yeah," I call out. "I need to plug my phone in."

My charger is already plugged into the wall. I have a bad habit of leaving it plugged in when I'm not using it. I plug the phone in and wait what seems like a month for it to come on. When it finally does, I call Rooter. He picks up on the third ring.

"Where are you?" He snaps.

"Home," I answer, irritated. Who cares where I am? Where are you? Before I can ask, he interrupts.

"Why haven't you returned any of my messages?"

I hear a muffled groan in the background. Something tells me it's Mike. I start pacing. "Is Mike with you?"

"Yeah," he answers flippantly. "Why haven't you called me?"

"My phone died," I answer impatiently and rake a hand through my hair. "Where are you?"

"Sophie, I need to be able to reach you at all times. Do you understand that?"

Seriously? I roll my eyes and huff. "I told you my phone died. How is Mike?"

"He's fine," he barks. "Tell me you understand that I need to be able to reach you."

"Yeah, yeah, I get it," I answer glibly, waving my hand, urging him to go on as though he can see me through the phone. "Where are you?"

"I can't tell you that."

Anger boils to the surface and my face gets hot. I kick a lone sandal across my floor. "The hell you can't! I need to know what's going on!"

"I have it under control. He'll live. I promise."

"Rooter, dammit! What did you do?"

"Not much." His voice is low and menacing. "Yet."

The Reckoning & Revelation

I stop moving. My body is so still that if someone stood right in front of me they might think I'm not breathing.

Wait. I'm *not* breathing.

This is what happens when I'm pushed beyond my limit. Right now I'm *way* beyond my limit.

I hate the person Mike has become. Everything about him. I've known him nearly my entire life, but I no longer consider him my friend. But somehow, against all odds, I still consider him family.

Miranda, on the other hand, I love with my whole heart. Our friendship isn't perfect. We've had our ups and downs. But that's because we're more like family than friends. She's the sister I never had.

Miranda loves Mike regardless of his faults or flaws. And as screwed up as our situation is, the three of us are joined, irrevocably, as family. So I can't knowingly allow harm to come to him, especially not on my behalf.

Another thing that happens when I'm beyond my limit: I speak in a deep monotone voice. "Don't. You. Dare. Hurt. Him." I snarl into the phone.

I think I hear Rooter gasp. "Sophie, he's going to pay for what he's done."

I close my eyes and inhale. "That isn't your decision to make. It's mine. And I'm telling you, you will not hurt him."

"Sophie—" he protests, but I cut him off.

"No." I shake my head and pinch the bridge of my nose. I am seriously out of patience with him and this conversation. "If you're smart, you'll listen to what I'm saying."

When I open my eyes, Sparrow stands in my doorway with his mouth hanging wide open, his eyes bulge from their sockets. He knows I'm talking to Rooter. No one talks to Rooter this way and gets away with it.

"Since when do you care what happens to this piece of shit?" The way his voice shakes tells me he's fighting to keep his composure.

Sparrow's presence distracts me, causing me to lose my nerve. I turn away and look at the opposite wall. "I don't need to explain anything to you. But you are going to listen to me."

"What?" He asks with a mixture of anger and astonishment.

I continue in my wrathful monotone. "I'm done with all this shit."

"Sophie?" He sounds scared now, and it empowers me to continue.

"You don't get to dictate everything anymore." I point at the air as though he's standing in front of me. "It's not all up to you anymore. I get a say in what happens."

"What is this really about?"

He's got to be kidding me. I no longer speak in monotone, but rather an ear-piercingly loud shriek. "It's about you! And me! And how everything is completely fucked up! My life is more fucked up now than it was before I met you!"

"I'm on my way." He's really panicking now.

"Not until you let him go."

"I'm not letting him go," he says, incredulous.

"Then I won't be here when you get here." I mean it. If he won't do what I say, I'm gone. I'm sure Ryan will let me stay with him for a while. He mentioned the other day his money is tight now that he's living alone.

"Babe—"

A tremor of anger surges through me. I'm back to my angry monotone. "Do. Not. *Babe*. Me. Just shut the fuck up and listen." It's kind of nice using his own words against him.

"I'm listening."

"I'm sure you've already done more than enough to scare him. Let him go. Then you and I are going to talk."

Rooter is quiet.

"Did you hear me?"

The sunlight floods through the window onto an upside down DVD and blinds me, but I don't turn away.

"I heard you," he mutters.

"Are you going to do what I've said?"

After a moment, he answers. "Yes. I'll be there in a half hour."

I tell Sparrow that Rooter is on his way, but he calls him anyway to confirm. Once he has confirmation he leaves, but not before wishing me luck.

Twenty minutes later, Rooter bursts through my door without knocking. Any other time, I'd be nervous about our impending confrontation. But right now as I sit crossed legged on the couch I'm fully confident. I'm much too agitated to be nervy.

For far too long, I have allowed others to dictate what happens in my life. I've let them govern how I feel and what I do. But not anymore. Relationships, be them romantic or platonic, should not be one-sided. It's time I stand up for myself. It's time I draw a line on what is and is not acceptable in my relationships, and I'm starting with Rooter.

Everything seems to move in slow motion, from the front door swinging open to Rooter marching toward me. The room has become dark from the impending storm outside and is briefly illuminated by a strike of lightening. I inhale deeply and count to ten.

I look around the room and memories of happier times come flooding into my mind. I'd give anything for Loraine to still be alive. If she was, so much would be different. Mike wouldn't have gone off his rocker and I probably wouldn't be with Rooter right now because Miranda and I'd be living in an apartment together somewhere.

I'm not saying I don't want to be with Rooter. I do want to be with him. Things are just so screwed up. I think I could get past Candace and even the pregnancy if I had more support from him; if I felt my feelings were understood and acknowledged. But ever since she told him about the baby, it's as if I barely exist. I don't want to come across as needy or clingy, but it'd be nice to feel as though I hold some importance to him.

"Babe?" Rooter stands before me still as a clay sculpture with his hands hanging at his sides. I take in his expression but it's unreadable.

"Did you let Mike go?" I ask point blank in monotone.

He clenches his jaw. "Yes. Are you okay?"

"No, Rooter, I'm not okay," I answer through gritted teeth. "What did you do to him?"

"Nothing much. Smacked him around a little, threatened him, and then you called."

"I think you should sit down." I motion to the chair beside me.

He doesn't bother to comment or ask why before taking a seat in the recliner. "Babe, you're freaking me out."

"Good! You should be. Because I'm beyond done with all the bullshit."

"Done? With me?"

That's not exactly what I meant, but... "If things don't change, yeah."

He squeezes his eyes shut for a short moment. "Is this about Candace?"

"Mostly, yeah, but it's also about how you've treated me through this. It's like I don't even matter."

His eyes go wide. "Of course you matter." He holds a hand to his chest. "How have I made you feel otherwise?"

He's got to be kidding. I wave my hands violently as I speak. "You run to her constantly. She could call you over a hang nail and you'd go rushing over there. It's getting to the point that I'm thinking your feelings for her are more than you've admitted to."

Rooter shoots forward in his seat. "I can promise you they're not. But what am I supposed to do? Ignore her? I can't do that. She's pregnant with my kid."

"Maybe. How do you know it's your kid?"

"I have to assume it is until it's born and I can get a DNA test."

I rub my hands on the tops of my thighs. "Fine. I can accept that. But I can't accept her calling every hour on the hour," I'm exaggerating, but it seems that frequent, "and you running over to her all the time. She's pregnant, not dying. Women get pregnant all the time for shit sake. It's really not that big of a deal."

Rooter narrows his eyes and tilts his head to the side. "What if you were pregnant? Would that be a big deal? Or should I ignore you?"

"Like I could even get pregnant!" I shriek. "At the rate we're going, we'll never get an opportunity to have sex in order for me to get pregnant because you'll be with Candace all the damn time!"

"What do you want me to do?" Rooter hollers and throws his hands in the air. "I'm trying, all right! I don't know what the fuck to do." He jumps up from the chair and paces the room with his hands clasped behind his head. "Do you think I *want* to go running to her every damn day? Do you think I *want* her calling me constantly? Because I don't. I don't want her to be pregnant, but I can't undo it. And I can't hide from it. And I won't ignore it, even if I want to, and trust me, I *do*!"

"I'm not asking you to ignore the baby. I'm asking you to stop giving in to her over every little whimper and whine when there's absolutely nothing wrong with her." I lean my elbows on my knees and hold my hands clasped in front of my face. "If we're going to be together, you need to make time for me. For us. It's like she knows exactly when to call so you'll run to her and leave me hanging, which you do all the time now."

Rooter stops pacing and sits on the coffee table in front of me. He takes my face into his hands and stares into my eyes. "All I fucking want is you. You're all I've wanted for as long as I can remember. You want truth? I'll give it to you. The truth is it would be so easy to choose you over the kid. It would be so fucking easy for me to walk away from both of them for you. The only thing stopping me is that's what my dad did to me and my mom. And I don't want to be like him."

What? When did Mick walk away? Did he leave and come back? They look like the perfect, happy family and when he speaks of them it's as though they are. "What are you talking about?"

Rooter leans away and looks at the floor, sullen. "Mick isn't my real dad. Or rather I should say, my biological dad. My bio-dad abandoned me. He walked out on my mom when she was pregnant. Left her for another woman."

"Oh my God, Rooter. I'm so sorry." I reach out and take his shaking hand into mine. Now things make a little more sense. I finally understand why he's doing what he's doing with Candace. He doesn't want to be like his dad.

Rooter looks back up at me. "Mom was just like Candace, trying to get by as a stripper. Had no family. She had one friend; Candace's mom." He exhales and sweeps a hand through his hair. His dark eyes convey a deep seated sadness. "Mick was already in love with her. He took her in when she could no longer dance. He told her he wanted to take care of me and be my dad. She eventually fell in love with him, too. He raised me like his own. Loved me like his own. There's no differentiation between me and Isa to him. To him, I am his blood. And if the kid Candace is carrying is mine, I'm going to love him or her just the way Mick loves me."

There's so much I don't know about this man. I had no idea Mick wasn't his biological father; that his father had abandoned him and his mother. I know the pain of abandonment. I wouldn't wish it on anyone. Not even my worst enemy. If only I'd known. Rooter is carrying around the same pain I carry. The same anger I carry. At this moment, I understand him in an entirely new way. Tears pool in my eyes and I fight to keep them back. The last thing he needs is for me to break down.

I say the only thing I can even though I know it won't make him feel any better. "I'm so very sorry."

"I know the situation is fucked up and that I'm asking way too much of you. I should let you go. This isn't fair to you."

"Rooter, no," I squeeze his hand and speak with conviction. "You can't let me go because I'm not going anywhere. I won't abandon you when you need me most."

"I do need you. But you're right." He looks away. "We can't go on like this. It'll never work."

I grab him by the chin and turn his face to mine. "Then we don't go on like this. We figure out a balance. Together."

He looks at me with a tormented expression; a mixture of hope of what could be and sorrow for what has been.

I continue since he can't seem to speak. "But you need to work with me."

When he finally speaks his voice is soft, yet passionate. "I can do that, babe. I can."

"I would never ask you to abandon your child. I'm only asking for you to make a little time for us."

Rooter's phone rings. It's Candace calling, naturally. As always, her timing is impeccable. Rooter closes his eyes and shakes his head, struggling with what to do. He keeps his eyes closed until the phone stops ringing.

He opens his eyes and focuses on mine. "I will make time for us."

"Uninterrupted time," I clarify.

He nods. "Uninterrupted."

"And there's something else."

Rooter looks at me seemingly exhausted. When he doesn't say anything, I go on.

"You need to give me a say in things that concern me. Like the situation with Mike."

"He deserves to pay for what he did."

"Yeah, but you don't get to decide the price on your own."

Rooter cracks his neck. "He deserves worse than he got."

I sigh with exasperation. He needs to stop fighting me on this. "Maybe so. But Miranda doesn't and she will feel any pain you inflict on him." He nods in understanding, but I can tell he doesn't like it. "Promise me, going forward we'll make time for each other and we'll make decisions that affect us both, together."

"I promise." He leans forward and rests his forehead against mine. "I'm going to get this right."

The Surprise

I've spent the entire day cleaning the house, mowing the lawn, and weeding the mulch beds. The house doesn't get as dirty as fast with Mike gone, but Miranda and I let the cleaning schedule go by the wayside. Therefore, things aren't being done as often as they should be. The problem is, Miranda doesn't mind a messy house as where I prefer things to be neat and orderly. However, she has been doing the dishes in the evenings so I must give her credit for that.

After showering and getting dressed, I lay on the couch and stare at the ceiling. It's so quiet. I love the quiet. I could use a little more quiet in my life.

The ceiling fan blades are coated with dust. I have half a mind to get the step ladder and clean them, but I don't. As I stare at them, it occurs to me they haven't been cleaned since before Loraine died. There's more than a year's worth of dust on those blades. Dust from when she was still alive. A lump forms in my throat and my chest aches. How can dust make me nostalgic?

I force myself to look away from the blades and check the clock on the wall. Rooter should be home from work in a half hour. We don't have any specific plans, but I'm sure we'll do something together since it's my day off. Maybe we can go for a ride along the lakeshore and then grab dinner somewhere.

Four days have passed since the Mike and Candace incidents. We never heard from Mike after Rooter let him go. Though Rooter and Bear have kept a close eye on me and Miranda just to be sure.

Things between me and Rooter have vastly improved. Candace still calls every day. In some ways, she's more demanding than ever. Probably because she feels she's losing her grip on him. But he doesn't answer her calls or texts when we're together. He waits and we listen to her messages together and decide whether it truly warrants an immediate return call. So far, none of them have.

Rather than him seeing her every day, it's turned into every other day, which is a fifty percent reduction, so I'll take it. I'm hoping over time, as Rooter sees she's just fine that his visits with her will become even less frequent.

She called all day Sunday—she must know Sundays are my day off—but he never answered. When we woke up that morning we made a vow not to discuss any of the prior day's events and decided not to attend the Russo family dinner. We needed a day of light and fun, which was ironic considering there was a raging tempest outside.

In light of our oath, we spent the entire stormy day in his house curled up on the couch watching comedies, laughing until our sides ached, and eating junk food. Well, I ate junk food. Rooter never eats junk food. Never. The closest thing to junk food he'll eat is lightly buttered popcorn. So we always make two separate batches because I like mine doused in butter and sprinkled with salt. As Rooter says, I like a little popcorn with my butter and salt.

Between my work schedule and his we barely see each other except for when I get off work. Naturally, we spend every night together. I still think it's way too soon for us to be spending every night together. But given our differing schedules and the situation with Mike, I go along with it.

Each night, he curls up against me from behind and we talk for an hour or so about our day, work, and Miranda and Bear. I'm itching to ask about his past and his real dad. I'm eager to learn more about him. But the middle of the night isn't the time for having such important conversations. And that specific conversation is better to be put off for a little while. I'm all for keeping things light and fun for as long as we can.

My cell phone pings. A text from Rooter: *Ur car is finished. I'll be by to get u in 15 minutes.*

I set my phone down, close my eyes and wait for him to arrive.

When I open my eyes, Rooter is passed out in the recliner. He's slumped over to his right with his mouth hanging open. I check the clock. I've been asleep for over an hour and never even heard him come in. The poor guy must be exhausted. He's only averaged four hours of sleep a night. By the time I get home from work and we talk for a little while, he doesn't fall asleep until around two in the morning. Then he has to turn around and get up at six o'clock to get to the shop.

When Rooter is asleep, he's completely adorable. His face is relaxed and sweet. I yearn to go over and touch his cheek, but I don't want to wake him.

With a severe case of cotton mouth, I'm in dire need of water. I stand and tiptoe toward the kitchen, but the moment I walk by the chair the damn wood floor creaks and wakes him up.

"Hey, babe," he mumbles with sleepy eyes and straightens up in the chair.

"I'm sorry," I whisper. "Go back to sleep."

He shakes his head and holds his hand out for me. I take it and he draws me onto his lap. "It's too late to get your car. Molly's is closed now."

"I can have Ryan take me to pick it up in the morning."

He grins mischievously and shakes his head. "You won't be here in the morning."

"What?" I ask, curious. "Where will I be?"

Rooter rubs his hands together rapidly. "You and I are going away for a few days."

My mouth falls open. "But I have to work."

He shakes his head and smiles. "I already talked to Randy. He's giving you the next three days off."

Oh my God. Is he serious? I lean back trying to process this unexpected information. "What? When did you talk to him?"

"Earlier today. He was totally cool with it."

I raise an eyebrow. Randy is probably the most easy going boss on the planet, but even he has his limits. Giving me three days off with zero notice doesn't sound like him.

Rooter wraps his arms around me. "Trust me. It's all good."

I stare at him, skeptical. "Are you sure?"

"Call him. He'll tell you."

I reach behind me and retrieve my phone from my back pocket and do just that. Randy confirms that yes, he has given me Thursday, Friday, and Saturday off. He laughs and says that Rooter can be very persuasive. When I ask him what he means by that, he tells me to ask the man with the plan.

"So, Randy says you," I poke him in the chest playfully, "are very persuasive. Care to tell me a little about that?"

Rooter shrugs. "I convinced a couple of your co-workers to work in your place. Hannah and Emily, I think their names were."

Randy said he was "persuasive." He had to have been extremely convincing. Hannah and Emily aren't my biggest fans. They wouldn't agree to work for me if I begged them. I know this because I've begged them in the past. "Exactly how did you convince them?" I fold my arms across my chest.

Rooter rubs the back of his neck, nervous to tell me. "I'm paying them."

"*You're* paying them?" I ask confused. "Why isn't Randy paying them?"

"He is." He clears his throat. "I agreed to double their earnings for each night."

He's doing what? "Oh my God, Rooter. You can't do that. They could earn as much as four hundred bucks each!"

He shrugs as though it's no big deal. "No worries, babe. We need this time away together. I don't care what it costs."

I laugh nervously. "You're crazy. I can't believe you did that."

Actually, when I think about it, I can. Nothing Rooter does surprises me. I should know this by now.

"Do you remember me telling you there's very little I wouldn't do for you?" He squeezes my thigh and nuzzles my neck.

I nod. Of course I remember. But I never expected anything like this; paying two girls—what will likely amount to hundreds of dollars—to work for me so he can take me who knows where to do who knows what. And knowing him it will be something extravagant.

"I'm trying to make things right so we can get back on track," he says and brings his lips to mine for a gentle, loving kiss. "I never want you to doubt your importance to me. You are priceless."

I gasp. *Did he really just say that?* This is the Rooter I'm crazy about. The one looking at me as though I am the most prized possession in the entire world. I've missed him. "I don't know what to say."

"Don't say anything." He smacks my ass and chuckles. "Go pack a bag woman. We need to get on the road."

I'm not sure which I like better, romantic or playful Rooter. Each is equally charming. "We're leaving tonight?" If I'd known I would've done laundry today.

He looks at the clock. "Yep, and we need to get going."

I start up the stairs to pack and Rooter follows me. "Don't you need to pack?" I ask.

He cocks his head to the side as if I should already know the answer. "I packed yesterday. All I need to do is load it into the truck."

"Oh." Of course he's packed. "What should I pack? I don't even know where we're going."

"It's a surprise. All I'll say is to pack that yellow bikini you were wearing the day we met." He winks and my heart flutters.

"That doesn't help much."

"Don't worry about it." He waves in the air nonchalantly. "If you need something when we're there, we'll buy it."

I stare at him with wide eyes. "You are too much."

"No, I'm not." He shakes his head and suddenly looks almost sad. "Sophie, there's no such thing as too much when it comes to you and from here on out, I'm going to prove it."

Most Beautiful Thing

After driving north for a little over two hours, a cheerful sign welcomes us to Ambrose, population 3,163. We drive through the "Downtown" which consists of three two story buildings, a tiny post office, a bank, and a diner called Pa's. Pa's is crammed with smiling joyous people.

During the drive here, Rooter kept looking at me with a silly, happy grin. He's so excited about wherever he's taking us. His hand rests on my thigh rubbing small circles with his thumb. At this moment, I am completely at peace.

Rooter removes his phone from his back pocket and makes a call. He tells whoever is on the other end we'll be there soon.

Once we've made it through downtown, he makes a left at a stop sign onto a gravel road. The road is tree lined with gated driveways leading to houses which are hidden from view. We follow the road for ten minutes until we come to the end and must choose to either turn left or right. In front of us is a mountainous hill, also tree covered. Rooter turns right followed by a quick left to an uphill winding road. When we make it to the top of the hill I see the expanse of Lake Michigan.

The sun hangs low in the sky casting an orange tint on everything. Along the road are extravagant homes with perfectly manicured lawns. I roll down my window and inhale the fresh lake air.

About a quarter mile down the road, Rooter pulls into a brick driveway. Sitting before us is a quaint, yet stunning white cottage style house with red shutters and a wrap-around porch with thick pillars. The evening sun is streaming in from the back windows to the front. We pull to a stop next to a red Mercedes and Rooter kills the engine.

"Welcome home, babe," he says and I gasp. "For the next three days anyway."

It suddenly occurs to me why Rooter brought me here. When we first started seeing each other, we had a conversation about dream houses. This house fits my description perfectly.

"We're staying *here*?"

"Yep," he leans over and gives me a quick kiss. "Wait until you see the back."

"You've been here?"

He nods eagerly. "I rode up the day before yesterday to check it out." He opens his door. "Stay here a minute."

Rooter jogs to the front porch and is met by an older, portly blonde woman. They talk briefly and she hands him a set of keys. He walks her to the truck and helps me out.

"Ella, this is Sophie," he says with a proud smile. His arm enfolds my waist. "Sophie, this is Ella, the owner of the house."

I extend my hand to her with a smile. "Nice to meet you, Ella. The house is beautiful."

"Thank you." She smiles, revealing a crooked incisor. "I hope you have a lovely stay."

"I'm sure we will," I tell her.

"I'll get out of your hair." She turns to Rooter. "If you need anything, please call me. My phone is on twenty four hours a day."

Once Ella pulls out of the driveway, we stroll hand in hand to the front porch. After opening the door, he steps aside allowing me to enter first. When I do, I can't believe my eyes. The place is exquisite with dark wood floors, light furniture, and a high vaulted ceiling. It's decorated in a lake and nautical theme.

I amble to the oversized white couch and run my fingers over the supple material. It feels every bit as expensive as it looks. In front of the couch is a great, matching ottoman, and on it lies a spread of all different magazines ranging from gossip rags to lakeside living and gardening. On the end table is a lamp and a bowl of black and white rocks. If I was to build my dream home, this would definitely be it. I turn to Rooter and jump up and down.

"I can't believe you brought me here."

"You like it?" He makes his way to me with a hopeful expression.

I wrap my arms around his neck. "It's amazing, Rooter. Thank you."

"You deserve this, especially after everything…"

I shush him and place my index finger against his lips. "Let's not talk about any of that."

I gently draw his face to mine for a kiss. His hands that were resting on my hips snake around my waist and pull me flush against him. His lips tenderly meet mine. First he kisses my top lip and then the bottom, pulling it into his mouth, prompting me to part my lips. I love the taste of his kiss. The way his tongue slowly glides against mine makes me weak. My hands slide into his soft hair and I press my body firmly against his. Both of his hands slide down my back and he grips my ass. The kiss turns into heated passion. He groans huskily and swiftly pulls away. Fire dances in his dark chocolate eyes.

"We need to stop," he says, breathless.

"No, we don't." I pull him back by the waist of his jeans. My finger grazes the skin just above edge of the denim. Feeling wanton, I lick my lips. *I want to taste him.*

Rooter flashes his perfect panty dropping grin. "Remember what I said on our first date about anticipation?"

"You're *not* playing that game with me again." I tug at his belt.

He chuckles and takes my hand into his. "It's not a game, babe. I'm not going to put my hands on you again until I know it's right, and the moment is perfect."

"Fine, don't put your hands on me. I'll put mine on you," I say and caress his ass with my free hand. He must be trying to kill me.

"You'll thank me later."

"I doubt it," I pout.

Rooter guides me through the living room and the kitchen to a pair of french doors leading to the sprawling backyard. The deck is expansive and is butted up to an in-ground pool and jacuzzi. To the right is a covered outdoor kitchen and dining area. We walk around the pool to the yard, and follow a stone path to a set of long stairs which lead to the beach below.

"We have our own private beach," he beams, "a boat, and a pair of jet skis." My mouth hits the ground as he continues. "You once said you wanted to try paddle boarding. There's two of those as well."

"Rooter, this is beyond perfect." I could burst into happy tears at any moment.

"But it gets better," he smirks.

"I don't know how it possibly could."

"Notice how my phone hasn't rung since we got on the road?"

Actually, yeah, I had noticed, but I didn't dare mention it for fear of jinxing my good luck. I nod in response.

He pulls a phone from his back pocket and shows it to me. It's not his usual phone. "This is a burner. Only my mom and pop have the number. I left my phone with them."

I squeal and throw my arms around his neck. Forget the house, the pool, and boat. Those have nothing on this. I would've been happy with him just getting rid of his phone. "Oh my God! Rooter, you do not understand what this means to me."

"Yeah, I do," he chuckles at my exuberance and pulls away. He places his callused hands on both sides of my face and stares lovingly into my eyes. "Babe, the next three days are for you and me alone. No world. No distractions. Just the two of us."

He places a featherlike kiss on my forehead, the tip of my nose, and lastly on my lips. I drape my arms around his waist and hook my fingers through his belt loops. All the tension and stress of the previous week washes away as I stand here gazing into his eyes. He tilts his head to the side and brings his lips to mine once again. His kiss is passionate, yet controlled, and he continues to caress my face as his skillful tongue dances with mine. My hands wander until they find themselves beneath his shirt. They trace the lines of his thick abdominal muscles and his sexy V. Rooter lets out a husky moan and I press my body against his. He's keeping the kiss slow and controlled, though he's not fooling me. I can feel his hardness against my belly. He's every bit as desirous as I am.

He pulls away, his chest heaving, and leans his forehead on mine. "You're not going to make this easy for me, are you?"

I shake my head. "No way."

Rooter kisses the tip of my nose again. "Come on, let's go see the rest of the house."

"How about a drink to celebrate," I suggest once we're back in the house. A drink sounds good, but the real reason I'm suggesting it is in hopes it will lessen Rooter's resolve to wait. "I wonder if there's anything here."

Rooter winks. "Already got you covered." He walks to a large wooden cabinet and opens the doors. Inside is every type of booze imaginable, including Jack Daniels, of course.

While he goes outside to get our bags, I make our drinks. Once he's back, I hand him his glass and hold up mine for a toast. "To the best three days ever."

"To making things right with my girl. And being a better boyfriend." After taking a sip, Rooter holds his hand out to me. "There's more to see."

He guides me through the rest of the house which is every bit as impressive as the living room and kitchen. He shows me a bedroom, a bathroom, movie room, and a billiards room before taking me to the master suite. We come to a stop in front of a pair of closed double doors. Rooter turns the handle and motions for me to step inside.

Simply stated, I've never seen anything so beautiful in my life. There are floor to ceiling windows galore. The wood floor in this room differs from the rest of the house. It's a deep brown, but it's shiny enough I can see my reflection in it. There's a massive wood burning fireplace with wood to burn. To the right, in front of the king size bed, is a flat screen television built into the wall with speakers for surround sound, and a built in book shelf. On the far side of the room, in front of the windows sits a plush, light gray sofa. All the wood in the room is dark and the furnishings light.

I set my drink on the bookshelf and throw myself onto the bed. When I do, I land on what I can only describe as a silken cloud. Rooter laughs and does the same, landing right next to me. He takes my hand and places a kiss on the palm.

"This is perfect." I turn to face him. "It's the most beautiful thing I've ever seen."

"It's not even close to the most beautiful thing I've ever seen," he says and climbs on top of me.

Rooter hovers over me and straddles my legs. I'd much rather he was between them. Images of our make-out sessions flash in my mind. God how I want to feel him between my legs, pressing himself into me over and over again until I'm left screaming his name. I want to feel his tongue on my skin and his fingers… My clit throbs at the thought.

"I want you," I murmur.

Rooter's mouth devours mine and just when I think he might give in to my request, he abruptly ends the kiss and rolls off of me. When

I stick out my bottom lip and pout, he chuckles and holds his hand out for me to take.

"How about a swim?" He suggests.

A swim? That's the last thing I want to do right now. All I want to do is rip his clothes off and touch, and lick, and play with every single centimeter of his rock hard body until the sun comes up.

"How about we stay right here," I pat the bed, "and play I'll show you mine?"

Rooter swallows. His resolve is so very thin. He shakes his head. "Not tonight, babe."

"Are you sure? I'm wearing that black and red bra and panty set you like so much," I tease.

He closes his eyes and takes a deep breath, steeling himself. "You're killing me," he groans.

"You know you want to." I bat my eyelashes and point at his growing bulge. "I can see how much you want to."

"Yes, I do. And we will. But not tonight." He takes my hand and pulls me upward. "Let's swim."

$\mathcal{A}$NTICIPATION

When I open my eyes, Rooter is no longer in the bed with me. I roll over to check the time and on the table is a cup of steaming hot coffee and a note: *Stay put. I'll be right back. R*

I pick up the coffee and take a sip. He made it with the perfect amount of my favorite creamer. I close my eyes and inhale the scent. This is heaven.

I'm halfway through my coffee when the bedroom door opens. Rooter carries a tray of food complete with a vase holding a single yellow rose. *Does he know yellow is my favorite?* He sets the tray in the middle of the bed and sits on the other side.

"Good morning." He smiles and leans in for a kiss.

"Breakfast in bed?" I press my hand to my chest, amazed.

"You like french toast, right?"

"I love it." *And I think I just fell in love with you.*

"Good," he sounds relieved and holds out a napkin for me.

He's dressed in a black and red Under Armour outfit making me wonder how long he's been up. "Have you been up long?"

"Just long enough to make breakfast." He hands me a fork and takes one for himself.

I cut a piece of the toast which is sprinkled with powdered sugar and topped with the perfect amount of maple syrup. I moan in delight the instant it enters my mouth. "This is delicious."

We go back and forth taking bites. I love watching Rooter eat. The way his mouth wraps around his fork and the way his strong jaw clenches as he chews. He's rugged and manly. Everything, and I mean everything, he does is sexy. And he's mine.

"What do you want to do today?" He asks and wipes his mouth.

"I think I want to try paddle boarding."

"Okay." He winks, and it sends a spasm straight to my core.

Good God. "New rule. You're not allowed to wink at anyone but me."

Rooter snickers. "Why?"

"Because it's ridiculously hot."

"Oh yeah?" He winks again, and it's like fire shooting straight to my center.

Holy hell he's gorgeous. "Like you don't know." As much as he does it, he must know. I cringe at the thought of how many girls he's gotten into his bed with that wink.

"Where'd you go just then?" He asks, all kidding aside, and tucks a stray lock of hair behind my ear. His warm eyes prod into mine.

"Nowhere." I smile, trying to play it off.

"Don't lie." His voice is tender with concern. "You went somewhere, and it didn't look like a very happy place."

I hesitate. I can't bring myself to tell him. "I'd rather not say."

"Sophie," he says and curls his fingers around mine, "I want you to be able to talk to me."

"I know I can talk to you. But sometimes I think things that are really... Stupid."

"Things like what?"

I sigh and look at the white comforter, too bashful to face him as I speak. "I sometimes find myself jealous of the girls before me."

I never realized how insecure I am until being with Rooter. I question everything about myself. Am I pretty enough? Funny enough? Smart enough? Am I too tall? Are my boobs too small? What does he see in me?

Rooter tilts my chin up to face him. His expression is thoughtful. "Babe, there's nothing to be jealous of. There was never anyone before you. It was just..." he trails off.

I nod because I know what he was going to say. It was just *sex*. But that doesn't make me feel much better.

"Sophie, you're the only one who has ever mattered to me. What you need to realize is," he waves his arms around and back and forth between us, "this has never happened with anyone else."

"I know that. But I still get jealous."

He scratches his head. "If it makes you feel better, I get jealous over guys who don't even exist."

My eyes go wide. "What?"

"Every day, especially lately," he slides his fingers through his hair, "I worry someone better will come along—someone without all the baggage I have—and that he'll steal you away from me."

His admission shocks me. Never in a million years would I imagine Rooter could ever be insecure. Even after the Hayden text incident. He's such an extremely confident person. But given his "baggage" and everything we've been through as of late, I can see why he feels that way.

"That's not even possible." I squeeze his hand. "You're the only guy I've ever wanted. Even with everything... I couldn't want anyone the way I want you."

Rooter leans in and caresses my cheek, stroking it lightly with his thumb. "And I have never and will never want anyone the way I want you."

After breakfast we suit up and hit the beach. Paddle boarding is not a success. For Rooter. The guy has zero balance, which takes me by surprise. The stiff wind doesn't help much either. He spends more time falling in the water and climbing back on the board than he does on the board. I don't have too much trouble. I only fall in twice when we first get going. Years of practicing yoga—although I haven't in a while—have surely helped with my balance.

After an hour of paddle boarding, we trade in the boards for the jet skis. I've been on jet skis before, but only as a passenger. Rooter offers for me to ride with him, but I want to try it on my own. He takes his time explaining all the buttons and how to work the throttle, warning me to press it gently to get going. Once I'm comfortable, we take off along the shoreline.

Rooter is a pro at jet skiing. He speeds, jumps waves, and throws himself off of his. Me on the other hand, not so much. I probably look like a grandma as I putter around on mine, but it's still fun and Rooter never makes fun of me. He's very attentive and stops to check on me every so often.

We spend the afternoon riding up and down the coast gawking at the mansions along the shore. At one point, we hop off and beach the skis so we can swim. On our way back to the cottage I gain a little courage and get up to forty miles per hour.

"That was so much fun." I beam at Rooter after we've secured the skis to the dock.

He laces his fingers with mine and is unusually quiet as we climb the stairs to the house.

"Did you have fun?" I ask, worried.

"Of course," he says and kisses the top of my hand.

"You're being quiet."

"Am I?"

"Yeah. Is everything okay?"

"Everything is perfect." His radiant smile eases my worry.

We take a couple more steps and I hear music playing. I don't think too much of it until we reach the top of the stairs and I see the reason for his silence.

The entire backyard has been transformed into a romantic oasis. It's decorated with what seems like thousands of red and white roses. Petals are scattered along the pathway leading to the deck where a magnificent table is set for a romantic dinner. A colossal, crystal vase of two dozen long stem red roses adorn the center of the table. There are candles everywhere although they're not yet lit. A man and woman are working in the outdoor kitchen preparing our dinner.

I clutch my chest and gasp at the sight. "Rooter, this is…" I trail off because there are no words to describe the beauty before me.

"Why don't you go inside and get a shower?" He suggests. "I need to talk to Vic and Martha."

When I enter the bedroom, I'm greeted by the sight of more roses and petals sprinkled throughout the room and on the bed. Also on the bed is a large white gift box topped with a red bow. On it is a note that reads: *Open Me, R.*

I take a deep breath and open the lid. Inside is a beautiful, white strapless gown. The skirt is layered and short in the front and long in the back and the top half is made of bunched satin. Also in the box is a pair of silver strappy heels, a gorgeous rhinestone necklace, and in the bottom of the box is a Victoria's Secret bag. Inside the bag is a white lace, strapless bustier and matching thong.

Rooter hasn't been waiting for a perfect moment to arise. He's been waiting for tonight. A night he has very carefully orchestrated.

When I step out of the shower, there's a note waiting for me on the bed: *Wear your hair down. I'll be waiting outside. R.* There's a heart drawn next to his initial. My pulse quickens at the thought of him waiting for me and in anticipation of what is yet to come. Although I hate to admit it, he was right about anticipation after all.

I hurry to the bathroom to apply my makeup and blow out my hair. I wish Miranda was here to help with the eyeshadow. I do my best, but am unable to recreate her famous smoky eyes. Instead of red lipstick, I go with an understated nude. Thankfully I brought my curling iron. I use it to turn my tresses into loose, flowing waves and top the look off with a little finishing spray.

I scurry to the bedroom to get dressed and stare at the bustier. I may enjoy fancy underwear, but I've never worn anything like this. The thought of having it on, and Rooter seeing me in it later, makes me giddy. It takes a few minutes, but eventually I'm able to get it secured comfortably. The dress is a little harder to manage having to zip it up on my own. Once I've finished adding the heels and necklace, I appraise myself in the mirror.

I feel like a princess and look like one too. The dress fits my body type perfectly, accentuating my long legs. The bustier even makes my girls appear bigger. *I might have to invest in more of these.* I twirl in front of the mirror and then take one last glance at my reflection.

The moment my hand clasps the door handle my heart races. Tonight is the night. Our night to make love for the first time. I want it to be perfect for both of us. I already know it'll be perfect for me. Rooter has put together such a beautiful evening. And he's outside waiting on me which is so incredibly exciting and yet nerve-wracking at the same time. I don't want him to be disappointed in me. He picked all of this out for me, and what if I don't look the way he hopes I will?

What if I'm no good in bed? He's used to being with girls like Candace who know what they're doing. I wonder if he's ever been with a virgin? Or a girl like me who seriously lacks experience. He could've gone to all this trouble just to be let down.

Get it together Sophie! I take a deep breath and turn the doorknob. I straighten my posture, open the door, step into the hallway and make my way to my man. *My man.* And tonight, he'll finally be mine in every way.

When I make it to the french doors leading to the deck, Rooter's sitting with his back to me. I open the door and step out onto the deck. Upon hearing my heels click on the wood, he stands and turns to face me. Not at all prepared for the vision standing before me, I come to a halt and gasp. He is in a tailored, charcoal gray suit paired with a black shirt and black tie. The fabric clings deliciously to his body, accentuating his muscular physique. We both stand and stare at one another for a long moment. Finally, he makes his way to me.

"You are gorgeous," he says and reaches for my hand.

"So are you," I breathe and eye him up and down.

"I clean up all right." He flashes a bashful smile and leads me to the table.

Rooter pulls out a chair for me and I spy his half-finished glass of whiskey.

"I think I need one of those," I say.

He fills the glass in front of me with ice from the silver canister on the table before pouring the Jack. He hands me the glass and then holds his up for a toast.

"To a perfect night with the most beautiful woman I've ever seen."

My heart skips a beat. I don't know how to follow that up. "To you, and what is sure to be the best night of my life."

Rooter and I each take a sip of our liquor without taking our eyes off of each other. I'm no expert on reading male desire, but with the way he's ogling me it's like he wants to have me for dinner.

The feeling is mutual. An hour ago I was famished, and as good as whatever Vic and Martha have prepared smells, I'm pretty sure I won't be able to eat a bite of it. My appetite for food has completely disappeared and has been replaced by a hunger for all that is Rooter.

"You're going to have to quit looking at me like that," he commands huskily and leans forward, "or we'll never make it through dinner."

"That's fine by me." I test him and take another sip of my Jack.

Passion flickers in his eyes. "You'll need to eat with what I have planned for you." He winks and I choke on my whiskey prompting him to chuckle. "You all right?"

"Mm-hmm." This is going to be a very, very long dinner.

I try to think of something to talk about, but all I can think about is Rooter naked, with me, in bed. I watch his muscles flex as he raises his glass to his lips. Those perfect, delicious lips. I need a taste.

"Do you like the dress?" He asks, breaking me from my spell.

"I love it." I graze the fabric with my fingertips.

He reaches down and captures a piece of the skirt between his fingers. The sleeves of his jacket squeeze his biceps. "When I saw it, I knew it was the one."

"When did you go shopping for all this?"

"On Monday." He leans back in his seat. "Isa went with me."

I shake my head. "You really went above and beyond with all of this." Then a question pops into my head. "But what if I hadn't been ready for... this?"

He traces the rim of his glass with his index finger. "Then tonight would've gone a little differently."

I raise my eyebrows. "You had a plan b?"

"I always have a plan b, babe." He takes a sip.

"Of course you do." I drink in the sight of him. "Would you have been disappointed?"

He shakes his head adamantly. "No. That's not what this trip is about, Sophie. It's about you and me reconnecting. If we make love that'll just be a bonus."

"If?" I raise an eyebrow.

"I never assume anything."

"And yet you've made all these arrangements." I wave my arms around and peer down at my dress recalling what's underneath it.

"I said I don't assume not that I don't hope." He winks, and it sets my skin ablaze.

BEST LAID PLANS

When Martha appears before us, I'm surprised. I would've thought they'd be gone by now. "Are you ready for dinner?" Rooter looks to me for the answer. I shake my head. "Not yet, Martha," he says with a smile.

"I'll check back in a few minutes."

"Thank you."

I swallow last sip of the liquor in my glass and Rooter pours me another.

"For a guy who's never had a girlfriend, you do romance very well."

For a fraction of a moment, his face turns a faint shade of red. "I can't take all the credit. I had help."

"Yeah?"

"After you told me I needed to make uninterrupted time for us, I came up with the idea of getting away. But I wanted to make it special." He strokes the top of my hand with his thumb. "I don't know what girls want so I went to my mom. We talked about you and the things you like. She helped me find this place and got me in touch with Vic and Martha. Isa gave me the idea for the dress."

"I'll be sure to thank them when we get back."

He smiles. "My mom loves you. Said you're the best thing to ever happen to me." He brushes a hand through his hair. "She was so pissed when I told her Candace is pregnant. She smacked me upside the head and cussed me out in Spanish." He chuckles, nervous.

I stare at him in silence, unsure know how to respond to that. To be honest, I don't want to talk about Candace or the baby tonight. Tonight is our night. Though something tells me he's bringing it up for a reason.

"Sophie, you were so mad. Honestly, I was afraid too much damage had been done. That things would never be the same with us. It scared the shit out of me. It still scares me."

"Things have changed," I admit and shift uncomfortably in my seat. "There's no denying that. But, my feelings for you haven't changed."

He breathes a sigh of relief. "We haven't been together very long, but I knew I wanted you a long time ago. I had it so bad that I'd sit in my room at night with the light out and watch you study in yours."

"Stalker," I accuse with a snicker. Not that I'm any better.

Rooter cocks his head to the side and shrugs before continuing. "I knew being with me wouldn't be easy for you, even without Candace and a kid. But I just couldn't stay away from you any longer."

I lace my fingers with his. "It took you long enough to change your mind."

"You deserve so much better than me. I struggle with that knowledge every day because I want better for you, but I want you for myself more."

"I already told you. You're all I want."

"I can't imagine why. But now I have you, I'll never let you go." His tone is light, but the intensity in his eyes conveys his meaning.

"I hope not."

Rooter shifts forward and motions for me to give him my other hand so that he's holding both. His eyes are piercing and when he speaks, his tone is intense. "I need to be real with you right now."

"Okay." I swallow.

"I'll try to give you everything you want and need. But life with me isn't going to be like the life you had planned."

"I don't care about those plans. I made them before I knew what I really wanted."

The corner of his lip curls in appreciation of my words, but he continues. "I'm going fuck up and piss you off... a lot."

I appreciate his candor and I know what he's doing. He's making sure I understand what I'm getting into before we take things any farther. What we have isn't a perfect fairytale. He has loads of baggage and he wants confirmation I won't bolt when the next catastrophe comes our way. "I'm beginning to figure that out. But even after everything that's happened, this is still where I want to be."

"Babe, I'll never do anything to purposely hurt or upset you. I'll never lie or cheat. But I am what I am. You understand?"

"Yeah. You're complicated."

He cocks his head to the side and sighs. "That's putting it mildly."

"Just promise me no more Candace's or surprise babies."

"I can definitely promise you that." Rooter looks down at the table and takes a deep breath. When he looks back at me his gaze is profound and unwavering. "You own me Sophia Noelle Holt. My heart is yours."

I gasp and I'm pretty sure my heart just skipped three beats. Rooter continues.

"I started falling for you way before that first conversation in your back yard. But that first moment I looked into your eyes, there was no going back. I'm in love with you."

A tear spills down my cheek and Rooter catches it with his thumb. "Rooter, I—" he puts his fingers on my lips to stop me.

"I don't know what you're getting ready to say, but if you're getting ready to tell me you love me, don't say it. Not yet. I haven't earned it."

I was going to tell him I love him. As crazy as it seems, I do. Even after everything and even though it seems way too soon, I do love him. Completely and irrevocably. He's the one for me. I can feel it in the depths of my being. After I nod he slowly lowers his fingers.

"We'll have tough days," he says, "but I promise to make more days like this for you."

"I don't expect days like this. All I wanted was a little time for you and me."

Martha clears her throat from a few feet away alerting us of her return.

"Ready to eat?" Rooter asks me. "I don't think the food will keep much longer."

Not at all. The man just told me he's in love with me. My heart feels as though it will explode from my chest. How the hell am I supposed to eat? "Sure."

Vic and Martha have prepared an exquisite meal: braised short ribs, garlic mashed potatoes, fresh bread, and a dark chocolate trifle for dessert. I eat a little of everything, but not nearly as much as I should. I'm just so overwhelmed.

Once we're finished, Martha clears our plates and she and Vic begin cleaning up. Rooter gets up from the table and peels off his jacket. His taut muscles flex underneath his fitted black shirt. He kicks off his shoes and crouches before me. His hands are hot as they gently unstrap and remove my sandals.

"Walk with me?" He stands and reaches out for my hand.

Walk? No I don't want to walk. I want you to throw me over your shoulder and carry me to the bedroom and... I slide my hand into his. "I'd love to."

The sun hangs low on the horizon as we stroll hand in hand to the beach. It'll be dark soon. We stand at the edge of the water and I close my eyes, enjoying the gentle breeze. I love the smell of the fresh lake air and the sensation of the sand between my toes. Even though my eyes are closed, I can sense Rooter watching me.

"Stop staring," I say and turn to see I'm right.

"I can't help it. I like seeing you happy and relaxed." He sits and motions for me to join him.

"I'll get my dress dirty."

"You won't be wearing it much longer anyway." He smirks causing my stomach to do somersaults.

I put my hands on my hips. "I thought you said you don't assume things."

"What?" He looks up, squinting from the low hanging sun. "All I said is you won't be wearing the dress much longer. That's not an assumption, it's a fact. It's not like you're going to sleep in it."

"Mm-hmm, we both know what you meant."

He tugs on my hand and pulls me into his lap. "Hey, I'm a guy. I can always hope."

"You don't have to hope." I gaze into his eyes. "I'm a sure thing."

Rooter rests his hands on my hip and nuzzles my neck. His breath is warm against my skin when he groans. "God you smell good."

I comb my fingers through his soft hair. "You didn't really want to go for a walk, did you?"

He regards me with hungry eyes and shakes his head. "Is it that obvious?"

I hold up my thumb and index finger about a quarter inch apart. "Just a little."

He chuckles. "Vic and Martha need time to clean up. I was going to try to play it cool like it was part of my plan to be romantic but…"

"You know what they say about anticipation," I toy with him.

"Fuck anticipation. This is agony." We both laugh.

"How long are we supposed to wait?"

"An hour," he groans and plays with the hem of my dress.

Great. We get to sit here for the next hour waiting to make love for the first time while trying not to think about it. This ought to be fun.

We spend the next fifty minutes mostly in silence. For me it's because I literally can't think about anything other than making love with Rooter. My brain is a pile of mush. I force myself to think of things to talk about and it all seems so trivial when compared to what is to come.

The sun has set in entirety and the only light we have comes from the lamps leading up our stairway. Rooter checks his phone for the time. He smiles and kisses the side of my head. His expression is a mixture of desire an angst.

After a few more minutes pass, he squeezes my hand and says we can make our way back to the house. We climb the stairs in silence, but every now and again steal glances at one another.

Once we reach the top of the stairs all signs of Martha and Vic are gone. The kitchen and dining table are clean. A few candles are still lit, but most of them have been blown out. On the table is a bottle of champagne sitting in a chiller alongside two long stem crystal glasses.

Rooter pours us each a glass and clinks his with mine. Neither of us says a word before tasting the sparkling wine. I've never had champagne before, so I'm not sure what to expect, especially since I'm not a fan of wine. I'm delightfully surprised at the flavor and nearly empty my glass.

"You really thought of everything."

"More?" He asks when he sees how much I drank.

"Please." I take another sip the moment he hands it to me. "This is really good."

He shows me the label: Dom Perignon. "It's supposed to be the best."

I've heard of Dom before and know it's expensive. "You're spoiling me."

"You deserve it." He winks, and it hits me like a wrecking ball right between my legs.

The sexual tension between us is palpable. Rooter licks his lips and his stare is penetrating. I squeeze my thighs together in an attempt to keep my desire at bay, but the pulsing between my legs remains. I watch his mouth curve around the glass as he takes another sip and long to feel it on my skin. I'm not sure how much longer I can keep this up.

Rooter takes a step forward and gazes directly into my eyes, his jaw is set. He cups my elbow and pulls me against him. "We're going to take this slow," he murmurs deep and raspy sending tingles from my head to my toes. "So slow that you'll be completely satisfied before you even feel me inside of you."

Oh my. My mouth parts and my eyes go wide. I'm not sure how to respond to that. But damn I like it when he talks dirty.

The First Time

Holy fuck, the way he's looking at me right now. My chest rises and falls with shallow breaths. He's so very close I can feel the heat radiating from his body. I don't know if I can take this slow. I want to rip his clothes off and lick every inch of his rock hard body. I need to see those sexy tattoos and chiseled abs right the hell now.

Rooter leans down and gives me a chaste, soft kiss and pulls away with a smirk, well aware of exactly what he's doing to me. He takes a half step back, tosses back the rest of his champagne and sets his glass on the table. He takes me by the hand and leads me at a seductively slow pace through the french doors into the dimly lit living room.

A slow, sensual instrumental song plays on the stereo. Rooter pulls my body against his and moves his hips in time to the slow song. "By the time this night is over, I'll have made love to every inch of your body."

He wraps one hand around the nape of my neck while the other travels slowly down my back to caress the curve of my ass. I roll my head to the side as he glides his tongue languidly across the sensitive skin of my neck. He backs away, removes his neck tie and opens the first two buttons on his shirt.

Keep going. Show me that gorgeous body.

He motions for me to finish my champagne and I quickly oblige, not the least bit gracefully. Once I've swallowed the last drop, he takes the glass and sets it on the table nearest us. He places his hands on my hips and resumes dancing with me, peppering my shoulder with soft kisses.

I drape my arms around his neck as we dance. His kisses move from my shoulder, to my collar bone, to my neck. When he reaches my earlobe he pulls it into his mouth and flicks it with his warm, wet tongue. I feel a spasm between my legs.

God the things I bet he can do with that tongue.

His mouth claims mine, demanding that I grant him entry. When I part my lips, his tongue slides deliciously into my mouth.

"You make me so hard." His fingers dig into my hips and he presses his erection against my belly.

"I can feel you," I say, breathless.

He flips me around so we're dancing with my back to his front. We sway side to side as his hands move from my hips up to my breasts. Keeping one hand on my chest, he uses the other to brush my hair to one side. He pulls away and then I feel the warmth of his tongue against the skin between my shoulder blades making its way up to my neck.

"You taste amazing," he groans. The heat from his hand brushes my skin as he tugs at the zipper of my dress. "I want to see you."

My heart is already racing, but my breath hitches at the thought of him seeing me in the lace lingerie.

Rooter backs away from me and pulls my zipper down unbearably slow. When the dress hits the floor he sucks in a breath. "Perfect."

He cups my bare ass and makes his way slowly to the front of me. Once he's facing me he pulls his bottom lip into his mouth and groans. He cups my left breast and flicks the nipple with his thumb. I close my eyes and shudder at the sensation of his warm touch through the thin material of the bustier.

"I love the color of your nipples," he declares and pinches me roughly, but I like it. "You're so fucking hot in this. I might not take it off."

Keeping it on sounds hot, but I yearn to feel his mouth on my bare skin. "But how will you put your mouth on me?"

"Don't worry," he says with hooded eyes. "I'm going to put my mouth on every millimeter of your body." He licks his lips and pinches my nipple again.

I moan in pleasure.

"You like that?" There's fire in his eyes and he pinches the other nipple.

I reach up and unfasten the buttons on his shirt. Once it's open I softly scrape my fingernails down his chest and abdomen to the waistline of his pants. I peel his shirt away from his skin, but I've forgotten to unbutton the cuffs. Without skipping a beat, Rooter does it for me and tosses it to the floor.

I trace the intricate design of the tattoo on his side with my index finger up to his shoulder and down his arm. His skin is warm to the touch. He takes my hand and tugs me against him, smashing my lips with his. For a moment we're a frenzy of tongues and hands, furiously exploring one another. But when my hand finds his erection he slows the kiss and takes my hands into his.

"Slow," he murmurs and kisses the top of my left hand. His breathing is erratic.

"But I want to touch you."

"And I want you to touch me, but if you do it now, I'll lose control."

"That's okay with me."

"Eager, are we?" He winks and a bolt of electricity shoots straight to my clit.

"Wink at me again and *I'll* lose control and you won't be able to stop me from putting my hands on you."

He arches a brow. "Is that right?" He winks again and my hands are pinned in his so I can't do anything about it.

"That's not fair," I pout. "Do you have any idea what that does to me?"

Rooter shakes his head but his rueful expression tells me he knows exactly what it does to me. "Why don't you tell me?"

Without giving me time to answer he turns my arm over and holds it up to his mouth. I throw my head back and shiver as he glides his tongue from the base of my wrist up to the inside of my elbow and then blows on the skin. His mouth is simply sinful.

"That's what I'm going to do to your entire body." He spins me around and points to the hallway leading to the bedroom. "Walk."

I obey, knowing he's following me and watching my ass with every step I take, making me feel bashful and brazen at the same time. I like that he's watching me, but I hope he likes what he sees.

"Turn around," he grunts upon reaching the bed. When I do I'm met by a pair of smoldering eyes. He definitely liked what he saw. His eyes drop to my chest and he grips his length. "Lay back on the bed."

I slide onto the bed and lay flat while Rooter unhooks his belt. I lick my lips in anticipation of seeing him naked. He slips his pants off and approaches me with his boxers still on, straining against his erection. He reaches for my foot and brings it to his lips and licks the instep. While it feels fantastic, my initial reaction is to pull away. He grips my ankle tightly and repeats the act.

"Oh!" I call out at the foreign sensation.

He crawls onto the bed and his mouth moves to my calf and he continues to lick and kiss all the way up to my inner thigh. "You taste so good, babe."

Rooter flips me over and before I know it, I feel the warm wetness of his mouth on my right ass cheek. He playfully bites and kisses the skin before moving to the other side. He places a trail of wet kisses down my leg to that foot's instep where he licks me once again.

"Does that feel good?" He asks in a raspy voice.

"So good," I pant.

He rolls me over and stares at me with hungry eyes. Leisurely, he crawls between my legs, presses himself into me and groans. He takes my left arm and nips and licks it all the way to my shoulder, across my collar bone to the other shoulder and arm. The man meant it when he said he was going to make love to every inch of my body.

"You're beautiful, Sophie," he rasps through ragged breaths.

Rooter lifts my hands above my head and begins to untie the bustier. By the time he gets to the end of the laces he seems as impatient to get his hands on me as I am to have them on me. Once the bustier is open, he places his right hand on the skin between my breasts and leans in to give me a wet kiss. His hand slides from my chest, down my stomach and back up before cupping my left breast. I arch my back in response as he plays with my nipple, twisting it gently between his thumb and index finger turning it into a stiff peak.

"I love how you respond to my touch," he murmurs before taking it into his mouth.

I cry out the instant his oh so talented tongue touches my delicate flesh. It swirls around and around as he nips and sucks until I can barely take anymore. And then he pulls away and blows cool air onto the skin giving me a chill. He leans down and roughly sucks the skin below my nipple to leave his mark. Once he's finished with that breast, he moves to the other. He looks up to see me watching him as he swipes his tongue across my pert nipple.

I writhe beneath him as he places a series of wet and dry kisses down my belly to the top of my panties. *Oh my God.* No longer able to resist, I lower my hands and rake my fingers through his silky hair. My body quivers in anticipation of feeling his hands and his mouth on my most sensitive spot. He smirks at me when he lifts my legs and kisses my inner thigh. My legs go slack as he grazes the delicate skin right next to my center, getting dangerously close to the fabric of my thong. I breathe in and out rapidly, desperate for that intimate contact.

"Touch me, please," I beg, unable to take another second of this torment.

He bows down and flicks his tongue against the skin next to the fringe of my panties. I whimper, a mixture of pleasure and desperation from the erotic sensation. If he just moved his tongue an inch to the left it would be right where I yearn for it to be. When he finally shifts his face to the left and presses against my entrance and inhales I nearly lose my mind. His face. Is. Right. *There*. Only a thin strip of cloth blocks his mouth from touching my sensitive skin.

"You smell so fucking good," he murmurs. "I bet you taste even better.

Using his thumb, he strokes my covered slit up and down causing me to cry out. I'm panting as he hooks his fingers on each side of my thong and pulls it down my legs.

This is really happening.

On his way back up he sprinkles my leg with kisses wet and dry and strokes the inside of my thighs before spreading them wide. There's a carnal hunger in his eyes as he gazes at my exposed pink flesh. He licks his lips and then looks into my eyes as though seeking permission.

"Please," I whisper.

He begins by gently stroking the skin on the outside of my entrance and works his way inward. Nothing could possibly prepare me for the sensation of his fingers coming into contact with the most delicate part of me. My back arches off of the bed when his thumb finds and circles my clit again, and again.

"You're so wet, babe," he rasps and continues to play with me, up and down and around.

My eyes screw shut and my legs begin to quiver as pressure mounts in my center. "Rooter," I moan. I'm teetering right on the edge when his fingers stop moving. "Please don't stop."

"Look in my eyes, babe," he speaks lovingly. When I do, he's wearing a serious expression. "When we're making love, I want you to call me Jace."

I pull my eyebrows together in confusion. Our eyes are locked when he reaches out and strokes my clit with his thumb. He dips just the tip of a finger into my entrance but it's enough to make me cry out in ecstasy.

"I want to hear you say my name, baby," he coos and leans his face into me.

And then his tongue is. On. My. Clit.

"Jace!" I squeeze my eyes shut and bask in the sensation of his tongue swirling around and around.

I grip his head and scream his name again as he glides his tongue up and down my wet slit. He works my swollen nub with his thumb and delves his tongue into me. A guttural groan escapes my lips as he brings me closer and closer to my peak, working me with his hand and his mouth. His glorious fucking mouth. Nothing has ever felt as good as his wet, velvety tongue dipping inside me.

Slight shockwaves begin to hit me as I become dangerously close to going off. He grips my outer thighs as he slows his pace and rubs and licks leisurely. I chant his name again and again. Everything falls away but the sensation of his tongue and thumb working me as I fall apart.

I lay for a moment with my hand on my chest, gasping for air, unable to fully comprehend the enormity of what I just experienced. When I finally come to, Rooter is laying alongside me with a proud smile on his glistening lips. I can't speak. I can't move.

He rolls on top of me and presses his cock between my legs. The only thing stopping him from entering me is the cotton of his boxers. He brushes his wet lips against mine and licks the seam, asking for entry. When his tongue finds mine it tastes of me, but I don't mind. He kisses me slow and tender, rolling his tongue along mine. I wrap my legs around his waist and ghost my fingertips up and down his back as we continue our sensual kiss.

Rooter pulls away and sits on his knees before me. My eyes move with his hands as he reaches down and grips his erection. My sex clenches with need as I watch him stroke his cotton covered length. His hand moves to the elastic of his boxers and he pulls the material down at an achingly slow pace. He's teasing me, knowing how I yearn to see him. Finally, his hard shaft springs forward. With his free hand he reaches for mine and places it around his girth. He hisses as he guides my hand up and down the smooth skin.

"Fuck that feels good," he grunts and closes his eyes continuing to move my hand up and down his length. After a few more strokes, he crawls off the bed and removes his boxers.

I marvel at the magnificence of his naked body. His broad shoulders, muscular arms and thick thighs are pure perfection.

Rooter slinks next to me and lies on his back, his dick standing proud. He reaches for my hand again and places it around the brick hard shaft. He never takes his eyes off of me as I stroke him the way he showed me. Pre-cum appears on the tip and I instinctively lower my head and swipe my tongue across the slit to taste it. He tastes good; salty and all man. I've never performed oral sex, but I've seen it done on porn and Miranda has given me lots of advice on the topic.

Rooter sucks in a breath and mutters a curse as I swirl my tongue around the head of his dick before taking it into my mouth. I pull back and lick him from the base back to the sensitive spot beneath the tip and flick back and forth causing him to buck off the bed.

"Fuck yeah," he groans and grabs a fistful of my hair.

His cock becomes even more engorged as I work him, gripping his shaft as I suck him up and down. With my free hand, I cup his balls and massage gently—a tip from Miranda. I glance up to make eye contact as I fondle him.

"I love the way your lips look wrapped around me." He throws his head back and groans. His cock twitches, warning me he's getting close. I stop sucking but continue to play with his balls.

"You taste so good," I murmur, proud of the pleasure I was able to give him. Not too bad for a novice.

"That was amazing, babe." Rooter pants for air. "Come here." He rolls to his side and pulls me against him.

His lips find mine and kiss me passionately. His hands wind into my hair as his mouth moves against mine. When I reach down and cup his firm ass, he rolls on top of me and seats himself between my legs. It would be so easy for him to slide into me. Instead, he rolls his hips and grinds himself against my bare flesh, up and down and around and around.

"I can make you come this way," he teases and nips at my neck.

"I know."

He pulls back to gaze in my eyes, but his hips continue to move. "I need to be inside you. Are you ready?"

"Yes."

Yearning swims in his deep brown eyes. He leans down and plants a sweet kiss on my lips before reaching over to the nightstand. He brings the foil packet to his mouth and winks as he rips it open with his teeth. My sex clenches at the sight of him rolling it onto his swollen length.

"Look at me, Sophie." His voice is tender and his hand gently caresses my belly.

When I peer up I'm met by soft, caring eyes.

"If at any time you're uncomfortable or want me to stop, tell me. Okay?"

I nod.

"I need the words, babe."

"I'll tell you."

He leans down and gives me a slow, loving kiss. He places the tip of his hardness at my entrance and pauses to look into my eyes. I grip his biceps and close my eyes as he slowly pushes in until he's seated fully inside me, filling me completely.

"You okay?" He asks and kisses my cheek.

It's uncomfortable, but not overly painful. It's a pleasurable discomfort. "I'm okay." I give him a reassuring smile.

Rooter pulls back and pushes in again at the same languid pace with which he entered me. I bite my lower lip and moan, prompting him to move again, but at a faster speed.

"You feel so good," he grunts and rocks into me with a bit more force.

I can tell he's straining to hold back. When he pulls back again I grab his ass and guide him forcefully back into me. "You don't have to be careful. I'm okay."

Rooter moans and moves inside of me with faster, stronger thrusts. He finds a delicious rhythm, pushing into me again and again and then rolls his hips, circling his hardness inside of me.

"You're so tight," he groans.

I arch my back, pressing my nipples against his chest prompting him to lean down and suck them. Our bodies move together as though they've done dance this a thousand times. He picks up the pace and rocks into me harder and faster until our bodies are slick with sweat. My breasts bounce up and down as I meet him thrust for thrust. His lips brush my jaw and his breath is warm against my skin. I drag my fingers up his back.

"Rooter," I call out as I feel my climax rising.

"Jace. Call me Jace, baby."

"Jace," I say and shudder, so very close to the brink.

"Come for me baby." He rocks into me. "I want to feel you come around my cock."

His dirty talk sends me flying over the edge. My sex tightens around his shaft and I shout his name as I come apart in his arms.

"Fuck, I'm going to come. You're gonna make me come, babe." Rooter stops thrusting and I feel him pulse inside me. His body trembles and he groans with his release. Several moments later he collapses on top of me, barely able to hold his weight up with his elbows.

We both lay together long enough to catch our breath. Rooter kisses my cheek before rolling off of me and gives me a "Yeah, that's right" grin.

BACK TO REALITY

My eyes are trained on Rooter's tight ass as he goes to the bathroom to discard of the condom. Even though he's no longer inside me, I can still feel him; a delicious reminder of what just took place. I'd often wondered what my first time would be like and the way he just made love to me far exceeds my fantasies.

Technically, it wasn't my first time, but it would've been had I been given a choice.

When he returns and crawls into the bed beside me I turn to face him. "That was..." I pause to come up with the right word to describe the experience. "There aren't words to describe how good that was."

He strokes my cheek. "Babe, you did so good."

I arch a brow. Had he expected me to suck?

"I don't mean to be condescending," he recovers and kisses my lips reassuringly. "With what you've been through, I didn't know if you'd freak out or..."

I nod, understanding his meaning.

"You didn't seem scared or nervous at all."

"I wasn't. I trust you."

He smiles. "I love you, babe."

I want to say it back because I love him so damn much. I want to scream it from the rooftop so that everyone knows. But he doesn't want me to yet. So instead, I say the next thing that comes to my mind. "I wish you had been my first."

"I was." He pulls me snug against him. "I was the first man to make love to you."

His words comfort and touch me deeply because what we did was indeed making love. It wasn't just sex. With every touch and every kiss, he gave as much as he took. He gave more.

"Yes, you were." I brush my lips across his chest.

"And I'll be the last." He plants a kiss on the top of my head. After a moment he speaks again. "You're the only one I've ever made love to, Sophie."

Tears threaten to spill from my eyes, but I keep them at bay. Once the emotion subsides, I pull back and look at him. "You surprised me when you told me to call you Jace."

He clears his throat and pauses before responding. "I surprised myself."

"Did you like it when I called you Jace?"

His adam's apple bobs up and down when he swallows. "Yeah. A lot."

"Should I call you by that name all the time?"

He shakes his head. "Only when we're making love, babe."

God I love it when he says making love.

I prop myself up on my elbow. "If you don't like the name, why do you want me to use it when we're making love?"

He rolls onto his back and rests a hand on his chest. "It's not that I don't like the name. It just represents a different side of me."

"A different side?"

"Jace is the person I want to be for you. Rooter is who I am."

"That's confusing." I pull my brows together.

He turns to face me with a sincere expression. "Jace is pre-club. Innocent. Good. Like you."

"I don't need you to be innocent."

"I know." He strokes my cheek and gazes into my eyes.

My mind goes back to a conversation we had on our first date when he said I had to earn the right to know the story of how he got his road name. "So, are you ever going to tell me how you got the name, Rooter? Have I earned that," I make air quotations, "privileged information?"

He chuckles and sweeps his hand through his hair. "I was hoping you'd forgotten about that."

"No chance." I giggle and playfully poke him in the side.

"I don't think this is the time for that discussion." He pulls me onto his chest and plays with my hair.

"Why not?"

"Because I want to lay here and bask in the afterglow of making love to my woman."

"Yeah right," I cackle and push away to look at him. "You don't want me to know how you got the name."

He closes his eyes and grumbles, "You're right."

My curiosity just shot up a hundred percent. "Now you have to tell me."

His face turns bright red, and he sighs. "Keep in mind this was years ago."

"Okay."

He clears his throat. "Bear's dad is Australian and in Australia rooting means fu—having sex. When I first got into the club, they were always finding me in the back room…" His voice trails off and he scratches his head. "One day, Bear was looking for me and he asked his pop where I was. His pop told him I was in the back room pouring the root to some girl. Bear knocked on the door and said, "Hey, Rooter we need to get going." It stuck with the guys and I've been Rooter ever since."

"That's not the story I was expecting."

"I bet not." We're both quiet a moment. "What were you expecting?"

"Well, when you say Rooter the first thing that comes to mind, for me anyway, is Roto-Rooter. So I always thought you got the name because you caused a lot of plumbing trouble." I burst out laughing.

Rooter is clearly mortified. "What? Please tell me that's not what you've been thinking this entire time."

I laugh even louder.

"Oh my God," he groans. "I should've told you the truth a long time ago."

"I think I prefer the Roto-Rooter story," I admit.

He rubs his face. "Sophie, I'm not the same guy I was back then. You believe that don't you?"

"I do. But if you're not that guy anymore, why continue to go by the name?"

"It's a part of me now. And while it may not have the same connotation it used to... Let me put it this way, what we just did, I plan on doing a lot more of." He winks. "Therefore, I am, in fact, still Rooter."

"And yet, you don't want me to call you Rooter while we do it. Makes sense," I say sarcastically and we both laugh.

For the next two days we do nothing but make love, only pausing to eat and shower. It turns out I like sex. A lot. No, I don't like it. I. Love. It. The more I have, the more I want. Forget the pool, the beach, the boat, and the jet skis. I have no interest in any of that. The hot tub, however, has definitely come in handy. If I had it my way Rooter would live naked, ready and willing to fulfill my every desire.

After cleaning the cottage and putting fresh sheets on the bed, we get in the truck to make the trip back home. I don't want to go back. With every mile tension builds in my neck.

We've spent the last three days in a perfect little bubble of happiness. Now we're on our way back to a very complicated reality.

The good thing is, I feel closer to Rooter than I ever have. We finally feel like a solid unit. It's us against the world and all it will try to throw at us.

"I never thought I'd say this," Rooter adjusts himself in the seat next to me, "but babe, I think I need a couple days off. My junk feels like hamburger."

I giggle. "What about your tongue? That still intact?" It got just as much of a workout as his dick.

His eyes go wide. "Do you ever get enough?"

"I'm thinking not."

"Damn woman," he chuckles. "Am I not doing the job well enough?"

I recall last night when he had me bent over the kitchen counter, pulling my hair as he slammed into me as hard as he was able. My clit throbs at the thought. It was the fourth time we'd had sex that day.

"The problem isn't you not doing it well enough. It's that you do it too well."

"Well, that I can't help." He winks.

I point at this face. "See that right there is what gets you in to trouble."

He smirks. "Dually noted."

He takes my hand and I lean back into my seat. I lay my head back and take a deep breath. We'll be home in a little over an hour. "I don't want to go home."

"It'll be okay, babe."

"I just don't..."

He brushes his thumb over my knuckles. "Don't what?"

"We've come so far these past few days. We're in a really good place and I'm afraid something will ruin it."

"Look at me," he commands and I turn to face him. "Nothing can ruin this. It's you and me, Sophie. I won't let anything come between us."

Candace is a force to be reckoned with. And being that she hasn't seen or heard from him in days means she'll probably be completely smacked out of her mind when we return. He'll likely have a thousand messages demanding he get his ass over to see her or else.

When we pull into his parent's driveway to pick up Dopey and get his phone, Candace's car is there.

"You've got to be kidding me," I groan, none too happy.

Rooter slows the truck to a stop and closes his eyes. It's obvious that he's no happier about this than I am. "Here we go."

We walk hand in hand into the house. The moment we cross the threshold Candace is in our faces. Rooter steps in front of me to keep us separated. As per usual she's in her typical slutty attire, shorty shorts, tank top and a pair of clog heels. She might as well tattoo the word "stripper" on her forehead.

"What are you doing here Candace?"

"I'll answer that as soon as you tell me where the hell you've been!"

Rooter's family leaves the room to give us privacy. Isa turns and looks at me sympathetically before disappearing through the doorway.

"It's none of your business where I've been," he tells her.

She takes a small step forward and holds a hand to her chest. "Do you have any idea what I've been through these past few days?"

"Oh, please," I groan and roll my eyes.

"Shut the fuck up, bitch!" She points at me. "This is none of your business."

"The hell it isn't!" I lunge forward, but Rooter grabs my arm and pulls me to his side.

"Stop it!" He snipes at us both. After a moment he speaks again. "What's going on Candace?"

"If you'd been here, you would know," she gripes and crosses her arms.

"I'm here now," his tone is gentle. "Tell me."

She sticks a hip out and shifts her weight to one foot. "I'm not talking to you with her around."

"Well, she's not going anywhere," he tells her. "So either talk or leave."

"That's how you talk to the mother of your unborn child?" She scoffs. "The child she almost lost yesterday because of the stress she's under?"

"What?" He freaks out.

"Yeah, that's right. While you were holed up in a hotel somewhere fucking your little princess," she waves in my direction, "I've been here trying not to lose our baby."

"What happened?" His concern is evident.

"I got fired because I've been too sick to work. Now I'm going to lose everything and be homeless. With all the stress I started cramping really bad and had a little spotting."

For some reason, I don't buy a single word of what she's saying, and it's not just because I don't like her. Everything about her screams liar. I knew she'd pull something like this when we got back.

"Jesus Candace." Rooter rakes a hand through his hair. He guides me over to sit next to him on the couch. Candace sits in a nearby chair.

"Did you go to the doctor? Is the baby all right?"

"You don't even give a shit about this baby. All you care about is her." Her voice is laced with venom.

"Of course I care about the baby. I'm sorry I wasn't here."

Great, now he'll regret going away with me. *Well played, bitch.*

She laughs, sarcastic. "Yeah, right."

"I mean it. I shouldn't have cut contact with you. It was wrong of me." His voice is cloaked in guilt. He sits hunched over with his elbows on his knees.

"Rooter," I start, "she's playing you. Do you really not see that?"

"You seriously need to mind your own business," Candace spews through gritted teeth.

"He is my business," I snarl and Rooter interrupts me before I can finish.

"Sophie, stop," he snaps.

But I don't listen. "You better stop with your fucking games!" I jump up from the couch and charge over to her. Rooter shoots up after me and grabs me by the arms.

Candace leans over and clutches her belly.

A BAD DAY

"Get her away from me!" Candace shouts.

"Goddamn it Sophie!" Rooter yells. "What are you doing?"

He rushes to Candace and crouches before her. Camilla, Isa, and Mick all come back into the room.

"What's going on?" Camilla asks, looking back and forth between me and Candace.

Candace points at me with one hand and keeps the other on her stomach. "She started to attack me!"

Everyone gapes at me, shocked. Everyone but Rooter. He hasn't taken his eyes off of Candace. I clutch the sides of my head unable to believe the scene before me.

"Get her out of here!" Candace shouts.

Rooter stands and Candace grabs him by the arm. "Don't leave me."

There are actual tears in her eyes. *Man, she's good.*

"I'm not leaving," he tells her and hands me his keys. "Take the truck home. I need to handle this."

I cross my arms. "I'm not going anywhere."

"Sophie," he whispers, "you need to go. Your being here is making things worse."

"How have I become the bad guy?"

"No one said that." He pinches the bridge of his nose and exhales sharply. "I can't have this conversation right now. Please, go home. We'll talk later."

I snatch the keys out of his hands. "Fine. But do me a favor and consider the fact that this is all an act to get your attention." I turn and glare at Candace. "Like everything else she's done."

Hours pass and I still haven't heard a word from Rooter. I'm dying to find out what happened after I left; what kind of bullshit guilt trip she's laid on him. About an hour ago I texted him asking him what's going on but didn't get a response. I keep analyzing the way he looked at me when I left. He was upset, for sure. But with me or with the situation in general?

I wasn't going to hit Candace. As much as I hate her for what she's done, I'd never hit a pregnant woman. But even I must admit the way I lunged at her would make anyone think I was going to. I groan and fling my head back on the couch.

Bear and Miranda are at my house so I'm waiting for Rooter at his house. The last thing I want to do is rehash the situation with them and I'm definitely not in the mood to see them all happy and lovey dovey with one another.

I turn the television on but can't concentrate on it. Rooter once told me he works out whenever he's angry or stressed out so I decide to give it a try. I go into his workout room, blast some hard rock and step onto the treadmill. After running two miles I'm bent over panting for breath. Yet I'm still as on edge as I was beforehand.

I look around the room in search of something else to try. His free weight bench sits across the room in the corner. Next to it is a set of hand weights ranging from ten to fifty pounds. I pick up the ten pound weight and do curls with my right arm. I get to ten and that arm wears out so I move to the other. So far I've found no relief and decide to do some of my regular exercises: three sets of twenty lunges on each leg, three sets of ten push-ups and my squat routine.

As luck would have it I'm more energized and pumped up than I was before working out. I turn off the stereo and go into Rooter's room and lie on the bed. I check my phone and still no call or text.

Come on, Rooter, call me already.

I turn on the television in his bedroom, but I don't know why. It has the same effect on me as before. Unable to sit still, I get up and mosey around his room. I'm not nosey nor am I one to snoop, but I'm bored as hell. I open the drawer to his nightstand and inspect the contents: a box of Magnum condoms, a motorcycle magazine, and a mystery novel. He always surprises me. I'd fully expected to find smut magazines.

I open the mystery novel and read. It doesn't take my mind completely off of the situation, but it helps. Somehow I simultaneously follow the story and think about Rooter, wondering when he's going to call.

By ten o'clock I still haven't heard from him which isn't like him at all. Either he's pissed at me or something bad happened with Candace and the baby. I'm not sure which is worse. I don't want him to be angry with me, but if something happens to the baby the guilt will eat him alive. He may not have planned on having a kid, but it would devastate him if something happened.

I text him: *Please call me. I'm worried.*

I hold the phone and stare at the screen praying for a response that never comes. By midnight I give up and turn out the light.

My eyes flutter open at seven twenty in the morning. The bed beside me is empty. I check my phone for a message even though I know there isn't one. I would've heard if he'd called or texted. Which he didn't.

This is bad.

I ponder whether to call him and decide against it. I've already left two messages. He knows I want him to call me. If he hasn't already done so there's a reason for it.

I decide to go to my house for a pot of coffee and a shower. When I get halfway down the stairs I hear snoring and snap my head toward the noise. Rooter is asleep on the couch. I stand and contemplate waking him up, but decide against it. Besides, I'm irritated he didn't get into bed with me.

He must be mad at me otherwise he would have.

Not wanting to wake him I try to tiptoe out of the room to the back door, but Dopey lunges at me and knocks my keys out of my hand.

"Sophie." Rooter jolts upright.

"Sorry, I was trying not to wake you up."

"Are you leaving?" He rubs his face.

"Yeah," I shift from foot to foot, unsure what to do. "I was going to get showered and let you sleep awhile longer."

"I'm up." He swings his legs over the side of the sofa.

"What time did you get in?" I ask and walk closer to where he sits.

"About three." He checks the time on his phone. "I didn't want to wake you so I stayed down here."

"You know I wouldn't have cared," I call him out on his lie.

He nods. "I was exhausted and didn't want to talk about what happened with Candace."

Great. So he was avoiding me. "How about now?"

"We should talk."

That doesn't sound good. I take a breath and sit next to him. "What happened? Is she okay?"

"She's really stressed out. Scared of losing the baby."

I roll my eyes. He can't be that gullible. "Don't you think she's exaggerating a little?"

He clenches his jaw and looks at me like I'm an asshole. "She's been sick, she's lost her job, and she's been cramping. So no, I don't think her freaking out over me being gone is exaggerating."

"She could be making up the cramping part," I point out.

He exhales harshly and shakes his head. "Could you give her the benefit of the doubt for once?"

My jaw goes slack. He can't be serious. "Excuse me for not trusting her after everything she's done. Did she even go to the doctor?"

He looks at me a moment before shaking his head.

"See!" I throw my hands in the air. "If there really was something wrong she'd have gone to the damn doctor."

"She thought everything would be okay once I got back and she could relax."

"Oh please," I groan. "And you buy that shit?"

"What choice do I have?"

I turn my entire body to face him, incredulous. "You're the father! Make her ass go to the doctor if something is wrong."

"I tried!" He shoots up and stares at me. "I spent the entire night trying to convince her."

"And it didn't work, did it?" I challenge and return his stare.

He looks to the window behind me and shakes his head, infinitesimally.

I jump up. "Of course it didn't because there's absolutely nothing the matter with her!"

"You know what?" He looks back at me. "I hope nothing is wrong with her. Do you have any idea what it would do to me if something happened to that kid, and I wasn't here?"

"Oh my god." I raise my eyebrows in disbelief. "Her guilt trip actually worked. She made you feel guilty for going away with me."

He sits on the couch with slumped shoulders and looks at the floor. "What I did was irresponsible. I left the mother of my child with no means of getting ahold of me."

Man, she did a number on him. He really feels guilty. I sit next to him on the couch and when I speak my voice is calm. "Your mother had your number. I'm sure she would've called you if she thought it was important."

He slaps his thighs, frustrated. "It's not up to my mom to decide what is and is not important."

So much for trying to be calm. "Camilla doesn't believe her shit either does she? That's why she didn't call you."

"Sophie," he sighs, "it doesn't matter if we believe her or not. If Candace says something is wrong and she needs me, I'm obligated to be there. Don't you get that?"

You're the one who doesn't get it. "As long as you're with me and not her, there will *always* be something wrong with her. Don't *you* get *that?*"

He rubs his face. "Fuck!" He kicks the side of the coffee table and sends it across the room. The dog yelps and trots to the far side of the room.

I flinch in reaction to his physical outburst and move away from the couch. "I knew this would happen. I knew she'd find a way to come between us when we got back. You said you wouldn't let it happen."

His phone rings. Thankfully it isn't Candace. He yanks it from his pocket and snarls into the phone. "What?" He listens to the caller. "I'm on my way."

"And now you have to go." Could our luck get any worse?

"It's the shop. There's a problem with a build." He stands up and reaches for my hand. "I'm sorry if I scared you."

"I wasn't scared." Surprised, but not scared.

He kisses the top of my hand and gives me a sad smile. "Remember those bad days I said we would have?"

I nod and look to the floor trying not to cry.

"This is one of them." He tilts my chin up with his index finger. His eyes are soft and sincere. "But it doesn't mean I'm going to let anything come between us. I love you, Sophie. Nothing will change that."

A lone tear spills down my cheek.

When we crawl into his bed later that night he pulls me against his chest and kisses the top of my head. I know it isn't a good time to ask, but I'm desperate for the answer to a burning question.

"Do you regret going away?"

He's quiet for a moment. "Yes and no. You and I needed the time together and I'm glad we had it, but I regret what it caused."

"Do you wish we hadn't gone?"

"No," he rakes his fingers through my hair, "but I wish I'd handled it different."

He wishes he hadn't cut communication with Candace. "It's like we took one step forward and three steps back."

He tilts my face up to look at him. "You and I will be fine, babe. I promise."

"What about Candace? Are you going to be back to running to her every time she calls?"

He looks up at the ceiling and sighs. "I'm just going to take it call by call, day by day. That's all I can do."

Choosing Us

The next two days pass in a haze. Rooter works during the day, I work at night. We exchange texts throughout the day and see each other when I get home. We don't talk about Candace or much of anything else for that matter. At night, we crawl into bed and he holds me until I fall asleep, then he wakes up at six for work and the day starts all over again.

We haven't made love since we've been back home. We're both too mentally, emotionally, and physically exhausted to do anything more than just... be.

I don't know what I'd do without Ryan. He listens and holds me as I scream and cry. He supports whatever decision I make, but he thinks Rooter and I need to take time apart to assess whether being together is really worth the pain and frustration. Will things ever get better where Candace is concerned? Because if not we better either learn to like our current predicament or cut ties and go our separate ways.

Candace will be a staple in Rooter's life forever now that they're having a kid together. Not to mention the history they have. As much as he and I care for one another, we're new to each other. They've known each other for years. Realistically, I need to accept the possibility that their bond is stronger than his and mine.

But I am stubborn. I am resolute. Rooter is mine and I will not let her take him away from me. Not without one hell of a fight, anyway. I've experienced how good he and I are together. We fit perfectly together in every way.

I wrack my brain trying to come up with a solution or at least a way to level the field with Candace. I find myself wishing she'd lose the baby and I hate myself for it, but it might very well be the only way to get rid of her. I've also had the crazy notion of getting pregnant myself. I'd never do that. I'm not ready to be a mom. But the thought has occurred to me in my moments of desperation.

I've had a lot of desperate moments these past two days.

Ryan says if I refuse to take a break I need to sit back and let the situation play itself out. Let Rooter deal with Candace and the pregnancy and do my own thing when he's not around. It'll work out the way it's meant to. Either we'll end up together or we won't.

But it's not in me to sit back and let things happen around me. I detest the feeling of powerlessness. However, that's exactly what I am here; completely and utterly powerless.

But I'm a fighter. I've had to fight my entire life. It's what I know best. So it's what I'm going to do.

I text Rooter: *I need some Jace time. 6:00. You, me, Jack, and pasta. S*

He texts back almost immediately: *Sounds great babe. Luv u.*

Rooter walks through the door eight minutes before six with frustration etched into his face. He throws his cut to the floor and pulls me into his arms. "Coming home to you is the only thing that got me through this day."

"Everything okay?" I ask, wondering if his agitation has anything to do with her.

"It's fine now." He strokes the sides of my face and kisses me tenderly. "It smells fantastic in here."

I go to the counter and fill a rocks glass with whiskey and hand it to him. "I made chicken alfredo. Garlic bread is in the oven. I also made a salad."

"Sounds perfect. I'm starved." He takes a long swig of the whiskey and leans against the counter.

I pull the bread out of the oven and make our plates. Rooter holds my hand while we eat though he doesn't say much. He asks about my day and listens as I tell him about my lunch with Ryan, but he's distracted. His mind is elsewhere. Something's wrong.

"Are you sure everything is okay?" I ask.

He looks at me. Whatever it is, he doesn't want to say. It must be about Candace.

"You can tell me," I encourage him and squeeze his hand.

"She went to the doctor today." He rubs the back of his neck. "She's still cramping and bleeding. Her blood pressure is through the roof. The baby is okay for now, but the doctor said absolutely no more stress or she could miscarry."

"I'm sorry." I mean it. I may hate Cand-ass but I'd never wish anything ill on an innocent baby.

"She's a wreck which isn't helping anything. She insists she needs me there with her. That it's the only way she'll get the stress under control."

I roll my eyes and start to speak but he continues.

"I realize part of it is her and her games, but I saw the paper from the doctor. This is real. I don't know what to do, babe."

"Were you with her before you came home?"

He nods.

"She probably wasn't too happy when you left."

He looks at his empty plate and shakes his head.

"And now you feel guilty."

He looks at me a moment. The answer is in his eyes.

"Do you think you should've stayed?" I ask, already knowing the answer.

He rubs his eyes with his thumb and index finger. "I feel split in two. I should do whatever I can to help the baby, but I don't want to risk losing you."

The last thing I want is for him to be torn between me and his baby. Now that I know she went to the doctor and something really is wrong, I can't be so selfish as to expect him to put me above the wellbeing of his unborn child. "If your being with me makes her so stressed that she miscarries... I can't let that happen."

"What are you saying?" His eyes go wide, stricken with panic.

"I'm saying you should go back there and get her settled down."

He breathes a sigh of relief and reaches for my hand. "Shit, you scared me."

"I'll clean this up and let Dopey out before I go home."

"You don't have to go home. Bear's there with Miranda and I seriously doubt they're playing scrabble."

Yeah. Because they get to have an actual relationship. I try to hide my envy. "I need to catch up on laundry. I can always put my iPod on."

"Do you want me to come over when I get back?"

I shake my head. "We could both use a good night's sleep."

Rooter leans forward and rests his forehead on his clasped hands. "You're mad."

"I promise I'm not." I'm really not mad. Sad and disappointed? Yes. I take my plate to the kitchen sink and Rooter follows me.

"Then why won't you stay?"

"Because I need a little me time." I rinse my plate and set it inside the dishwasher. I walk toward the dining room table to clear it off but he puts his hand on my shoulder to stop me.

"Earlier you needed Jace time."

I try to hide my disappointment when I look into his eyes. "Candace needs you more."

"I'm staying."

I shrug his hand away and gather the dirty dishes. "Rooter, you need to go. I'll see you tomorrow night."

"I refuse to leave things like this."

"Things are fine." I lie, trying to convince myself as much as him and carry the dishes to the sink.

Once my hands are empty Rooter pulls me into a tight embrace. "I love you. I'm staying."

And then his phone rings. It's her. I pull away.

"You should answer it and tell her you're on your way."

Rooter takes his phone out of his back pocket. "Yeah?"

I dig through his cupboards looking for containers for the leftovers.

"Of course I care," he says into the phone, "but I can't be there every second of every day."

I hear her scream, "You care more about your princess than you do your own kid."

"This is exactly why you're in this condition," he tells her. "You refuse to accept the situation for what it is and you're getting yourself all worked up."

She screams something unintelligible and then the phone goes quiet. Rooter stares at the screen a moment before putting it back in his pocket. "She hung up on me."

"Don't you think you should go?"

"I honestly don't know, Sophie." He sweeps a hand through his hair. "I'm worried about the kid. But my going there won't fix anything because the same thing will happen tomorrow and the next day and the day after that. She won't be happy unless she and I are together and that isn't happening."

"I agree, but if you stay you'll spend the entire night worrying."

He leans against the counter and stares at the floor. "My pop once told me that ninety nine percent of the things we worry about never come to pass. That I shouldn't drive myself crazy worrying about all the things that could go wrong."

"What if something happens and you aren't there?"

"I don't know." He looks in my eyes. "All I know is that I need to pick my battles wisely. Something may or may not happen with

Candace and the baby tonight." He walks over and takes my hands. "But what I'm sure of is if I leave you'll start giving up on me. So I'm going to stay here and believe everything will be okay with the baby."

"If something happens..."

He puts two fingers on my lips to quiet me. "The only thing that's going to happen tonight is you and me cuddling in bed and talking until we pass out."

After we clean the kitchen, Rooter takes me upstairs and gives me an hour long back rub which nearly puts me to sleep. Afterward he cuddles with me exactly the way he said he would. As much as I miss making love with him, I'm glad we're just lying here, side by side talking about our day: A geriatric woman in an old Caprice Classic ran me off the road. Business is booming at the shop. One of the guys nearly sliced three fingers off working on a build. His mom called him earlier and told him it's imperative we attend this Sunday's family dinner. He laughs when I tell him she called me too.

Camilla also called me on Monday to discuss the incident at their house. She told me she knew I wouldn't have attacked Candace and didn't want me to worry about what she thought. She knows Candace is out of her mind. We had a pleasant conversation, and she said she'd like to get together soon, just the two of us.

I'm not sure what time it is when we fall asleep hand in hand, but the clock reads two-oh-six when I'm awoken by kisses on the small of my back.

"Mm, that feels nice," I murmur sleepily.

"I've been dying to do this since I gave you the back rub," Rooter chuckles lightly against my skin, "but I was trying to be chivalrous."

He brushes his lips against my skin so lightly that it almost tickles, planting kisses from my lower back up to my neck. I begin to roll over to face him but he tells me to stay the way I am. His bare, hard length is pressed against my backside. I slide my hand behind me to stroke him and he sucks in a breath.

"I need to be inside you," he hisses in my ear.

He pulls my panties down part way with his hands and then removes them the rest of the way with his foot. I feel him pull away and then hear the drawer of the nightstand open followed by the crackle of a condom packet. A moment later he's pressed up against my back again. He drapes my top leg over his giving him full access to me. It's like a bolt of electricity when his finger slides into me.

"So wet already," he whispers and slips his finger in and out.

He pulls his finger out and then positions the tip of his cock between my legs. When he enters me it's at an agonizingly slow pace. He pulls back and enters again just as slowly. Once he's seated fully inside me he rotates his hips. We've never made love in this position. I like it. A lot.

He keeps up the same slow pace and reaches down to stroke my clit, up and down, around and around.

"I love you, Sophie." Settled all the way inside me he stops moving and circles my clit with his middle and index fingers. "I want to feel you come like this, while I'm still inside you."

He nips my neck and continues to stroke me. The fullness of him being motionless inside me adds to the pleasure he gives me with his fingers. He knows just how to touch me. I squeeze my eyes shut and delight in the sensation.

"That feels so good. You're so big inside me."

"That's right, baby. Talk to me." His voice is gruff and full of lust. "Are you getting close?"

"Yeah," I bite my lip.

His fingers make faster circles around my clit. "Say my name when you come."

Every now and then I feel him twitch inside me as he works me with his hand and it pushes me higher and closer to my peak. My center throbs with aching need as the first wave crashes over me. I grab his hand and slow the movement of his fingers. I want this orgasm to last. I want it to feel so good it hurts. When it hits me my toes curl and I scream his name.

"Oh yeah, baby. You're so tight around me."

The moment my orgasm subsides Rooter moves frantically inside me. His fingers dig into my hips as he pounds into me again and again. The room is filled with the sounds of moans, his and mine, and our wet skin slapping together.

Before I know it I'm rocked by the shockwaves of another orgasm. When I scream his name a strangled curse escapes Rooter's lips, and he stops slamming into me. He draws me into his arms and shudders with his release.

"I love you so much, Sophie," he says in a strained voice as he comes.

When the alarm clock sounds at six I wake with a giant smile on my face, remembering last night. Rooter stayed. He held me. He made love to me.

He chose me.

Finding Our Way

Thursday and Friday pass much the same as Monday and Tuesday had with Rooter and me only seeing each other after I get off work. Candace has reached out to him each day, and he's gone over to check on her. She claims she's still as stressed as ever, though nothing has happened with the baby.

Rooter doesn't know what else he can possibly do to improve the situation. I try my best to console him by telling him he's doing everything he can. He's been supportive and present for her. Short of him moving in with her—and I'll be damned if that happens—there's nothing else he can do.

I'm getting used to our predicament and with each passing day it gets a little easier. I admire him for the way he cares for and worries about the baby. He'll make a great dad.

Last night as we laid in bed we talked about turning the third bedroom into a nursery. I recommended he gets started on it now. We could paint the walls a gender neutral color such as yellow and get a crib and whatever else a person needs for a newborn baby. I may not have envisioned this for us, but it's happening so I might as well be a helpful participant.

Rooter likes it when I speak in terms of "we." Although it isn't my baby, and he doesn't expect anything from me in terms of raising him or her, it makes him happy to know he has my support.

I still wish things were different and that he wasn't going to be a dad. I never wanted a ready-made family. But I do fully support him and I'll be there for him with whatever he needs.

When we get to his parent's house for Sunday dinner Camilla scuttles to us and hugs me first.

"I'm so glad you're here." She pulls back with a radiant smile. Camilla is a beautiful woman. I see so much of her in Rooter. They have the same eyes and smile.

"I'm happy to be here," I tell her and return the smile.

This time I brought a bathing suit with me so I go into the house to change. I take my time as I walk to Rooter's old room and pause to look at family photos along my way. I find one of Rooter when he was much younger, in high school. Even as a young man he was built and obviously strong. He's standing with Bear in front of an old, black convertible Camaro. As per usual, Bear isn't smiling.

"My boy was always handsome," Camilla says, startling me.

I jump and spin around to face her. "Yes, I see that."

"He always had a heart of gold." She smiles with pride. "So protective of me and Isa."

"I imagine so."

"I always knew he was capable of loving deeply," she says, misty eyed. "And I believe you are too, Sophie. I can see it in your eyes."

"Yeah?"

She nods and rubs my arms in a comforting, motherly fashion. "I realize this isn't easy for you, sweetie. And I won't kid you, it'll get even harder some days."

She's spot on. I rub my eyes with my thumb and index finger. "We've had some bad days."

"He loves you so much, Sophie." She stares into my eyes as though trying to convince me.

"I love him, too."

Camilla leads me up the stairs to his room and closes the door once we're inside. "Be patient with him, but be firm, too. He'll mess up and make you mad, but I know he'll try hard to give you what you need."

"He has been trying," I admit and take a seat on the bed. "But it's hard for him. He feels torn between doing what's right for the baby and what's right for me and us."

Camilla sits beside me and appraises me in a maternal manner. The way Loraine had done on many occasions. "Having a relationship means finding balance and compromising. You need to help each other as you find your way together. If you can do that, everything will be just fine."

"It's been difficult to find balance," I admit and pick at the bedspread.

She sighs and rubs the top of her thighs. "My mama always said nothing worth having comes easy. We have to work for what we want. My life has been a testament to that."

Her words make me recall the story Rooter told me about her past. "Nothing in my life has been easy, either."

"He hasn't given me any details, but he told me you've had it pretty tough." She tucks a stray lock of hair behind my ear. "It's why he was initially hesitant to be with you. He didn't want to make your life harder."

The idea of us never being together makes my chest ache. Regardless of everything, I simply can't envision never having been together. "I can't imagine him not being in my life."

Her brow furrows with worry. "I hate to think what would happen to him if you broke up."

I reach for her arm to comfort her. "You don't need to worry about that, Camilla. I don't give up easily."

"I'm glad to hear that, baby girl," she says and pulls me into a tight embrace. "But if you call me Camilla one more time, I'm gonna put you over my knee and swat that tiny behind."

"Sorry, mama." We both laugh.

Later that night, Rooter and I cuddle in bed after making love. It's been a mostly perfect day. Candace called after dinner and cried about how it should be her there with him instead of me. He didn't know what to say to her so Camilla got on the phone and told her she needed to stop putting herself through this. It isn't healthy for the baby and the sooner she can make peace with the situation, the better. She didn't argue with Camilla, probably because she knows better, but she told her Rooter was making a mistake with me. Camilla said, "Love is never a mistake." That was the end of that conversation.

Rooter and I lay on our sides facing one another. His hand is on my hip, mine is on his chest. I remember seeing the photo of him and Bear and am sparked by curiosity. There's still so much I don't know about him. "Tell me something about you I don't know."

He stares into my eyes while he thinks. "I have a younger brother and sister by my biological father. Thomas and Ashley. He was named after my dad." He blanches, apparently hating calling him dad. "Thomas isn't even a year younger than me. Ashley's your age."

"Wow." I wasn't expecting such a heavy confession.

"I met them a couple years back. They didn't know who I was."

"You didn't tell them?"

He shakes his head. "Nah. They didn't seem very interested in me."

"They probably would've been if they knew you were their brother."

"I doubt it. They were every bit as stuck up and shallow as their father."

I stroke his cheek with the back of my hand. "I'm sorry."

"A glutton for punishment, I went to his house—my dad's—when they were all there. I watched him with them." He swallows. This is hard for him. "The fucked up part of it all was that he seemed like such a good dad. The way he looked at them with love and pride. One big happy family."

"That had to have been difficult to see."

"Yeah. I think I'd rather he was a deadbeat dad to all of us. As fucked up as that sounds." He rubs the back of his neck. "But the hardest part for me was that I felt like I'd betrayed Mick. I went there to see what I'd missed out on when in truth, I haven't missed out on anything because Mick has been a phenomenal father. I wouldn't change that for anything in this world. I'm glad Thomas O'Shea abandoned me. I love Mick and I'm glad to be his son."

His name would've been Jace Alexander O'shea if Thomas hadn't abandoned him. Or maybe he'd be Thomas O'Shea Junior. I can't imagine that at all. He isn't Jace O'Shea or Thomas anything. He is Rooter, the man he was always meant to be. The man I love. I lean forward and kiss his forehead.

"You're right, you didn't miss out on anything. You have a wonderful family. I wish I had a family like yours."

His eyes soften. "Babe, you do. You have my family now. The more they get to know you, the more they love you."

Tears pool in the corner of my eyes. For him and for me. Not for our past, but in hope of letting go of the past and creating a future full of love and happiness. "The feeling is mutual."

He swallows. "I don't just love you, Sophie. I consider you my family. You're a part of me now. You always will be."

"When do I get to tell you I love you?"

He smiles and kisses my hand. "I'm still working on earning it, babe."

The next morning, after Rooter leaves for work, I go home and Miranda and I talk about our men while she gets ready for work.

She and Bear are hot and heavy. He's spent as many nights with her as I've spent with Rooter. They haven't exchanged I love you's yet, but she's pretty sure she's in love and that the feeling is mutual. Evidently, Bear's the one who made things official. He flat out told her she was his, and that she needed to cut ties with any other guys if there were any.

I never in a million years would've imagined Miranda would end up with a biker, but she seems happier than ever. Everything about her is lighter and brighter. She's like a ray of sunshine whenever I see her. She isn't even fretting about her brother anymore. Miranda said she's come to peace with it all but still holds out hope he'll get clean and be the Mike he used to be.

After she leaves for work, I hop in the shower. As soon as I finish blow drying my hair the doorbell rings. I trot down the stairs and pull the curtain aside to see who it is before opening the door. My breath catches and fire lights within my veins at the sight of Candace standing on the other side of the door.

The Fallout

O*h hell no!*
I jerk the door open so hard it slams into the wall. There will be a hole in the drywall from the doorknob but I don't care. Seeing Candace at my door in her short skirt and playboy bunny tank top have my blood boiling.

"What the fuck are you doing here?" I shout.

The tears in her eyes do not play on my sympathies. It's one thing for her to harass the father of her baby but it's absolutely one thousand percent not okay for her to come here with her bullshit.

"We need to talk, Sophie." Her voice is meek which only pisses me off more.

I roll my eyes. "Cut the bullshit tears, Candace. They don't work on me."

She straightens up right away proving me right. "I'm not going to let you take my family away. The Russo's are my family. Mine."

I cross my arms and shift my weight to one foot. "That may very well be true, but according to Rooter, they're my family, too."

She narrows her eyes at me. "They're *not* your family. You've barely known them a month. I've known them my entire life."

"I'm not disputing that, but Rooter loves me. We're together and we're staying together. There's nothing you can do to change that."

She tosses her head back and laughs. "Honey, if I had a dollar for every girl who told me that I wouldn't need to work for a year."

She's just messing with you, Sophie. I try to slam the door in her face but she puts her hands against it. "Leave. Now," I growl, out of patience.

"Do you think you're the first girl he's done this with? He falls into infatuation with someone new every month."

She's trying to psyche me out, but I can't let it work. I turn the tables. "If that's true, why do you want him? Why chase after a guy who doesn't want you?"

"He obviously never told you our story or you would understand."

I narrow my eyes. "He told me all about you."

"Oh?" She cocks her head to the side. "Did he tell you I was his first love? That we lost our virginity to each other when we were sixteen?"

That, he did not tell me. "Take your bullshit lies and get the hell out of my face."

She scrolls through her phone, I imagine to call him. Good. I hope she does so he can put an end to this. She holds the phone up and her voice blares through the speaker. It's a recording.

"I love you, Rooter," she cries. "I always have. I'm sorry I hurt you back then. Are you going to hate me forever?"

"I don't hate you Candace. I'll always care about you." His voice is tender. Rage spreads through my veins at the sound of him talking to her that way.

"Then why are you doing this?" She asks him. "Are punishing me for what I did?"

"No. Of course not." He sounds offended.

"You know we belong together, baby." My skin crawls at the sound of her calling him baby. "You and I make more sense than you and her."

"You're right, we do make more sense—"

What the hell? Unable to listen to another word I snatch the phone from her hand and throw it with all of my might into the street. She retreats toward the steps and I follow like a predator getting ready to pounce. "Get the fuck away from my house!"

I puff my chest and fling my hand in the air. She takes a quick step backward and loses her balance. Everything happens so fast. I reach for her, but it's too late. She has fallen down my front porch stairs. I wasn't going to hit her. I was just going to point at her car and insist she get in it and leave before I call the cops.

"You crazy bitch," she shouts and clutches her stomach. "I'm pregnant!"

I run to her side but she kicks me in the shin. I grimace and reach for her. "I wasn't going to hit you."

"Stay away from me!" She scrambles to her feet, still clutching her stomach, and limps to her car.

"Are you okay?" I chase after her with genuine concern. "Do you need to go to the hospital?"

"I don't need your help!" She gets in her car and slams the door.

"I didn't mean to hurt you," I say through the window. "I'm sorry."

"Yeah right. Wait until Rooter finds out what you've done!"

She peels away and I scramble into the house and sprint up to my room to get my phone. I must get ahold of Rooter before she does.

"Babe?" He answers on the first ring.

"Candace was just here," I say, out of breath.

"What? What was she doing there?"

"Trying to talk me into leaving you." I pace back and forth in my room with one hand clasped to the side of my head. "Rooter, she fell."

"Fell?" His voice is panicked. "Is she okay?"

"I think so. She wouldn't let me help her."

"Shit, I better call her."

I squeeze my eyes shut. "You can't. I threw her phone into the street."

"Dammit, Sophie! What happened?"

"She was playing a recording of a conversation you had with her and it pissed me off." My heart feels like it will explode from my chest. "I swear to God I didn't touch her."

"Fuck. I need to find her. Stay put. I'll call you later."

Hours pass and I still haven't heard from Rooter. I tried calling him about an hour ago and he didn't answer so I texted, but he never responded.

I hear the rumble of a motorcycle and dart outside, but it's just Bear. "What happened? Rooter won't answer my calls."

"Let's go inside," he says and leads me into the house. He motions for me to sit on the sofa and takes a seat in the chair. "Sophie, it isn't good. She lost the baby."

"Oh, God no." The poor baby. Poor Rooter. I never meant for this to happen.

"She says you attacked her." I detect skepticism in his voice. He must not believe her. "That you pushed her down the stairs."

"That's not true! I never laid a hand on her."

"But she fell down the stairs?" His voice isn't at all accusatory.

"I screamed at her to leave and she backed away and fell." I hold my hand to my chest. "I tried to help her."

"That's not the story she gave Rooter. He's furious, Sophie."

I sit forward with my head in my hands and let the tears fall. "She came here and got in my face, Bear. She did this. Not me."

He reaches out and rests his hand on my shoulder. "For what it's worth, I believe you. I just thought you should be prepared when Rooter gets here."

I look up at him. "Prepared for what?"

"I've never seen him like this. He's angry, and he blames you."

I sit up straight and take a deep breath. Rooter knows me. He knows I wouldn't do anything to hurt his baby. "Then I'll make him understand that I didn't do anything."

"I don't think he'll believe you. He said you went after her at his parent's house. Did you?"

"I jumped up at her, but I wasn't going to hit her." *Does Rooter really not know that?*

"Sophie, I know how much he cares about you, but she has painted a very ugly, convincing picture. She said she came here to try to mend fences so the three of you could come to an understanding and move forward."

"Bullshit! She wasn't trying to mend fences! She came here trying to get me to leave Rooter." I stand up and pull my hair. *This cannot be happening.* "She played a recording of a conversation they had where she apologized for hurting him and he said how much he cared about her. She told me he lost his virginity to her!"

"She didn't say anything about that, but it probably won't help your case any. He'll think it was your motive for pushing her."

"I didn't push her!"

He holds his hands up in surrender. "I believe you."

"What am I going to do?" The question is rhetorical. I don't expect Bear to have the answer.

"I don't know. But you need to prepare yourself for an entirely different guy when he gets here. Which is why I'm here. To make sure things don't get out of hand."

My chest squeezes and my eyes go wide. "Do you think he'd actually hurt me?"

"Rooter has never hit a woman in his life, but Sophie, he's out of his mind right now. I'd tell you to leave and give him time to cool off, but if you hide from him he'll take it as an admission of guilt."

I've never been afraid of Rooter. I have a hard time believing he'd do anything to hurt me. But Bear, his lifelong friend, is here to protect me. If he thinks there's a chance I could get hurt, there must be a real possibility of it. My stomach churns as hot tears continue to spill down my face. I choke, gasping for air and Bear pulls me into his arms.

"He has to believe me." I grip the leather of Bear's cut in a tight fist. "He has to."

Bear and I watch the clock in silence for a little over an hour. The sound I once loved, that I lived to hear, now causes me panic as Rooter pulls into his driveway. We turn our attention to the door, waiting for it to open. When it does, Rooter steps in wearing an angry scowl. His jaw is set, his eyes are narrowed. His posture is rigid. He looks from me to Bear who sits in the chair across from me.

"What are you doing here?" Rooter barks at him.

"Just trying to keep things on an even keel, brother."

I lurch up with the intention of going to Rooter but the glare he shoots me stops me in my tracks. "Bear told me about the baby. I'm so sorry."

"Don't you dare say you're sorry." He takes a step forward and his nostrils flare. "You are not sorry."

I hold my hands up in front of me and speak calmly. "Rooter, I swear I didn't lay a hand on Candace."

"That's not what she said." He widens his stance and purses his lips.

It hurts he believes her over me. I take a small step forward. "How many times has she lied? Do you honestly believe her over me?"

"I saw the way you went after her the other night!" He screams, angry and accusatory.

"I'd never hit a pregnant woman. It was an accident. We were arguing. She said things. I got in her face and screamed for her to leave," I point toward the porch, "she lost her footing on the stairs and fell."

"So you admit you are to blame." He clenches his fist.

"No," I shake my head vehemently. "I don't admit to that. She came here and got in my face. She did this."

He strides toward me, stopping a few feet away and points in my face. "You got in her face, you were going to hit her and she fell down the stairs! You did this! You killed my kid!"

"No. No, I didn't," I sob. "You have to believe me."

He stands before me shaking, with his hands balled into fists at his side. There's a violent gleam in his eyes making the hair on the back of my neck stand up. Bear gets up and stands between us.

Rooter takes a small step sideways and peers around Bear. When he speaks it's through gritted teeth. "I'll never believe another word you say. I never want to hear your voice again." He points at me again. "If you're smart, you'll stay away from me and you sure as hell better stay away from Candace."

"Rooter, please don't do this," I beg and step forward, but Bear holds his arm out to stop me from reaching him. "Please. You know I'd never do anything to hurt you. I love you."

"I can't even stand to look at you," Rooter spits. "I could never love someone who could take the life of an innocent child. I never want to see you again. If you have half a brain, you'll make sure I don't."

With that he turns on his heel and stalks out the door, slamming it behind him. I drop to my knees and sob uncontrollably calling after Rooter to come back. Begging him not to leave me.

THE AFTERMATH

I always thought I understood what people meant when they say their heart is broken. I didn't. Not even a little bit. I'm not just sad. This shit actually hurts physically. It's like someone sliced my chest open and shredded my heart with a fork. Now it lays open bleeding out.

I spent the entire night curled in fetal position bawling my eyes out. Miranda stayed and held me until morning when she had to get ready for work. I can't work. I called off last night and I'm sure I'll end up doing the same today.

I can't get the way Rooter looked at me out of my mind. Any love he felt for me, if he ever felt any at all, was gone entirely and had been replaced by sheer hatred.

Nothing has ever hurt as much as the words that came out of his mouth when he said he never wanted to see me again. Nothing my mom ever did—none of her cruel words, not one blow from her fist—ever hurt me half as much as the contempt Rooter feels for me.

I keep replaying the event over and over in my mind. Had I been responsible for her fall? I scared her when I flung my arm up. If only I'd kept calm none of this would've happened. Candace wouldn't have lost the baby and Rooter and I would still be together.

I'm such an idiot! Why did I let her get to me?

I knew better. I knew what she was doing. She was trying to goad me. Trying to get me to distrust Rooter so it would cause a rift between us. Boy did she cause a rift. No. She didn't just cause a rift. She caused an explosion. And I wasn't the only casualty. The baby died and Rooter is crushed. I may hate Candace, but I even have sympathy for her loss. No matter how crazy she is, no one deserves to suffer the pain of losing a child.

It may not have been all my fault, but I must take half of the blame. I could've controlled myself. Rooter has a right to be angry with me. If I was him, I'd never talk to me again either.

Just when I think the pain can't get any worse, I watch Rooter and Candace pull into his driveway in the truck. He helps her out and into his house. When he comes back out he retrieves bags and boxes from the bed of the truck and carries them into the house.

Candace is moving in with him.

The pain hits me like a heart attack, square in my chest. It's like a vice grip squeezing my already bleeding heart. I'll not survive this. There's no way I can.

My doorbell rings and I jump out of my skin. I don't bother going to the door. It didn't do me any good the last time. If I hadn't opened the goddamn door none of this would've happened. I wouldn't be sitting here miserable, Rooter's baby would still be alive, and Candace wouldn't be moving in with him, taking my place in his life.

Oh my God… I no longer have a place in his life.

A gut wrenching wail escapes my lips. My phone pings and I want to throw it out in the road like I did Candace's. It's a text from Ryan: *Let me in or I'll bust the damn door down.*

I run down the stairs as fast as I can and nearly bust my ass on the last step. That would be some fitting karma. Maybe I should take a tumble down the stairs. I swing the door open and fling myself into Ryan's arms.

He carries me in and sits us down on the sofa. "How are you, Soph?"

I clutch my chest and drag in a jagged breath. "It hurts so bad, Ry. And now he's moving her in."

"Fuck him, Soph. If he's going to take her word over yours you're better off without him."

"But I'm partially to blame in this. I scared her." I wave toward the front porch. The image of her falling down the stairs is vivid in my mind. "I'm the reason she fell."

"Bullshit! She had no business being here." He points toward Rooter's house. "This is on her and if he can't see that he's bloody stupid."

I wrap my arms around myself and sob. "I killed his kid. I killed an innocent baby."

"No, you didn't." He grabs each side of my face and glares into my eyes. "Listen to me. You did not do this. You are a victim here. He should've left you alone. You should've never been together to begin with. He's not good enough for you. Do you hear me?"

But he is. I want him. I don't want to live without him. "I love him."

Ryan takes me in his arms and holds me tight. "I know, honey. I know."

By Thursday I don't feel any better. If anything, I feel worse. I keep watching them from my window. Last night they stood in the kitchen talking while he cooked dinner. Every now and then he'd hug her or wipe a tear from her eyes.

The blinds to his bedroom window stay drawn. I can't help wondering if she's sleeping in his bed with him.

Randy called me this morning to ask if I'd be able to work today. He doesn't know the details of what happened, he just knows I'm a complete and total wreck. I don't think he'd fire me, but I can't risk it. No matter how devastated I am I can't risk my livelihood, so I told him I'd be in.

The bummer of it all is that Ryan doesn't work Thursdays so I have no one to lean on in my weak moments. And there's a lot of them. But, being at work is a good thing because it forces me to think of something other than Rooter and my broken heart.

When the night comes to an end I dread going home. I don't want to be there so close to the one thing I want more than anything in the world, but can never have again. As stupid as I am for it, when I make the turn onto my street, I hold out hope I'll see Rooter waiting on his front porch to make sure I get in safe.

He isn't there. Just like I knew he wouldn't be. All the lights are off in his house. I look up at his window and an image of Candace lying next to him creeps into my mind. My nine hour stretch without tears comes to an abrupt end.

On Saturday, Rooter is outside unloading groceries from his truck when I get into my car to go to work. We lock eyes and all I see in his is disdain.

The next morning, I sit in the dining room and watch him play with Dopey in the backyard. A few minutes later Candace walks out with them and tries to play with the dog, but Dopey ignores her and heads for my yard. At least the dog misses me.

Rooter corals him and looks toward my back door. I can't make out his expression. It's not quite the disdain from yesterday. I want to say he looks sad, but I'm sure that's not the case. I'm just trying to make myself feel better because I want him to miss me as much as I miss him.

"This has to stop," Miranda says from behind.

I jump and spill a little of my coffee on my shirt. I didn't know she was standing there. "What?"

Miranda sits in the chair diagonal from mine. "You sitting by the windows watching Rooter. It isn't healthy, Soph."

"I can't help it," I admit, staring at the white siding of his house.

"You'll never get over him sitting here watching him day after day."

"I don't want to get over him." I take a sip of the coffee. It burns my tongue, but I don't care.

"Sophie, you have to." She takes my hand and looks at me with concern. "It's over. Bear told me there's no chance for you two."

I shrug. *Tell me something I don't know.* "I know that."

"I never thought I'd say this, and please don't take it the wrong way, but I think you should move out. It's for your own good. I already talked to Ryan, and he said you can move in with him."

I don't get mad at her because I know she's doing this for me. She's sad for me. "What about you? You can't afford this place on your own."

She shrugs. "I'll figure something out, don't worry."

Over the next two days I move my clothes and other belongings into Ryan's house. I don't bother with my furniture because his guest room is already fully decorated with much nicer furniture than my own.

I must admit being away from the house makes me feel better. Somewhat freer and more relaxed. I can actually function rather than sit and stare at Rooter or his house when he's not there.

After a week has passed, I still feel the crushing pain of the breakup, but Ryan has helped me realize I'm not the bad guy. The situation was completely messed up from the beginning.

In the end, Rooter is the one who lost the most, but it was his own fault. He's the one who got involved with Candace. He's the one who got her pregnant. Ryan thinks I dodged a major bullet.

I'm in the kitchen making a sandwich when my phone rings. It's Miranda.

"Oh my God, Sophie." She's freaking out. "You'll never believe what I just heard."

"What?" I absentmindedly spread mayonnaise on my bread.

"I was on the back porch when Candace pulled into the driveway." The sound of her name prickles my skin. "She was on her phone. Sophie the whole thing was a lie. The pregnancy, the miscarriage, everything was a lie to break you and Rooter up."

I blink and drop the butter knife onto the counter. "What?"

"I heard her tell whoever was on the phone how easy it was, how you played right into her hands that day on the porch. She meant to get you worked up so she could fall down the stairs to fake the miscarriage."

All the air has escaped my lungs, and I'm frozen in place.

"Are you there, Soph?"

"Yeah." My hands tremble as I stare at my unfinished sandwich.

"I called Bear. He's telling Rooter right now."

I run to my purse on the table next to the entryway and fumble around for my keys. Leaving all the food on the counter I race to my car. "I need to go. I can't be here when he finds out."

"Why? Where are you going?"

"I don't know. But I can't see him." I throw my car door open and jump inside.

"What are you talking about? Why not? This changes everything, Soph."

"No, Miranda, it doesn't." I put the car in drive and speed away not knowing where I'm going. All I know is I can't see Rooter until I've had time to process this new information. I need to find a place to go where he won't be able to find me.

*L*ETTING *G*O

I have no idea where the hell to go to hide from Rooter. Miranda knows all of my friends. By the tone of her voice, I know she'll tell him where to look for me. The only person I can trust to keep my secret is Ryan and unfortunately, Miranda knows where his house is. Not that Rooter wouldn't figure it out for himself. All he'd have to do is follow him home from the Grand.

I pull into a local park and call Ryan's cell.

"Hey, think of something you want from the store?" He answers. Shortly before Miranda's call he'd left for the grocery and told me to call him if I thought of anything that wasn't on the list.

"I need a place to go where Rooter can't find me."

"What's going on, Sophie?"

"Everything with Candace was a lie." I crank the air conditioning and fan myself. It's not even that hot out. "The pregnancy and the miscarriage. Bear's telling Rooter now. He's going to come looking for me, Ryan, and I don't want to see him."

"Shit, Soph. Let me think a minute."

His minute feels like a damn eon. I scan the immediate area like a maniac even though I know Rooter isn't tailing me. Bear's probably still telling him about Candace. Maybe he won't even believe it since there isn't any proof. It's Miranda's word against Candace's. He didn't take my word over hers. Still, I'd feel better if I had somewhere to go where he can't find me. I'd go to a hotel, but I can't afford it.

"I'll call my friend Josh and tell him you're on your way. I can meet you there in less than twenty minutes."

Ryan gives me Josh's address and I break nearly every driving law known to man to get there as fast as possible. I've never met Josh, but I've heard of him. He and Ryan have been friends for years. When he opens the door he's wearing a kind smile that meets his eyes. He's a good looking guy; short brown hair, tall, good body like Ryan, but he is seriously tan. Too tan. It takes away from his good looks.

"You must be Sophie," he says and welcomes me inside.

"Thank you so much for letting me come here, Josh. I had nowhere else to go."

He gives me a quick hug and leads me to a recliner in his living room. He's very effeminate in his speech and mannerisms. Graceful even. "Ryan told me you're one of his best friends and any friend of Ryan's is welcome here."

"You have no idea what this means to me." I smile, but I'm panicking on the inside.

"He said something about man problems." He straightens his perfectly pressed shirt. "You're hiding out."

"I need a little time to think."

"I realize you don't know me," he leans forward and puts his hand on mine, "but I promise you I'm a good listener and I've been known to give some pretty stellar advice."

Josh doesn't realize what he's asking. I don't even know where to start. "It's a long, complicated story."

"I've got nowhere to be." He sits back and crosses his legs.

"I'll give you the cliff's notes version. I got involved with a guy who was in a friends with benefits situation—which I had no idea of at the time—with a crazy slut who ended up pregnant and accused me of causing her miscarriage. The guy told me he never wanted to see me again and today it turns out she wasn't even pregnant to begin with."

"And you don't want to get back with this gentleman?"

"She better not," Ryan says from the front door.

I jump up and run to him. "Ry!"

"I left everything at the store and came straight here. Tell me everything."

"You basically know everything." I tell him and Josh the other small details about how Miranda overheard Candace talking while outside and that she called Bear and now he's telling Rooter.

"He didn't believe you. Why would he trust Miranda?"

"I don't know if he'll believe it. But I know he'll question Candace to get to the truth and then he'll come looking for me. I can't talk to him until I figure out how I feel about everything."

Ryan's face turns a deep shade of red. "I swear I want to murder them both!"

After an hour, Ryan has to leave for work. He doesn't want to go. He wants to stay and keep an eye on me to make sure I stay strong in my conviction not to give in and see Rooter if he calls. But I tell him there's a chance he won't even call.

"So, would you like time alone to think or do you want me to try to distract you from your thoughts?" Josh asks me once Ryan is gone.

I'd love for Josh to distract me, but I need time to think. I need to be prepared if Rooter calls me and right now I'm so unprepared. "I'm sorry, I don't want to be rude, but I think I should be alone."

"It's not rude at all. I have a few things I need to do so please make yourself at home. There's soda, water, and food in the kitchen. Help yourself to anything. I'll be back in a few hours."

"Josh, thank you. You're a godsend right now."

"No worries." He winks.

I cry at the sight and he dashes over and crouches before me. "Are you sure you want to be alone?"

"Yeah, it's just that saying "no worries" and winking was kind of his thing. It brought back memories."

"Noted. I won't say or do that again."

"I'm such a mess." I sniffle and wipe my face with the hem of my shirt.

"Yeah, but at least you're pretty when you cry. I turn into Willem Dafoe when I cry."

I laugh a real laugh. It feels really good. But in no time whatsoever I'm right back being a blubbering mess.

I spend the next two hours staring at my phone dreading Rooter's possible call. It wasn't too long ago that I used to stare at it hoping he'd call me. Things have changed a lot in such a short period of time.

In a way, I'm curious as to what happened when Bear told him. He obviously didn't believe him right away or he would've called me by now. He undoubtedly went to confront Candace, which I imagine he's already done. He's had plenty of time to do it by now. That I haven't heard from him gives me hope that maybe I won't. Perhaps he's come to the same conclusion as me.

It doesn't change anything. What's done is done.

Or maybe he knows better than to reach out to me now.

No, that wouldn't be it. If Rooter wanted to talk to me nothing would stop him from calling.

My phone pings with a text from Miranda: *I'm watching Rooter toss that slut's shit out of his house. Bear's making sure he doesn't kill her.*

Well, that answers my question. I stare at my phone unable to come up with a reply when my phone pings again with a text from her: *Are you there, Soph?*

Me: *Yeah. I just don't know what to say. I'm glad he knows the truth, but it doesn't change anything.*

Fifteen minutes later my phone rings. It's Rooter. My heart races and I can barely breathe as I stare at the screen. I can't make myself answer. I can't talk to him. The phone rings until it goes to voicemail. He calls right back.

I still can't answer. The sound of his voice will kill me. It goes to voicemail again. A minute later I get a notification of a voicemail followed by a text. I don't listen to the voicemail, but I read the text.

Rooter: *Please answer. I know you have ur phone. I saw ur text to Miranda. Sophie, I'm so so so so so sorry. Please talk to me.*

I text him back before I even know what I'm doing: *I can't talk to you. Not right now. I need time.*

My phone rings. It's him. He's not going to give me time because he knows it won't work out in his favor if he does. He wants to get me to talk to him while I'm emotional. While there's still a chance I'll give into him. I lay the phone on the sofa and stare at his name on the screen as it continues to ring. He texts again.

Rooter: *I'll just keep calling and texting until u answer.*

Of course he will. I grit my teeth and pound my reply on the screen: *I'll block your number.*

Rooter: *I'll get another phone, and then another, and then another. Just answer and talk to me.*

He's serious. He will get one phone after another until I talk to him. I shake my head exasperated and respond to his threat: *I'll change my number. Leave me alone.*

Rooter: *Just hear me out and if u still want me to leave u alone, I promise I will.*

Me: *I can't.*

Rooter: *I don't want to do this, but if u don't answer I'll be at the Grand tomorrow when u get there. Either way, we're talking. We can either do it now on the phone or tomorrow in person. U pick. If u don't call I'll assume u want to talk in person.*

It isn't like Rooter to stir up trouble at a person's job, but he's desperate to talk so I know he'll follow through with his threat. I must go to work tomorrow so that leaves me with one choice. I swallow, inhale a deep breath to steel myself, and call his number.

"Baby, I'm so sorry." His voice is shaky and contrite.

It takes everything I have not to cry at the sound of him calling me baby. "Rooter, this doesn't change anything."

"How can you say that? It changes everything."

I shake my head and fold my leg underneath me. I can't get comfortable. "No, it doesn't. What happened still happened. I scared her and she fell down the stairs. If she had been pregnant, she could've lost the baby and you'd still hate me."

"But she wasn't pregnant, babe. She set us up. This is all her fault," his voice cracks. "I never hated you."

"Yes, you did." I recall the look on his face when he told me he never wanted to see me again. That he could never love me. "I saw it in your eyes. I heard it in your voice. You meant it when you said you never wanted to see me again."

"Babe, I was mad. I lost it and said things I didn't mean."

Rooter doesn't say things he doesn't mean. I decide to challenge him. "Let me ask you something. This morning, before you found out the truth, how did you feel? Did you hate me this morning?"

He's quiet a moment. "This morning, I was still grieving the loss of a child, but I've missed you every second you've been gone."

His voice sounds so sincere and I long to believe him, but I can't. "You moved on rather quickly for someone who misses me. You moved her in the very next day."

"It wasn't like that, Sophie. She was staying in the guest room. I was helping her recuperate and get back on her feet."

I hate that this makes me feel better. I must stick to my conviction. "Too much damage has been done. There's no coming back from this."

He chokes. He's crying. "No baby, don't say that. I can make this right. I can fix it. I'll do whatever you say. Just come home."

I can't hold back my tears any longer. "Rooter, do you care about me?"

"Baby, I love you so much that it's breaking me in two." It sounds like his entire body is shaking. "And you love me."

"If you love me, let me go." I'm crying so hard I can barely get the words out and they turn into a whisper. "Please just let me go."

I listen to him cry for several long moments. "That's what you really want?"

It's not what I want at all. "It's what I need."

"I'm so sorry I hurt you. I'll never forgive myself."

I know he's sorry. But it doesn't change anything. "I have to go. Goodbye, Rooter."

"Goodbye, Sophie."

SEEING THINGS

Three days have passed since my conversation with Rooter and he hasn't attempted to contact me once. The tone of his voice when he said goodbye told me I wouldn't hear from him again. I asked him to let me go and that's what he has done. I did the right thing. But it doesn't make it any easier. The finality has hit me like a boulder falling from the sky. There's no going back. Rooter and I are done.

But I can't stop thinking about him. I constantly try to picture what he's doing at different times of the day. Does he still wake up at six every morning for work? Does he still exercise after work like he always did on the days I work? Is he back to running first thing in the morning? Miranda told me he's become reclusive. He goes to work, goes home, takes care of Dopey and that's about it. Bear tried to get him to have drinks with him last night and he refused.

About an hour after that last conversation with Rooter, Miranda called me freaking out. Bear heard a ruckus and went to check on him. Apparently he obliterated his house. It was an ugly scene. He smashed a bunch of dishes, threw some tables and chairs, one of which went through a window. As bad as it sounds, knowing he's hurting as much as me makes me feel better. It's a retribution of sorts.

Ryan has been a saving grace for me. He finds ridiculous ways to make me smile and has even managed to get a few laughs out of me. The poor guy has next to no life now because he spends all his time with me trying to keep my spirits up.

This morning we hit a flea market for the hell of it. He thinks it'll be a fun hobby for us to find old furniture to refurbish and sell online. An idea he came up with watching the home and garden channel a couple nights ago.

I told him I'd rather hit the gym and punch my frustrations away, but he thinks that isn't a good idea since I'm hardly eating. It's not on purpose. I just can't remember to eat. It's like my hunger switch is turned off. So he watches the clock and makes sure I eat at the appropriate times. If we're not together he texts me a reminder. His way to motivate me to eat was by playing on my small boob insecurity. He said, "If you don't eat you'll lose what little boob you have and once they're gone, they never come back." It almost worked.

Miranda, God love her, has tried to be supportive. She calls and texts regularly to check on me. But every time we talk she ends up telling me how bad Rooter's doing and that she really believes now Candace is out of the picture he and I'd be happy. Yes, Candace was our only real problem, but that doesn't undo the damage that's been done. Every time I close my eyes I still see him glaring at me with pure, utter hatred.

Since Sundays are the only day Ryan and I have off together we decide to go out and have a good time. He thinks I need to start living like a normal twenty-something. So we're headed to the Red Door for dancing and drinks. Josh is coming along and I've invited Abby since she lost her job and doesn't have anywhere to be in the morning.

By my third drink the Rooter sightings start. Abby and I are out on the dance floor when I swear I see his cut by the front door. I stop dancing, shake my head and try to focus, but it's gone.

"You okay?" Abby asks.

"Yeah," I say and resume dancing. "Just thought I saw something."

I look to the spot where Rooter and I danced and am hit by a wave of new memories from that night. I remember being in his bed and him kissing me and the way he stared at me with lust filled eyes as I gave him the lap dance. *Stop thinking of him, Sophie.* I shake my head again trying to clear my mind.

"I need to go to the bathroom," I tell her. I need to splash some cold water on my face.

"I'll come with."

On our way to the bathroom I see a guy go around the corner in the back of the bar and swear I see Rooter's tattoo on his arm.

"Did you see that?" I ask Abby.

"See what?"

"That guy go around the corner." I point in the direction of what I saw.

"I didn't see anyone," she giggles. "I think you should switch to beer."

"You're probably right."

In the bathroom I splash water on my face and tell myself Rooter isn't here. It's all in my head because I miss him so much and this place holds memories for us. But on our way back to the booth I scan the area for him. He isn't here, just like I already knew.

Ryan catches on to my funk and insists on another drink and more dancing. After downing a shot of Jack he drags me to the dance floor. Ryan is a ridiculously good dancer. Josh follows us out to the floor and the two of them dance together. I wave for Abby to come out and dance with me, but she's chatting it up with a not so attractive guy.

I start to walk off of the dance floor but am stopped when a warm hand clasps my arm. My heart skips a beat. It's silly, but the first thought I have is that it's Rooter. He really has been here watching me this entire time and can't help himself. He has to talk to me. But when I turn around, it's not him. The cute guy asks if I want to dance. I turn him down. There's only one guy I want to dance with. If I can't dance with him, I don't want to dance at all.

As we're leaving the bar a car pulls out of the parking lot. It happens so fast, but it looks like the driver has a tattoo on his arm like Rooter's. But his hair is longer. And Rooter hates cars. He definitely wouldn't be driving a little girly car.

The next morning while I'm nursing a monstrous hangover my phone rings. When I see the number I feel a pang in my chest. It's Camilla.

"Hello?"

"I hope it's okay that I'm calling."

"It's fine." I adjust the wet rag on my forehead.

"How are you doing, sweetie?"

"I've been better." In more ways than one. I swear I'm never drinking again. If Rooter had been with me he would've seen to it that I ate and took ibuprofen before I went to bed. *Dammit Sophie, stop thinking about him.*

"I've been worried about you. This whole thing with Candace. I'm flabbergasted."

"Me, too," I sigh. *I really don't want to talk about her.*

"What my son did to you, the things he said, were awful. He should've given you the benefit of the doubt."

"Yes, but he didn't." *And I don't want to talk about that either.*

"I'm going to sound like one of those annoying mom's begging you to forgive her boy. But, is there no way you can try?"

"Camilla..." I sit up. I need to brace myself for the rest of this conversation. "So much damage has been done."

"I know, baby, I know. But is there anything he can do? Because he'll do it."

I shake my head, and immediately regret it because it makes the throbbing even worse. "What's done is done."

"Do you still love Jace?"

Her use of his given name catches me off-guard. I don't bother to lie. "Yes."

"He loves you so much Sophie. He hates himself. He was here for a little while yesterday. Barely ate. Barely spoke. I've never seen him this bad. My boy cried in front of me and he has *never* cried in front of me."

"I'm sorry this is hurting you." I put the wet rag around my neck. "But, no, I really don't think there's anything he can ever say or do to fix this."

That's not true. If he showed up right now and asked me to take him back, I would. In a heartbeat. I miss him and love him too much not to. Which is why it's a good thing he hasn't tried. If I tell her, she'll tell him and then he will try. I don't need that. It's hard enough to stay away.

"When he left here yesterday, I was scared. For the first time in my life, I was scared for him. I wanted him to stay, but he said he couldn't be here without you. He said he couldn't be anywhere without you."

All I can think about as I'm walking out of the pharmacy an hour later is my talk with Camilla. That woman really knows how to play on one's feelings. She didn't mean any harm. She genuinely believes Rooter and I belong together and thinks we'll both be happier if we get back together. Perhaps she's right, but I can't ignore everything that happened.

As I open my car door I see a car exactly like the one from the bar. At least I think it is. I was pretty drunk so I can't be sure. There doesn't appear to be anyone in it. *Get a grip, Sophie. Rooter is not following you.* I can't get over how entirely hung up I am on the guy. It's ridiculous.

But later that night, I see what appears to be the exact same car parked across the street when Ryan and I are leaving work.

"I've been seeing that car since last night." I point at the shiny, silver vehicle.

"It's not him, Soph." He unlocks the car and we both climb in. "There's a million of those cars. They're like the most popular car right now."

"I'm sure you're right."

"I am." He starts the car and puts it in reverse. "Can you actually picture Rooter driving one of those?"

"No, I can't. I'm just losing my mind." I stare the car down as we pull out of the parking lot. "I miss him."

"I know you do."

I see a similar car five times over the next two days and each time it's either a young girl or old woman driving. Rooter definitely hasn't been following me around in one of them. I'm just sad and completely pathetic.

Wednesday night rolls around and Ryan's at work. Miranda calls to invite me out to dinner with her and Bear. I'm honest when I decline and tell her it'd be too hard to be a third wheel with Rooter's best friend. She says she understands, but she misses me so we make plans to do a little shopping together on Sunday.

I put a bag of popcorn in the microwave and pour myself a soda when there's a knock on the front door. I look at the clock. It's after nine. Who would be here at this time of night? Rooter would definitely show up at this time of night. But I know it's not him.

I walk to the door and look through the peephole. I gasp and smack my hand over my mouth when I see who is standing on the other side.

STAY WITH ME

This cannot be happening. My shock sends me stumbling backwards and I nearly fall to the floor.

"I know you're in there," Mike taunts. His slow speech tells me he's either drunk or high or worse yet, both. "I could see you in the kitchen from the street when I pulled up. Looked like you were making popcorn. You know how much I love popcorn."

What should I do? Should I respond? I run to the kitchen counter, grab my phone and call the first person I think of.

"Sophie?" Rooter answers on the first ring. He sounds so happy that I'm calling.

"Mike's here," I whisper. "I'm scared."

Mike beats on the door. "It's really rude to leave me out here! Open the damn door!"

"Oh my God, he's kicking the door." I stand frozen, staring at the door.

I hear commotion on the other end of the phone. "Stay on the phone with me. We're on our way."

But he doesn't know where I am. "I'm at Ryan's. He lives on—"

"I know where it's at."

Mike shouts through the door. It sounds like he's ramming his shoulder into it now. "You're going to pay for what you've done. You've taken everything from me!"

"I don't know what to do," I mutter into the phone with a shaky voice.

"Grab your gun and lock yourself in a room," Rooter instructs. "The more barriers you put between you the longer it'll take him to get to you."

My gun! Why didn't I think of that?

My self-defense instructor told me that in an actual attack most people freeze from fear and forget a lot of their training. I was sure I wouldn't be one of those people. This makes twice I was wrong. Thank God for Rooter. I run to my purse and grab my gun. Ryan's bedroom has a master bath. That will put two extra doors between us. I lock the bedroom door then run into the bathroom and do the same.

"I'm in Ryan's bathroom," I whisper even though Mike can't hear me from here, but I can still hear him. He's yelling about how I broke his heart, took his home and his sister away. "I can hear him screaming. He's going to break in."

"Stay where you are and keep your gun at the ready. If he gets into the bathroom before I get there you fire immediately. Do you hear me?"

"Yes." My voice cracks. As scared as I am that Mike will hurt me if he gets to me, I'm not sure I can shoot him. I'm not sure I could actually shoot anyone, but especially not someone I grew up with.

"Sophie, he's dangerous. He isn't the Mike you used to know." It's as though he can read my mind.

"I know."

"I'm only ten minutes away. Hold on, babe. Everything will be okay."

I can't wait ten minutes. I need him here with me now.

I hear a crash in the living room and Mike's voice is suddenly louder. My entire body is wracked by tremors. I hold the gun with shaking hands and point it at the bathroom door.

"He's inside the house," I cry.

"Stay calm, Sophie. Remember the night when those guys broke into your house? You were so calm and collected. I need you to be that way now."

"I was only calm because you were there." Now I'm alone and terrified.

I hear several loud thuds and the sound of busted glass as Mike screams about how he's going to make me pay for everything I've done to him.

"I'm driving as fast as I can," Rooter tells me. "Just hold it together until I get there."

"Please hurry."

"Baby, I'm coming." His voice is gentle and soothing.

Mike's voice gets closer and then I hear him kicking the bedroom door. "No sense hiding from me, Sophie. You might as well face what you've done."

"He's kicking Ryan's bedroom door." I can feel my heartbeat throughout my entire body.

"I'm going to fucking kill him," Rooter seethes.

I hear another crash followed by Mike cursing and begin to hyperventilate. I grip the butt of the gun so tightly I lose feeling in my fingertips. "Oh God, he's in the bedroom."

"He's probably going to make it to you before I get there. Do not hesitate to shoot him."

There's a light tap on the bathroom door. "Sophie, if you make me bust through another door, I'll be really pissed off."

"Tell him I'm on my way," Rooter says.

"Rooter's on his way, Mike. He'll be here any minute. You better leave before he gets here."

Mike's laugh is an evil sound. "Yeah right. He doesn't want anything to do with you. He left you high and dry like I knew he would."

"I'm serious Mike. I'm on the phone with him right now."

"Well, it won't matter because you'll be dead before he can get here." He kicks the door and I flinch. "Now open the motherfucking door!"

"If you hurt me, he'll kill you!"

Mike laughs again. "Like it would even matter."

"Mike, please don't do this," I cry.

"I didn't do this. You did," he says and rams the door.

"He's going to break the door down," I cry to Rooter.

"Put the phone down and aim. You shoot the moment he comes through the door."

I do as I'm told and lay the phone on the sink counter. I aim the gun at the door. My pulse races and I hold my breath. I can't steady my trembling hands. The quaking door will give away any second.

"I have my gun." I holler. "I swear I'll shoot you."

Mike laughs and then I hear a loud bang. The shower door glass shatters behind me. I scream and Mike laughs. His shot barely missed me. I fall to the ground and squeeze my trigger. The sound is ear-piercing in this enclosed space. The wood of the door splinters as Mike fires three more rounds and I continue to pull my trigger until the gun clicks in my hand.

I stay crouched on the floor and listen, but hear nothing. Panicked, I scramble for my phone. Rooter is shouting when I put it to my ear.

"I shot him through the door. I can't hear anything."

"I heard over five shots. Are you okay?"

"Yes. He didn't hit me."

He breathes a sigh of relief. "I'm almost there. Can you see him?"

I peek through one of the holes and see Mike's body. There's blood on the floor. "He's on the floor, not moving. I think I killed him." I clasp my hand on my mouth and fall to the floor, gasping for air. "Oh my God, I think I killed him."

"It's okay, Sophie. Stay put until I'm with you."

"O-kay," I choke on a sob.

I hear the sound of tires screeching to a halt followed by the sound of Rooter and Bear's voices.

"Sophie!" Rooter hollers as he makes his way into the house.

He's so close. I want to run into his arms where I'll be safe. "Rooter!" I swing the door open and run out of the bathroom.

And then it all happens in slow motion. Rooter appears in the doorway and our eyes lock. Something must catch his attention because his eyes twitch to where Mike lays behind me.

"Sophie!" Rooter yells and reaches for me.

He pulls me forward, spins us around. I hear two loud bangs and Rooter's body falls to the ground before me. I scream and drop to my knees at his side. Several more shots are fired from behind us and I watch as the life disappears from Mike's hateful eyes. Bear crouches to me and Rooter and hollers, but I can't focus on what he's saying.

"Rooter!" I cry and clutch his body.

A small pool of blood forms beneath him. Pain is etched on his face as he smiles at me. *Why is he smiling?* He tries to reach for me, but he's weak.

"Call 911," I yell.

"No." Bear refuses. "The hospital is less than two miles from here. I'm not waiting on an ambulance."

Rooter groans as Bear hoists him up. I try to help as Bear hurries him to my car. We won't all fit in Rooter's truck. I run into the house and grab my keys. Bear props Rooter up on his side in the backseat. There are two gunshot wounds in his back.

"Keep pressure on the wounds," Bear orders.

Rooter's body is limp, seemingly lifeless, but his eyes are open and fixed on mine. He tries to say something but I put my lips on his to stop him.

"I love you," I cry. "Stay with me. Don't leave me."

The drive to the hospital seems to take a lifetime although it probably isn't any longer than four minutes.

Twenty minutes later, Camilla, Mick, and Isa come running to us in the emergency room. They're all three frantic.

"How is my boy?" Camilla cries and I throw myself into her arms.

"We don't know yet," Bear tells them. "He has two bullet wounds in his back."

"What happened?" Mick asks.

I pull away from Camilla. "Mike, my old roommate, showed up at my house and I was scared so I called Rooter. I shot Mike and thought he was dead. When Rooter got there I ran out of the bathroom to him and he saw Mike was going to shoot me so he spun us around and took the hit."

"Mike's dead now," Bear says.

Mick nods. "I knew that fuck was going to be a problem."

Mick's words leave me feeling guilty. If I'd let Rooter handle things his own way when Mike vandalized my car this might not have happened.

Isa runs into Bear's arms and sobs. He wraps his arms around her and tells her everything will be okay.

We give our statements to the police. They're classifying it as self-defense and will get Rooter's statement when he comes out of recovery. Evidently, Mike was arrested a week ago for assault and possession of narcotics.

"Someone needs to go to Miranda," I tell Bear. "I don't want to leave Rooter."

"I'll go. She should hear this from me anyway."

He is, after all, the one who fired the kill shot, even though it was in defense of Rooter and me. She'll want to hear from him exactly how it happened. I hope she's able to understand the gravity of the situation and why Bear shot him.

"This is all my fault." I turn to Camilla after Bear has gone. "I should've never called Rooter."

Camilla takes my hand and leads me to a set of chairs so we can sit. "If something happened to you and he hadn't been there, it would've killed him."

I shake my head adamantly. Being there is what could kill him. She shouldn't be consoling me. She should hate me. I hate me. "This was my problem. Not his."

"Sophie, he loves you. Your problems are his problems."

I point toward the doors leading into the emergency room. "That should be me in there," I cry. "He would've been better off never knowing me."

Camilla takes me firmly by the chin and glares into my eyes. "That isn't true. My son had never been happier than when he was with you."

I collapse into her arms. "Rooter has to make it. He has to."

"He will." Mick asserts and rests a comforting hand on my shoulder. "My son is strong. He will survive this."

An hour passes and we still haven't heard anything. Camilla tells me this is good news. It means he's hanging on while the doctors work on him. I don't care if it's good news or not, I want answers. I sprint to the information desk and inquire on his condition.

"Are you family?" The nurse asks. "I can only release information to his family."

Camilla is now standing by my side. "She is family. She's my daughter."

"Oh, I wasn't aware Mrs. Russo. I'll make a note of that." The nurse turns back to me. "What's your name?"

"Sophie." I huff. "Now can you please tell us how he is?"

The nurse pulls up his information on the computer. "It shows he's still in surgery. I don't know anything more."

I pound my fist on the counter and shout. "Then find someone who does!"

"Miss Russo, I'm sorry. I'll see what else I can find out. Please give me a few minutes."

The nurse's few minutes turns into an eternity. It feels like days have passed when she finally appears before us.

"Jace is still in surgery. They estimate he'll be in for another three hours. They'll move him to the ICU when they're finished. You can go there now. The doctor will find you there after surgery."

"You can't tell us anything else about his condition?" Mick asks.

"Not at this time. I'm sorry."

It's amazing how when something happens to someone you love all you can think of is the good times you spent together. You forget all about the arguments and bad days. All that matters is how much that person means to you. A crisis like this has a way of revealing what's most important.

Rooter and our love is what's most important to me.

I close my eyes and cry, remembering all the time we spent together. How I laughed so hard when he kept falling off of the paddle board. The way it felt to be in his arms after making love the first time. The taste of our first kiss. I can remember every single detail about every single second of the time we spent together right down to the taste and smell.

The time passes excruciatingly slow. I check the clock every ten to fifteen minutes feeling as though an hour has passed each time. He can't leave me. Not now. Not like this. We need more time together. I need more time with him to hear his voice and his laughter. I need to feel the safety of his arms around me and hear him tell me he loves me. Most importantly, I need him to tell him how very much I love him.

Camilla pulls me into her arms and murmurs comforting words about how he'll be just fine and we'll be back home with one another in no time. She has to be right. If he doesn't pull through it'll be the end of me. I don't want to live in a world in which he doesn't exist. I refuse to live without him.

A little over two hours later, the doctor appears before us.

A Long Night

The somber expression on the doctor's face sends me into a panic. I jump from my seat to face him directly. Mick, Camilla, and Isa join me. Before I can ask about Rooter, the doctor extends his hand to Mick to introduce himself.

"I'm the surgeon who worked on your son. My name is Doctor Gallagher."

"I'm Mick Russo." Anxiety looms in his eyes as he shakes the doctor's hand. "How is my son?"

"He suffered two gunshot wounds, both of which hit his left lung." The way the doctor speaks is so careful it's almost robotic. "He suffered major blood loss, a collapsed lung, and went into respiratory shock."

Camilla chokes back a sob and clasps a hand to her mouth.

"Is my son alive?" Mick barks, apparently as irritated with the explanation as I am.

"He's in critical condition," Doctor Gallagher begins, "unable to breathe on his own. But yes, he's alive. He's in recovery at this time and will be moved to the ICU where he'll be sedated and connected to a ventilator."

"Is he going to be okay?" Camilla cries.

"I assure you we're doing everything we can." The doctor stands with his hands in the pockets of his lab coat. "We were able to remove both bullets and have put a tube in place to aid the collapsed lung. It's our hope he'll regain the ability to breathe on his own within the next twenty four hours."

"And if he doesn't?" I ask.

"I prefer not to speculate. We have every confidence he'll regain the ability to breathe on his own by that time." For a moment seems that's all he will say on the matter, but when he sees the scowl on my face he continues. "If not, we'll reassess his condition and treatment at that time."

"When can we see him?" Isa asks. It was going to be my next question.

"He should be in ICU within an hour. However, only one visitor may be in the room at a time." The doctor looks at Isa and then to Camilla. "Please be warned that the sight of Jace in his current condition may be... overwhelming."

"We understand," Camilla says. "Thank you, Doctor Gallagher."

An hour later on the button a nurse lets us know we can see Rooter. I want to run at full speed into his room, but only one visitor may go. I turn to Camilla and tell her to go ahead. She shakes her head.

"You're the first one he'd want to see," she tells me.

"He isn't awake," I insist. "He's your son. You should be the first to see him."

"You are his love, Sophie. And he is yours. If it was Mick in there, nothing and no one would keep me away."

"Are you sure?" I ask.

"I'm sure."

I look to Mick and Isa as well who both nod in agreement. I turn and follow the nurse through the ICU doors wishing Camilla could come with me. I'm not sure I can do this alone. The doctor warned us about how he will appear. My hands become slick and I wring them nervously as we approach his door. I look to the nurse in search of comfort and strength. She gives me an understanding smile before pulling back the curtain and stepping aside. I close my eyes and take a deep breath in an attempt to prepare myself for what I'm about to see.

But there's nothing that could possibly prepare me.

Rooter—my invincible love—lays in the bed with a myriad of wires and tubes connected to him. I follow the tube in his mouth to the machine that is breathing for him. His chest rises and falls in time with the sound of the machine. Tears fall from my eyes as I make my way to his side. His skin is pale and cool to the touch when I press my lips to his forehead.

"I'm here, babe." I cry and take his hand into mine. "I love you so much. Can you hear me? I love you and I'm so very sorry."

My legs fail me and I grab the bed rail to keep from falling. There's a rolling stool behind me and I pull it up so I can sit at his side. His hand is limp in mine as I entwine my fingers with his. With my free hand I trace the design of the tattoo on his arm. I remember all the times he reached for me with this arm. The way it felt to wake up in the morning being held by this arm. My body shakes as I sob quietly. Several minutes pass until I'm composed enough to speak again.

"The doctor says you should be able to breathe on your own within twenty four hours," I stroke his forehead with the back of my fingers, "but I can't wait that long. I need you to wake up and come back to me."

I tell him about what happened with the cops and that Bear is with Miranda explaining what happened.

"You saved me, Rooter. I'd be dead if not for you," I choke. It's a while before I can speak again. "Why didn't you let him shoot me? Seeing you like this... the fear that you won't wake up is killing me. I can't live without you. Please, please come back to me."

A half hour passes. I don't want to leave his side, but it'd be selfish of me to stay any longer when his family are all in the waiting room, probably going crazy as they wait their turn to see him.

"They're only allowing one person in here at a time. I'm going to leave for a little while so your mom, Mick, and Isa can see you." I kiss the cool skin of his forehead again. "I'll be back soon, I promise."

When I step out into the waiting room it's filled with members of the club. I try to remember if they've been here the entire time, but everything from the moment Rooter was shot is fuzzy.

"Sorry I took so long," I tell Camilla.

"No need to apologize, sweetie." She squeezes my hand.

Over the course of two hours, the four of us take turns visiting with him. The one visitor at a time rule seems ridiculous. What would it hurt for the four of us to be in there? It's not like we can disturb him, he's sedated for God's sake.

After my third time visiting with him I remember to call Bear to find out how it went with Miranda. I'd call her directly, but am not sure that's a great idea. When I turn my phone on there's a multitude of voicemails and texts from Ryan. Before I can check on Miranda, I need to call him.

"Jesus, Sophie, are you okay?" His voice is laden with fear.

I should've called him a long time ago, but I haven't been able to think about anything other than Rooter and whether he'll survive. He's probably in his house amid all the destruction wondering what the hell happened.

"I'm so sorry Ryan." I rub my face with my free hand. "I'll find a way to pay for the damage."

"Babe," his voice is tender and kind, "you have nothing to apologize for. I've been so worried. Are you okay? Are you hurt?"

"I'm fine, but Rooter was shot." I turn and gaze in direction of the ICU doors. Isa is in with him now. "He's in critical condition."

"Where are you?"

"I'm at Memorial in the ICU waiting room."

"I'm on my way."

As soon as I hang up with Ryan I dial Bear's number. He picks up on the third ring.

"Are you with her now?" I ask, biting my thumb nail.

"Yeah. Here she is." He sounds exhausted.

"Hi." Her voice is thick with emotion.

"How are you?" A stupid question, but I don't know what else to say.

"I don't know," she sniffles. "It's all so hard to believe."

"Yeah, it is." I stare absentmindedly at a cheap painting on the waiting room wall.

"How are you? How is Rooter doing?"

"I'm okay," I pace, look to the floor. "Rooter is sedated. He's hooked to a ventilator because he can't breathe on his own."

"Oh, God, Sophie," she sobs. "I'm so sorry."

"It's not your fault."

"I should've kicked Mike out a long time ago. He could've killed you."

"This just would've happened that much sooner."

Mick hands me a steaming cup of coffee from the vending machine. I put it to my lips and swallow. It's so hot it burns all the way down, but I welcome the sensation as it temporarily gives me something to focus on other than the gaping hole in my heart.

"I'm so glad you're okay. I don't know what I would've done if... I love you Sophie."

"I love you, too." The lump in my throat threatens to choke me. "How are things with you and Bear?"

"We'll be okay. I understand he did it to save both of you and I'm glad he did."

After saying goodbye, Bear gets back on the phone and asks about Rooter's condition. I give him the details and promise to call as soon as there's an update. Before hanging up I ask him to please take care of Miranda.

Poor Miranda; in a year's time she's lost her father, her mother, and now her brother. I know what it feels like to have no family, but it's different when you lose family members whom you love. Mike may have turned bad, but he wasn't always so. There was a time, not all that long ago, when they were close. I'm sure as she mourns her loss she's thinking about the Mike of old and all the good times they shared.

At present, the only memory I have of Mike is the sound of his threats as he tore through Ryan's house intending to kill me.

Only spouses and parents may spend the night in an ICU patient's room so Camilla stays with Rooter. Before going in she urges me to try to sleep and promises to come get me if there's any change in his condition.

Sometime after four in the morning I doze off. When I open my eyes it's only six thirty. Isa and Mick are both asleep in chairs to the right of mine. Ryan sleeps in the chair to my left. I keep my eyes on the clock for two hours until Mick stirs.

"Did you sleep?" He asks and rubs his face.

"For a couple hours."

Ryan sits up in the seat next to me and Isa wakes up as well.

"It's probably going to be a long day." Mick's voice is full of concern.

I have no doubt it will be. But, I'm not the one to worry about. Sometime today we will find out if Rooter can breathe on his own. The ICU doors open and Camilla appears. Her eyes go straight to me.

"Did you sleep at all?" She asks, concerned.

Do I look that bad? "A little."

"Sophie, you need to rest. If Rooter wakes up and sees you like this…"

I guess I do look that bad. "I can't sleep until he wakes up."

"He's going to wake up today, sweetie. Why don't you go on back and talk to him for a while." It isn't a question.

When I enter his room, he looks exactly the same as he did the last time I was in here, though his color is a little better. His skin, though, is still cool to the touch. I press my lips to his forehead and then to his eyelids.

"Good morning, babe. I missed you." *I still miss you. Come back to me.* I wipe a tear from my cheek.

Doctor Gallagher walks in and stands at Rooter's side, opposite of me. "He's healing rapidly. The pneumothorax is improved and he won't be needing the tube anymore. We'll remove it shortly."

I breathe a sigh of relief at the good news. But now what about his breathing?

The doctor answers my unspoken question. "We will also try to take him off the ventilator to see if he's able to breathe on his own."

A shot of relief and fear run through me at once. I want to know if he can, but what if he can't? What then? But I don't dare ask. No sense in considering the worst. I need to be positive right now.

"The nurses will be in shortly," he says. "You'll need to leave the room at that time."

"Thank you doctor." I kiss Rooter's temple as the doctor leaves the room. "Did you hear that? The doctor says you're healing rapidly. You need to breathe on your own, okay? You have to come back to me."

I stroke his soft hair and notice it's longer than usual. A moment later a team of nurses appear before me. The older, round, brunette speaks.

"We're going to take him off sedation. If he's able to breathe on his own, we will remove the ventilator. We'll need you to leave the room while we work on him. Someone will come out with an update as soon as we're finished."

I lean in and whisper in his ear. "Breathe for me, babe. Please breathe for me. I'll be waiting."

*J*ACE

Over an hour later, we're still waiting for someone to tell us what's going on. I've chewed my thumb nail so much it's bleeding and I'm surprised I haven't worn a hole in the floor from pacing.

"What are they doing in there?" I snap.

"I'm losing my mind," Camilla groans.

"It can't be too much longer," Mick tries to reassure us.

I throw my head back and huff, impatient. I can't wait much longer. What's going on? How is he? Have they taken him off of sedation? Can he breathe on his own? Why the fuck is it taking so long?

I wish Ryan was still here. His nearness has a calming effect on me which I could use right now. But he has to handle some things at his house. When I turn around there's a nurse scurrying toward me with a tense expression. A pain rips through my chest.

"I need Sophie," she says, frantic.

"That's me." I close the distance between us.

Camilla, Mick, and Isa jump from their seats.

"Come with me," she orders and tugs my hand.

"Is he okay?" I ask with a shaking voice.

"He's demanding to see you."

I suck in a breath of relief as she leads me at a hurried pace into the ICU. The moment I'm through the doors I hear him hollering.

"Sophie! Where's Sophie?"

"He woke up in a panicked state, yelling your name."

When we round the corner into his room a team of nurses, male and female, try to hold Rooter down in the bed. He's trying to rip at his wires and IV.

"I'm here!" I call out and run to him, unable to stop the tears pouring from my eyes.

"Sophie?" He peers around one of the bodies.

A tall male steps out of the way giving me access to him.

"I'm here, it's okay, calm down."

Rooter reaches out and pulls me to him. "Babe, you're okay."

His warm hands give me an immediate sense of calm. I stroke the side of his face as I whisper, "You saved me."

"Will you relax now?" The male nurse asks, out of breath.

Rooter nods without taking his eyes off of mine. The team of nurses leave us alone in the room.

"I've never been so scared in my life," he says and tugs me onto the side of the bed. His voice is raspier than usual.

"You?" I shake my head. "You have no idea what fear is. You were shot and have been sedated on a ventilator since last night."

"He could've shot you." He grimaces. His eyes are damp with unshed tears.

"It should've been me."

"No. Never say that." He wipes my tears away with his hand.

"You could've died," I sniffle.

"Better me than you."

I shake my head vehemently. "I'd rather be dead than live in a world where you don't exist," I choke. "I love you."

He smiles. "I love you, too."

I want to wrap my arms around him and hold him tight, but don't want to hurt him. Instead, I lay my forehead against his and whisper, "Please don't leave me again."

"I'll never leave you baby." He clutches the side of my face and presses his lips to mine. "I swear to fucking God, I will murder anything and anyone who tries to come between us."

Three days later Rooter is released from the hospital. I've agreed to stay with him while he recuperates.

"I could get used to this," Rooter says with a smirk as I set his breakfast, a bowl of oatmeal and fresh fruit salad, in front of him.

"Forget it. I'm not June Cleaver." I take a seat across from him at the dining room table.

"That's a shame." He chews a bite of pineapple. "You make a good rendition."

"Ha ha." I fake a laugh.

"Are you sure you don't want me to go with you?" He asks, turning serious.

Mike's funeral is today. I'm attending, but the weird thing is, Miranda isn't the only reason I'm going. Mike was a big part of my life. If not for the drugs and alcohol, things may not have gone the way they did. He might be still the Mike I grew up with. That's the Mike I will memorialize. That is the Mike I'm mourning.

I swallow my bite. "You should stay here. The doctor said to take it easy for a week."

"It's not strenuous to sit in a chair," he gripes. He hasn't been a very diligent patient.

"No, but it'll be stressful." I stir bits of strawberries into my oatmeal. "Miranda isn't doing well, so I'll be comforting her the entire time. I can't take care of both of you at the same time."

"I'm fine, Sophie." His spoon clangs the side of his bowl.

"You're not fine," I snipe. "You have two holes in your body."

He takes my hand and strokes my knuckles with his thumb. "I want to be there for you."

"I know." I smile at him. "But it would make me feel better if you stayed here and rested."

"All I've been doing is resting," he whines.

I arch a brow and scowl. He's lying. I've found him tinkering with things around the house three times already. Last night I caught him out in the garage lifting a heavy box. "Don't argue with me, Rooter. Please just do what I ask."

Later that night we lay in bed watching a rerun of an old sitcom. Rooter turns on his side and gazes at me with a thoughtful expression.

"I don't want you to call me Rooter anymore."

"What?" I gape.

"I want you to call me Jace from now on."

"You do?" I roll over to face him.

He kisses the top of my hand. "I haven't been able to talk about it before now, but losing you did something to me. It changed me. When you called me that night… When he pointed his gun at you I knew nothing in this world means as much to me as you do. The only thing that matters is making you happy and being what you need."

I reach for his face and caress his cheek. He's been different since the incident with Mike; quiet and overly attentive. "You are what I need. You do make me happy. You don't need to change."

"I'm not changing. Rooter will always be my alter ego. Hell, I'm sure the guys in the club will always call me that. But when you look at me that's not what I want you to see. I want you to see the good in me."

"I've always seen the good in you." *I saw it before we even met.*

He pulls me into his chest and kisses the top of my head.

"I never felt pain like I felt when you asked me to let you go. And it wasn't just the pain of losing you. It was knowing the pain I caused you." He leans away and gazes into my eyes. "I know I made this promise before and failed, but I swear I'll never hurt you again, Sophie. You're everything to me. I love you."

"I love you, Rooter," I cry.

He wipes away my tears. "Jace, baby. Call me Jace."

*E*PILOGUE

It's my graduation day and I don't know who's more excited; me or Jace. He's been begging me to move in with him ever since he got out of the hospital last year. When he wants something, he can be very persistent. And annoying as hell. Three months ago I gave in and agreed to move in after I graduated.

There are movers packing up my things at Ryan's and delivering them to his—our house—at this precise moment. Camilla and Isa are overseeing everything. I'd rather they were here, but Jace wants everything to be set by the time we get home.

"You did it, babe." He scoops me up in his arms and spins me around, kissing me in front of Miranda, Bear, and other friends.

"Longest four years of my life," I chuckle.

"I finally have you all to myself," he smirks.

Not only am I finished with school, I have a new job working as a customer service representative at a bank. Not the most glorious job, but it's a step up from waiting tables.

"Congrats, Soph," Ryan says and pulls me in for a hug.

Ryan has become the brother I never had, but always wanted. I love the guy. He and Jace have also become good friends. It's rather strange watching a badass biker hanging out with a gay guy, especially when Ryan's new boyfriend Tom is around. Tom is a tad flamboyant and doesn't bother hide his appreciation for Jace's svelte body. The first time Tom smacked his ass—a drunken lapse in judgment—I thought I'd die from laughter. Jace just stood, frozen, with wide eyes. But he's used to it now. The joke is if Tom wasn't in love with Ryan, I'd have some stiff competition. Pun intended.

"Congratulations," Miranda says with a gigantic smile and hugs me. She understands my happiness more than anyone since she just graduated from her online course.

"Congrats." Bear flashes his bright white teeth and pulls me in for a hug.

They're living together now. I admit I was worried for them after Mike's death, but Miranda was a trooper. Sure, they had bad days, but they always pulled through. Bear stayed by her side through it all. He loves her so much it's sickening. She has a way of reducing the guy to a whimpering baby. If she told him to strip and ride his Harley naked through rush hour traffic, I believe he'd do it.

Thank God Jace has more pride than that. There isn't much he wouldn't do for me, which he's proven to be true, but at least the guy has boundaries.

The club is throwing Miranda and me a blow-out party in our backyards. After a leisurely ride along the lakeshore, the four of us pull into our driveways. Everyone is already there, music is playing and Mick is at the grill. Camilla stands next to him chastising him about burning the hotdogs. He argues that everyone likes them that way. Jace and I laugh at the sight. I imagine that'll be us in twenty years.

Isa darts to my side.

"Hey sis! We're all done. If you don't like where we put things, I can always come over tomorrow and help rearrange."

"I'm sure it's fine, Isa." I smile.

"You know, since you're living together now, you might as well get married." She shoulder bumps me. She's been begging us to get married for months now so I'll "officially" be her sister.

I choke and Jace doubles over in laughter. He's made it perfectly clear he'd love to get married. And I've made it clear I will marry him. One day. But, there are things I want to do before we get married. I want to enjoy being young and in love and have fun as a normal twenty-something. And hopefully by the time I'm twenty five I'll be well on my way in a career in business management.

Besides, for now, I have everything I need. Great friends and a wonderful, loving family. Life will never be perfect, but I don't think it can get any better than this.

ABOUT THE AUTHOR

Teiran is obsessed with the written word. When she's not writing, she's reading. She can get so lost in a story, be it one of her own or someone else's, that she won't even break away to eat, drink, or take a bathroom break. By the time she gets up from a story, she's usually dizzy from low blood sugar, suffering blurred vision, and hunched over from a painfully full bladder.

Whenever she's not writing or reading, you will find her working out, trying her hand at landscape photography, and spending time with her husband, Scott, and their four legged child, Sasha.

Please visit:
Author website: www.teiransmith.com
Email: teiransmith@gmail.com
Facebook: www.facebook.com/TeiranSmith
Twitter: @TeiranSmith

Made in the USA
Charleston, SC
15 October 2015